"I shall take the heart," returned the Tin Woodman;
"for brains do not make one happy, and happiness is
the best thing in the world."

—L. Frank Baum,
THE WONDERFUL WIZARD OF OZ

IDW

COVER ART BY
DREW ZUCKER

COVER COLORS BY
VITTORIO ASTONE

SERIES EDITS BY
DAVID MARIOTTE

COLLECTION EDITS BY
JUSTIN EISINGER
AND ALONZO SIMON

COLLECTION DESIGN BY
JEFF POWELL

Chris Ryall, President & Publisher/CCO

Cara Morrison, Chief Financial Officer

Matthew Ruzicka, Chief Accounting Officer

David Hedgecock, Associate Publisher

John Barber, Editor-in-Chief

Justin Eisinger, Editorial Director, Graphic Novels and Collections

Jerry Bennington, VP of New Product Development

Lorelei Bunjes, VP of Technology & Information Services

Jud Meyers, Sales Director

Anna Morrow, Marketing Director

Tara McCrillis, Director of Design & Production

Mike Ford, Director of Operations

Rebekah Cahalin, General Manager

Ted Adams and Robbie Robbins, IDW Founders

ISBN: 978-1-68405-621-7   23 22 21 20   1 2 3 4

CANTO, VOLUME 1: IF I ONLY HAD A HEART. MARCH 2020. FIRST PRINTING. © David M. Booher and Andrew Zucker. The IDW logo is registered in the U.S. Patent and Trademark Office. IDW Publishing, a division of Idea and Design Works, LLC. Editorial offices: 2765 Truxtun Road, San Diego, CA 92106. Any similarities to persons living or dead are purely coincidental. With the exception of artwork used for review purposes, none of the contents of this publication may be reprinted without the permission of Idea and Design Works, LLC. Printed in Korea.

IDW Publishing does not read or accept unsolicited submissions of ideas, stories, or artwork.

Originally published as CANTO issues #1–6.

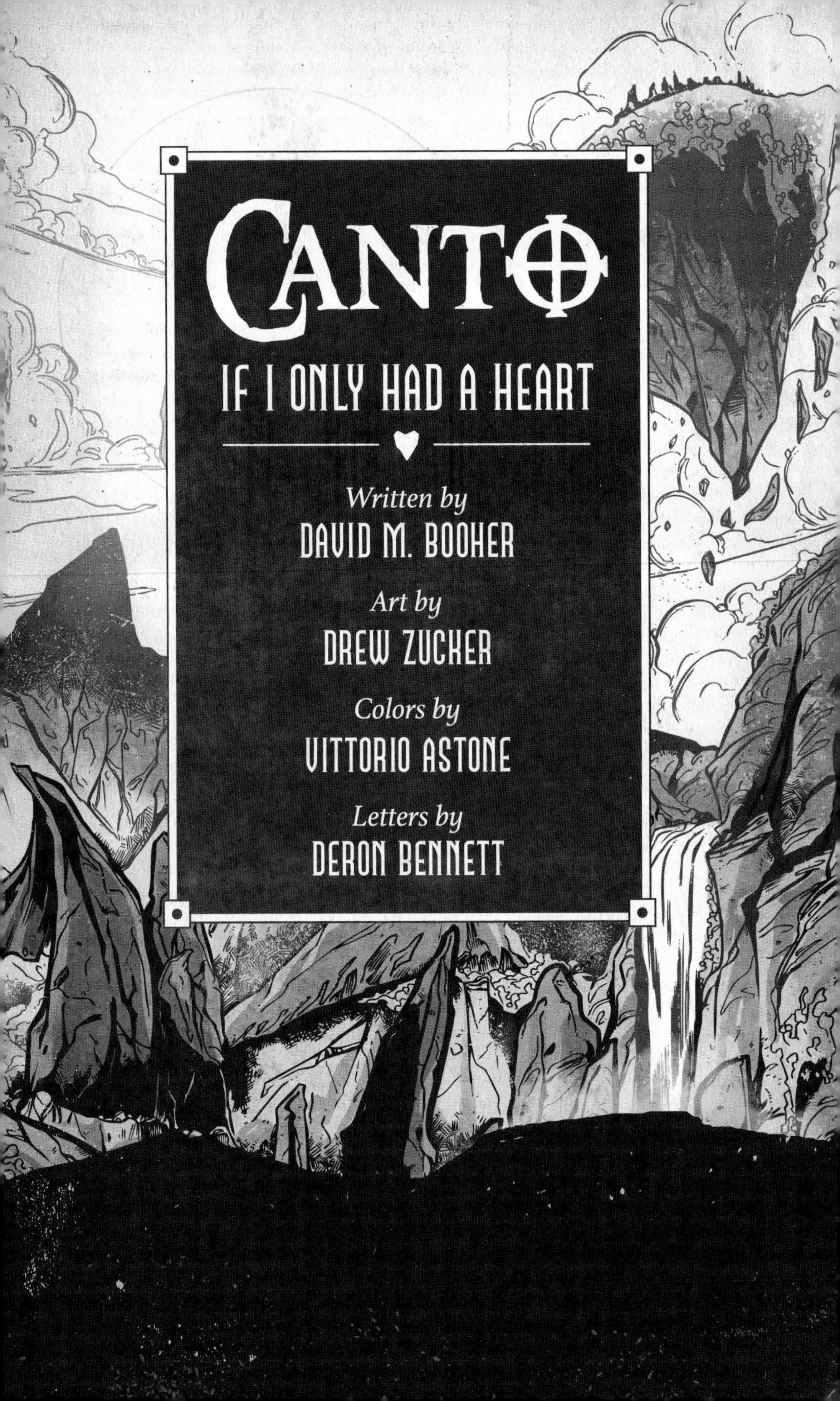

CANTO

IF I ONLY HAD A HEART

Written by
DAVID M. BOOHER

Art by
DREW ZUCKER

Colors by
VITTORIO ASTONE

Letters by
DERON BENNETT

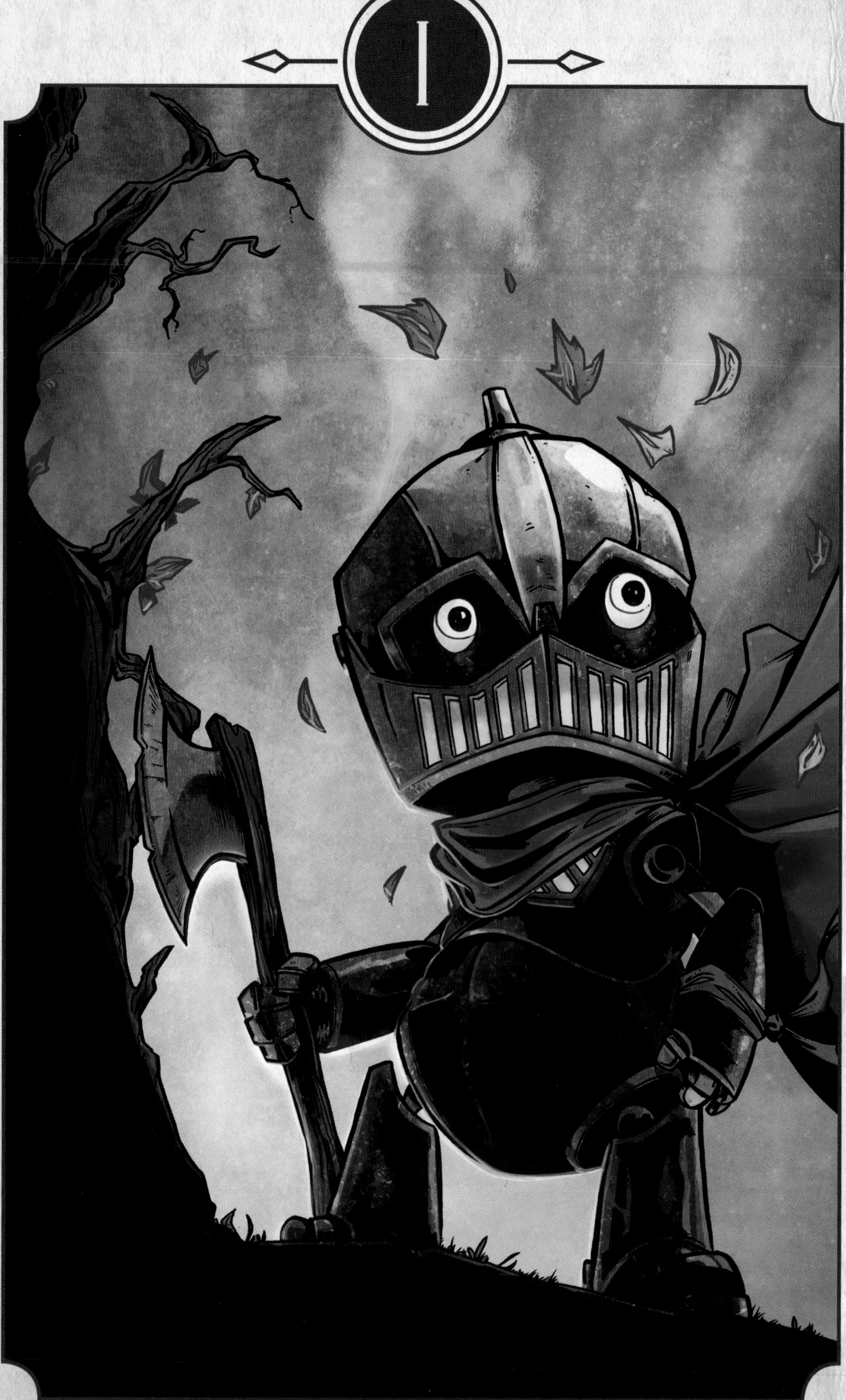
I

Art by **Drew Zucker**, *Colors by* **Vittorio Astone**

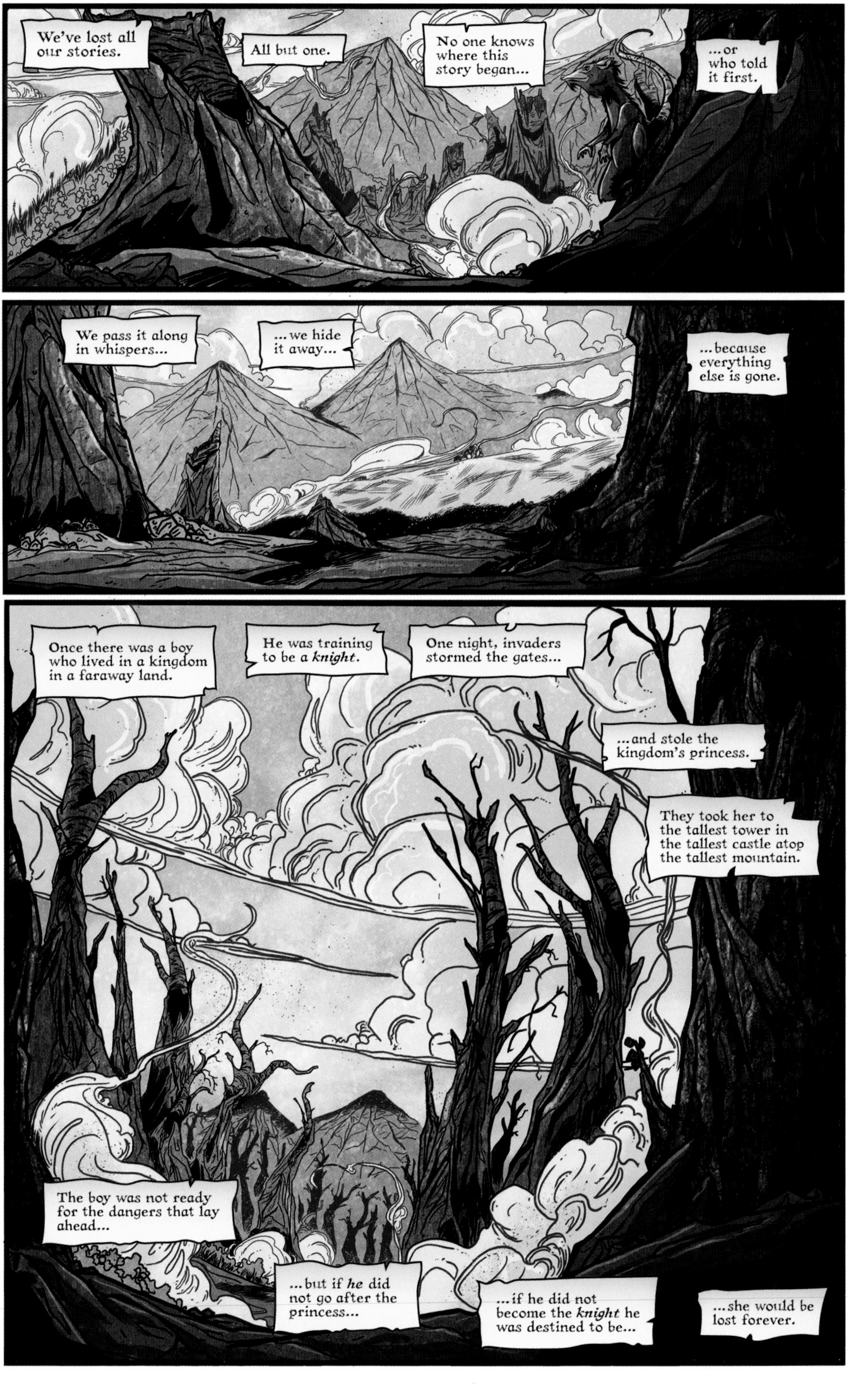
We've lost all our stories.
All but one.
No one knows where this story began...
...or who told it first.
We pass it along in whispers...
...we hide it away...
...because everything else is gone.
Once there was a boy who lived in a kingdom in a faraway land.
He was training to be a *knight*.
One night, invaders stormed the gates...
...and stole the kingdom's princess.
They took her to the tallest tower in the tallest castle atop the tallest mountain.
The boy was not ready for the dangers that lay ahead...
...but if *he* did not go after the princess...
...if he did not become the *knight* he was destined to be...
...she would be lost forever.

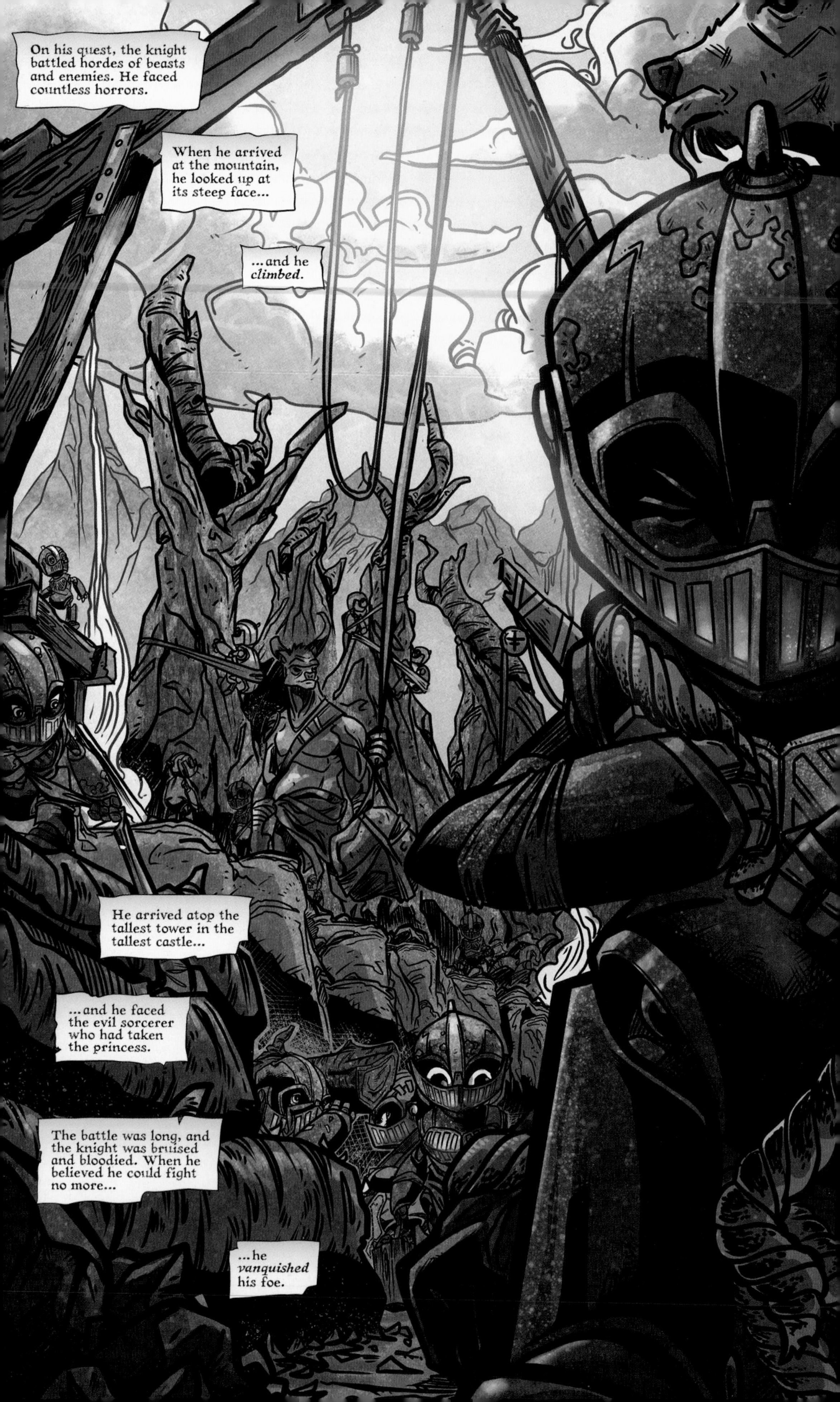
On his quest, the knight battled hordes of beasts and enemies. He faced countless horrors.
When he arrived at the mountain, he looked up at its steep face...
...and he *climbed.*
He arrived atop the tallest tower in the tallest castle...
...and he faced the evil sorcerer who had taken the princess.
The battle was long, and the knight was bruised and bloodied. When he believed he could fight no more...
...he *vanquished* his foe.

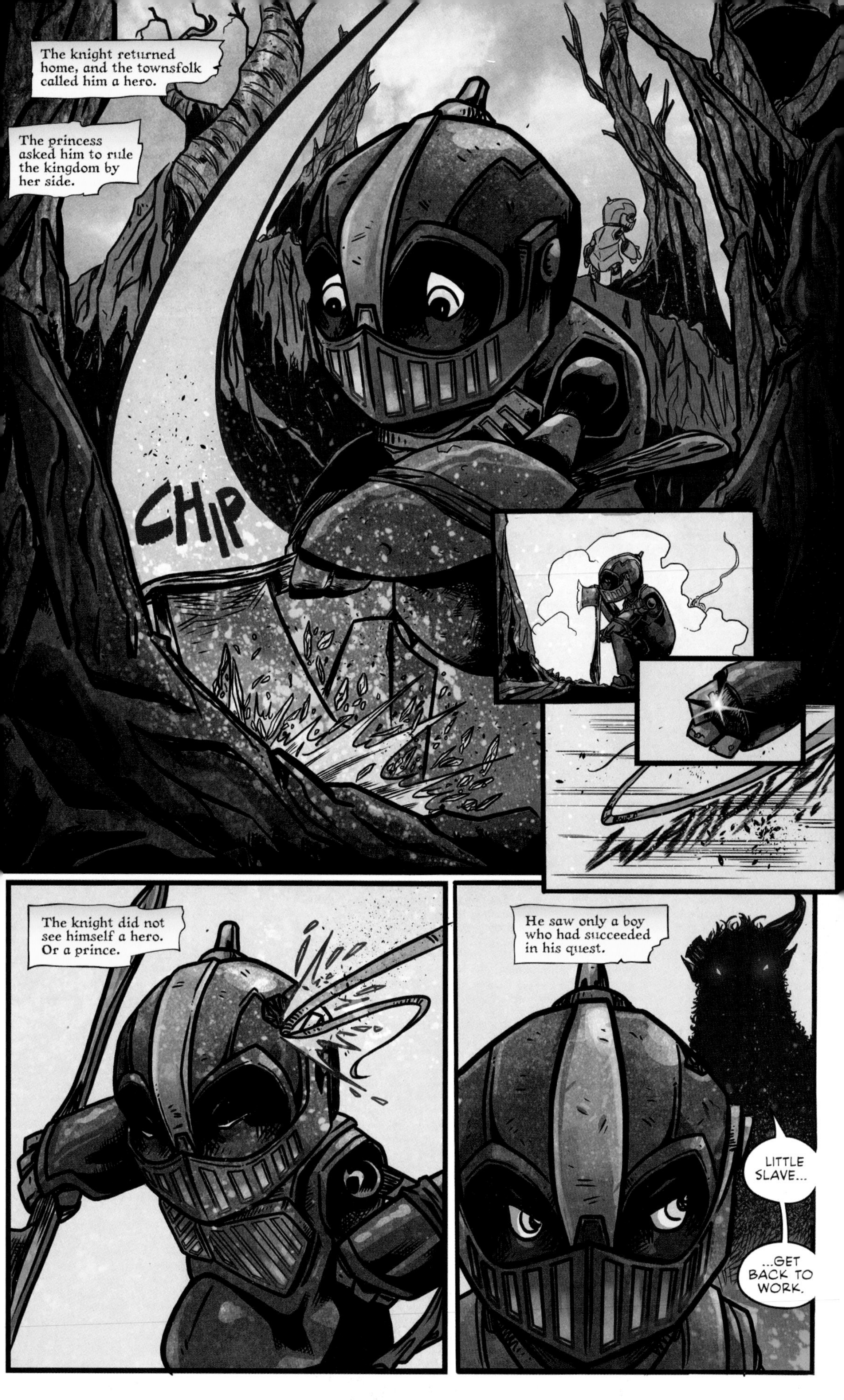
The knight returned home, and the townsfolk called him a hero.
The princess asked him to rule the kingdom by her side.
CHIP
The knight did not see himself a hero. Or a prince.
He saw only a boy who had succeeded in his quest.
LITTLE SLAVE...
...GET BACK TO WORK.

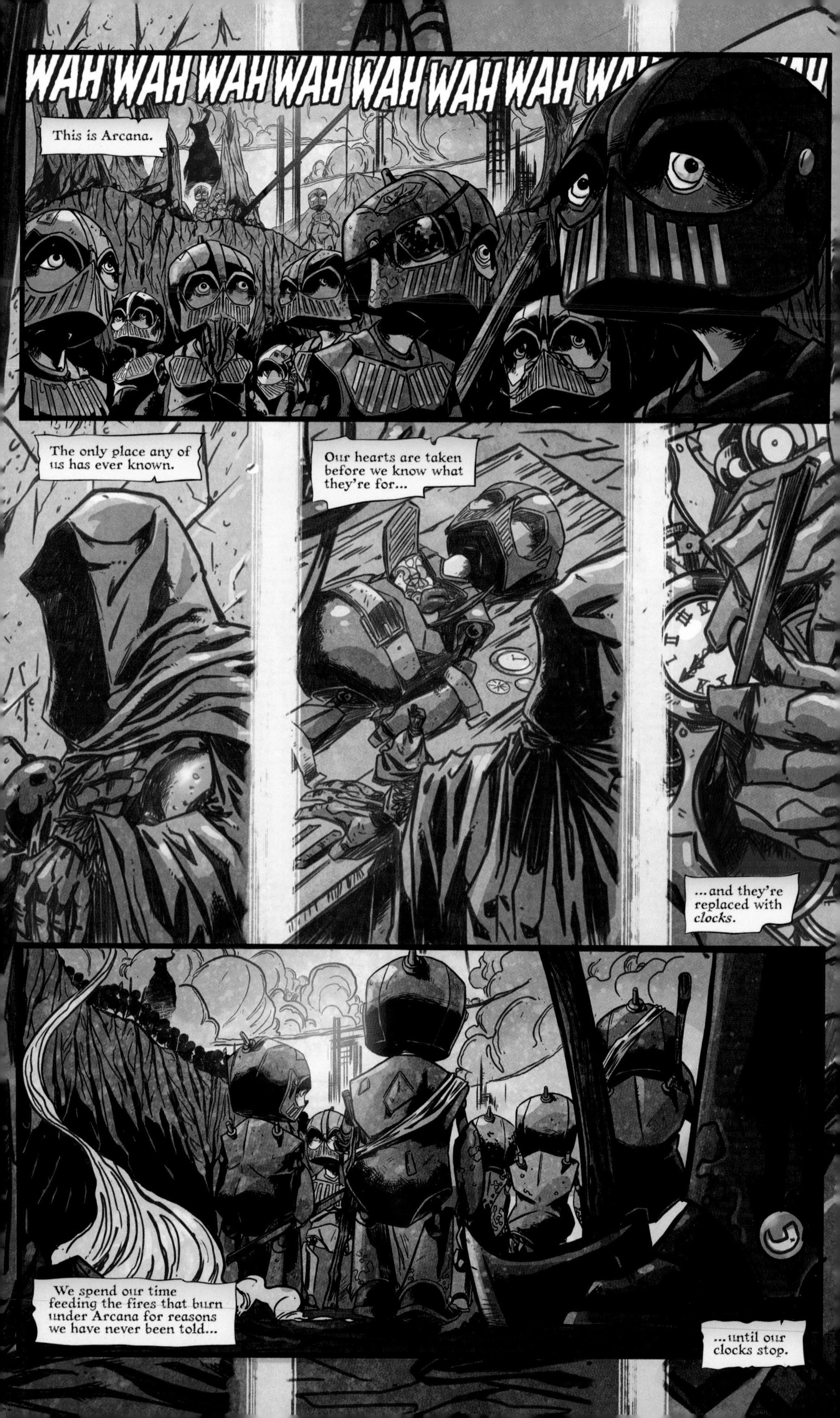
WAH WAH WAH WAH WAH WAH WAH WA
This is Arcana.
The only place any of us has ever known.
Our hearts are taken before we know what they're for...
...and they're replaced with *clocks*.
We spend our time feeding the fires that burn under Arcana for reasons we have never been told...
...until our clocks stop.

They've forbidden us to have names...

...forbidden us to care for one another...

...forbidden us to feel love.

But I care for others...

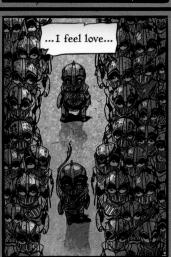

...I feel love...

...I have a name.

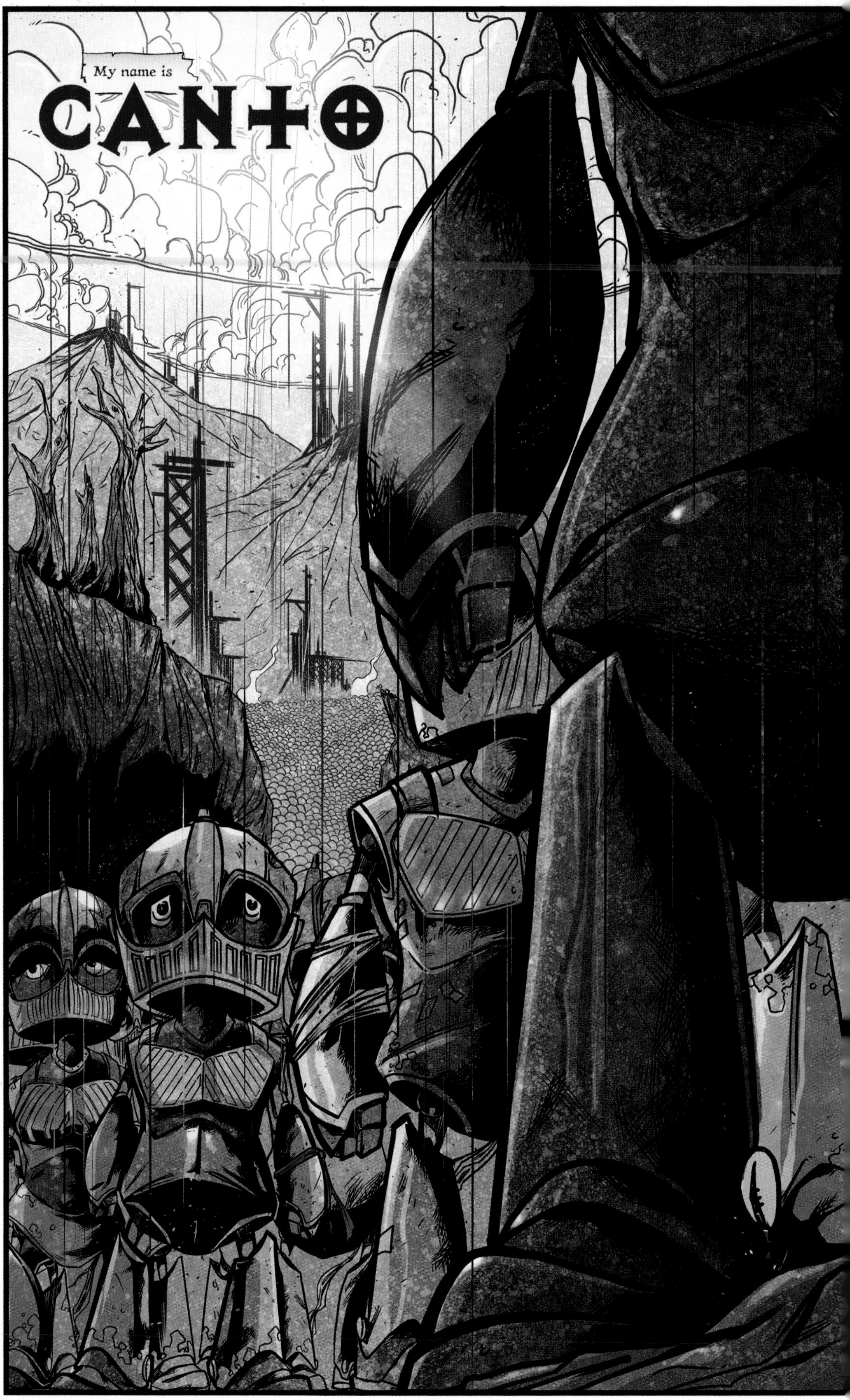
My name is
CANTO

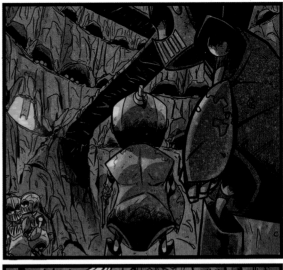

WHAT IS IT? WHAT'S WRONG?

THE SLAVERS DAMAGED HIS CLOCK BEYOND REPAIR.

COULDN'T YOU FIX IT? HE WAS YOUNG! HE HAD TIME LEFT!

IT WAS BEYOND MY SKILL.

BURY HIM IN THE FOREST OR THEY WILL THROW HIM IN THE FURNACES.

BE QUICK. THE MALOREX ARE ACTIVE TONIGHT.

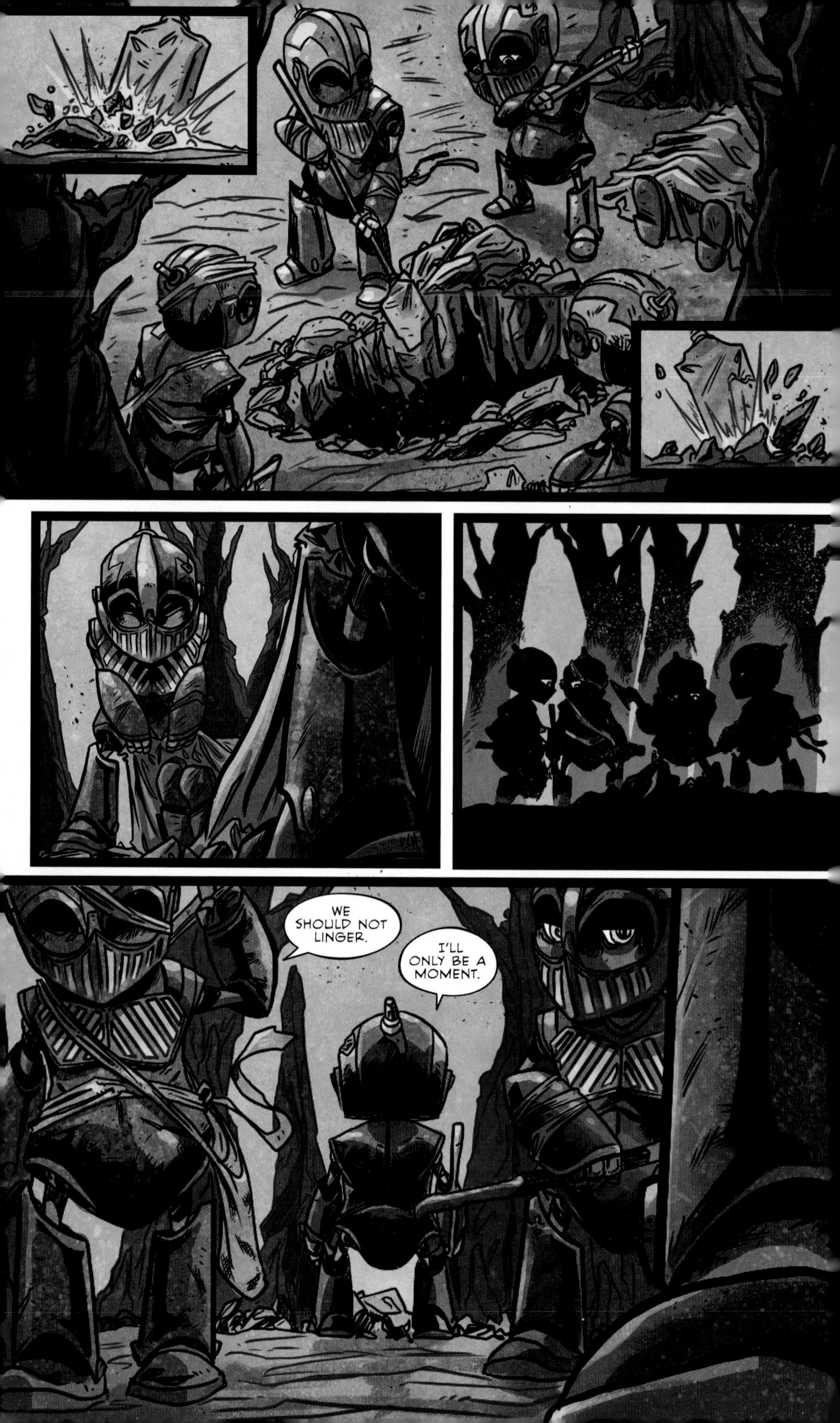
WE SHOULD NOT LINGER.
I'LL ONLY BE A MOMENT.

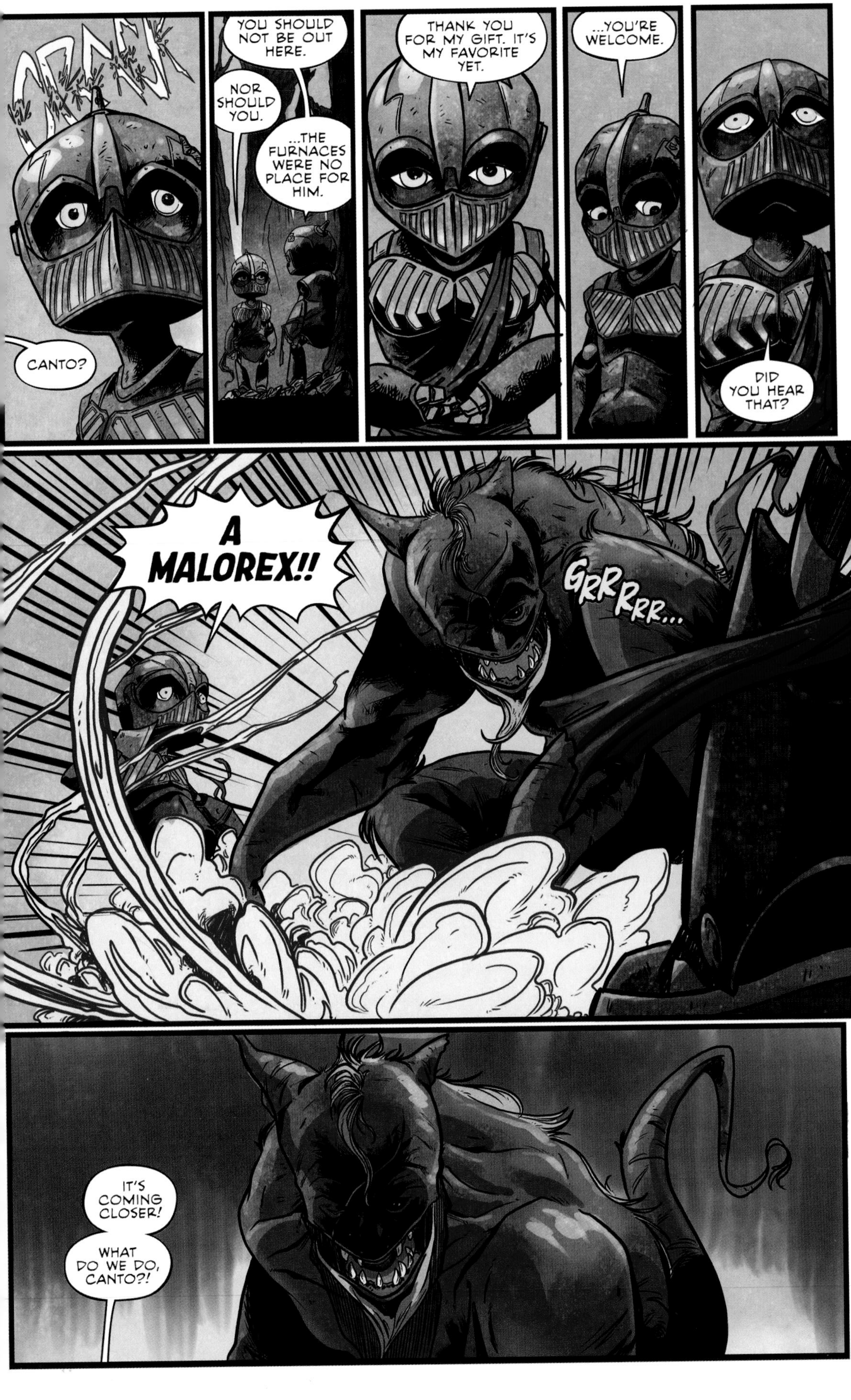
CRACK
CANTO?
YOU SHOULD NOT BE OUT HERE.
NOR SHOULD YOU.
...THE FURNACES WERE NO PLACE FOR HIM.
THANK YOU FOR MY GIFT. IT'S MY FAVORITE YET.
...YOU'RE WELCOME.
DID YOU HEAR THAT?
A MALOREX!!
GRRRRR...
IT'S COMING CLOSER!
WHAT DO WE DO, CANTO?!

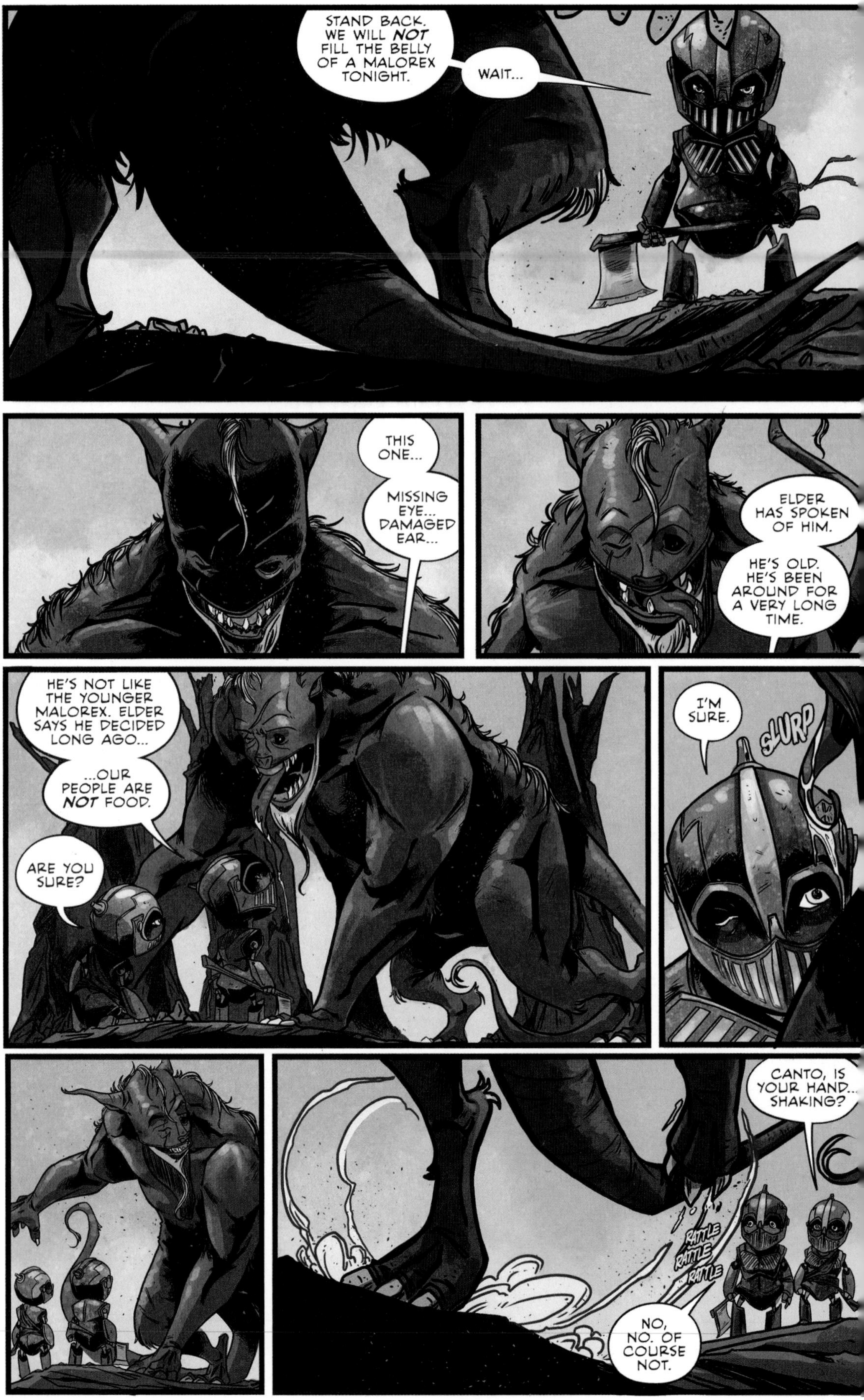
STAND BACK. WE WILL *NOT* FILL THE BELLY OF A MALOREX TONIGHT.
WAIT...
THIS ONE...
MISSING EYE... DAMAGED EAR...
ELDER HAS SPOKEN OF HIM.
HE'S OLD. HE'S BEEN AROUND FOR A VERY LONG TIME.
HE'S NOT LIKE THE YOUNGER MALOREX. ELDER SAYS HE DECIDED LONG AGO...
...OUR PEOPLE ARE *NOT* FOOD.
ARE YOU SURE?
I'M SURE.
SLURP
CANTO, IS YOUR HAND... SHAKING?
RATTLE RATTLE RATTLE
NO, NO. OF COURSE NOT.

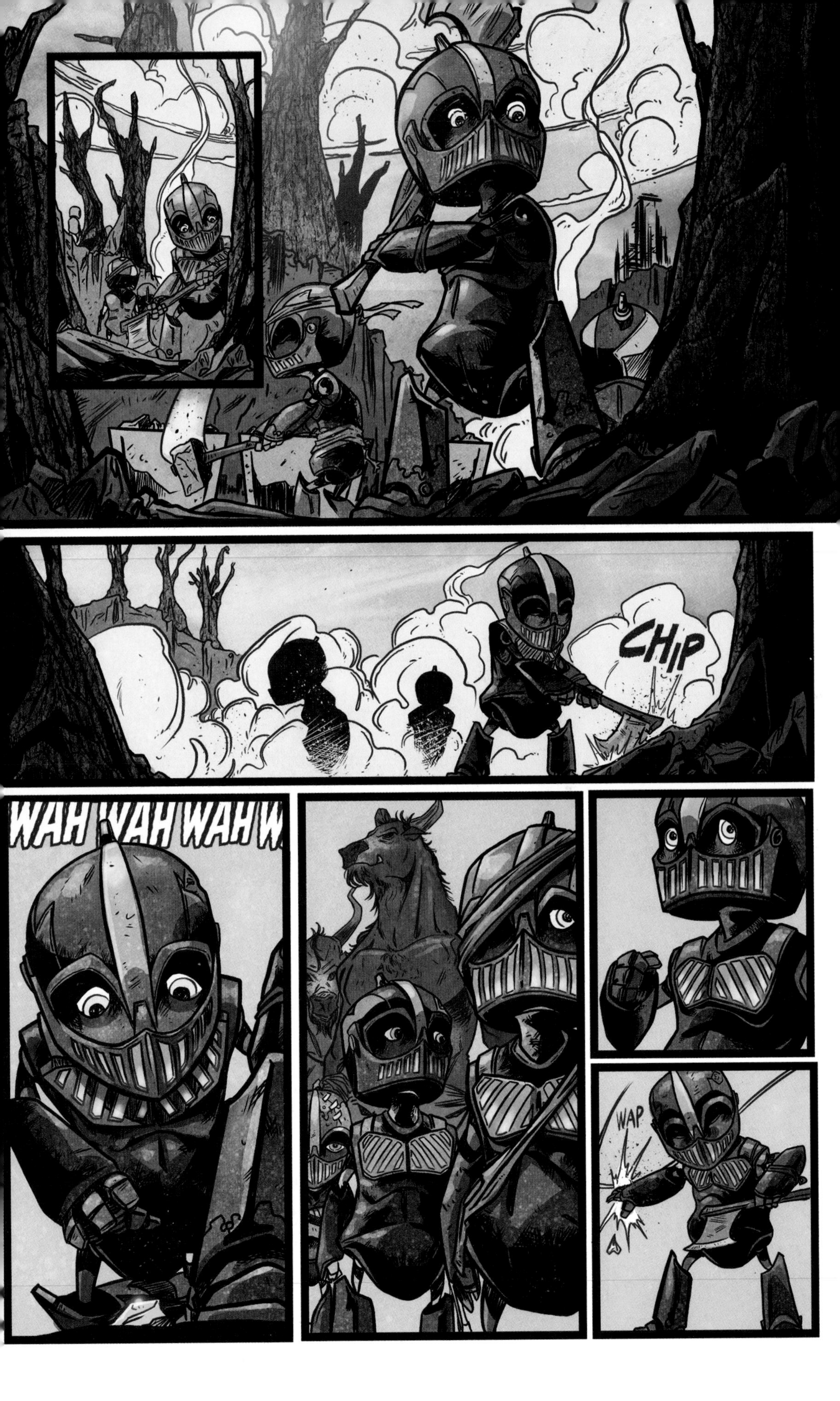
CHIP
WAH WAH WAH W
WAP

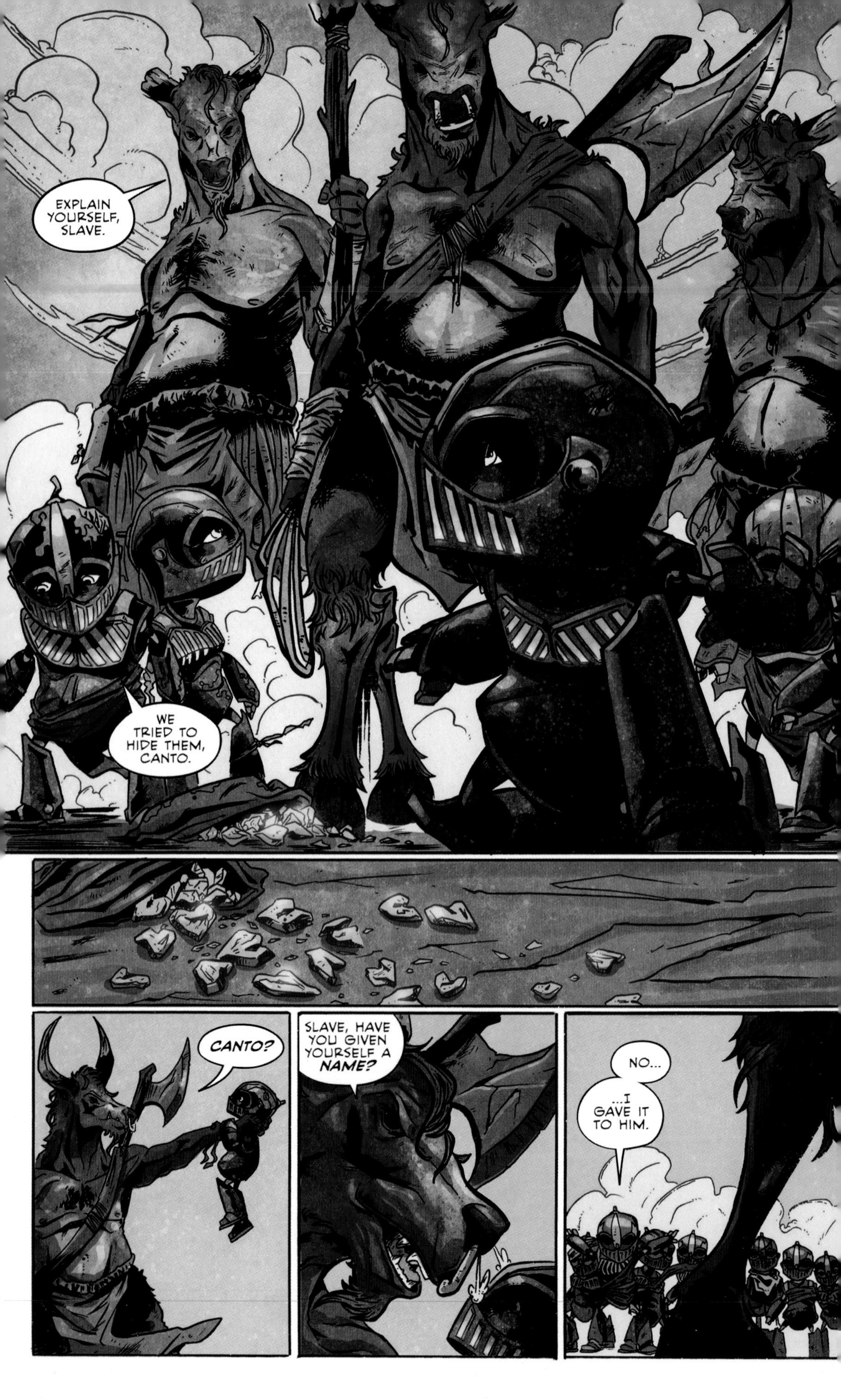
EXPLAIN YOURSELF, SLAVE.
WE TRIED TO HIDE THEM, CANTO.
CANTO?
SLAVE, HAVE YOU GIVEN YOURSELF A NAME?
NO...
...I GAVE IT TO HIM.

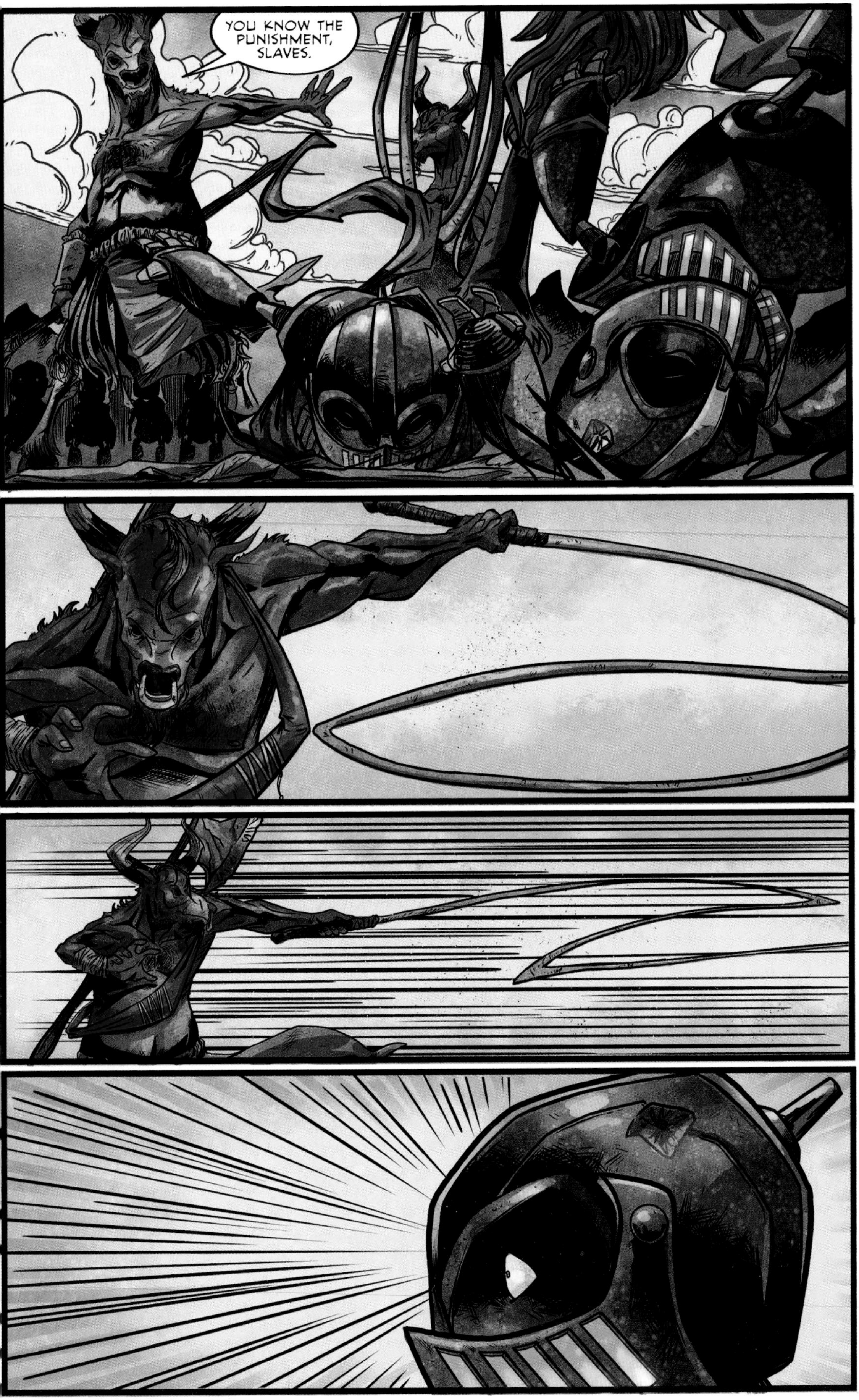
YOU KNOW THE PUNISHMENT, SLAVES.

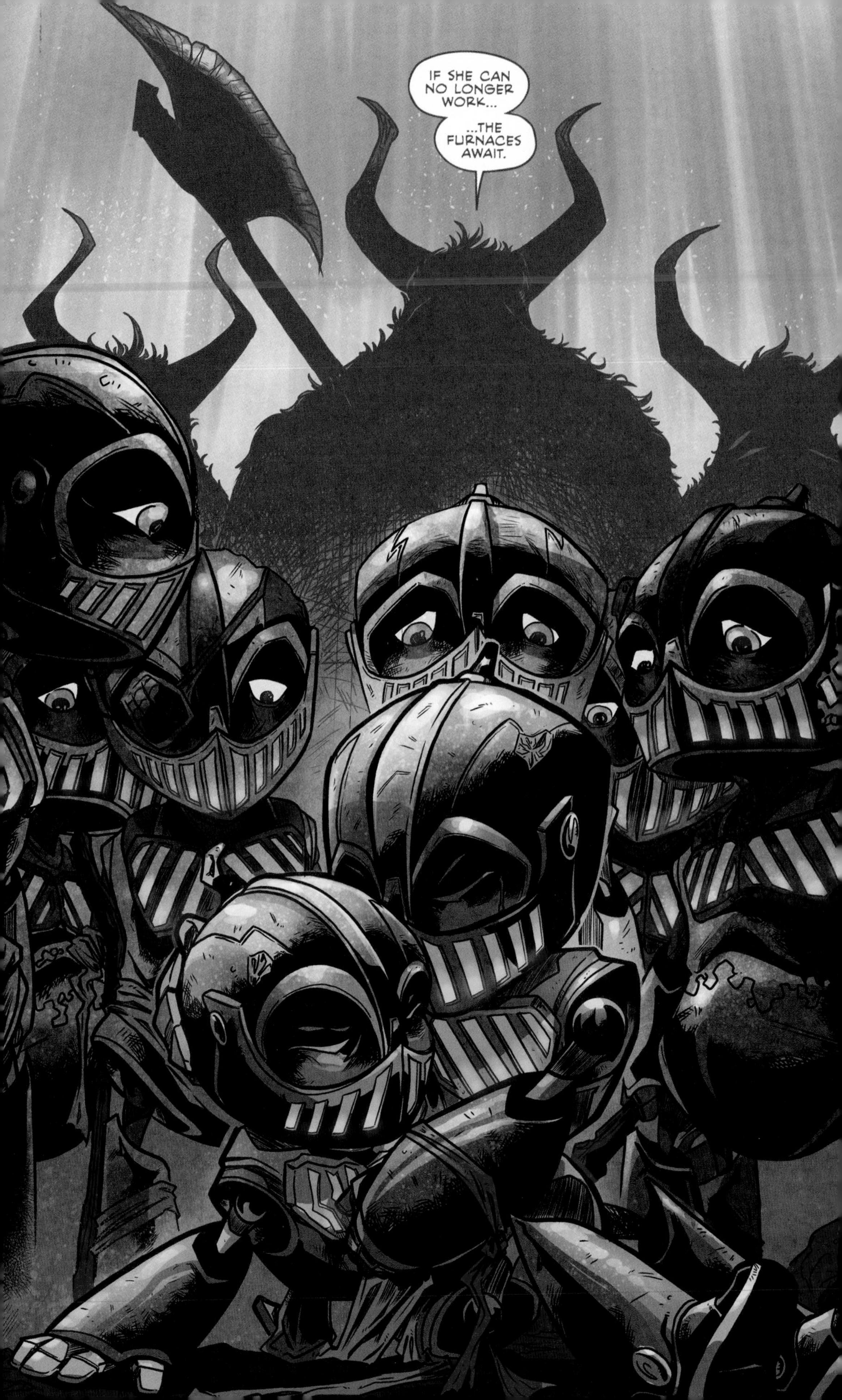
IF SHE CAN NO LONGER WORK...
...THE FURNACES AWAIT.

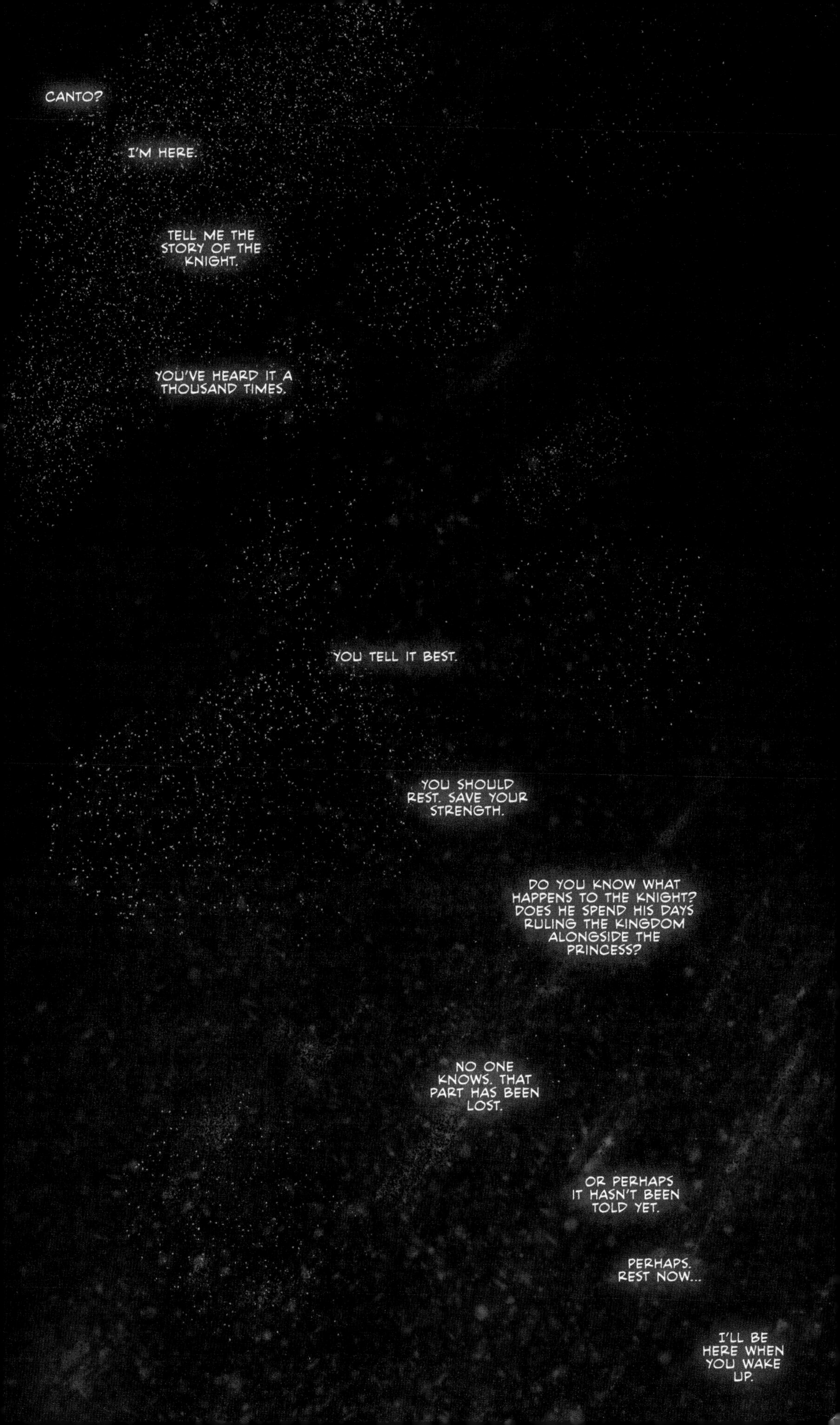
CANTO?
I'M HERE.
TELL ME THE STORY OF THE KNIGHT.
YOU'VE HEARD IT A THOUSAND TIMES.
YOU TELL IT BEST.
YOU SHOULD REST. SAVE YOUR STRENGTH.
DO YOU KNOW WHAT HAPPENS TO THE KNIGHT? DOES HE SPEND HIS DAYS RULING THE KINGDOM ALONGSIDE THE PRINCESS?
NO ONE KNOWS. THAT PART HAS BEEN LOST.
OR PERHAPS IT HASN'T BEEN TOLD YET.
PERHAPS. REST NOW...
I'LL BE HERE WHEN YOU WAKE UP.

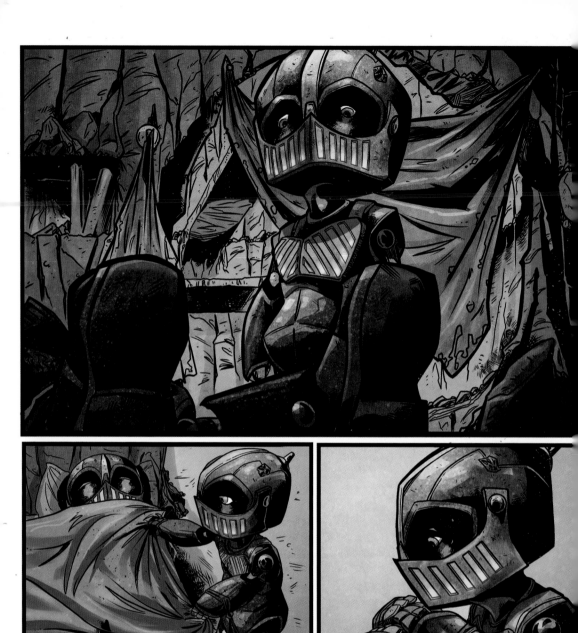

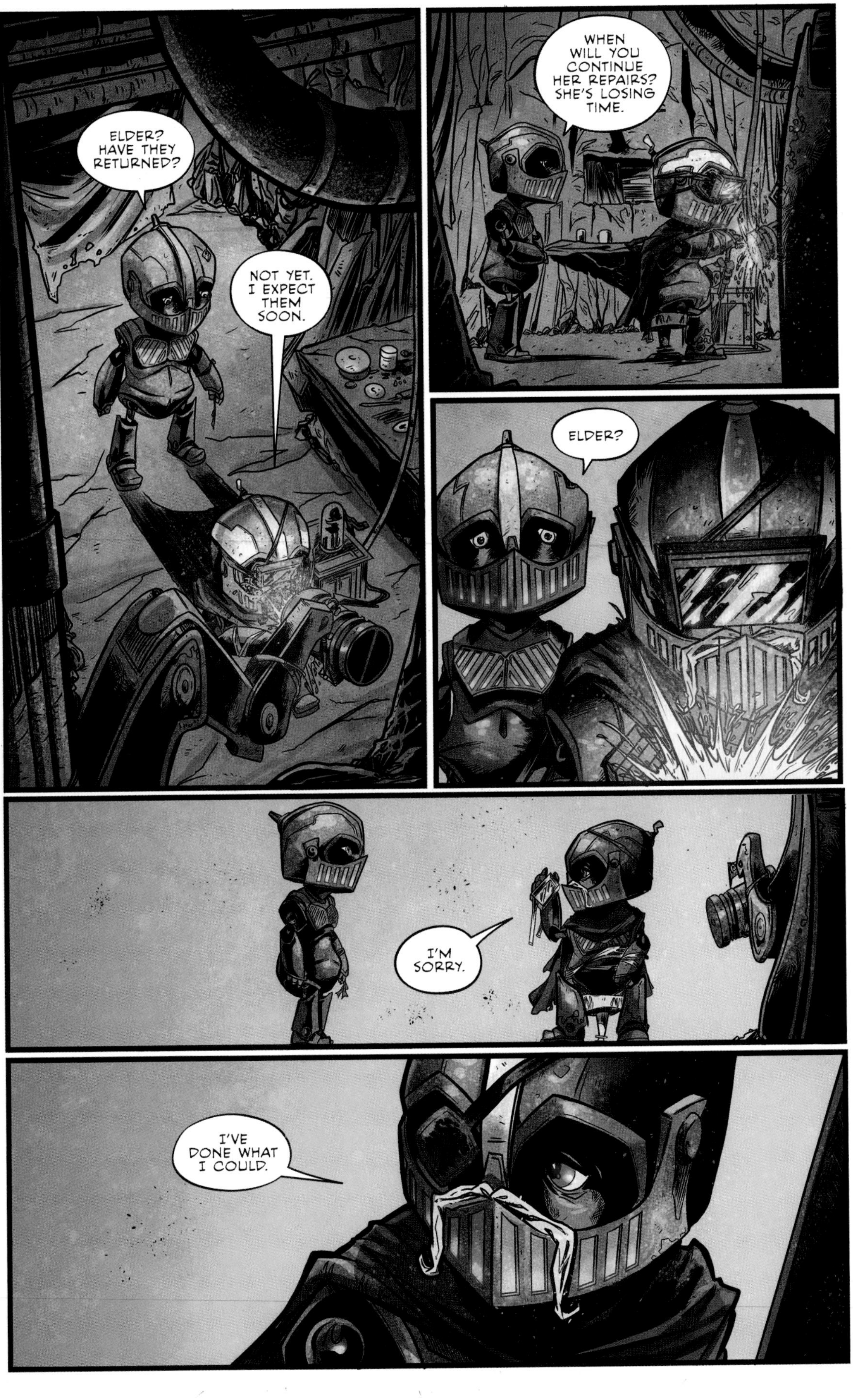
ELDER? HAVE THEY RETURNED?
NOT YET. I EXPECT THEM SOON.
WHEN WILL YOU CONTINUE HER REPAIRS? SHE'S LOSING TIME.
ELDER?
I'M SORRY.
I'VE DONE WHAT I COULD.

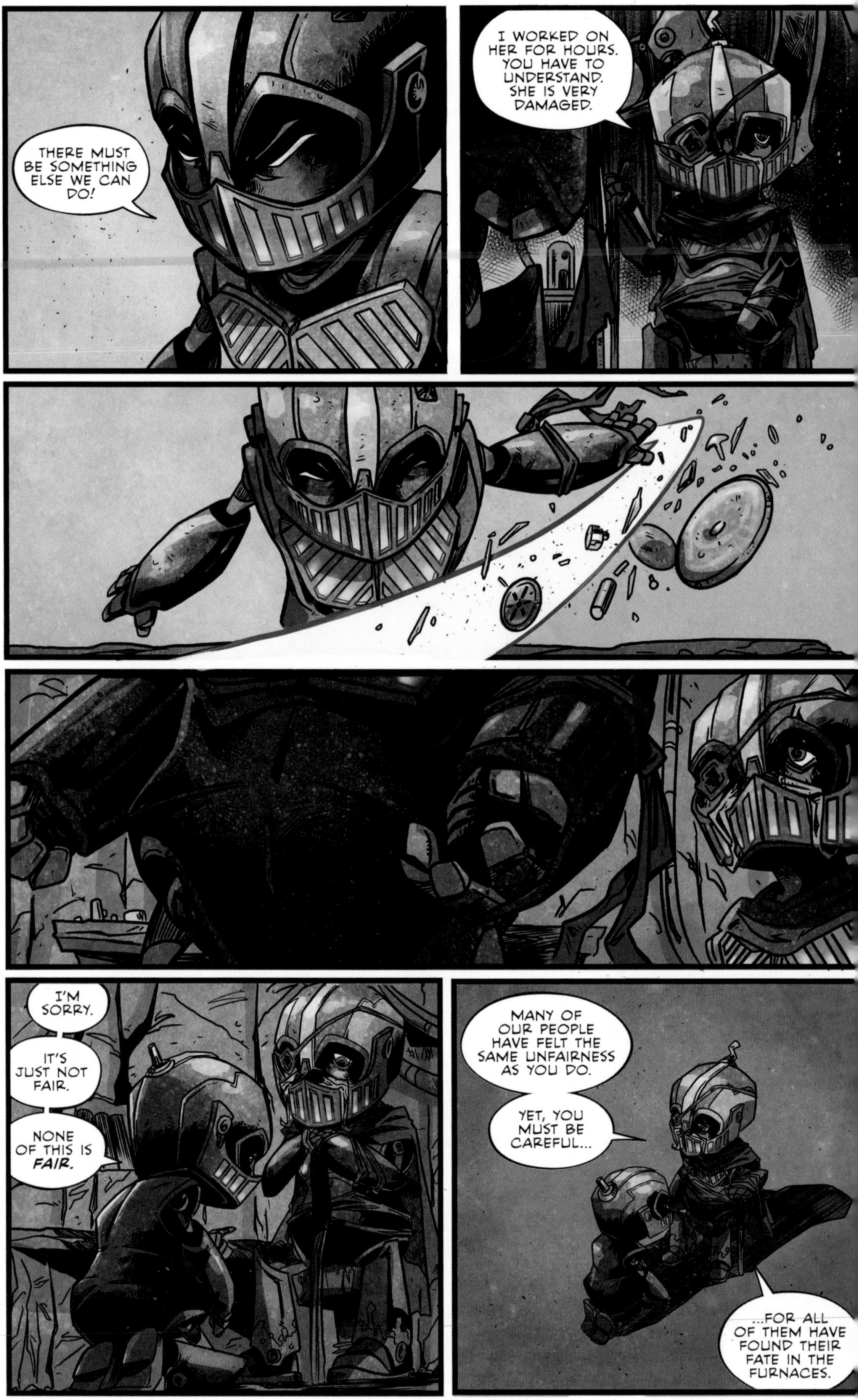
THERE MUST BE SOMETHING ELSE WE CAN DO!
I WORKED ON HER FOR HOURS. YOU HAVE TO UNDERSTAND. SHE IS VERY DAMAGED.
I'M SORRY.
IT'S JUST NOT FAIR.
NONE OF THIS IS *FAIR.*
MANY OF OUR PEOPLE HAVE FELT THE SAME UNFAIRNESS AS YOU DO.
YET, YOU MUST BE CAREFUL...
...FOR ALL OF THEM HAVE FOUND THEIR FATE IN THE FURNACES.

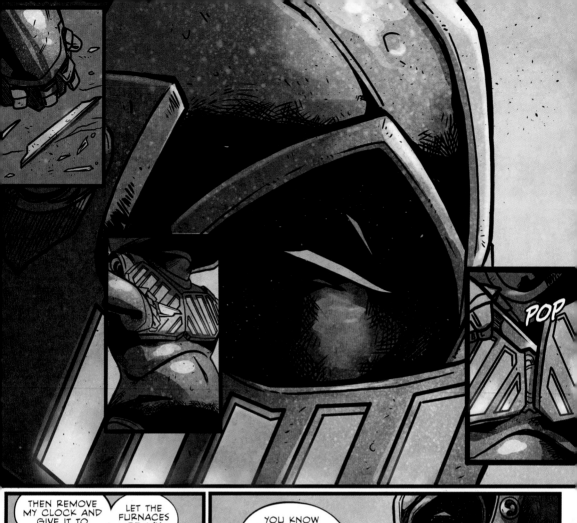

POP

THEN REMOVE MY CLOCK AND GIVE IT TO HER.

LET THE FURNACES BE *MY* FATE...

...NOT *HERS.*

YOU KNOW I CANNOT DO THAT, CANTO. OUR CLOCKS CAN NEVER BE SWITCHED.

THE SLAVERS HAVE MADE QUITE SURE...

...OUR TIME IS OUR OWN.

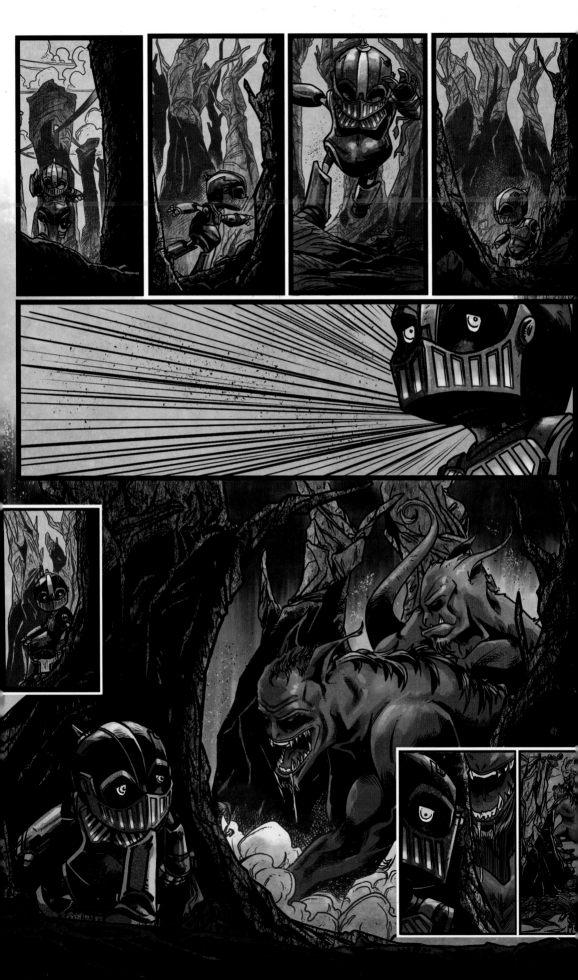

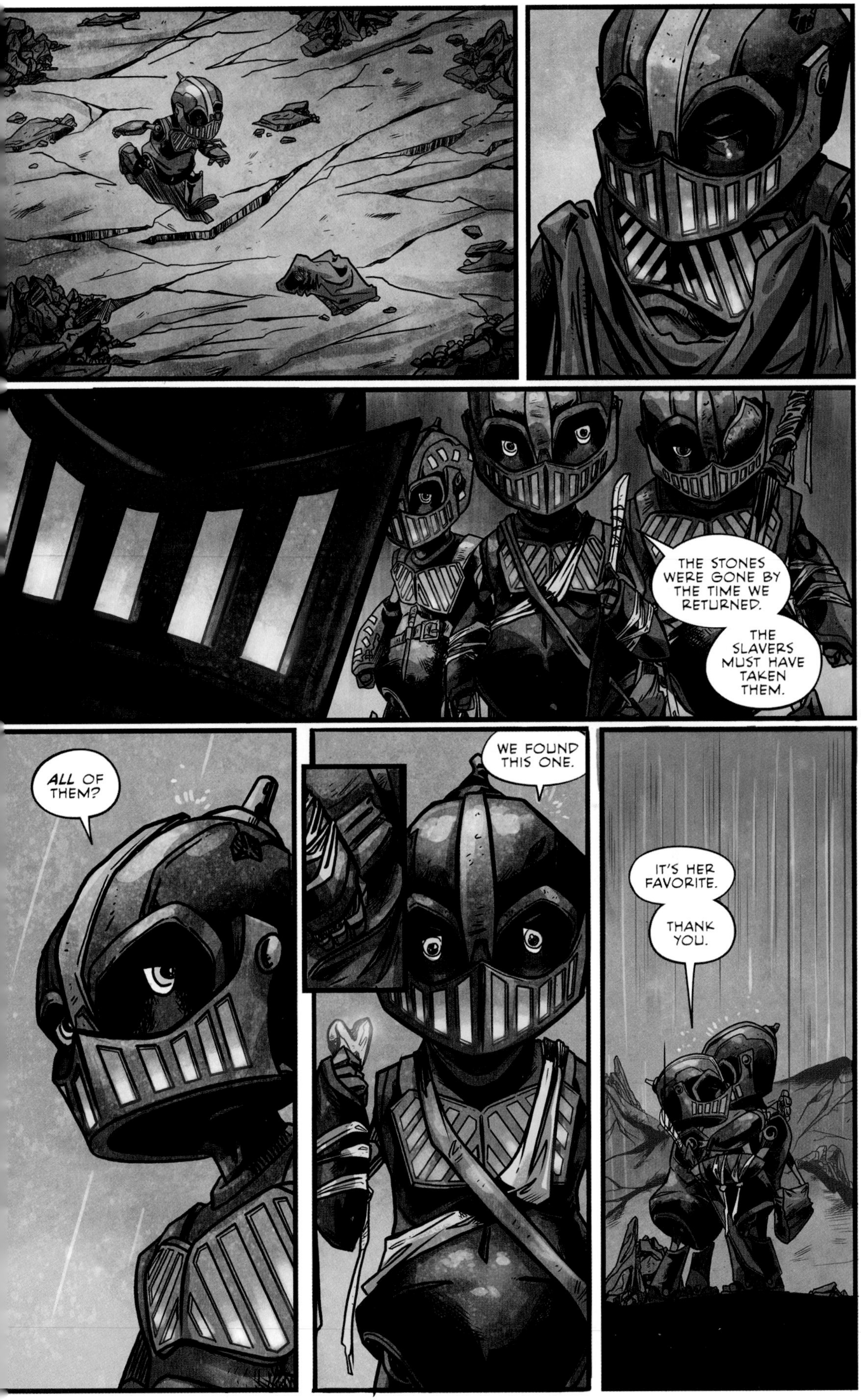
THE STONES WERE GONE BY THE TIME WE RETURNED.
THE SLAVERS MUST HAVE TAKEN THEM.
ALL OF THEM?
WE FOUND THIS ONE.
IT'S HER FAVORITE.
THANK YOU.

ELDER!

IT'S NOT SAFE FOR YOU WITH ALL THE MALOREX--

MY TIME OF FEARING THE BEASTS OF THIS WORLD HAS LONG PASSED.

CANTO, SHE HAS GIVEN YOU A NAME... ALTHOUGH IT WILL COST HER LIFE.

YOU LOVE HER... ALTHOUGH IT IS FORBIDDEN.

YOU OFFER TO GIVE HER YOUR OWN CLOCK... ALTHOUGH YOUR TIME WOULD END.

I WAS NOT FORTHRIGHT WITH YOU, CANTO.

BEYOND OUR BORDER, THERE IS A LAKE. THERE ARE RUMORS OF A HERMIT LIVING THERE WHO KNOWS WHERE WE CAME FROM AND WHY WE ARE SLAVES.

WE DID NOT COME INTO THIS WORLD WITH CLOCKS IN OUR CHESTS. WE CAME WITH HEARTS.

THE RUMORS SAY THE SLAVERS STILL KEEP THEM... SOMEWHERE. THE HERMIT WILL KNOW.

THE ONLY WAY TO SAVE HER...

...IS TO BRING BACK HER *HEART*.

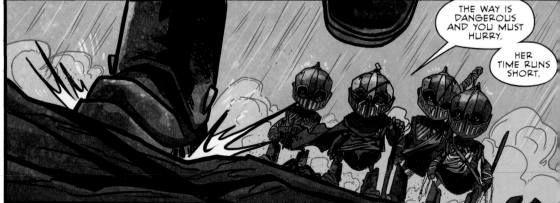

THE WAY IS DANGEROUS AND YOU MUST HURRY.

HER TIME RUNS SHORT.

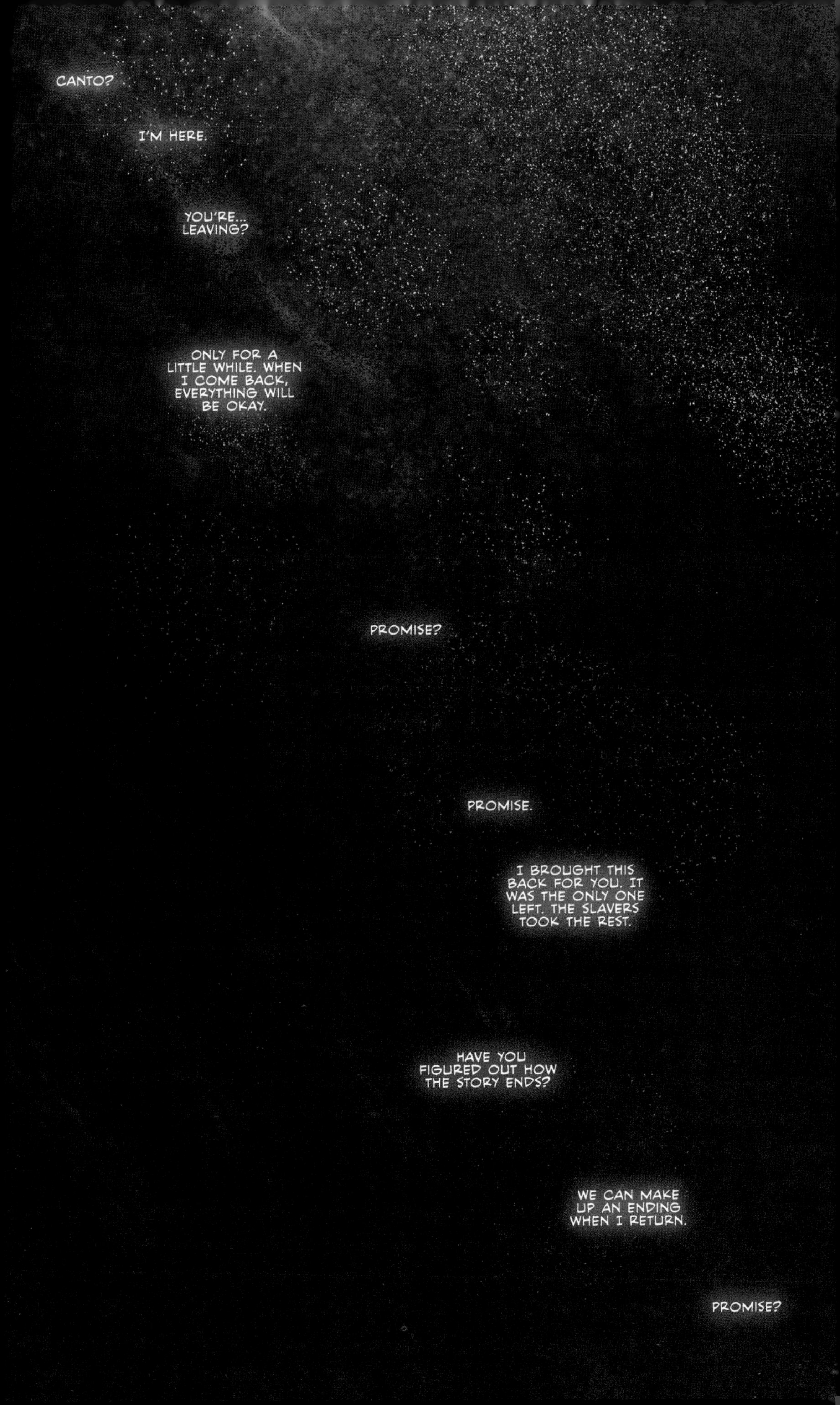
CANTO?
I'M HERE.
YOU'RE... LEAVING?
ONLY FOR A LITTLE WHILE. WHEN I COME BACK, EVERYTHING WILL BE OKAY.
PROMISE?
PROMISE.
I BROUGHT THIS BACK FOR YOU. IT WAS THE ONLY ONE LEFT. THE SLAVERS TOOK THE REST.
HAVE YOU FIGURED OUT HOW THE STORY ENDS?
WE CAN MAKE UP AN ENDING WHEN I RETURN.
PROMISE?

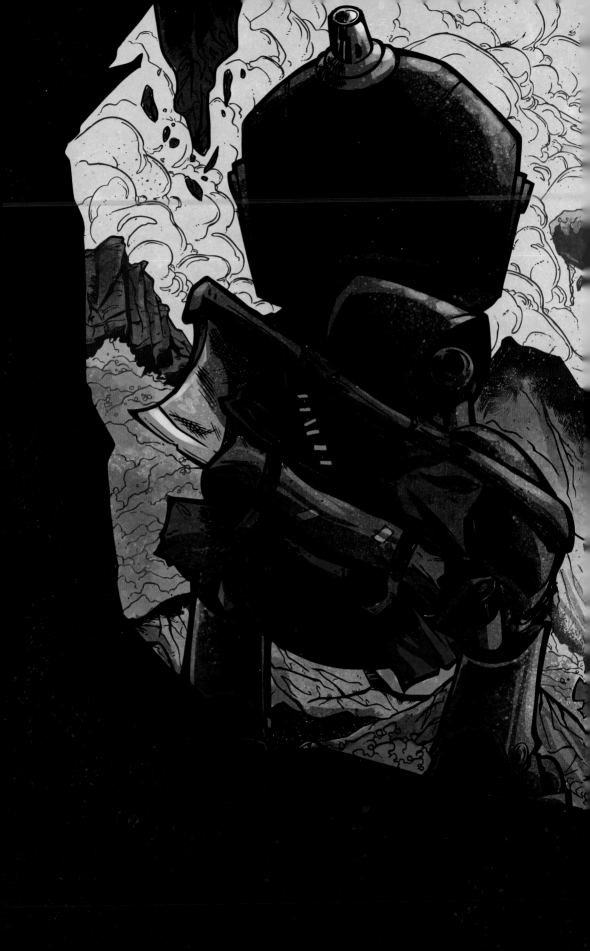

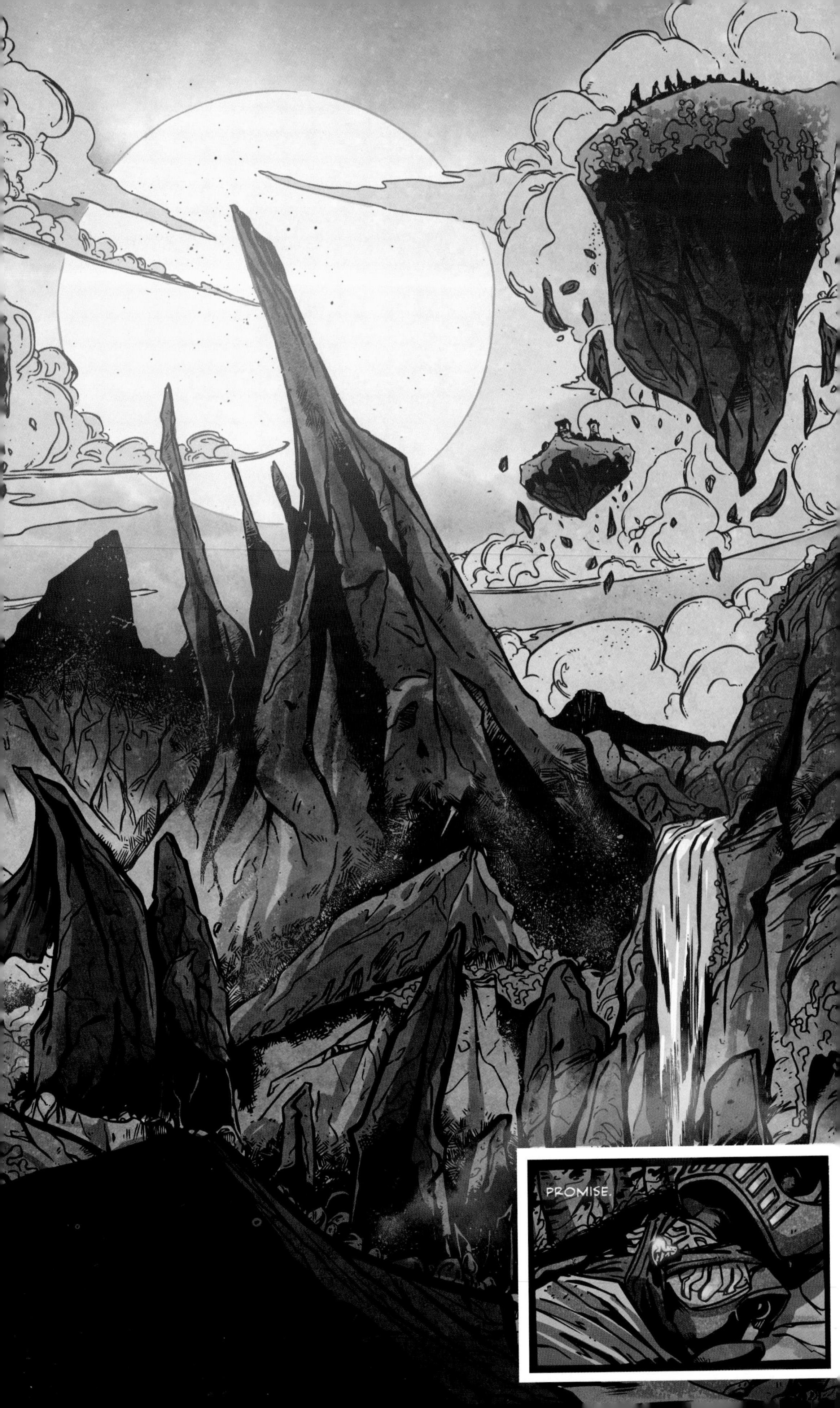
PROMISE.

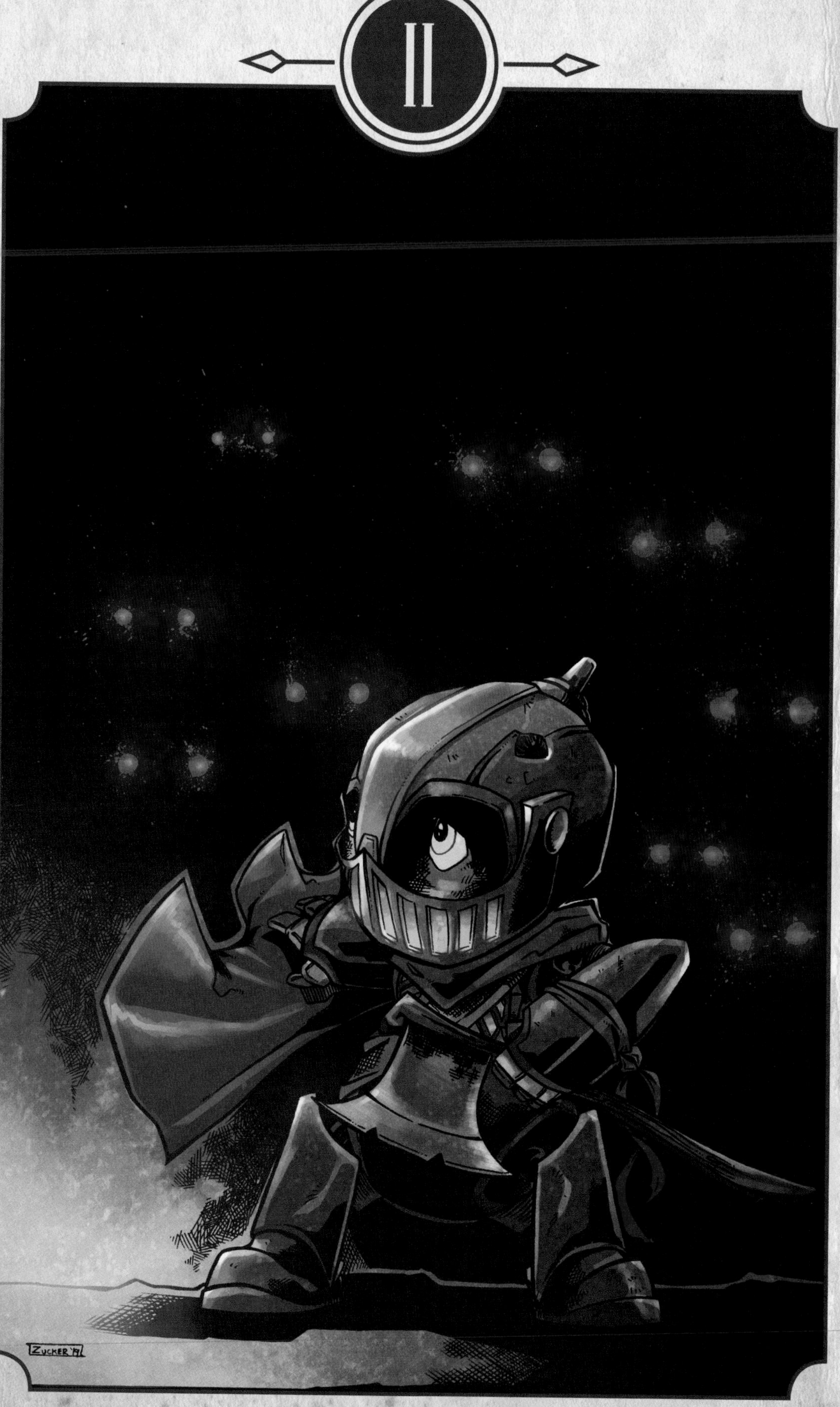
II
ZUCKER '19

Art by **Drew Zucker**, *Colors by* **Vittorio Astone**

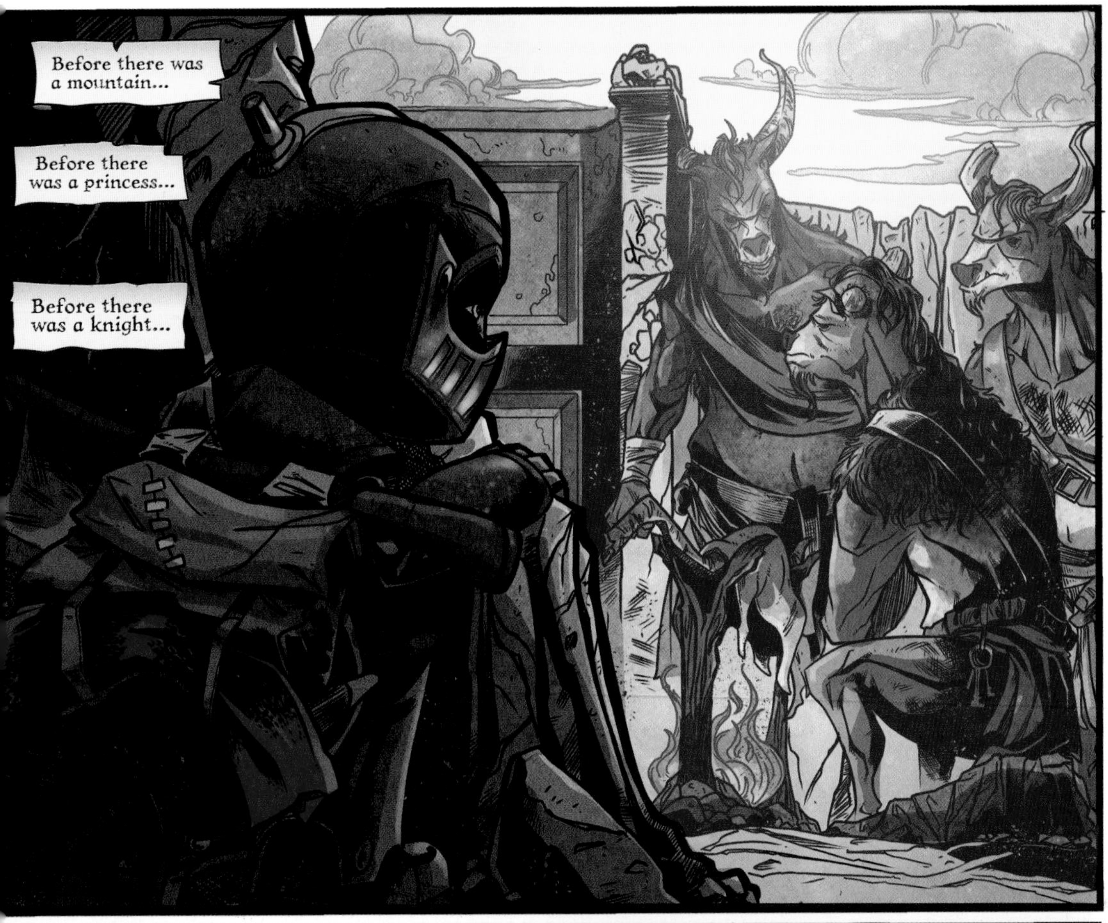
Before there was a mountain...
Before there was a princess...
Before there was a knight...

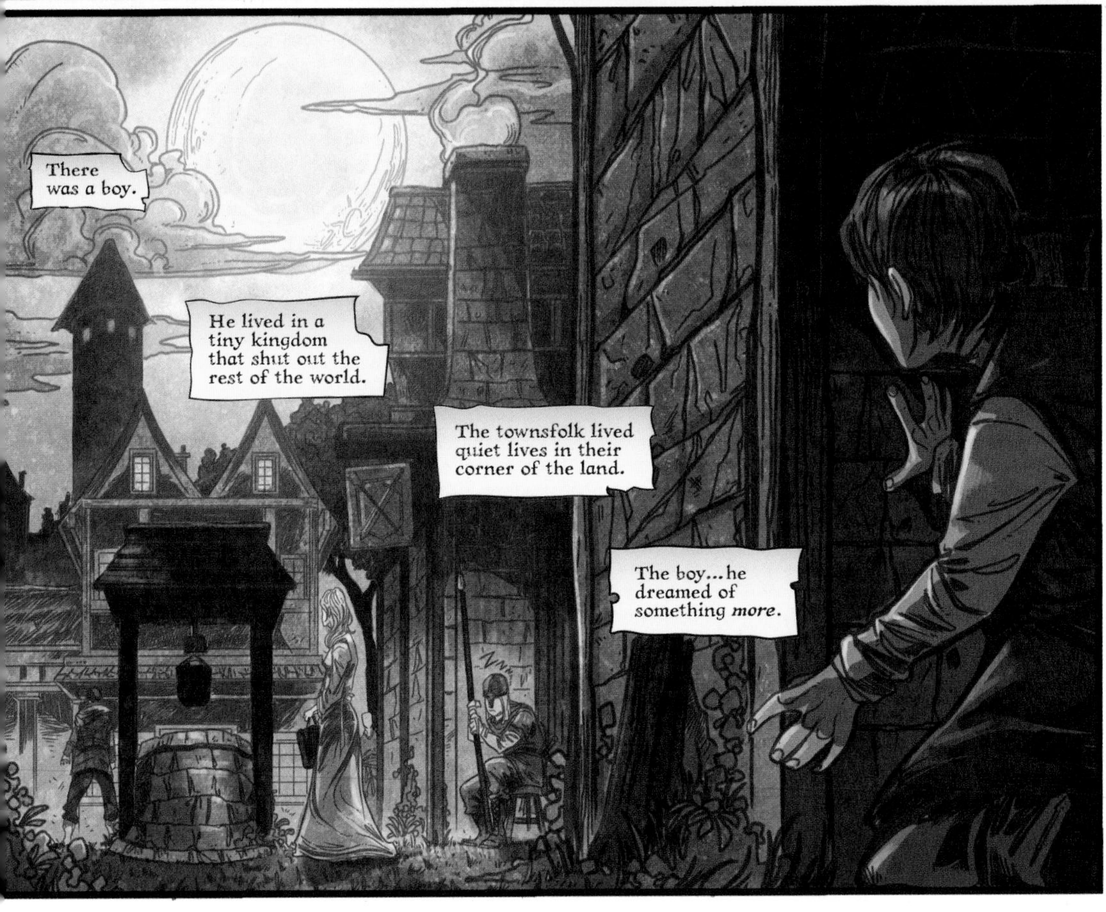
There was a boy.
He lived in a tiny kingdom that shut out the rest of the world.
The townsfolk lived quiet lives in their corner of the land.
The boy... he dreamed of something *more*.

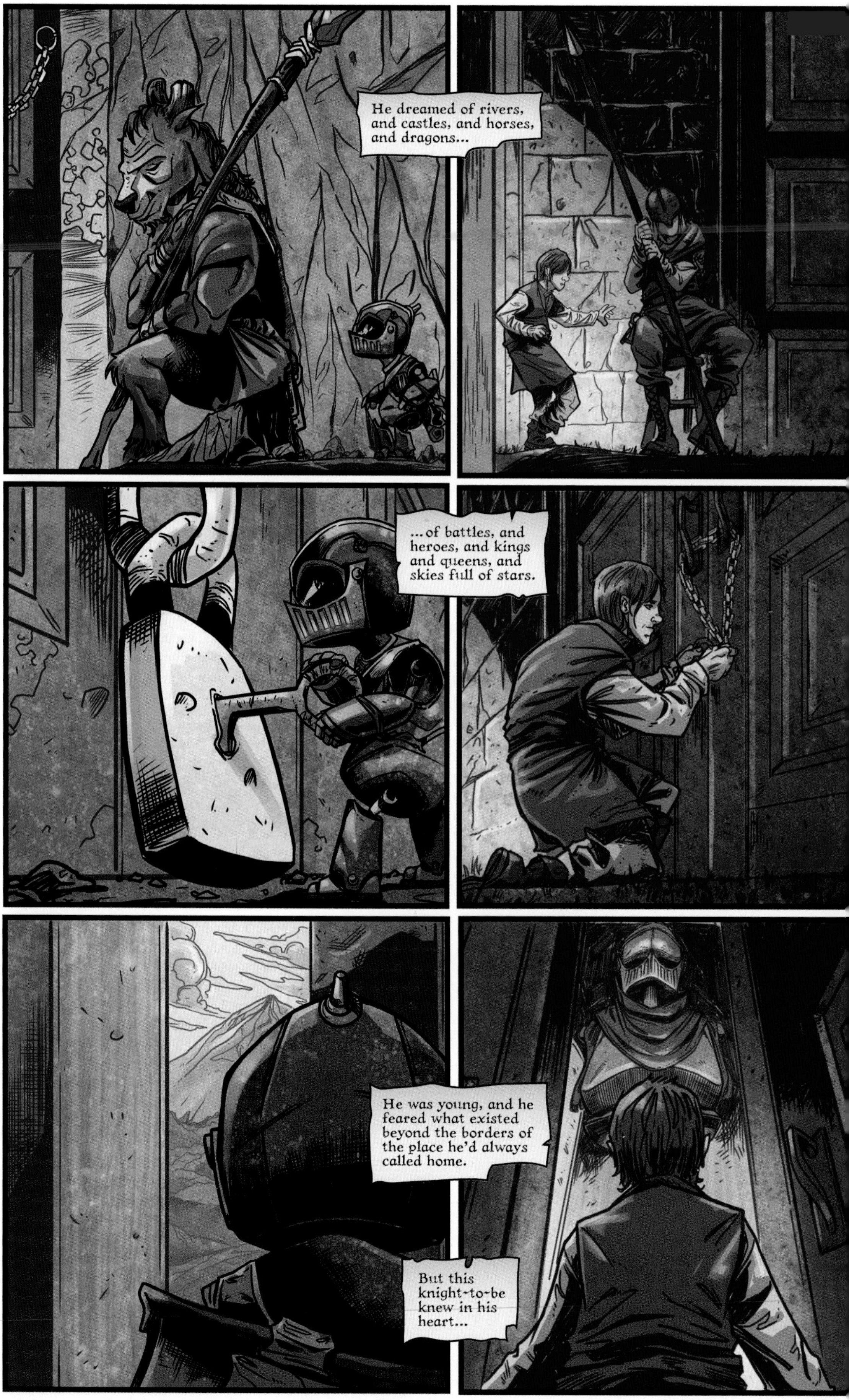
He dreamed of rivers, and castles, and horses, and dragons...
...of battles, and heroes, and kings and queens, and skies full of stars.
He was young, and he feared what existed beyond the borders of the place he'd always called home.
But this knight-to-be knew in his heart...

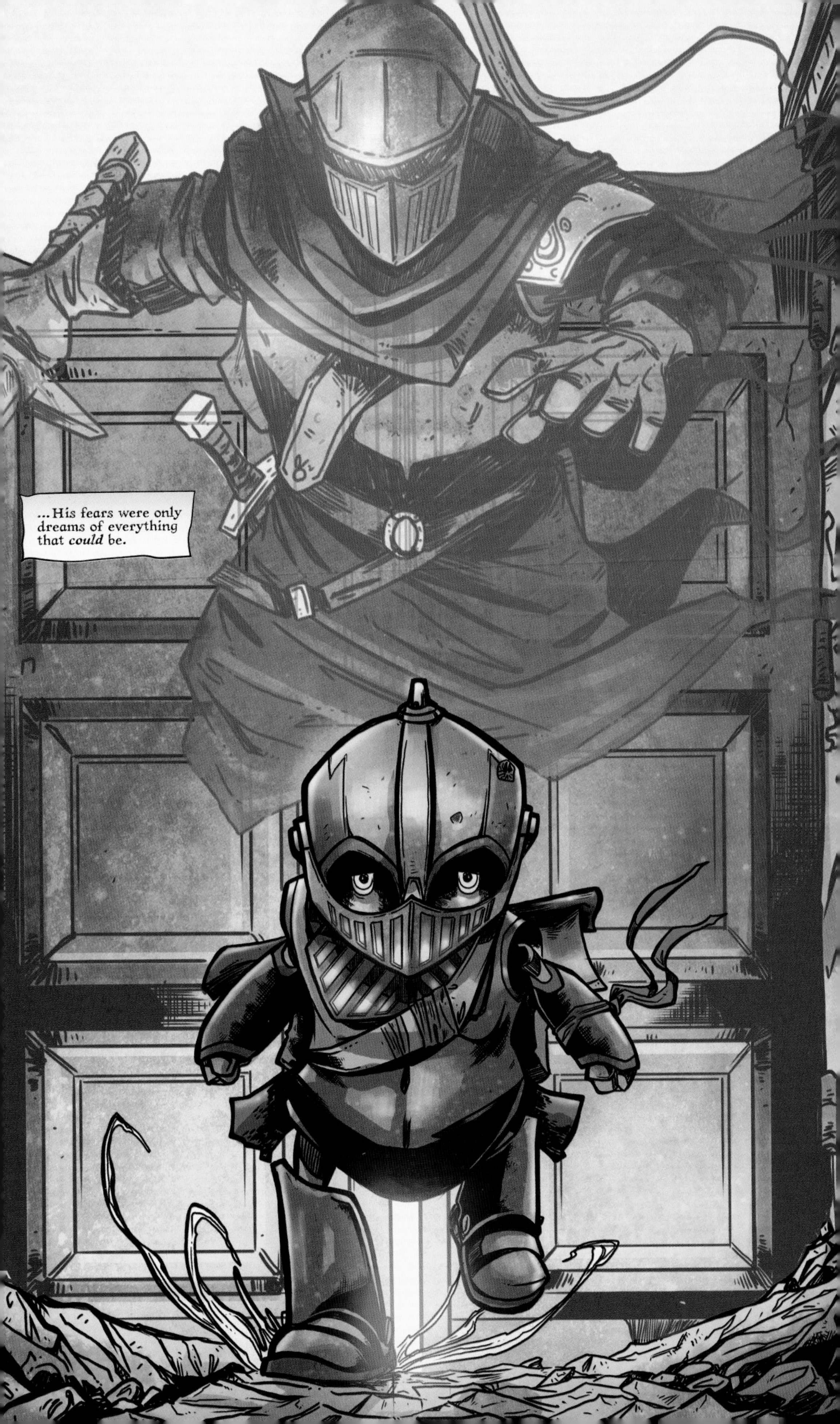
...His fears were only dreams of everything that *could* be.

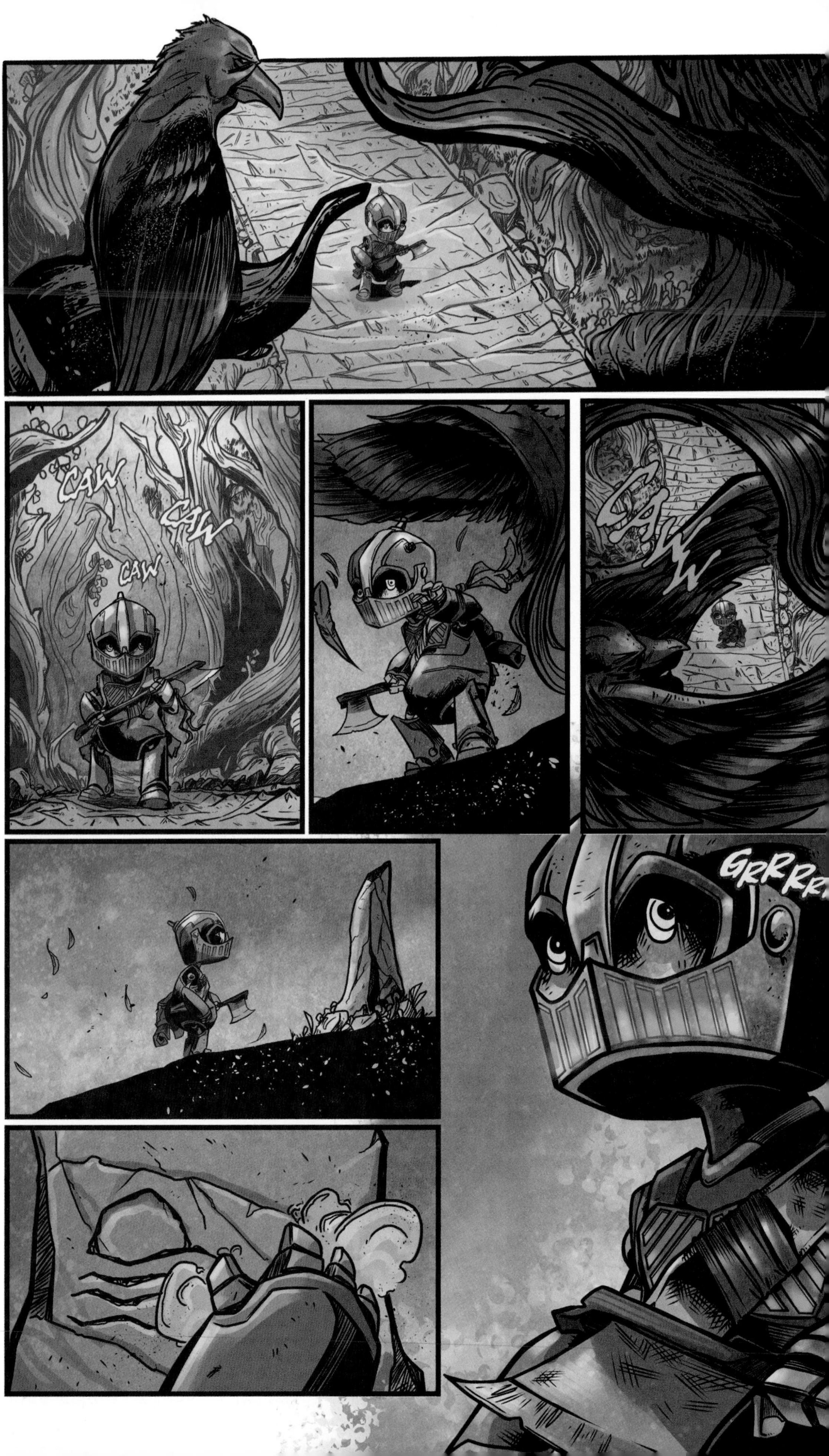
CAW
CAW
CAW
CAW
GRRR

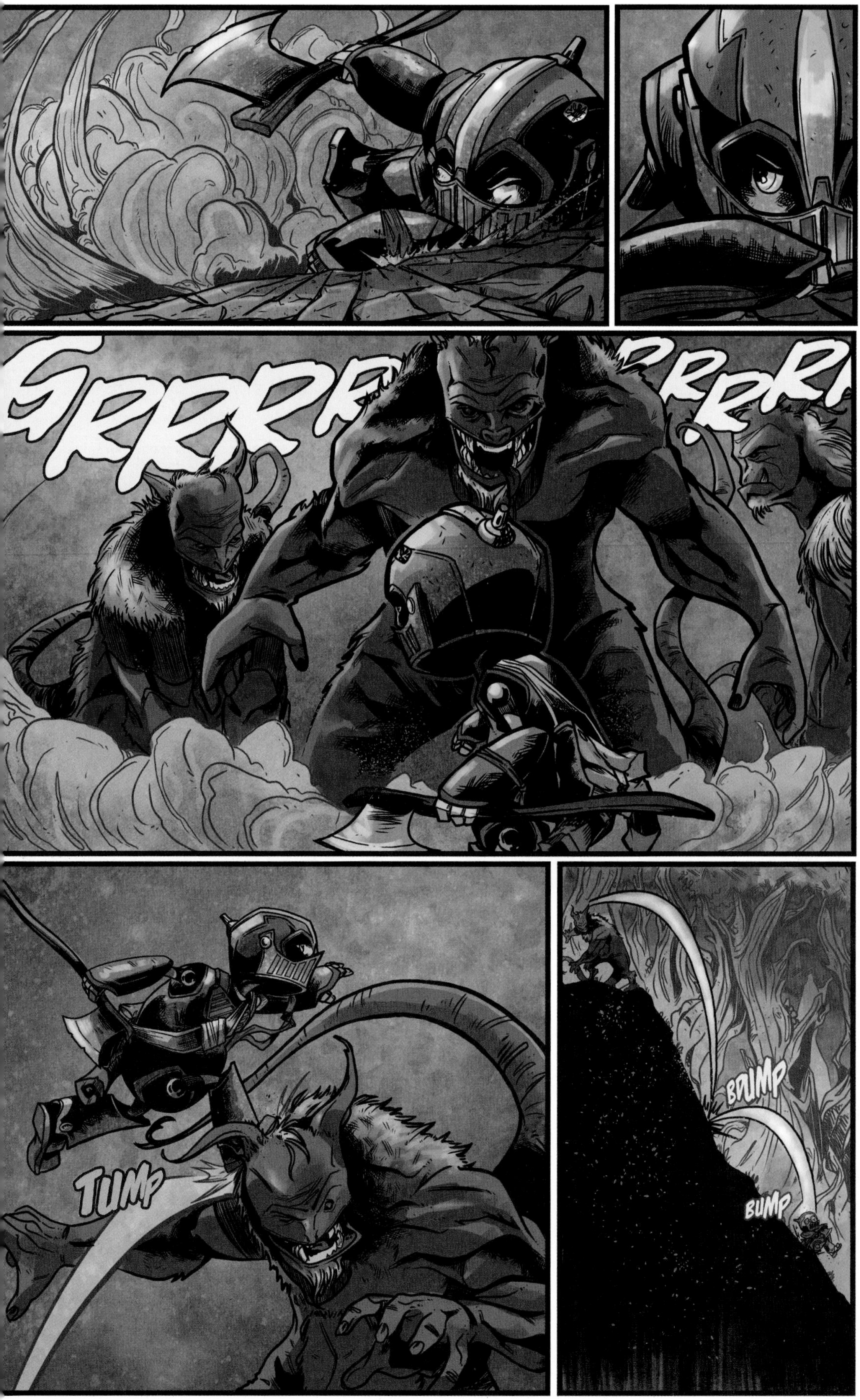
GRRRRRRRRRRR
TUMP
BDUMP
BUMP

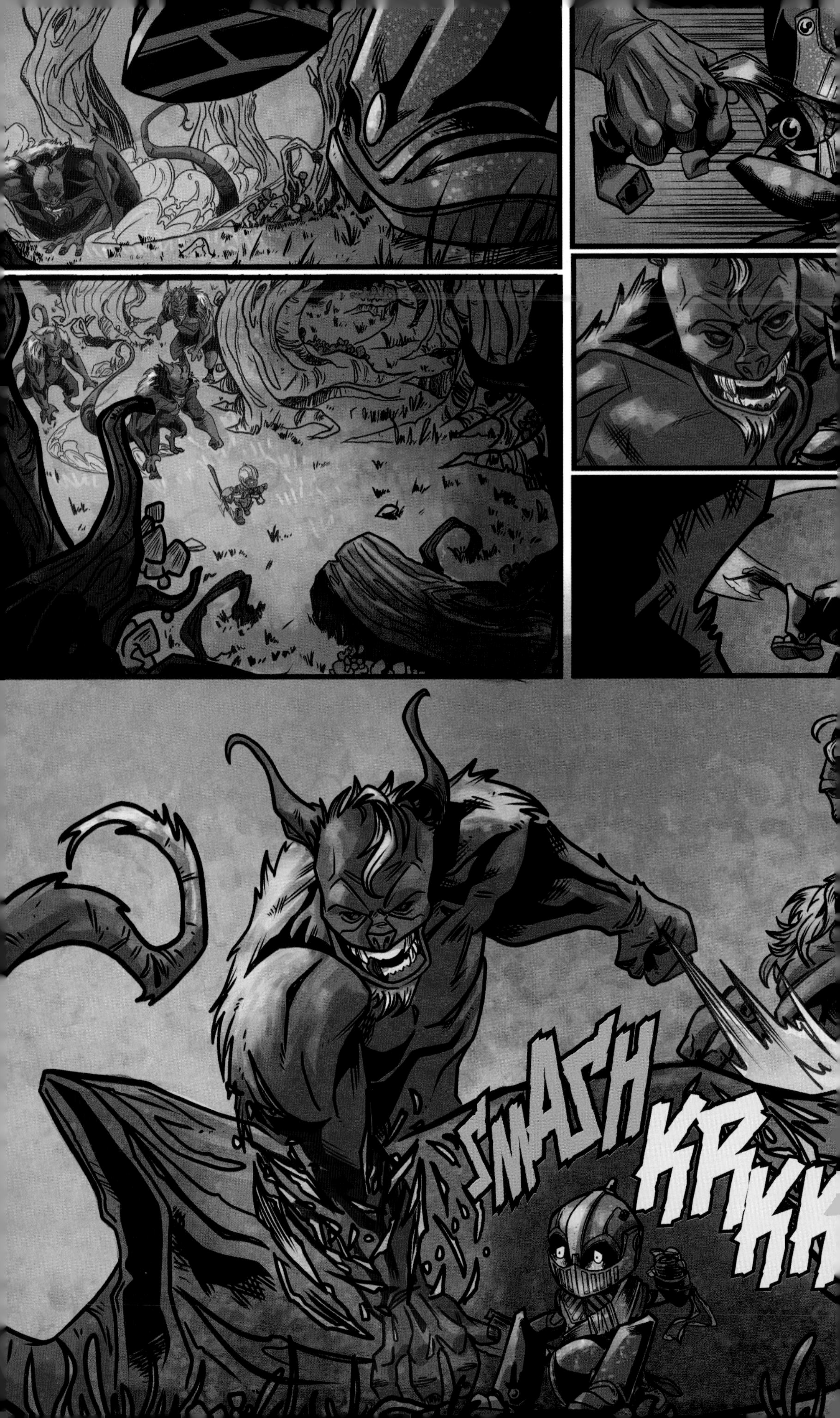
SMASH
KRKK

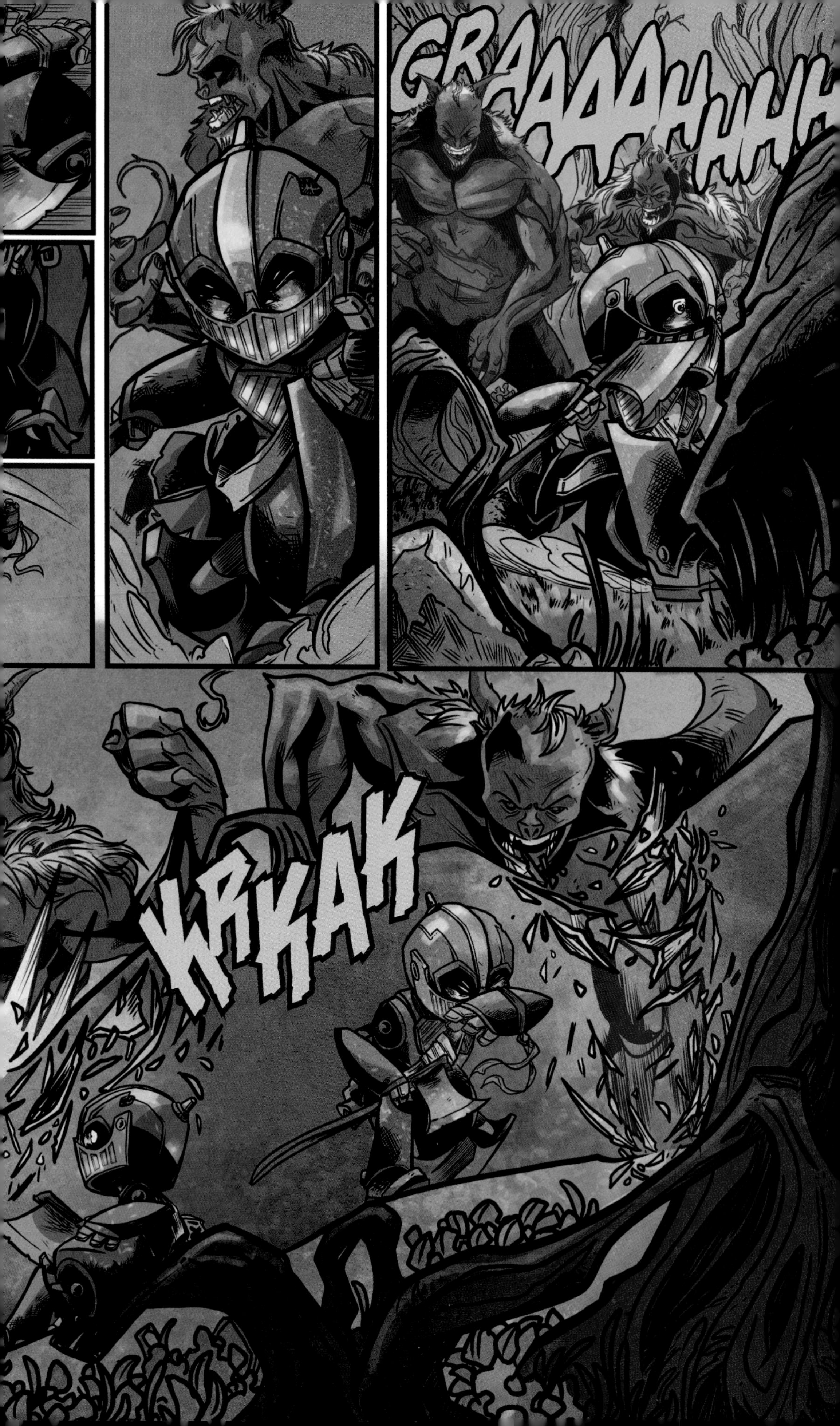
GRAAAAHHHH
KRKAK

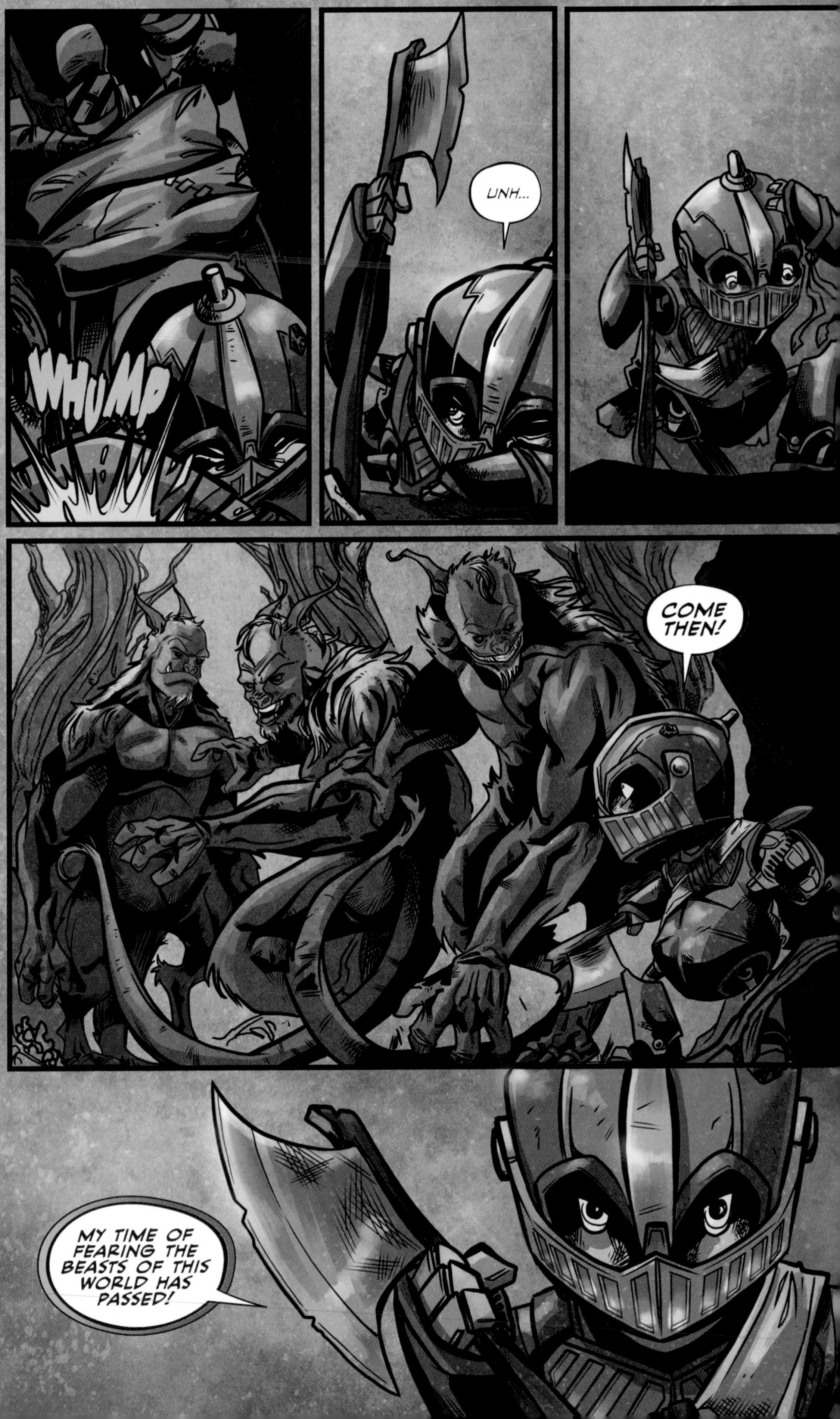
WHUMP
UNH...
COME THEN!
MY TIME OF FEARING THE BEASTS OF THIS WORLD HAS PASSED!

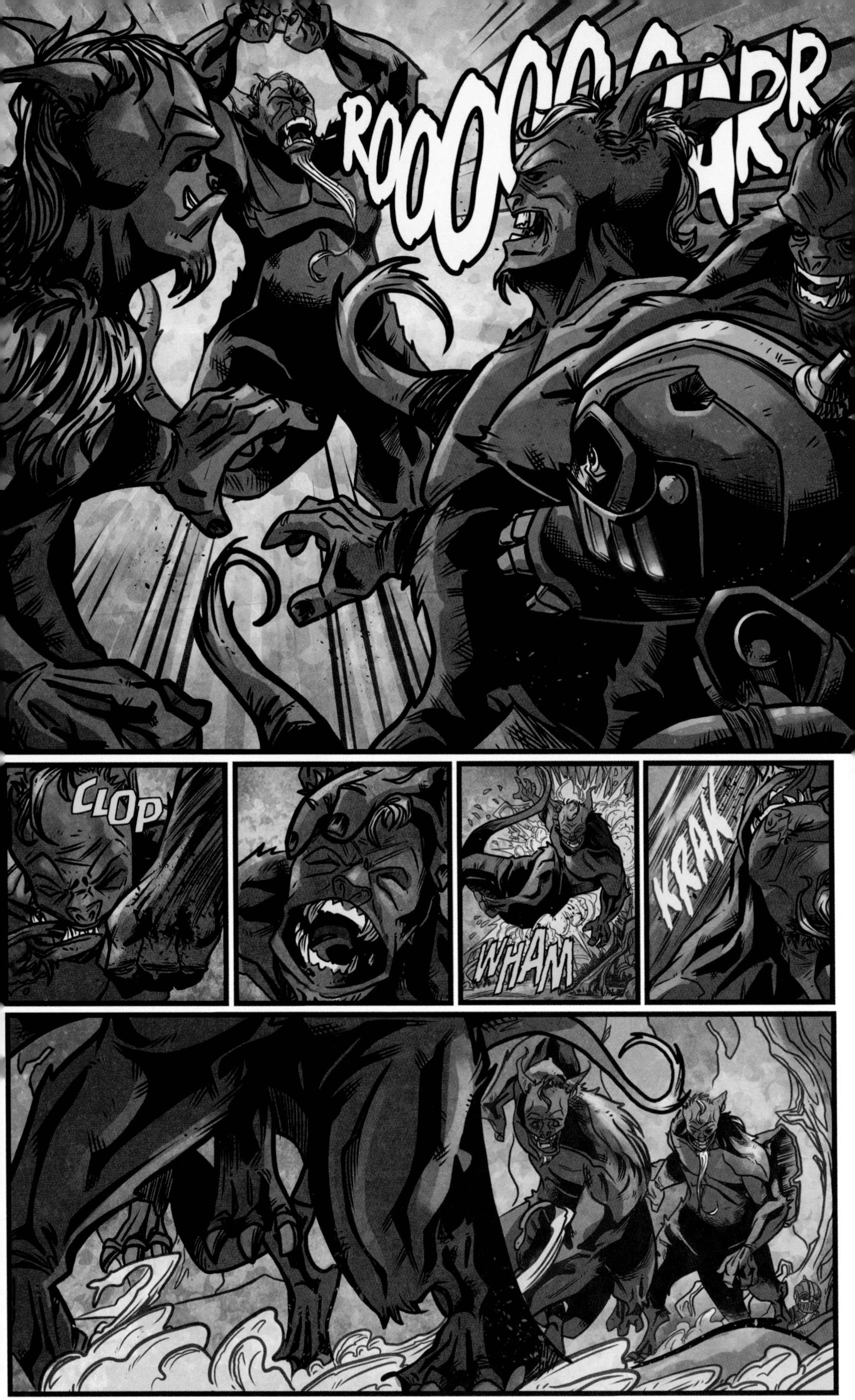
ROOOOOOOARR
CLOP
WHAM
KRAK

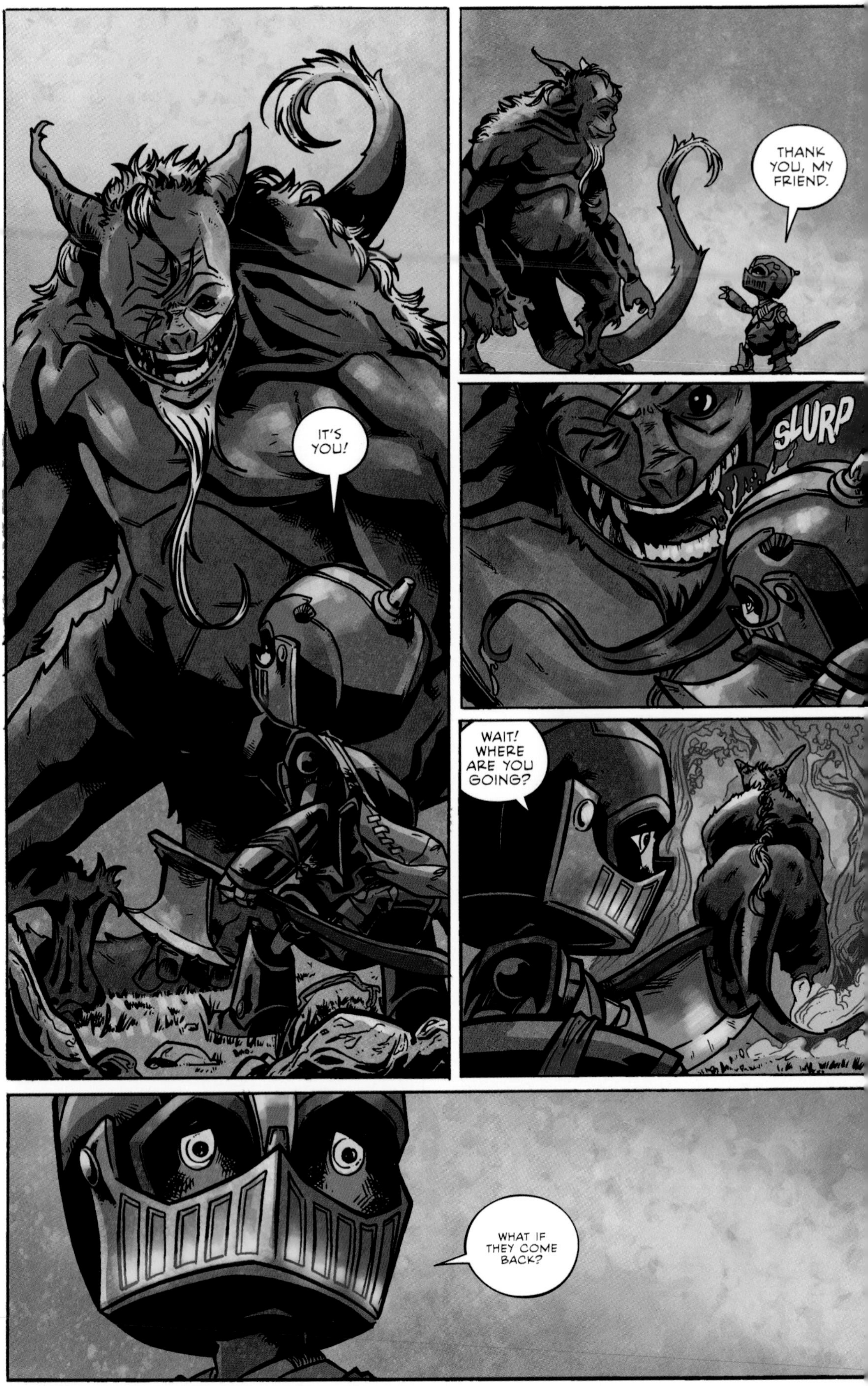
IT'S YOU!
THANK YOU, MY FRIEND.
SLURP
WAIT! WHERE ARE YOU GOING?
WHAT IF THEY COME BACK?

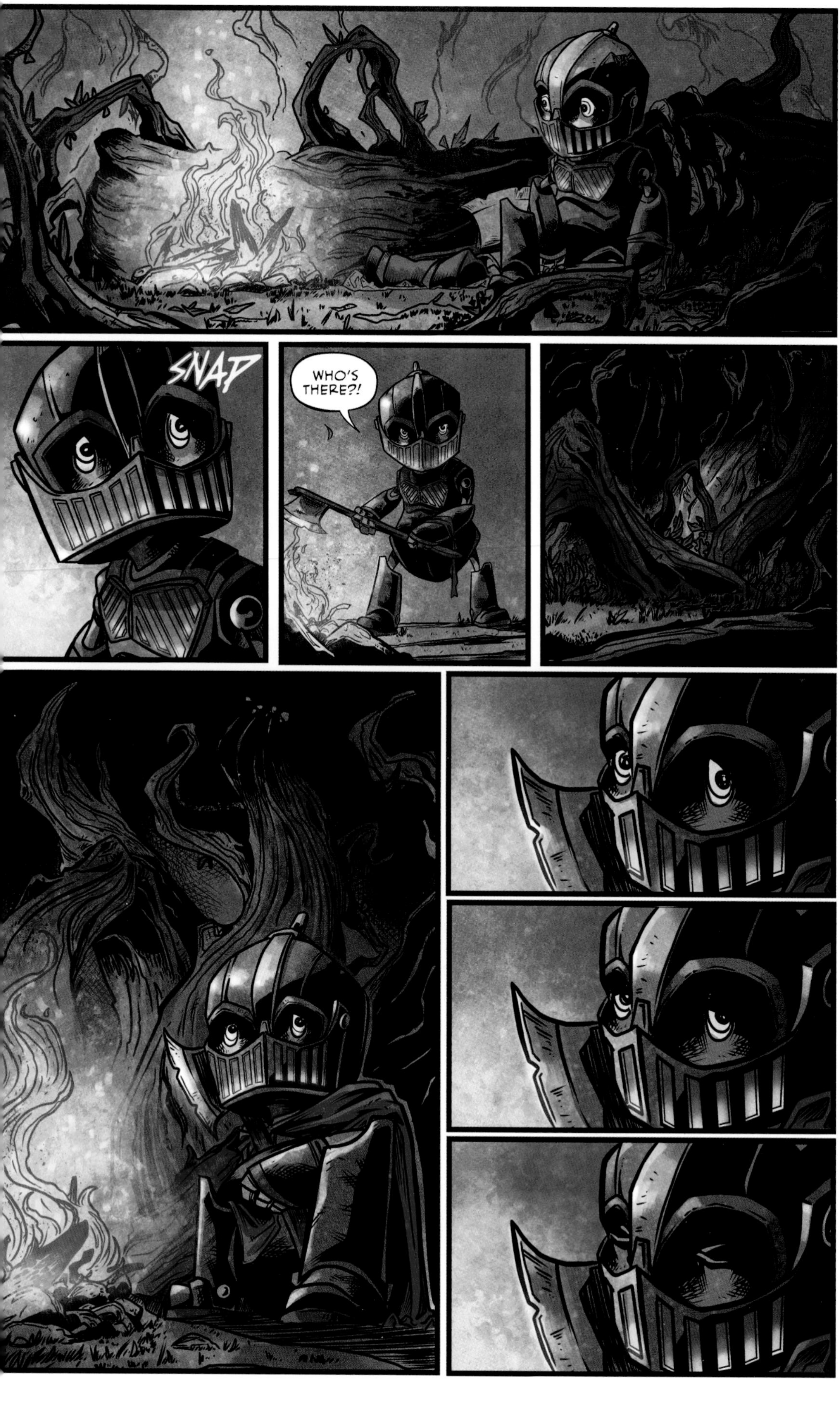
SNAP
WHO'S THERE?!

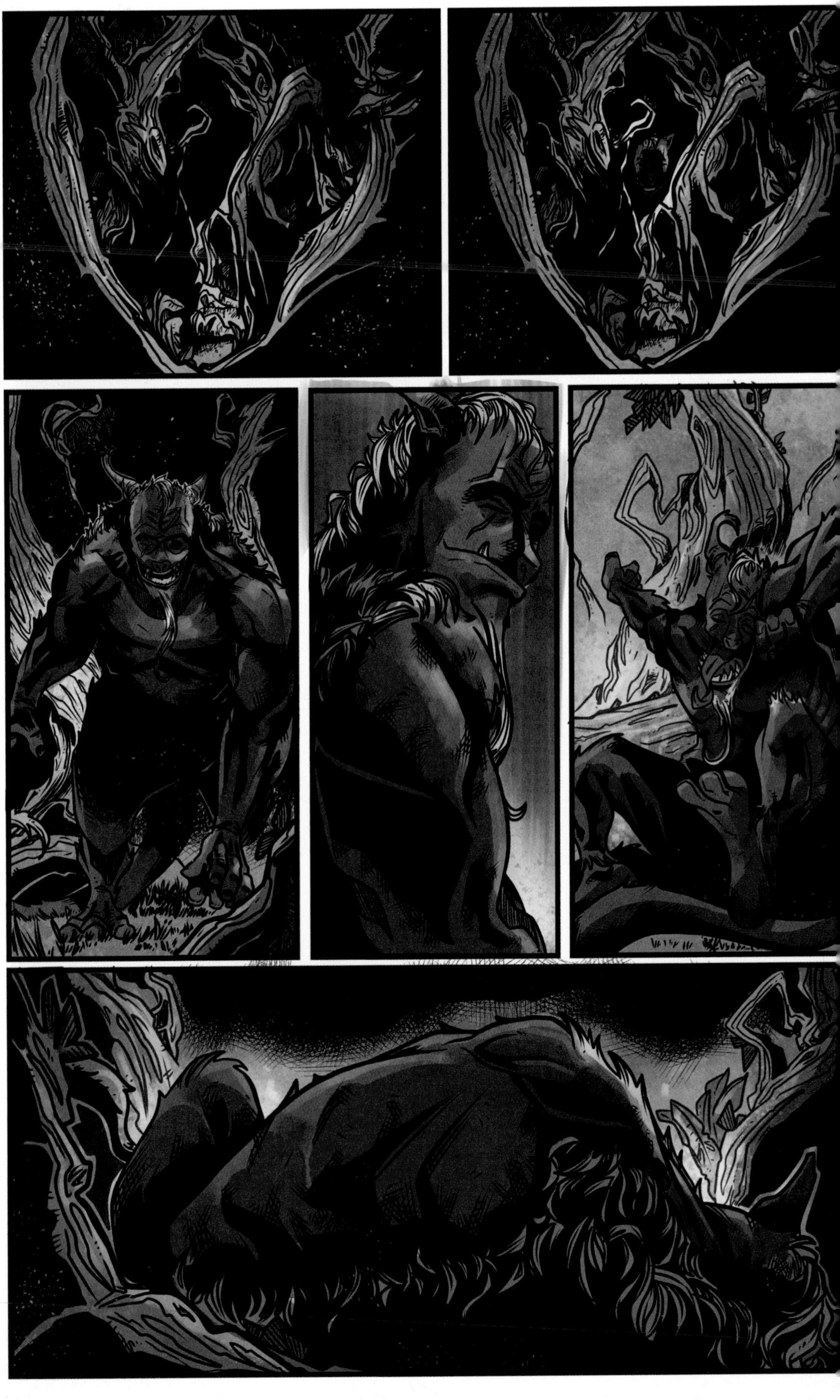

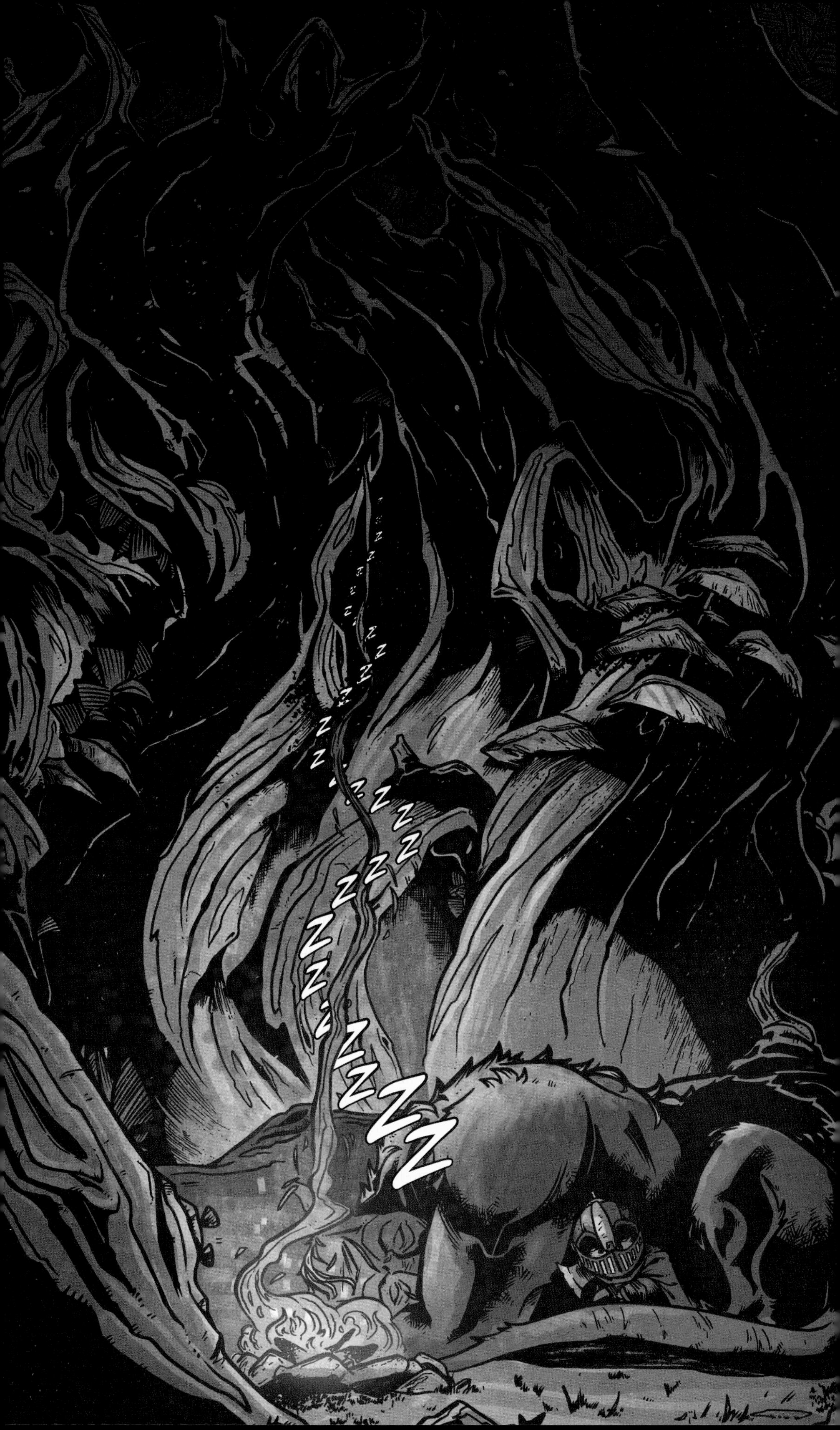

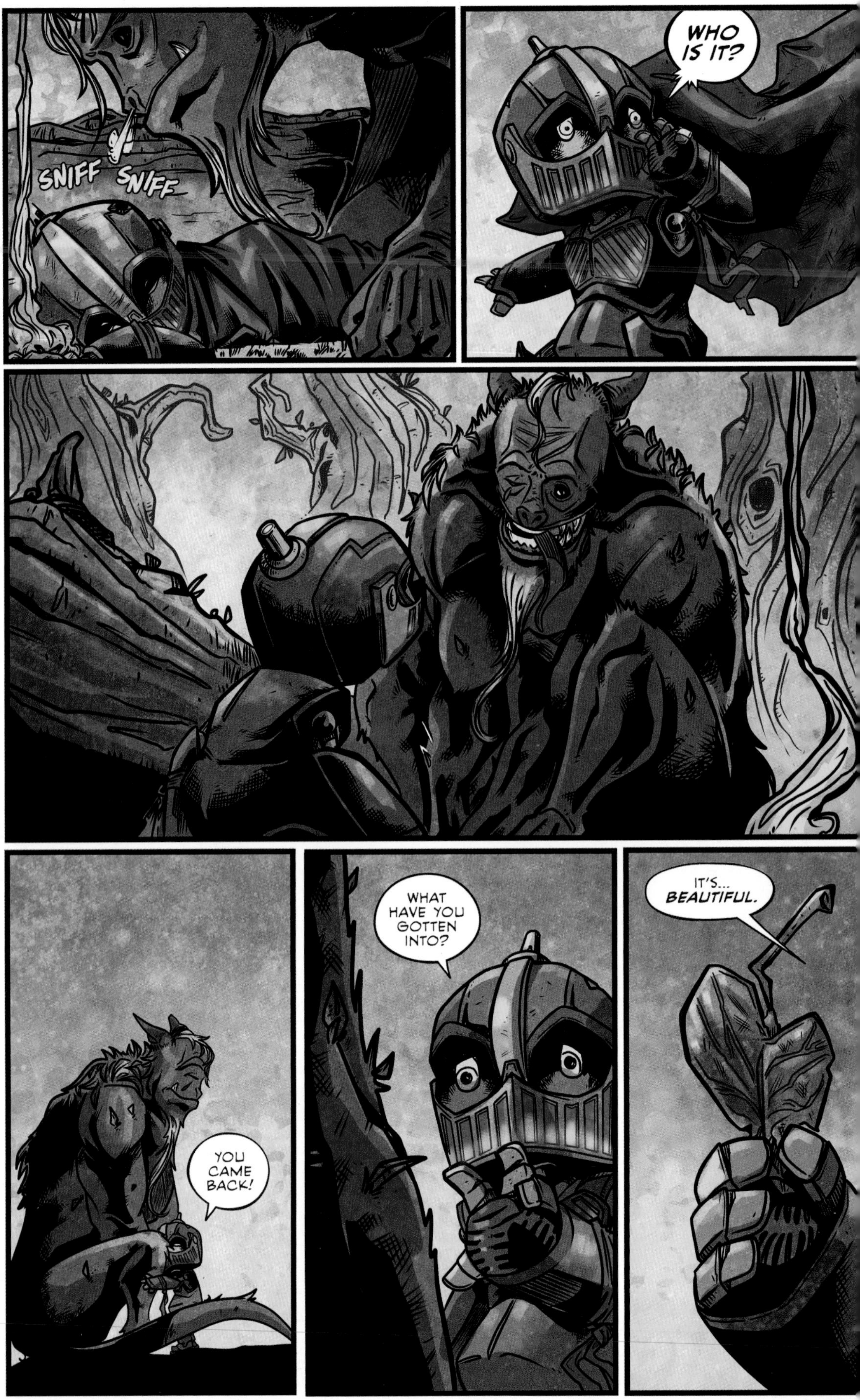
SNIFF SNIFF
WHO IS IT?
WHAT HAVE YOU GOTTEN INTO?
IT'S... BEAUTIFUL.
YOU CAME BACK!

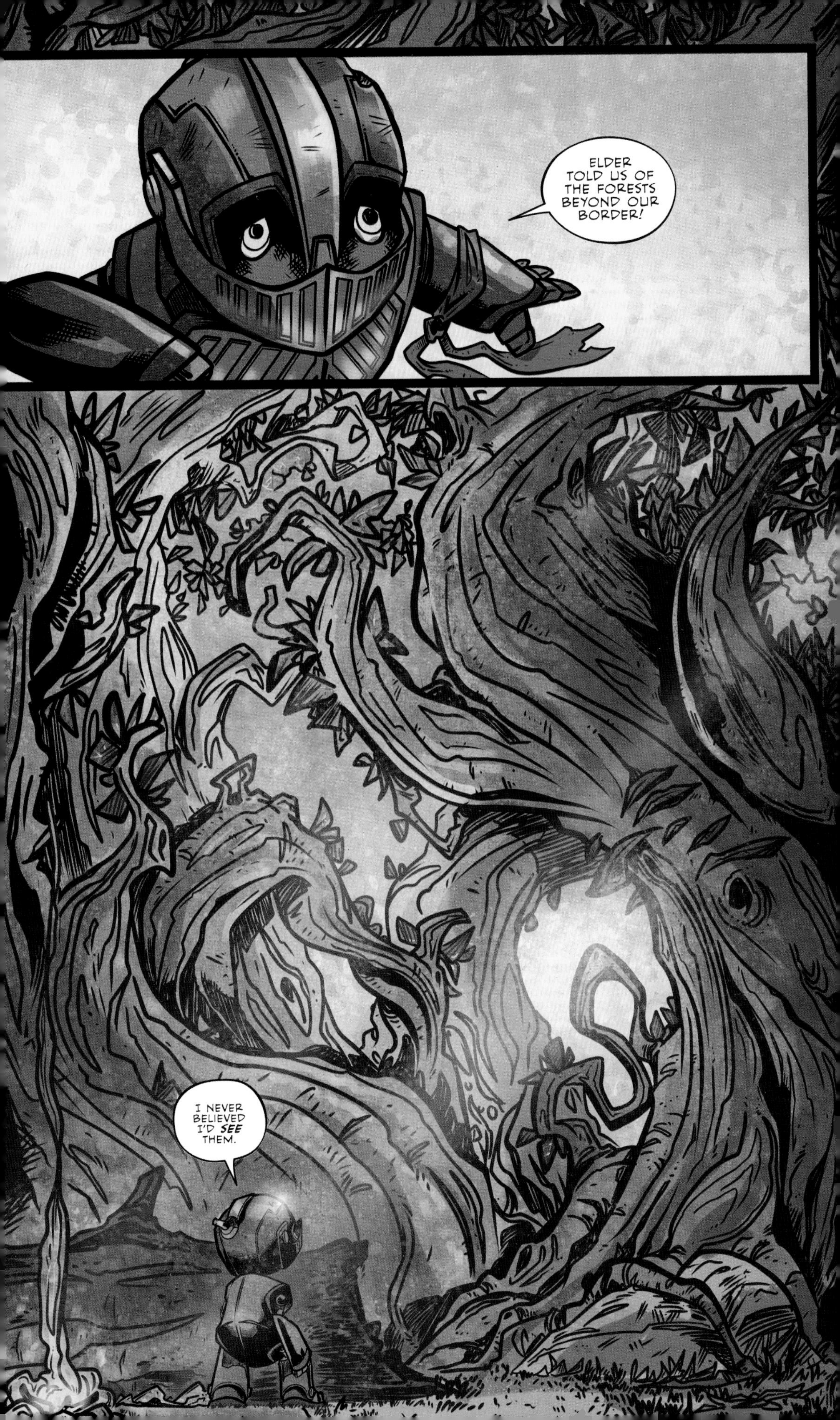
ELDER TOLD US OF THE FORESTS BEYOND OUR BORDER!
I NEVER BELIEVED I'D *SEE* THEM.

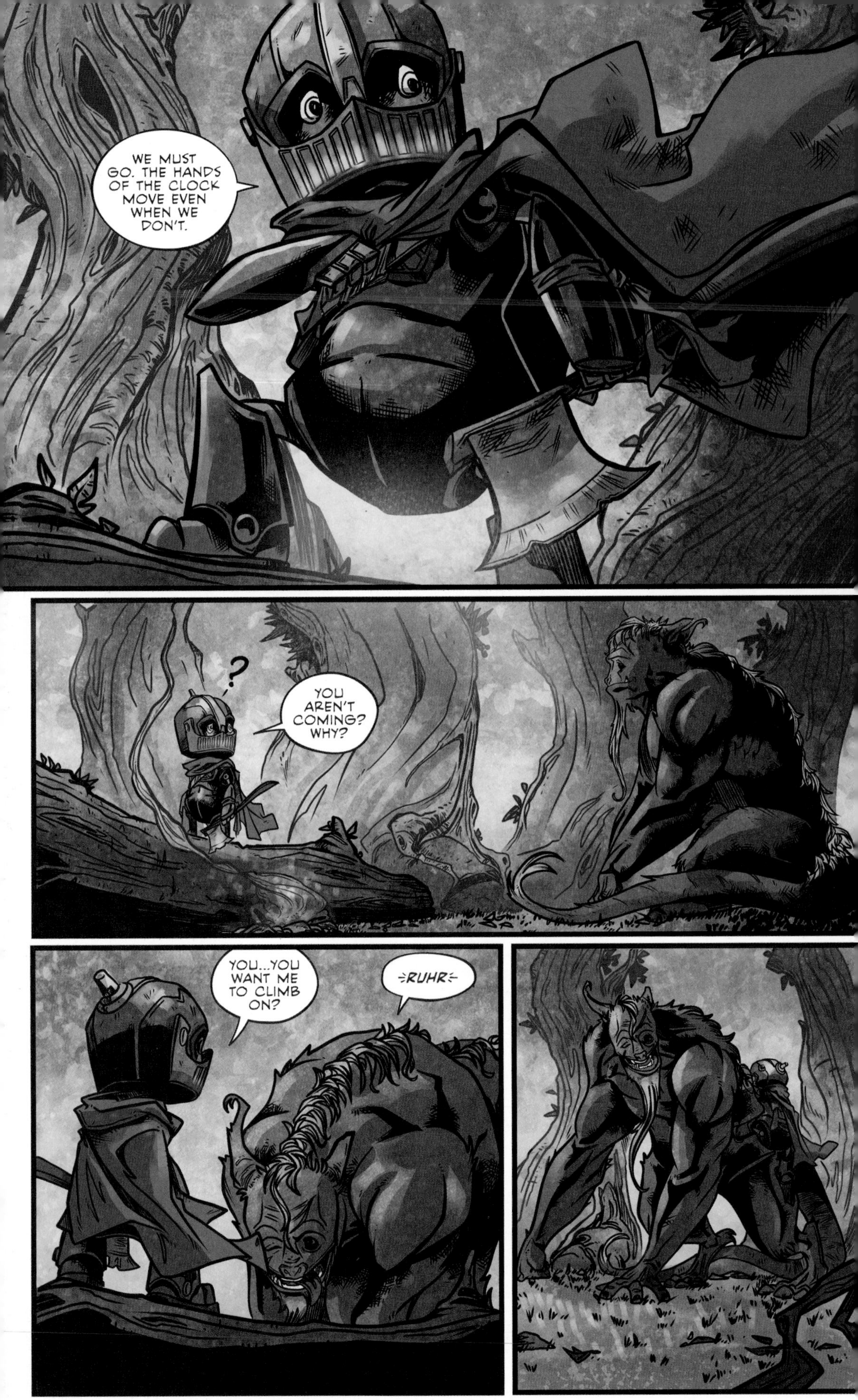
WE MUST GO. THE HANDS OF THE CLOCK MOVE EVEN WHEN WE DON'T.
?
YOU AREN'T COMING? WHY?
YOU...YOU WANT ME TO CLIMB ON?
RUHR

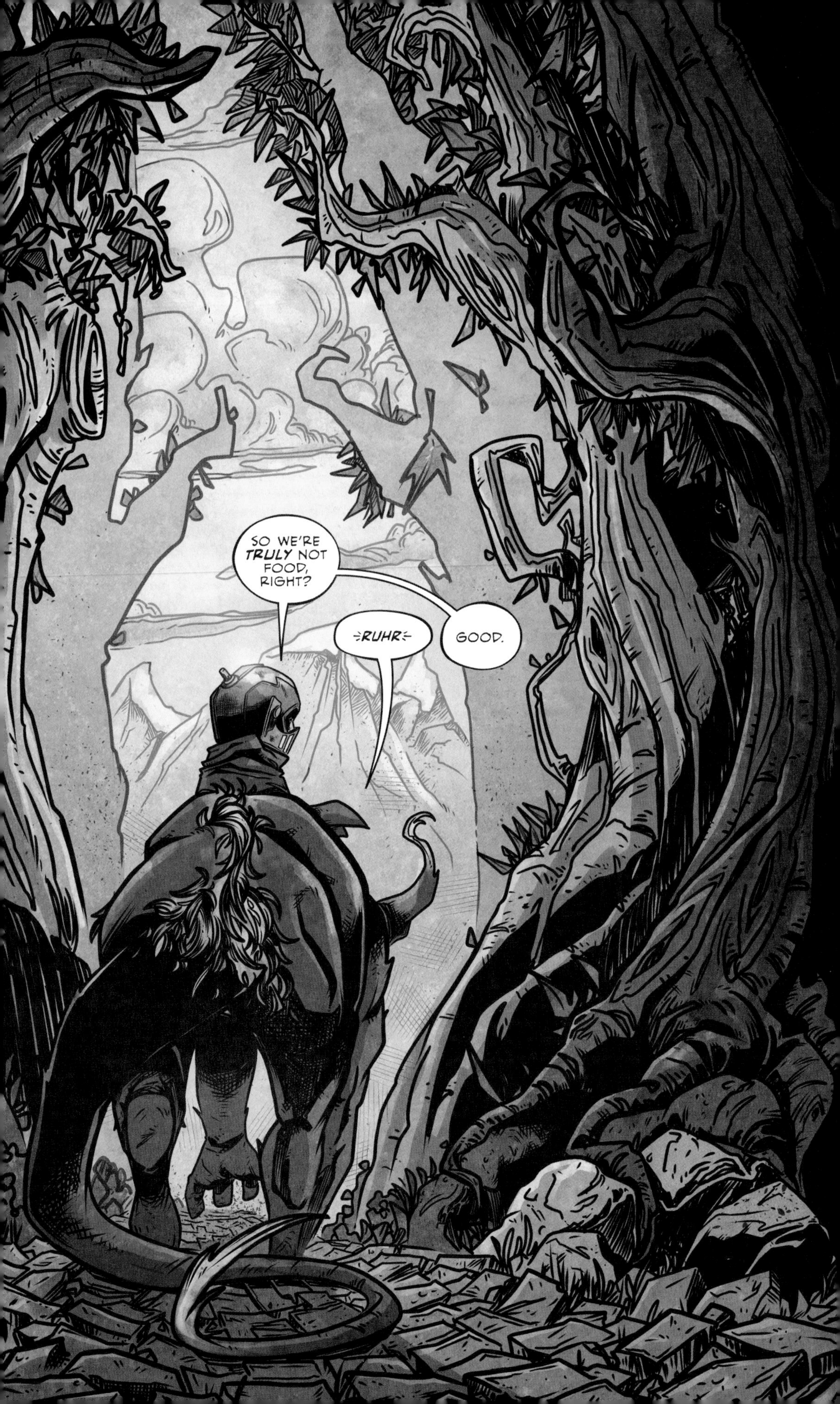
SO WE'RE TRULY NOT FOOD, RIGHT?
RUHR
GOOD.

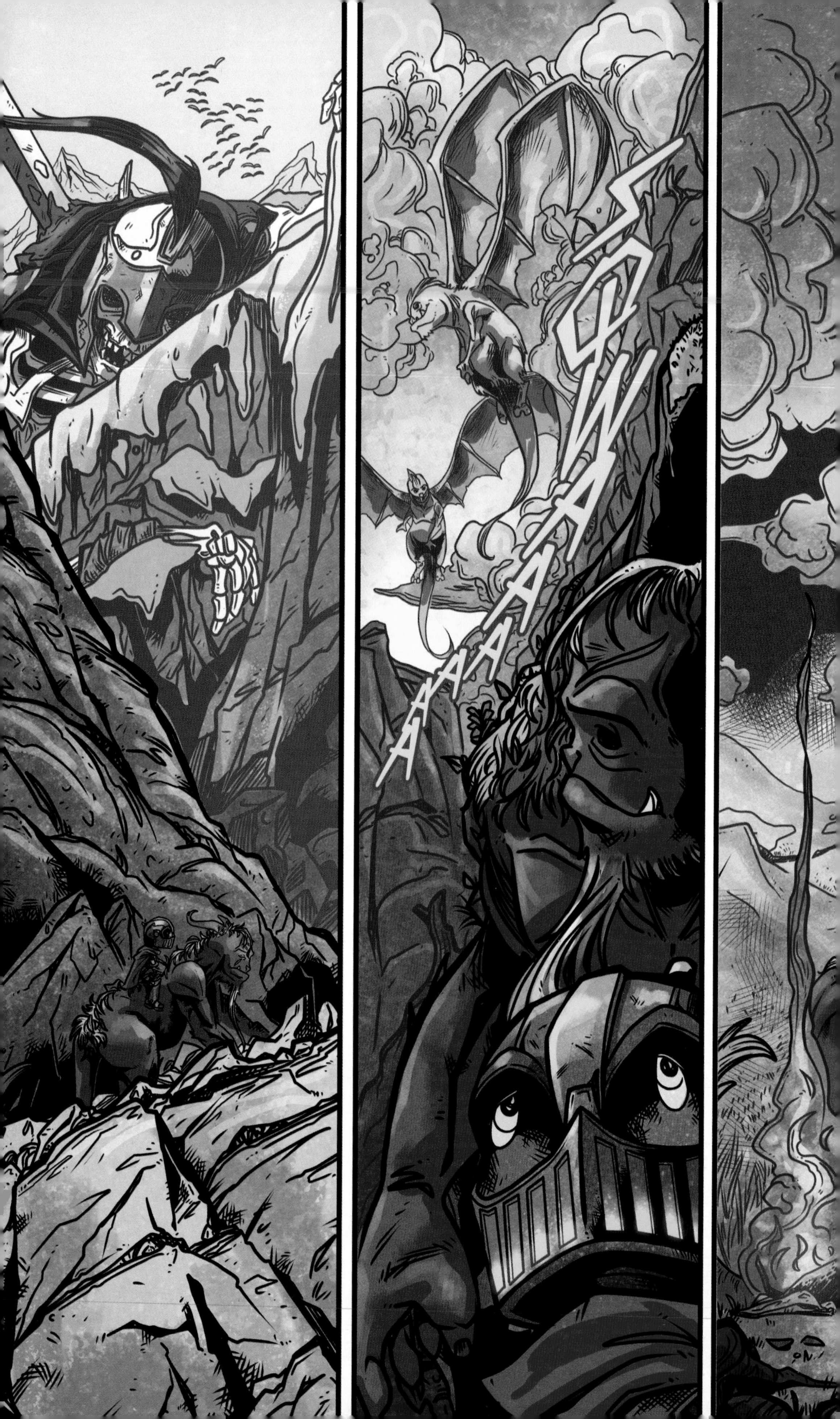
SQWAAAAAAAA

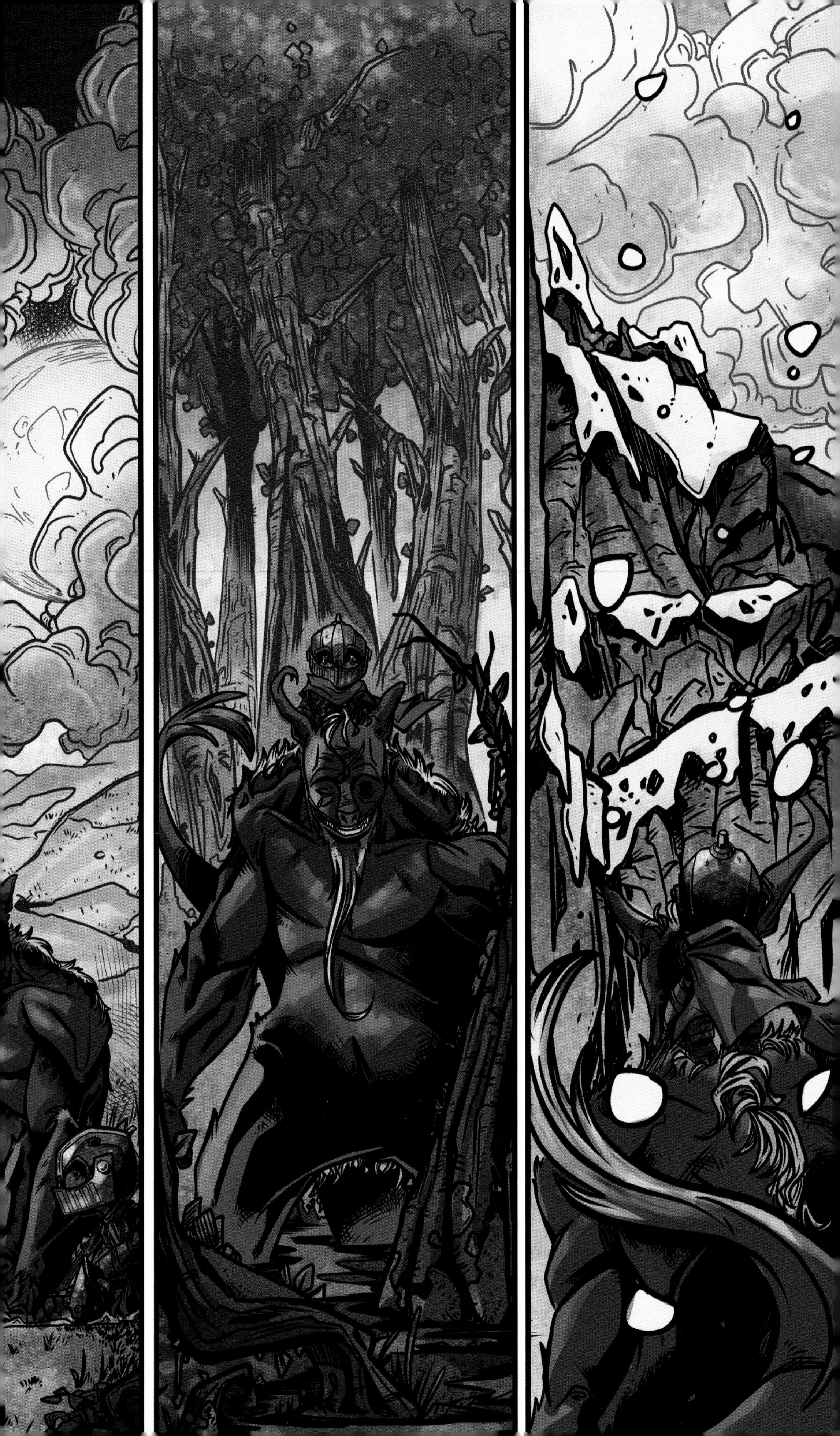

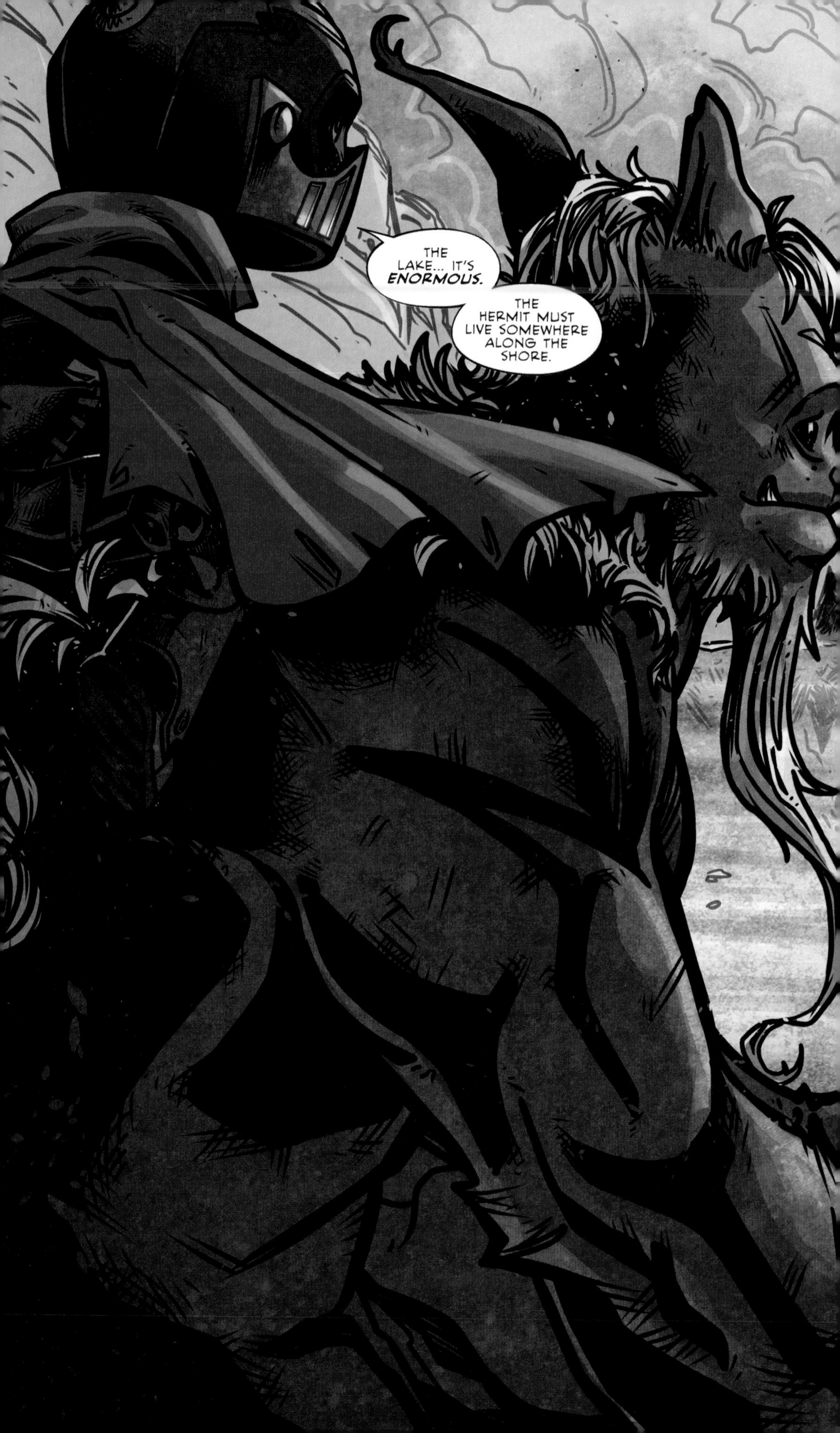
THE LAKE... IT'S *ENORMOUS.*
THE HERMIT MUST LIVE SOMEWHERE ALONG THE SHORE.

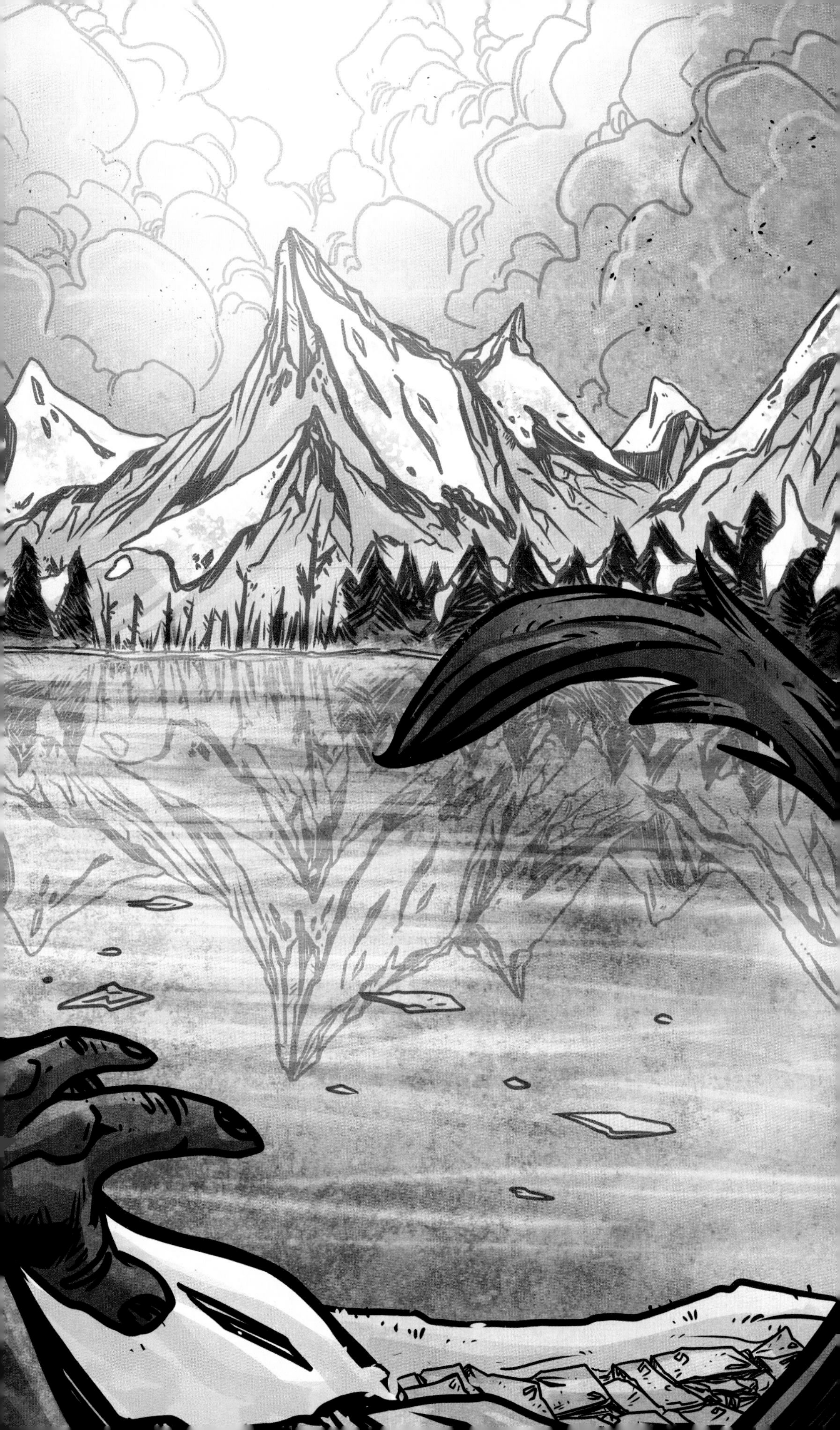

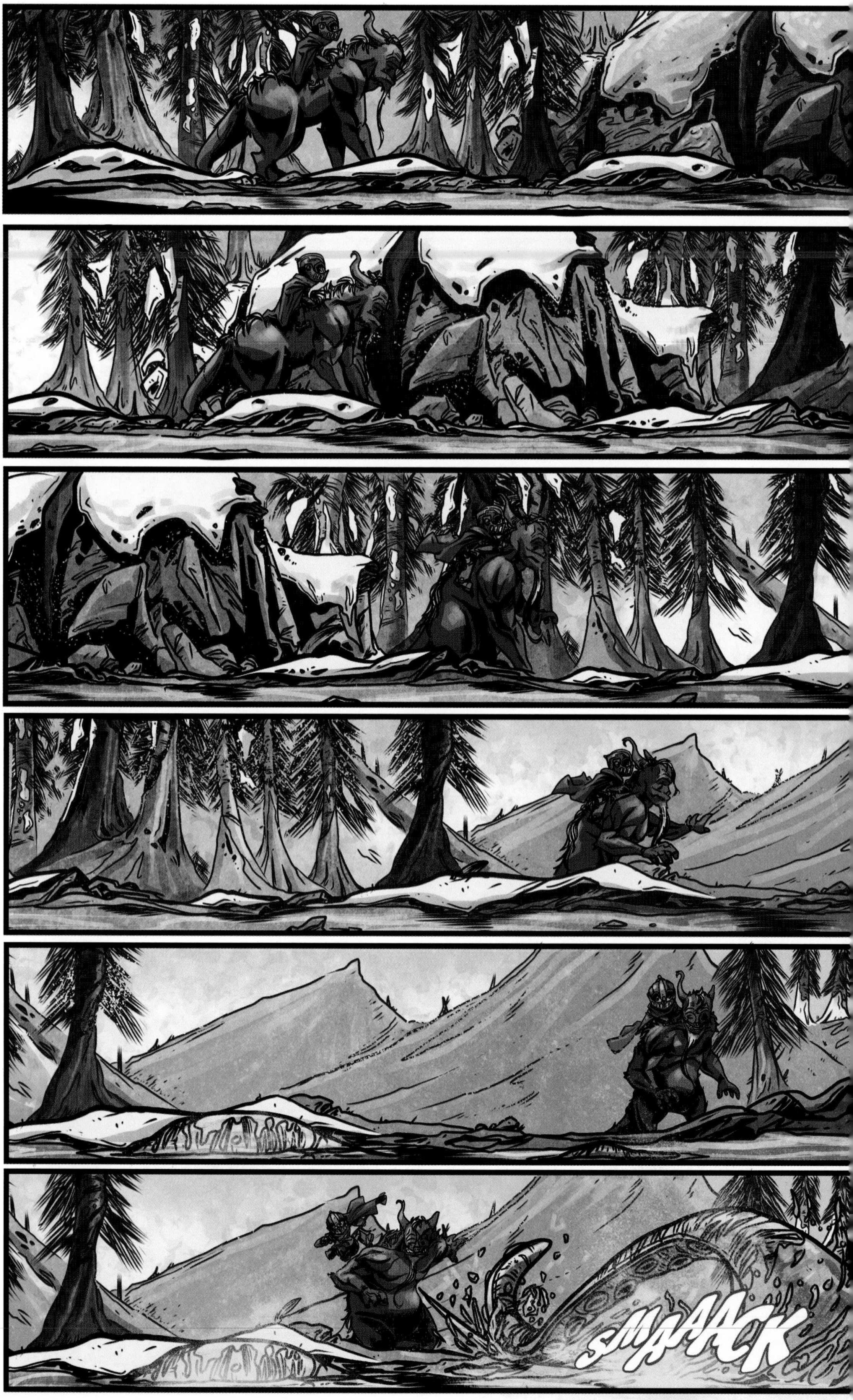
SMAAACK

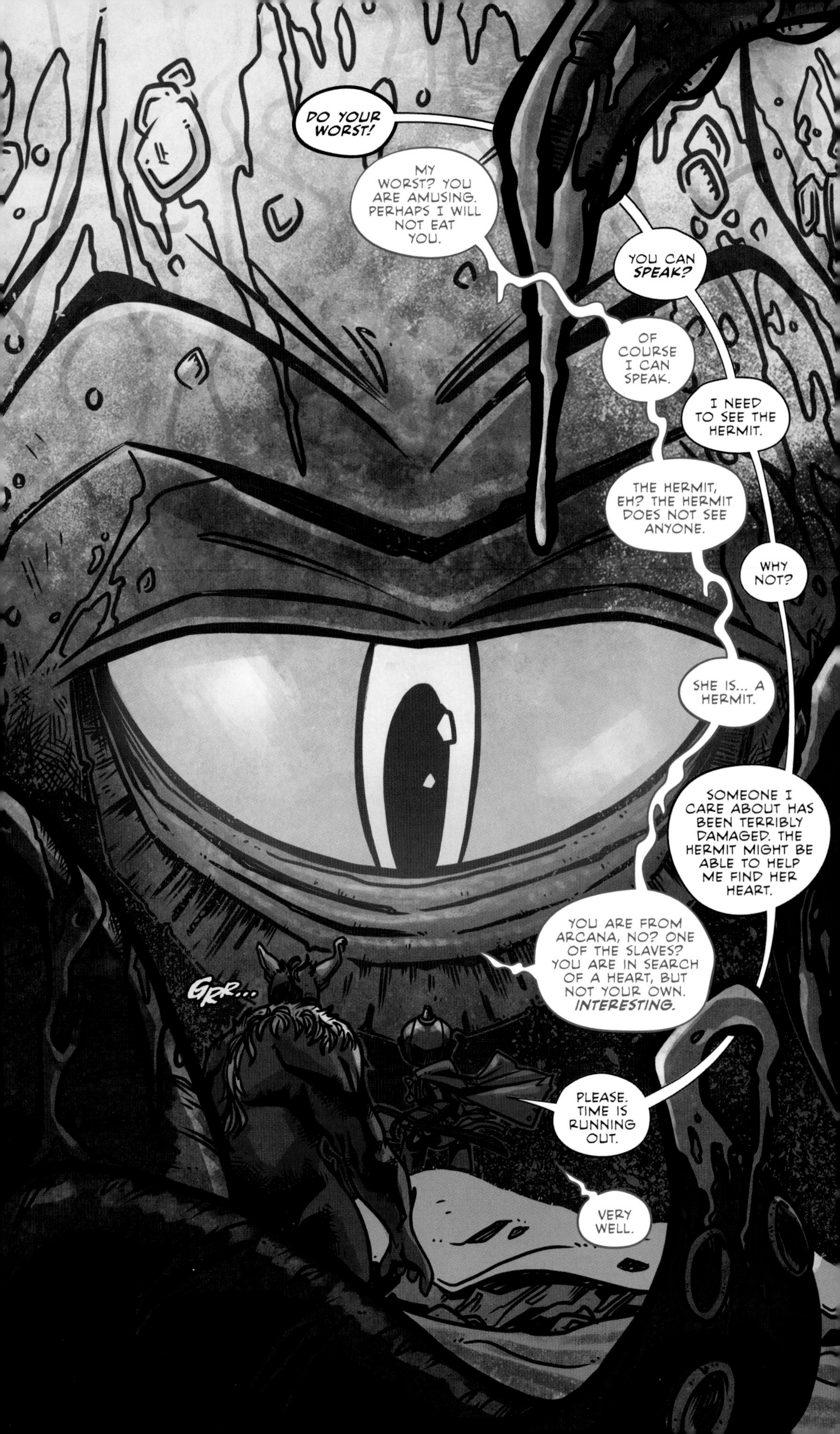
DO YOUR WORST!
MY WORST? YOU ARE AMUSING. PERHAPS I WILL NOT EAT YOU.
YOU CAN SPEAK?
OF COURSE I CAN SPEAK.
I NEED TO SEE THE HERMIT.
THE HERMIT, EH? THE HERMIT DOES NOT SEE ANYONE.
WHY NOT?
SHE IS... A HERMIT.
SOMEONE I CARE ABOUT HAS BEEN TERRIBLY DAMAGED. THE HERMIT MIGHT BE ABLE TO HELP ME FIND HER HEART.
YOU ARE FROM ARCANA, NO? ONE OF THE SLAVES? YOU ARE IN SEARCH OF A HEART, BUT NOT YOUR OWN. INTERESTING.
GRR...
PLEASE. TIME IS RUNNING OUT.
VERY WELL.

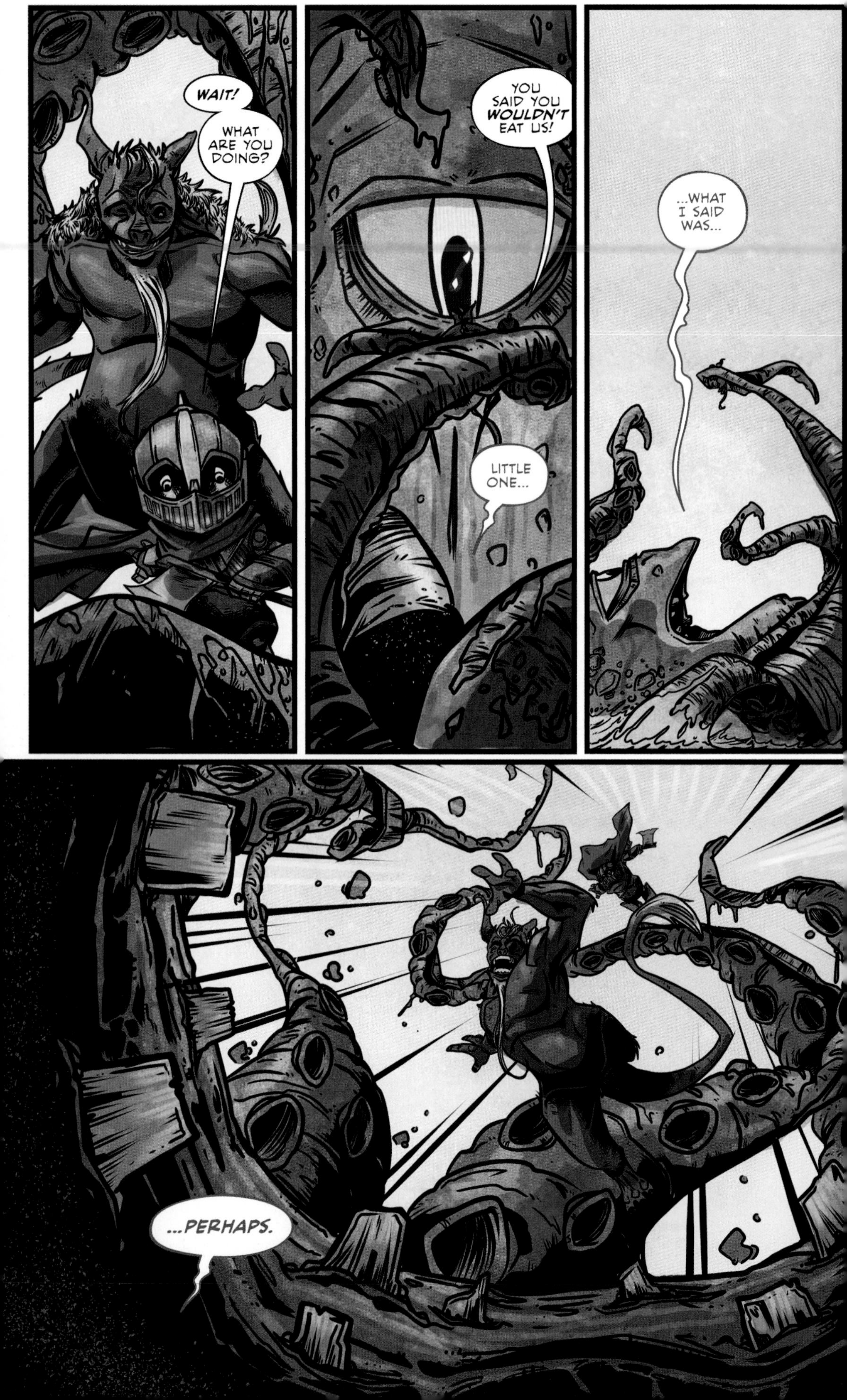

WAIT!
WHAT ARE YOU DOING?
YOU SAID YOU WOULDN'T EAT US!
LITTLE ONE...
...WHAT I SAID WAS...
...PERHAPS.

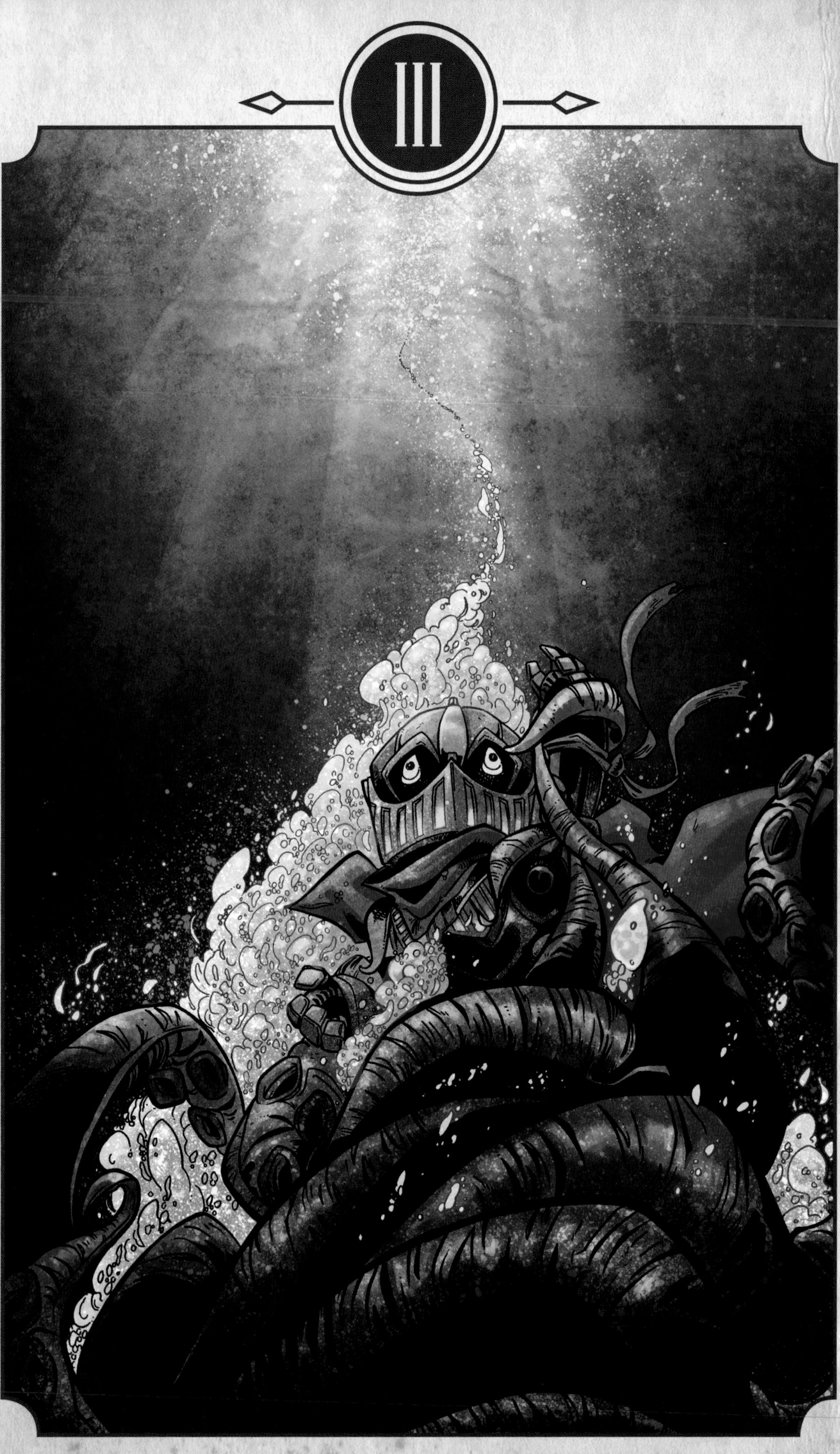
III

Art by **Drew Zucker**, *Colors by* **Vittorio Astone**

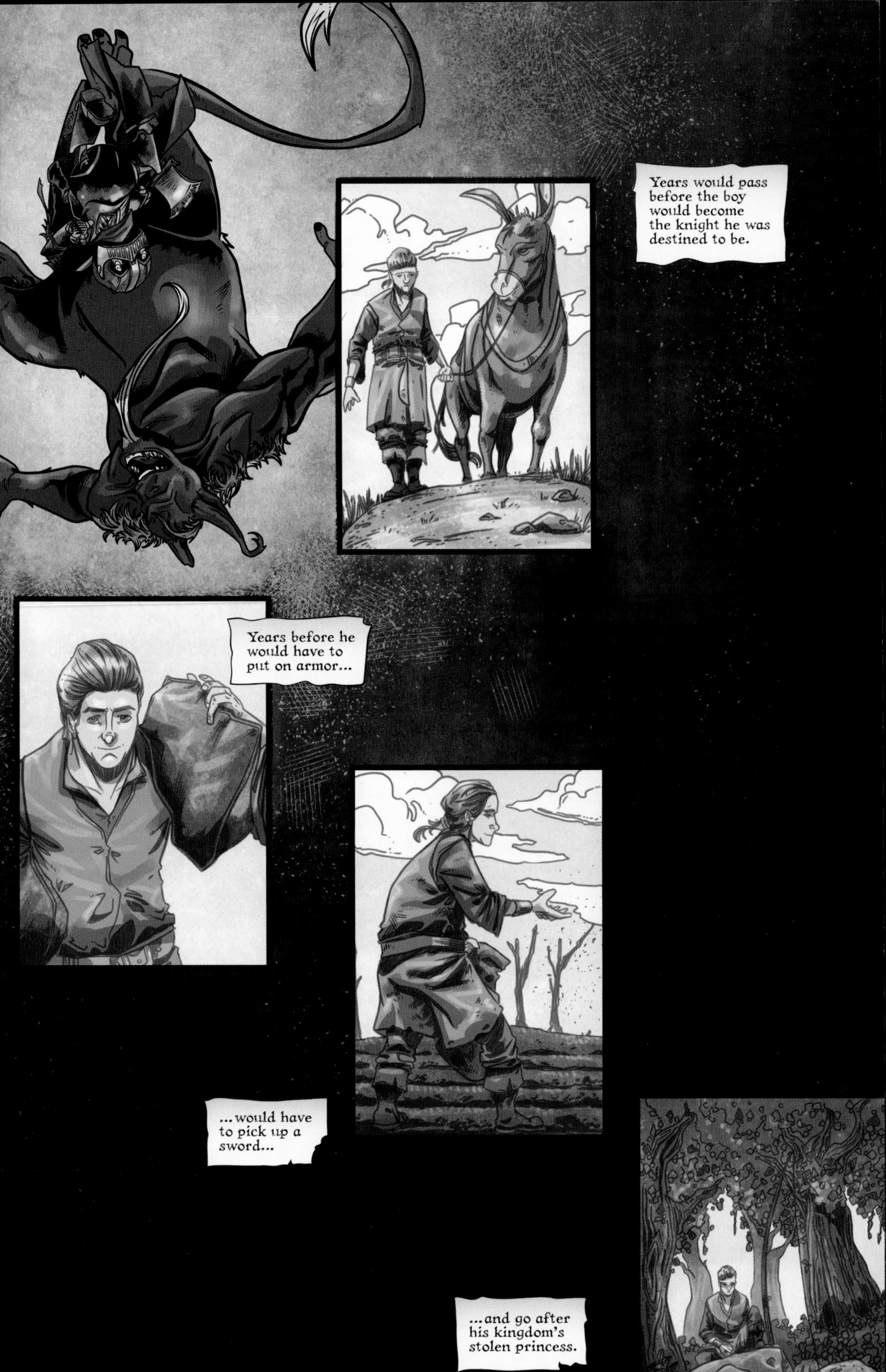
Years would pass before the boy would become the knight he was destined to be.
Years before he would have to put on armor...
...would have to pick up a sword...
...and go after his kingdom's stolen princess.

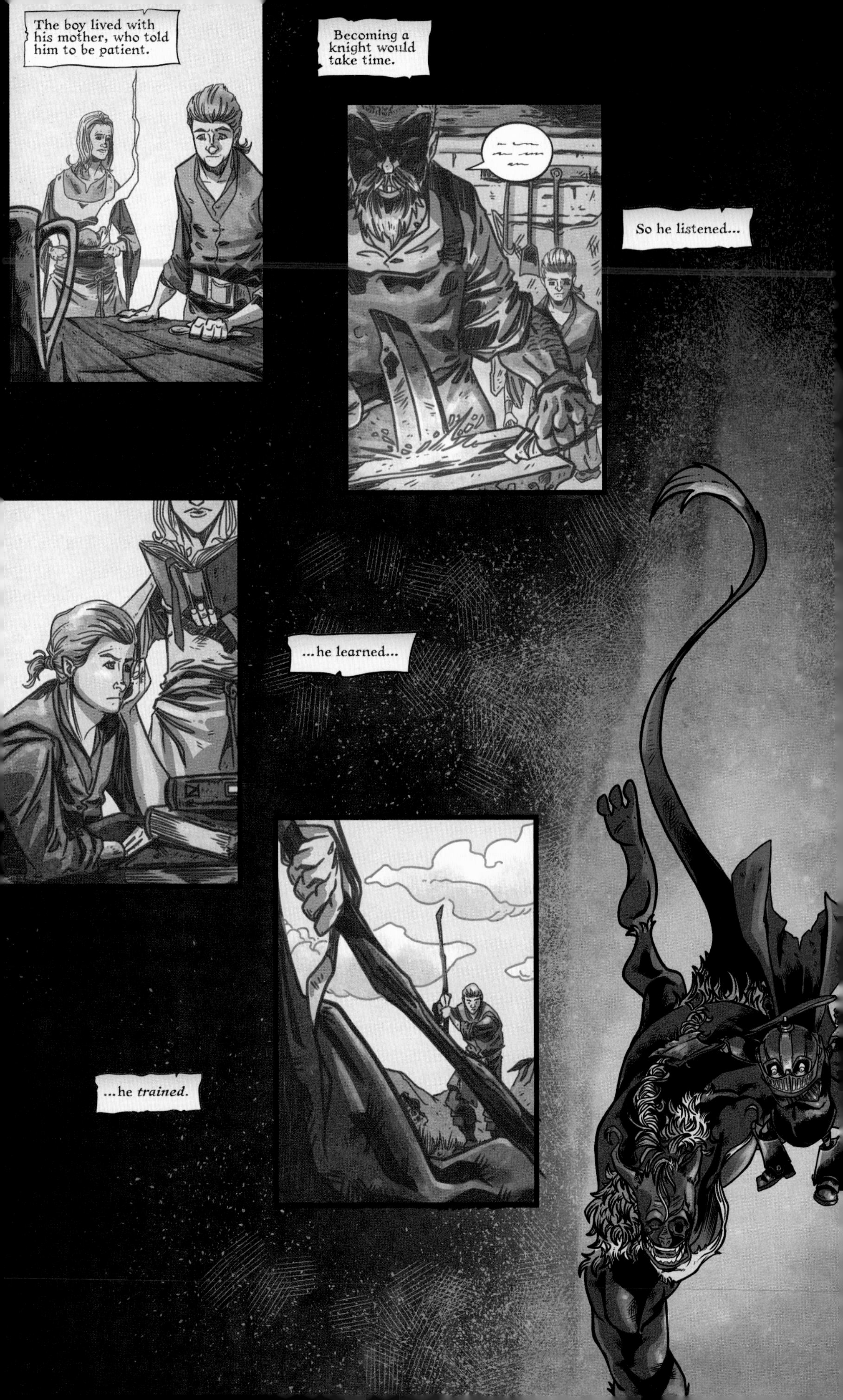

The boy lived with his mother, who told him to be patient.
Becoming a knight would take time.
So he listened...
...he learned...
...he *trained*.

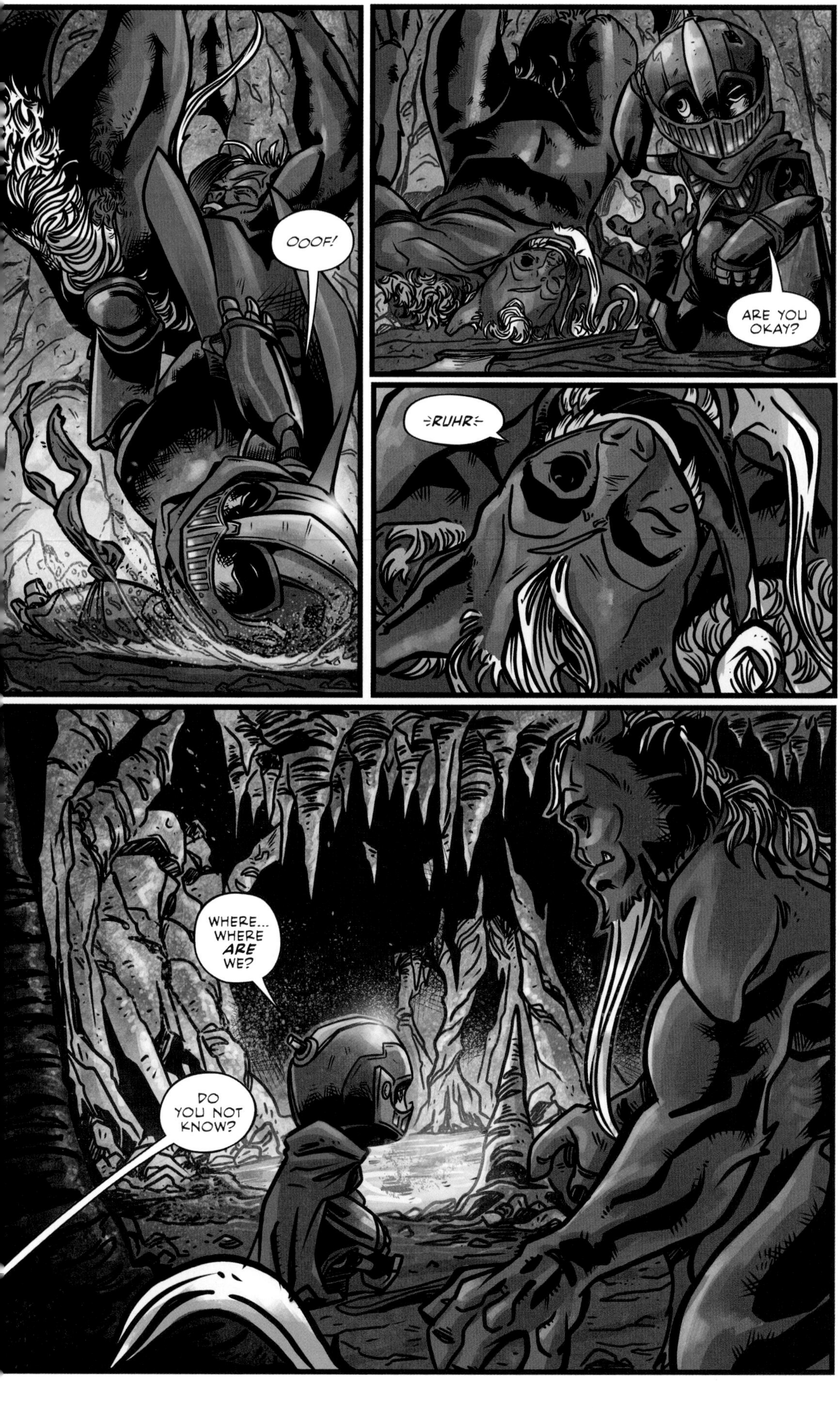
OOOF!
ARE YOU OKAY?
RUHR
WHERE... WHERE ARE WE?
DO YOU NOT KNOW?

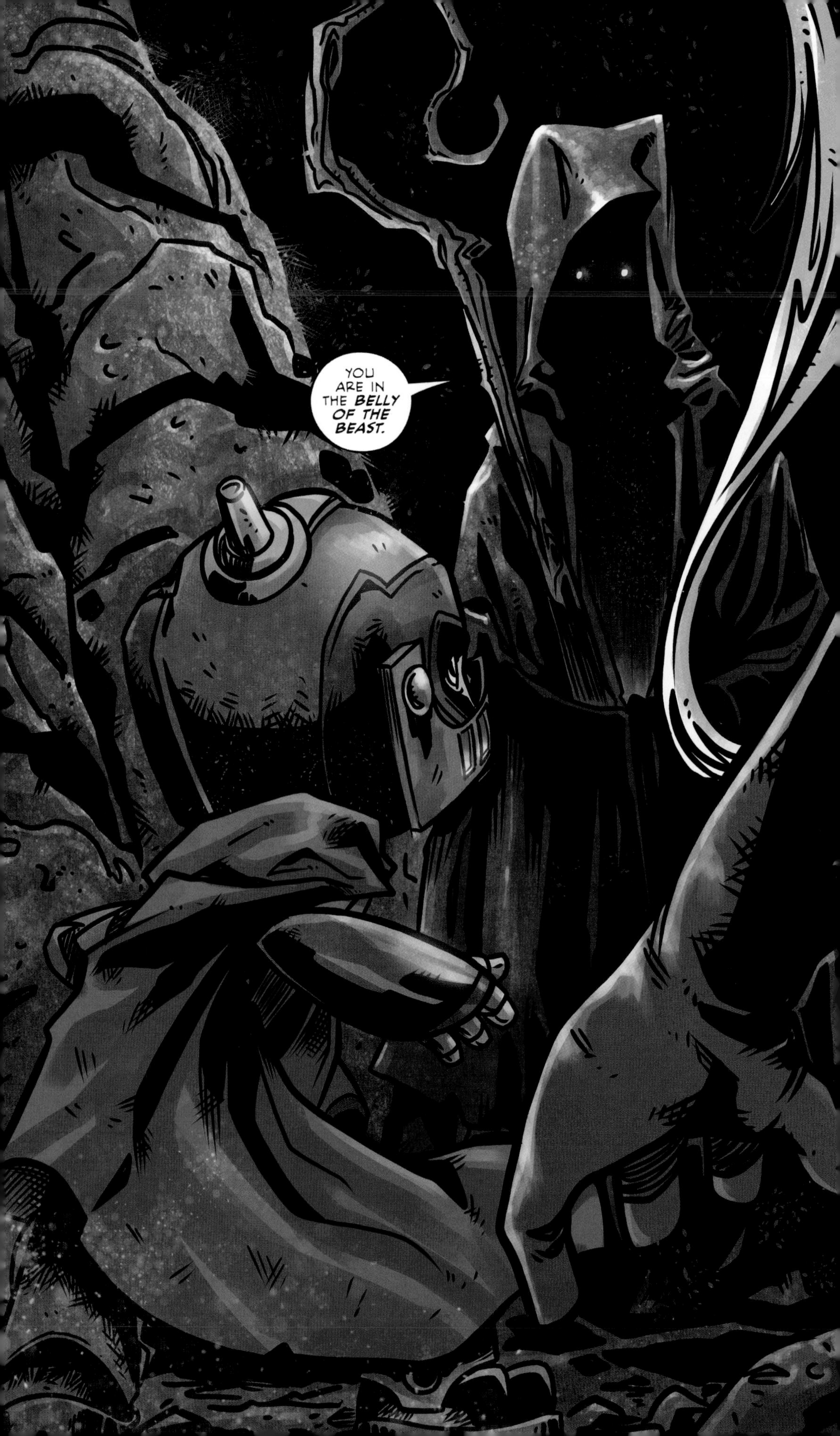
YOU ARE IN THE BELLY OF THE BEAST.

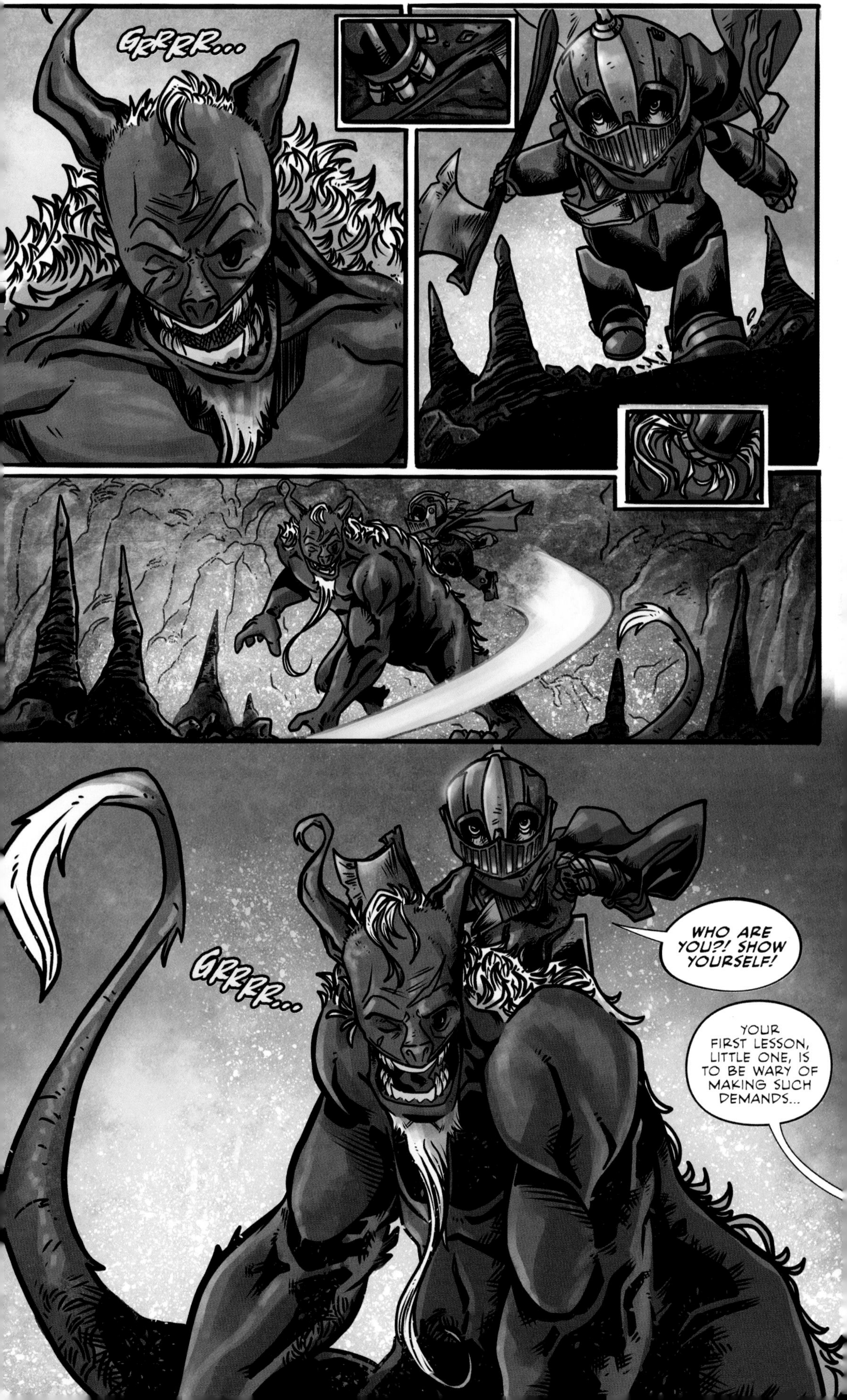
GRRRR...
GRRRR...
WHO ARE YOU?! SHOW YOURSELF!
YOUR FIRST LESSON, LITTLE ONE, IS TO BE WARY OF MAKING SUCH DEMANDS...

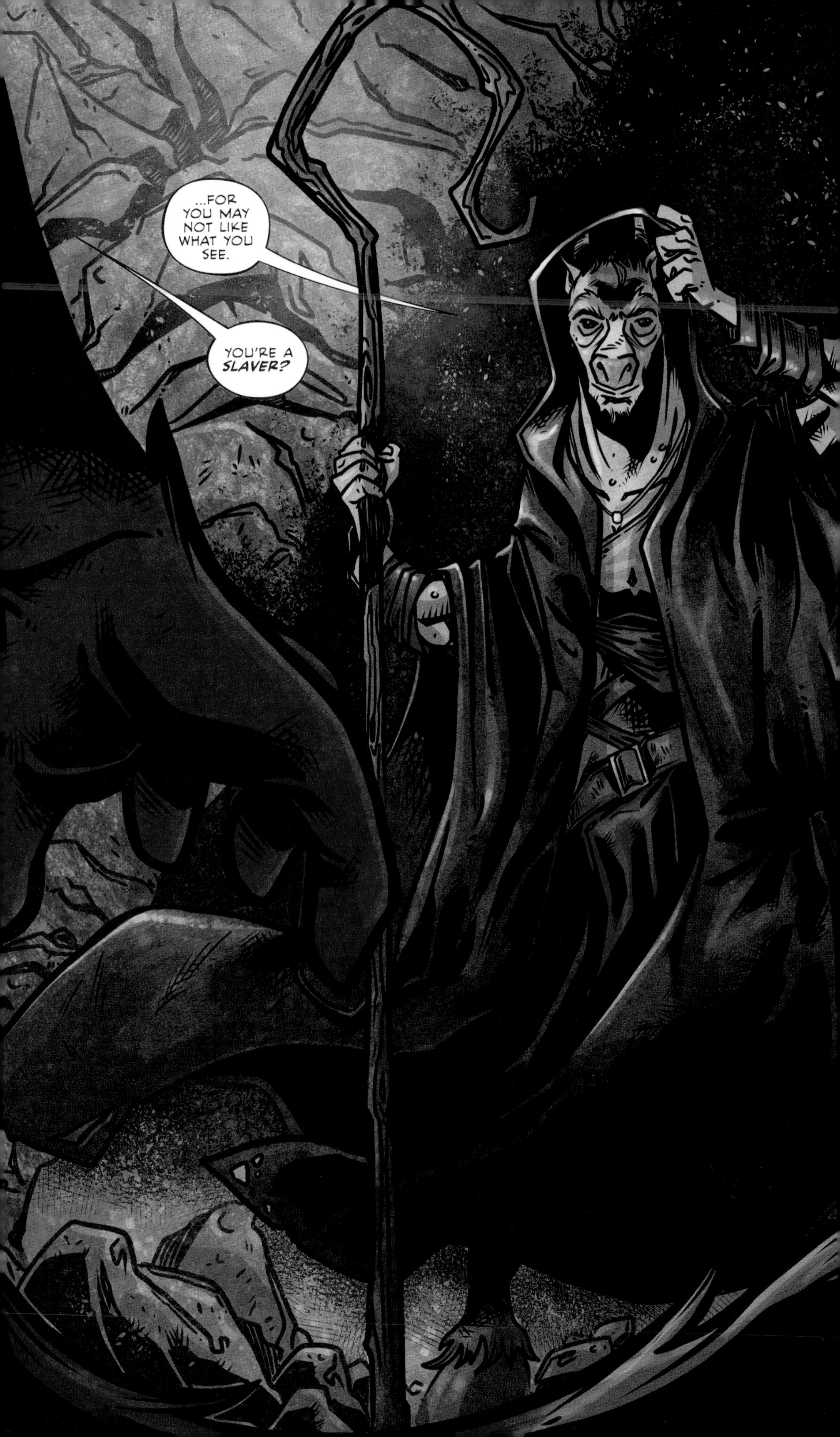
...FOR YOU MAY NOT LIKE WHAT YOU SEE.
YOU'RE A *SLAVER?*

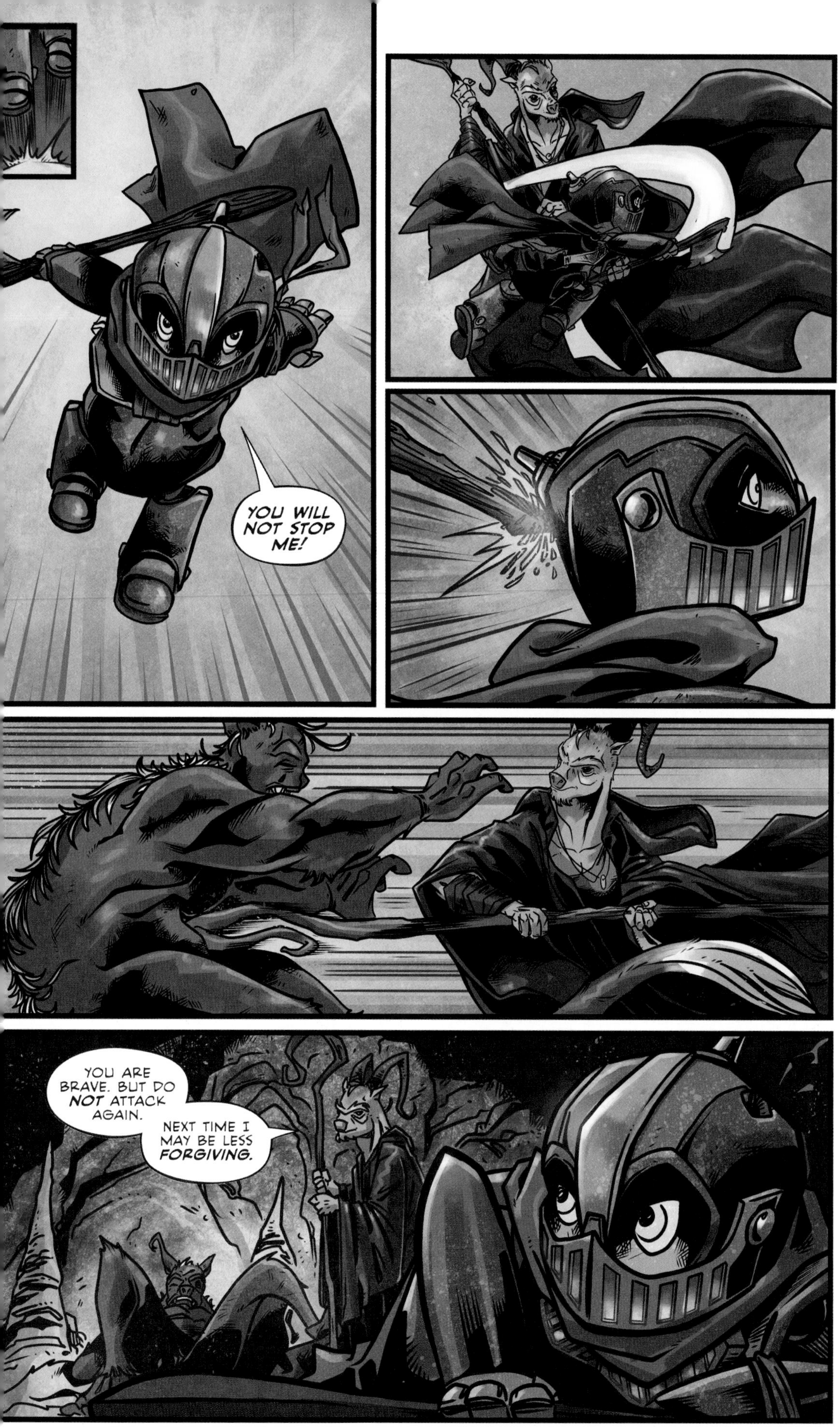
YOU WILL NOT STOP ME!
YOU ARE BRAVE. BUT DO NOT ATTACK AGAIN.
NEXT TIME I MAY BE LESS FORGIVING.

WHAT HAVE YOU DONE WITH THE HERMIT?

AH, YES. *THE HERMIT.* THEY HAVE CALLED ME THAT FOR LONGER THAN I CARE TO REMEMBER.

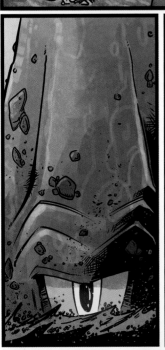

YOU? BUT YOU'RE A SLAVER.

AND YOU ARE A SLAVE.

YET NEITHER OF US APPEARS TO BE SERVING OUR PURPOSE JUST NOW, ARE WE?

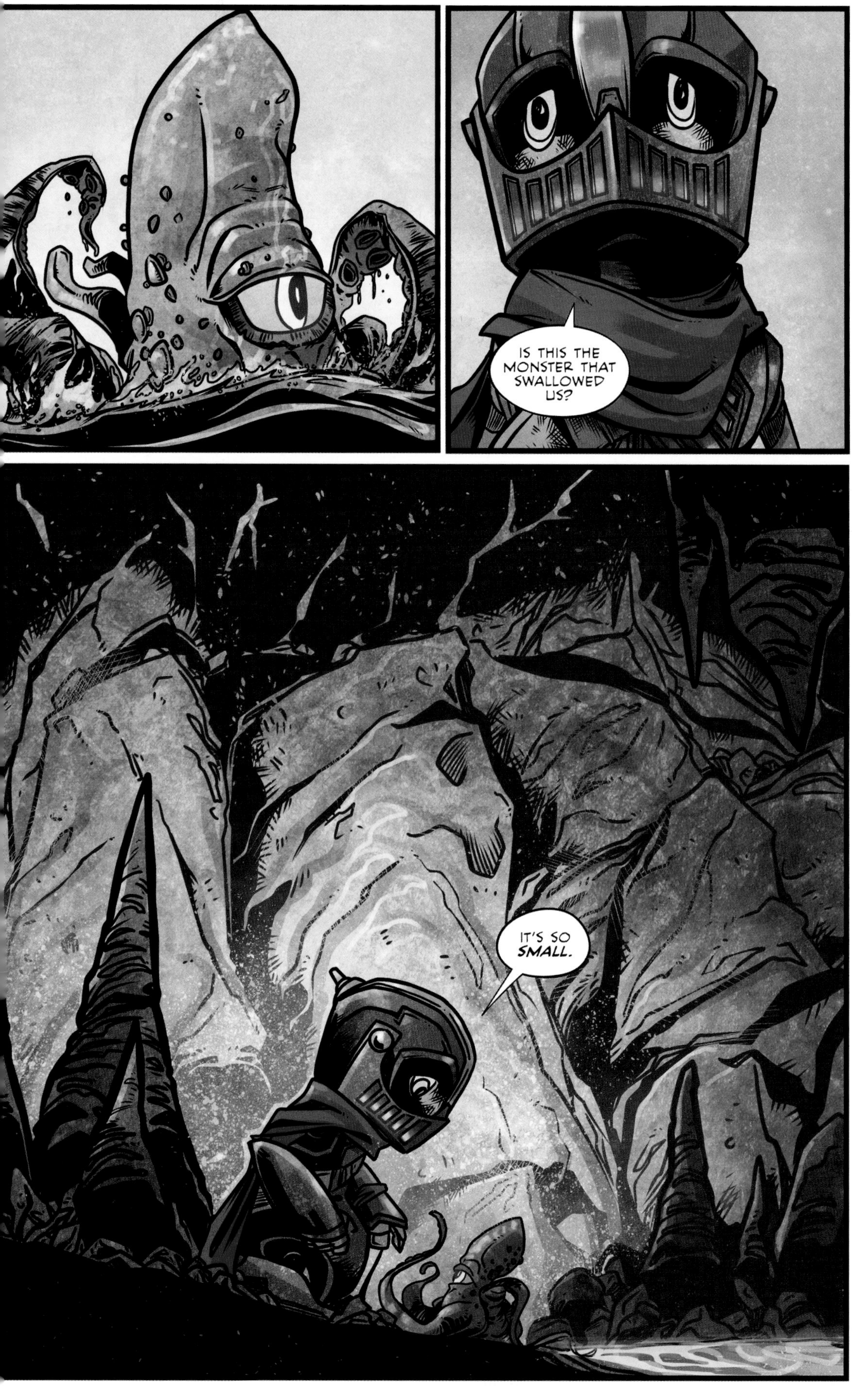
IS THIS THE MONSTER THAT SWALLOWED US?
IT'S SO SMALL.

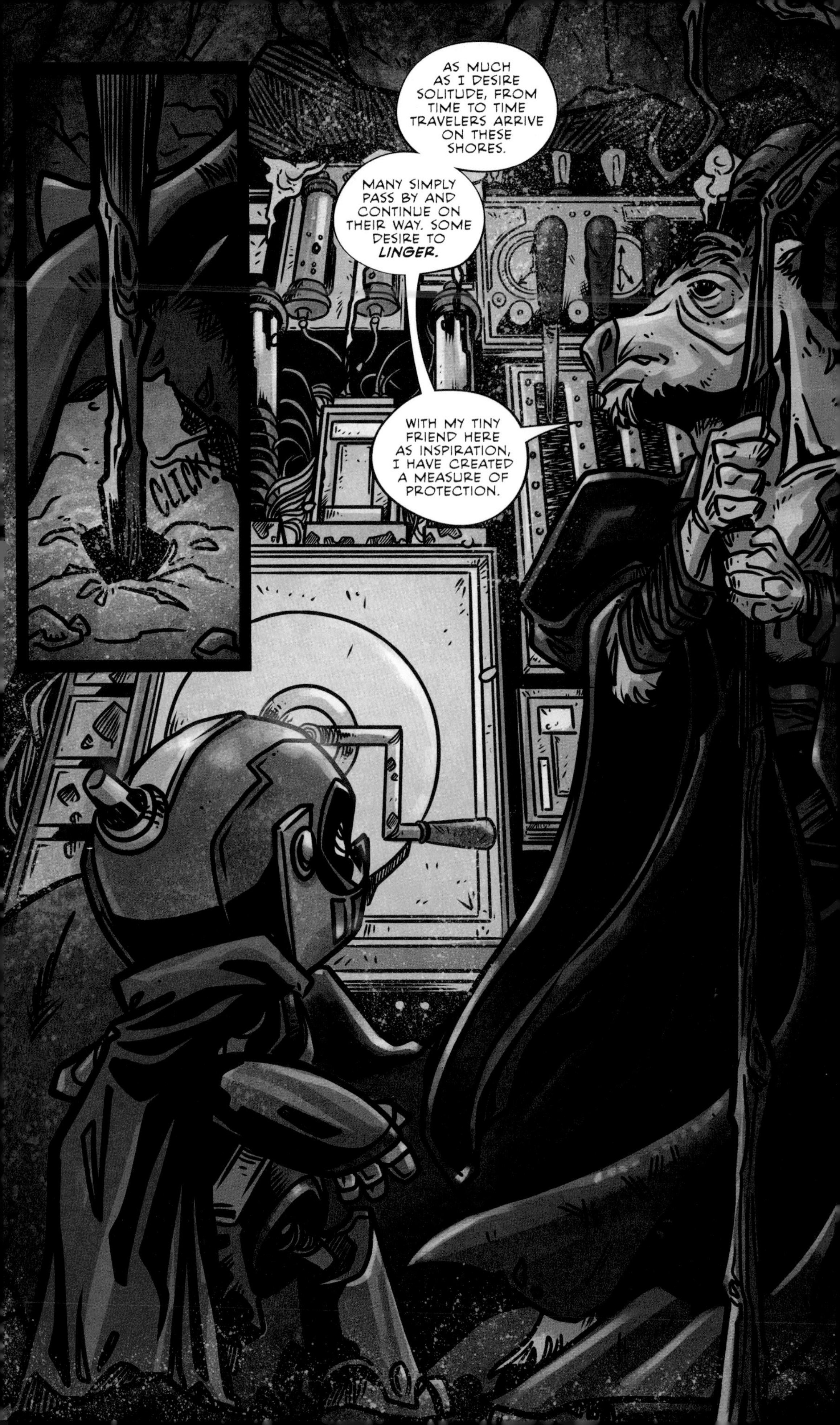
CLICK!
AS MUCH AS I DESIRE SOLITUDE, FROM TIME TO TIME TRAVELERS ARRIVE ON THESE SHORES.
MANY SIMPLY PASS BY AND CONTINUE ON THEIR WAY. SOME DESIRE TO ***LINGER.***
WITH MY TINY FRIEND HERE AS INSPIRATION, I HAVE CREATED A MEASURE OF PROTECTION.

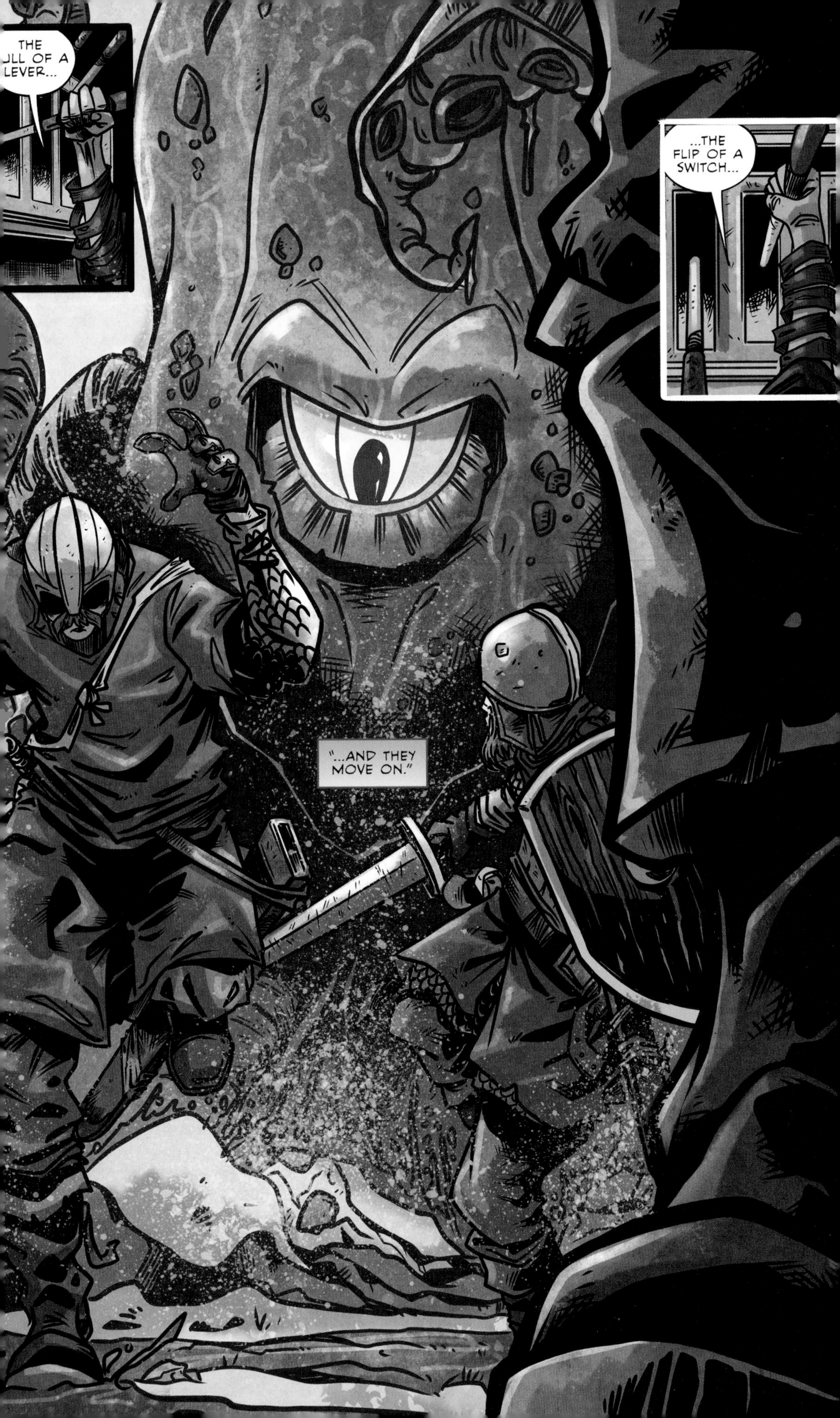
THE
ULL OF A
LEVER...
...THE FLIP OF A SWITCH...
"...AND THEY MOVE ON."

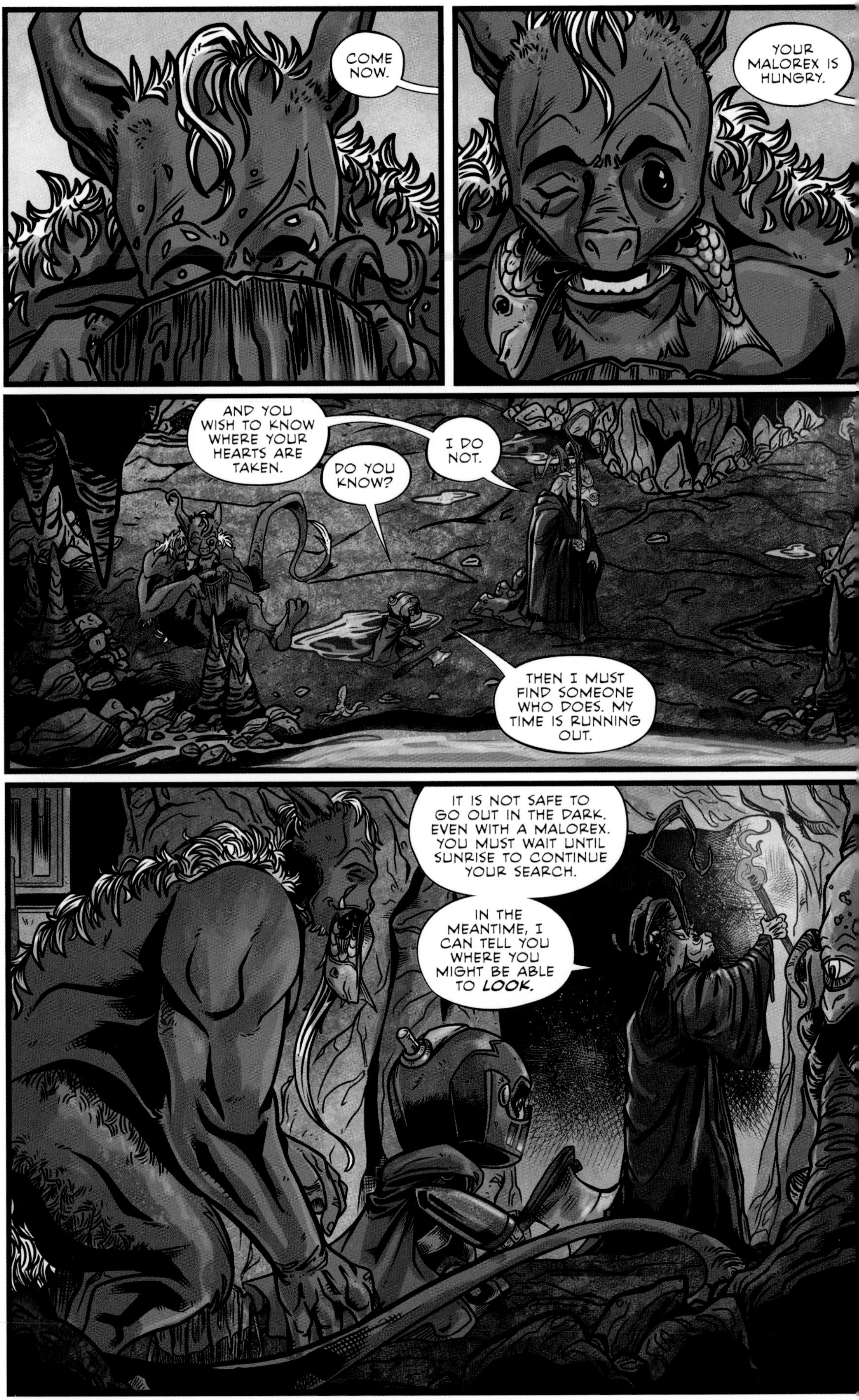
COME NOW.
YOUR MALOREX IS HUNGRY.
AND YOU WISH TO KNOW WHERE YOUR HEARTS ARE TAKEN.
DO YOU KNOW?
I DO NOT.
THEN I MUST FIND SOMEONE WHO DOES. MY TIME IS RUNNING OUT.
IT IS NOT SAFE TO GO OUT IN THE DARK. EVEN WITH A MALOREX. YOU MUST WAIT UNTIL SUNRISE TO CONTINUE YOUR SEARCH.
IN THE MEANTIME, I CAN TELL YOU WHERE YOU MIGHT BE ABLE TO ***LOOK.***

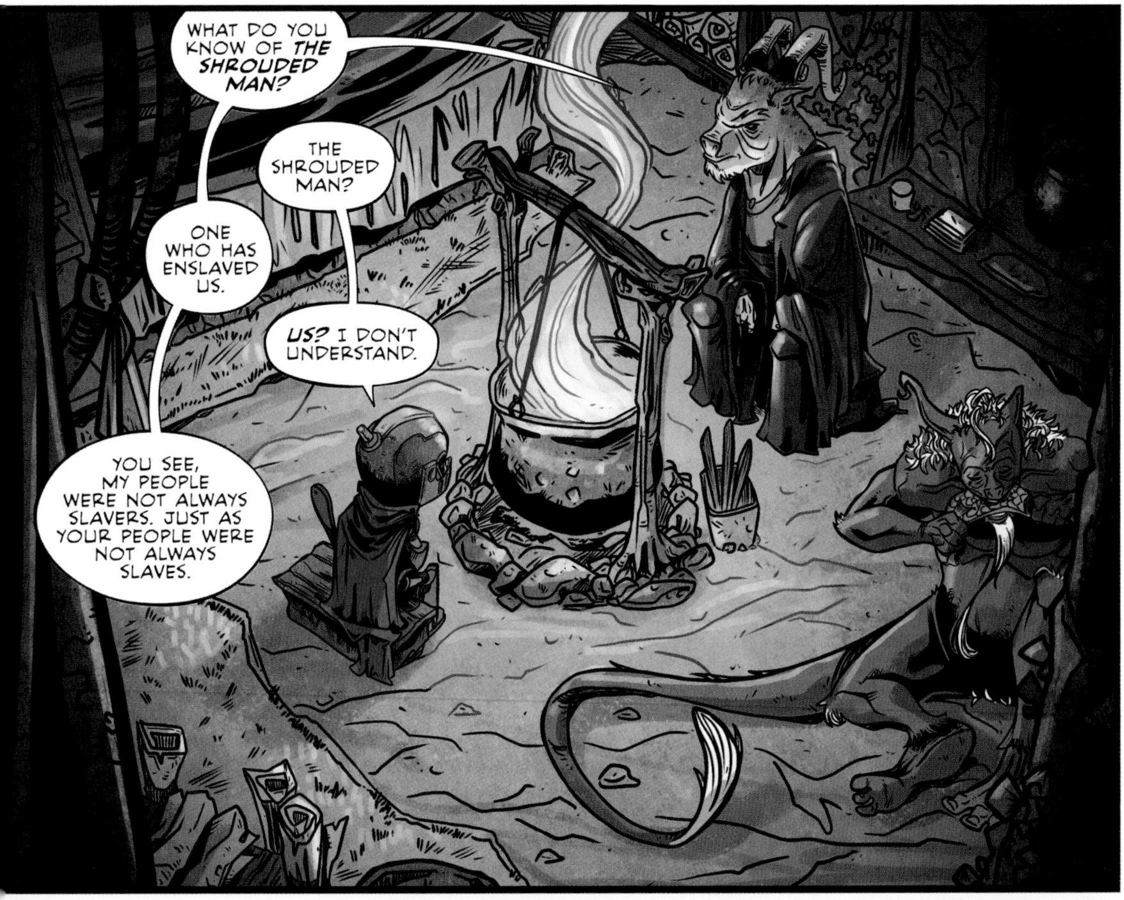
WHAT DO YOU KNOW OF *THE SHROUDED MAN?*
THE SHROUDED MAN?
ONE WHO HAS ENSLAVED US.
US? I DON'T UNDERSTAND.
YOU SEE, MY PEOPLE WERE NOT ALWAYS SLAVERS. JUST AS YOUR PEOPLE WERE NOT ALWAYS SLAVES.

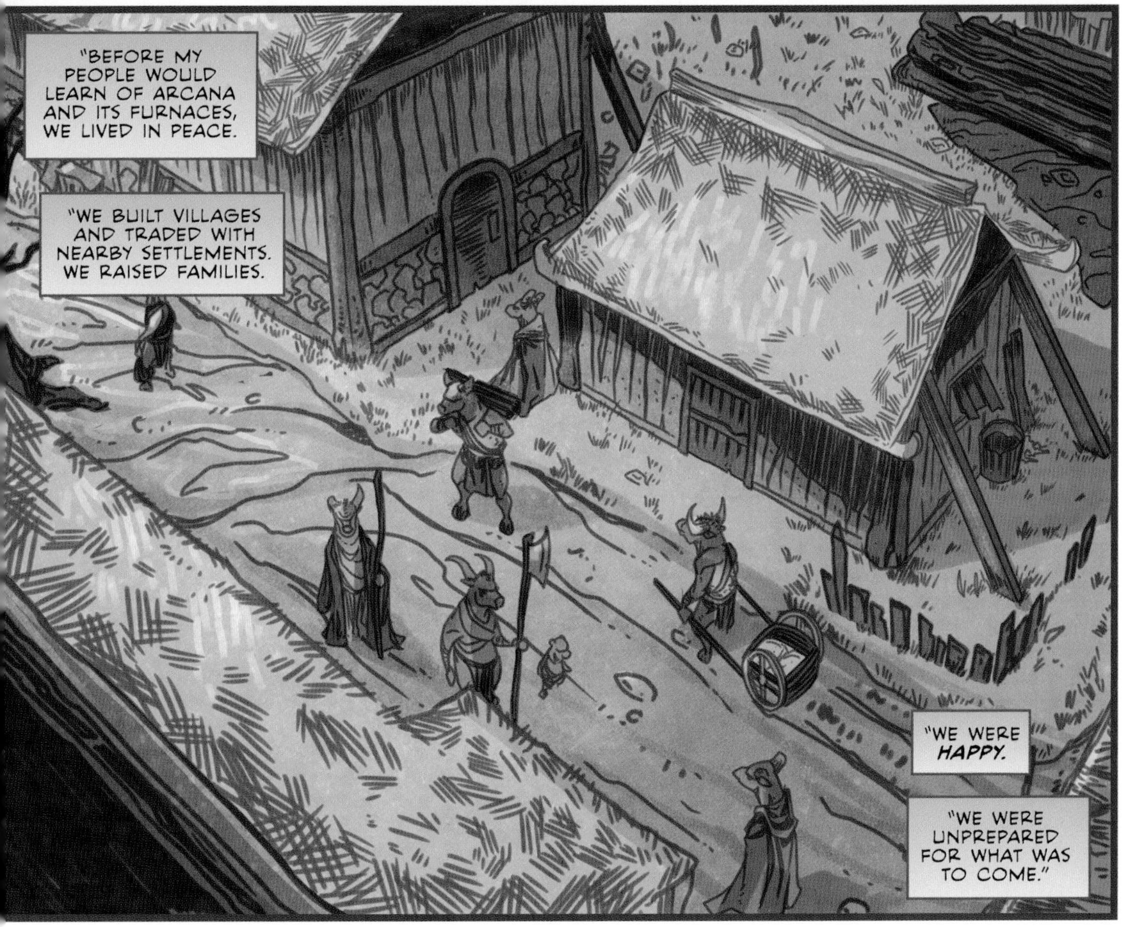
"BEFORE MY PEOPLE WOULD LEARN OF ARCANA AND ITS FURNACES, WE LIVED IN PEACE.
"WE BUILT VILLAGES AND TRADED WITH NEARBY SETTLEMENTS. WE RAISED FAMILIES.
"WE WERE *HAPPY.*
"WE WERE UNPREPARED FOR WHAT WAS TO COME."

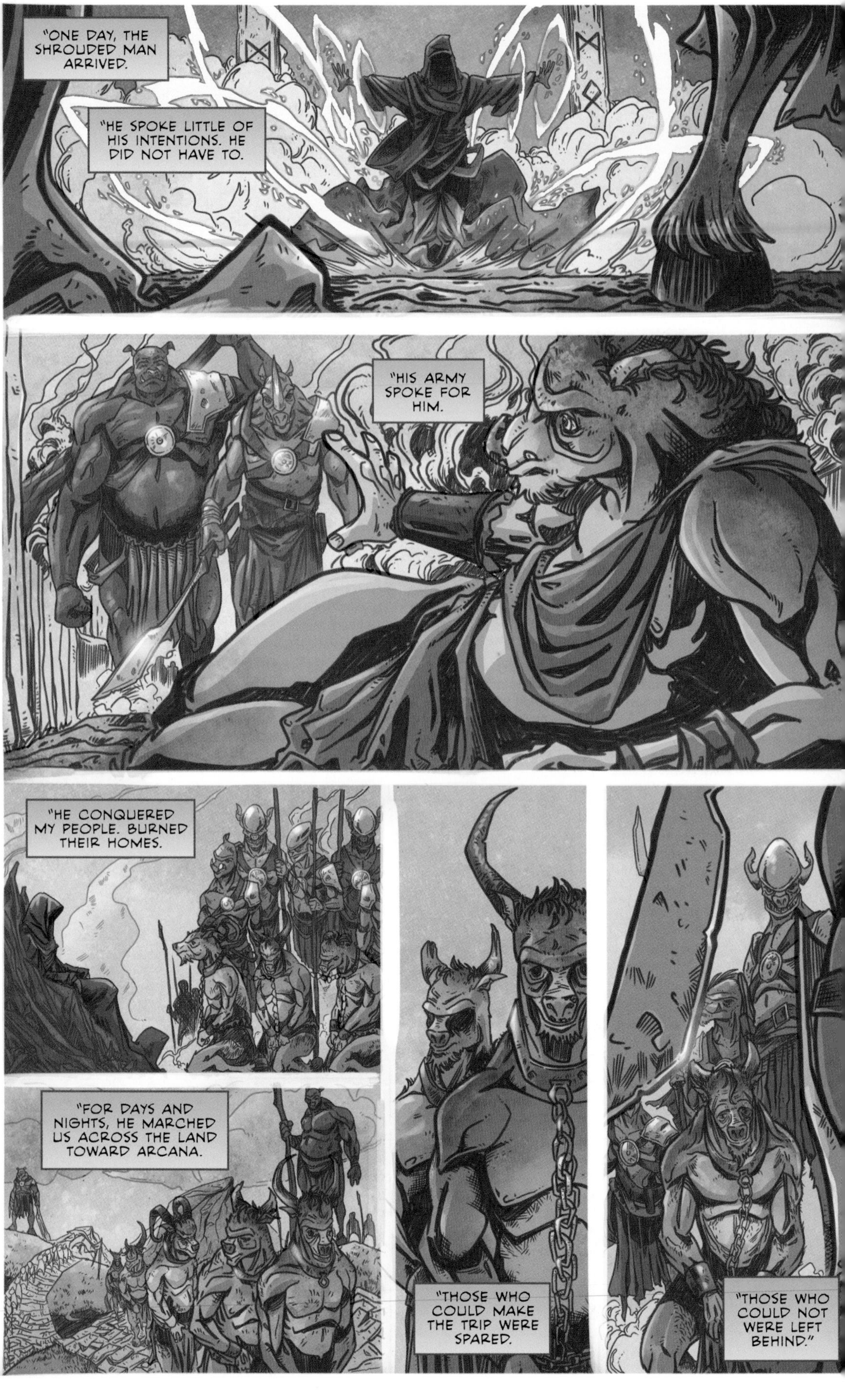
"ONE DAY, THE SHROUDED MAN ARRIVED.
"HE SPOKE LITTLE OF HIS INTENTIONS. HE DID NOT HAVE TO.
"HIS ARMY SPOKE FOR HIM.
"HE CONQUERED MY PEOPLE. BURNED THEIR HOMES.
"FOR DAYS AND NIGHTS, HE MARCHED US ACROSS THE LAND TOWARD ARCANA.
"THOSE WHO COULD MAKE THE TRIP WERE SPARED.
"THOSE WHO COULD NOT WERE LEFT BEHIND."

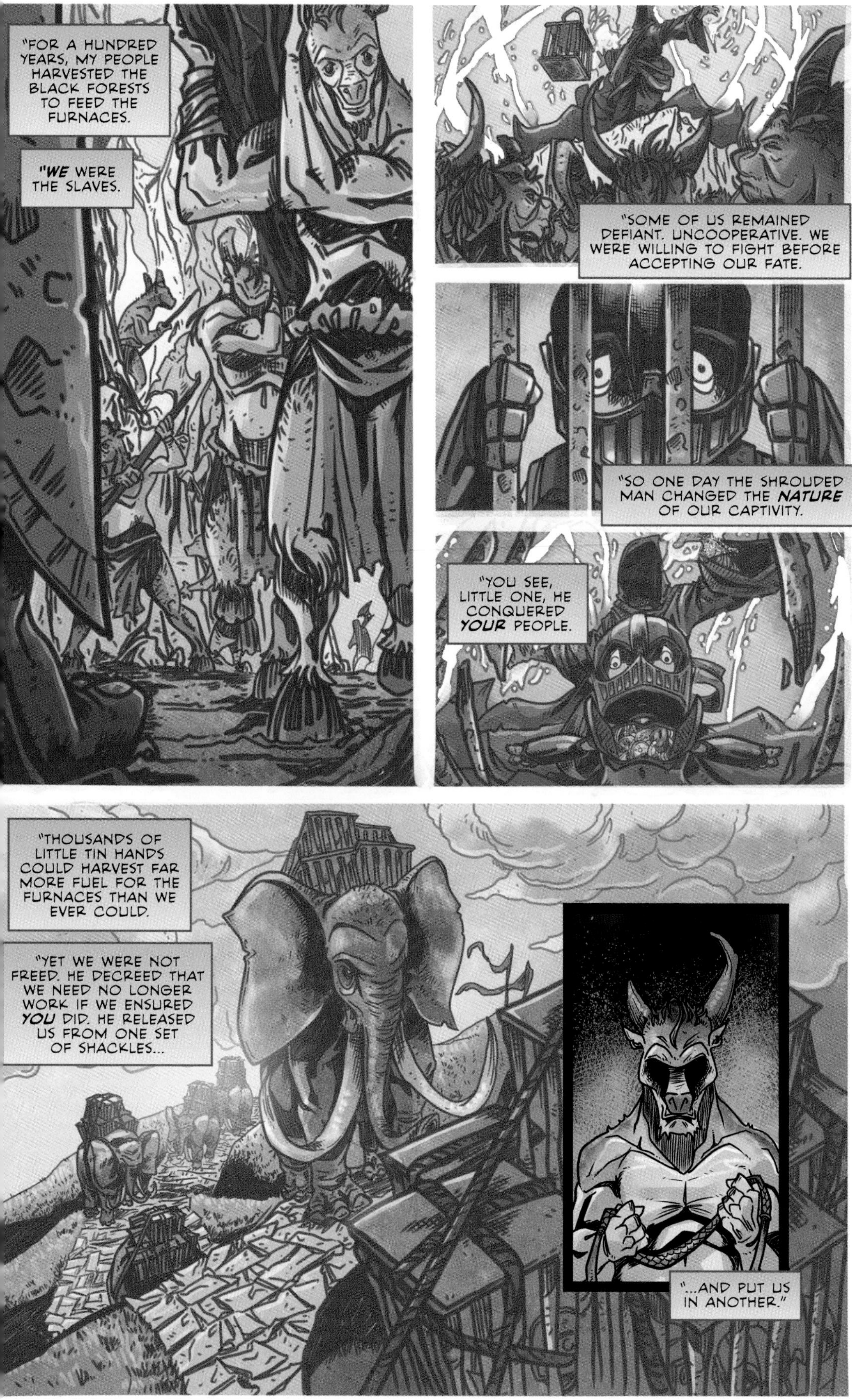
"FOR A HUNDRED YEARS, MY PEOPLE HARVESTED THE BLACK FORESTS TO FEED THE FURNACES.
"*WE* WERE THE SLAVES.
"SOME OF US REMAINED DEFIANT. UNCOOPERATIVE. WE WERE WILLING TO FIGHT BEFORE ACCEPTING OUR FATE.
"SO ONE DAY THE SHROUDED MAN CHANGED THE *NATURE* OF OUR CAPTIVITY.
"YOU SEE, LITTLE ONE, HE CONQUERED *YOUR* PEOPLE.
"THOUSANDS OF LITTLE TIN HANDS COULD HARVEST FAR MORE FUEL FOR THE FURNACES THAN WE EVER COULD.
"YET WE WERE NOT FREED. HE DECREED THAT WE NEED NO LONGER WORK IF WE ENSURED *YOU* DID. HE RELEASED US FROM ONE SET OF SHACKLES...
"...AND PUT US IN ANOTHER."

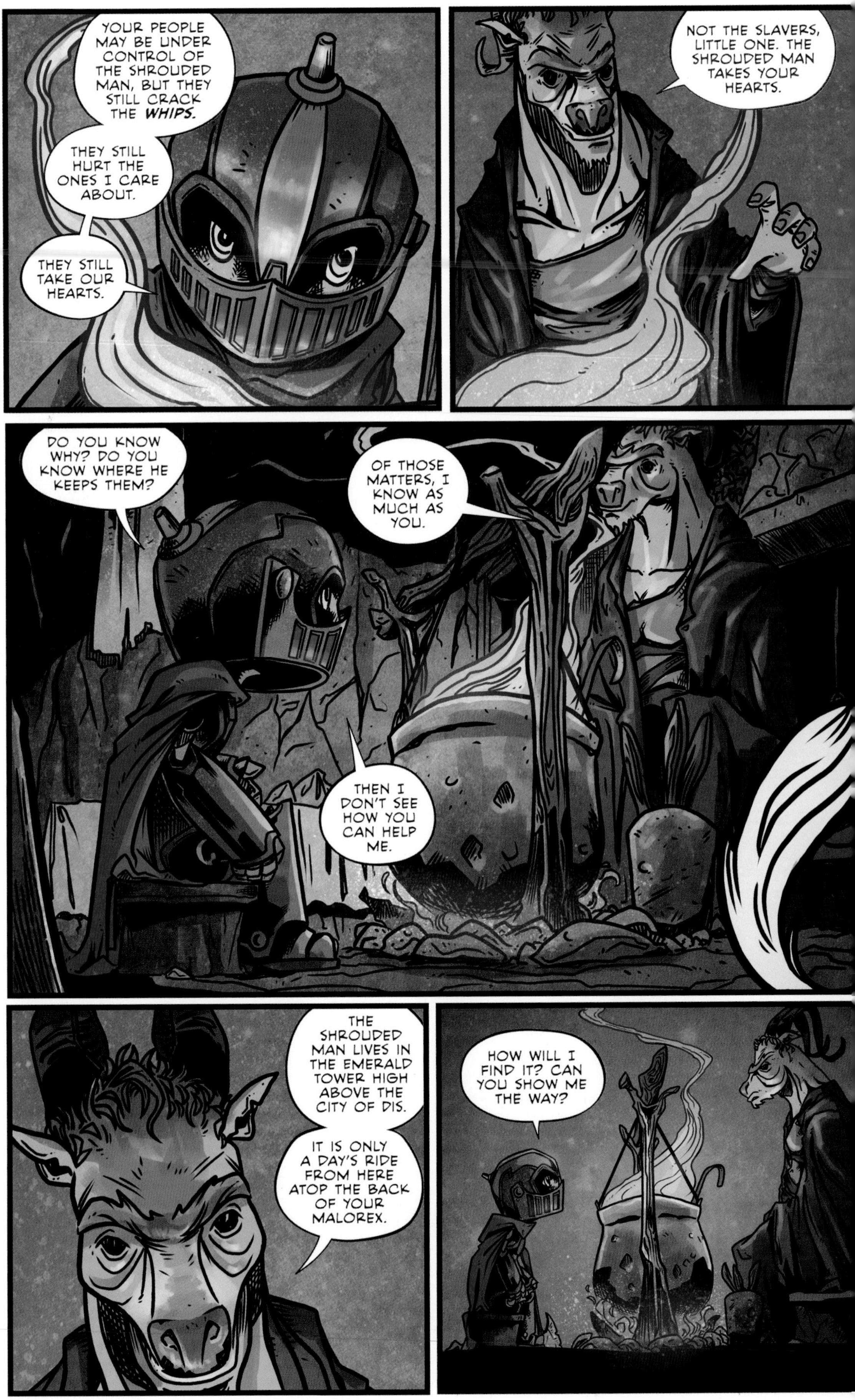
YOUR PEOPLE MAY BE UNDER CONTROL OF THE SHROUDED MAN, BUT THEY STILL CRACK THE *WHIPS.*
THEY STILL HURT THE ONES I CARE ABOUT.
THEY STILL TAKE OUR HEARTS.
NOT THE SLAVERS, LITTLE ONE. THE SHROUDED MAN TAKES YOUR HEARTS.
DO YOU KNOW WHY? DO YOU KNOW WHERE HE KEEPS THEM?
OF THOSE MATTERS, I KNOW AS MUCH AS YOU.
THEN I DON'T SEE HOW YOU CAN HELP ME.
THE SHROUDED MAN LIVES IN THE EMERALD TOWER HIGH ABOVE THE CITY OF DIS.
IT IS ONLY A DAY'S RIDE FROM HERE ATOP THE BACK OF YOUR MALOREX.
HOW WILL I FIND IT? CAN YOU SHOW ME THE WAY?

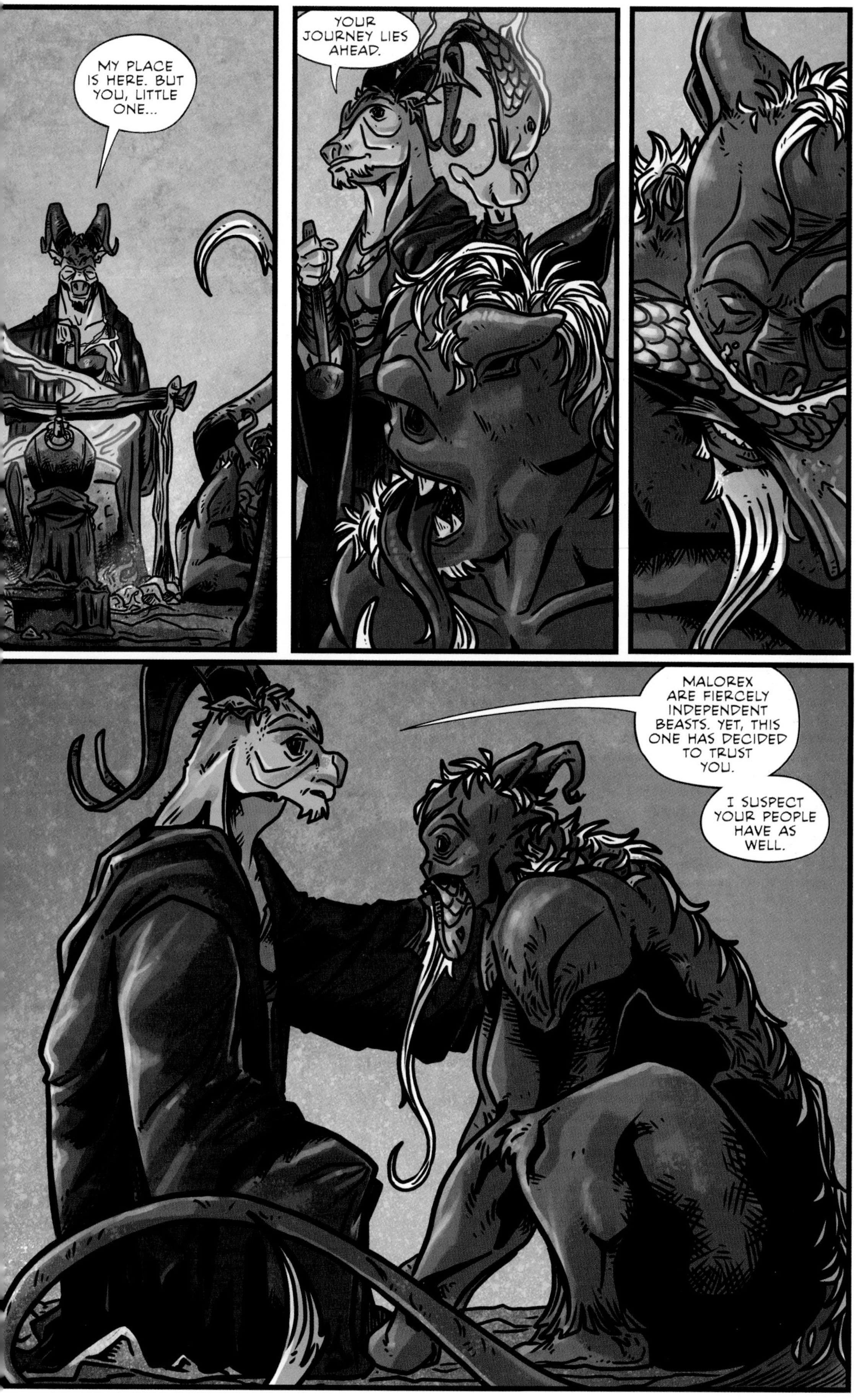
MY PLACE IS HERE. BUT YOU, LITTLE ONE...
YOUR JOURNEY LIES AHEAD.
MALOREX ARE FIERCELY INDEPENDENT BEASTS. YET, THIS ONE HAS DECIDED TO TRUST YOU.
I SUSPECT YOUR PEOPLE HAVE AS WELL.

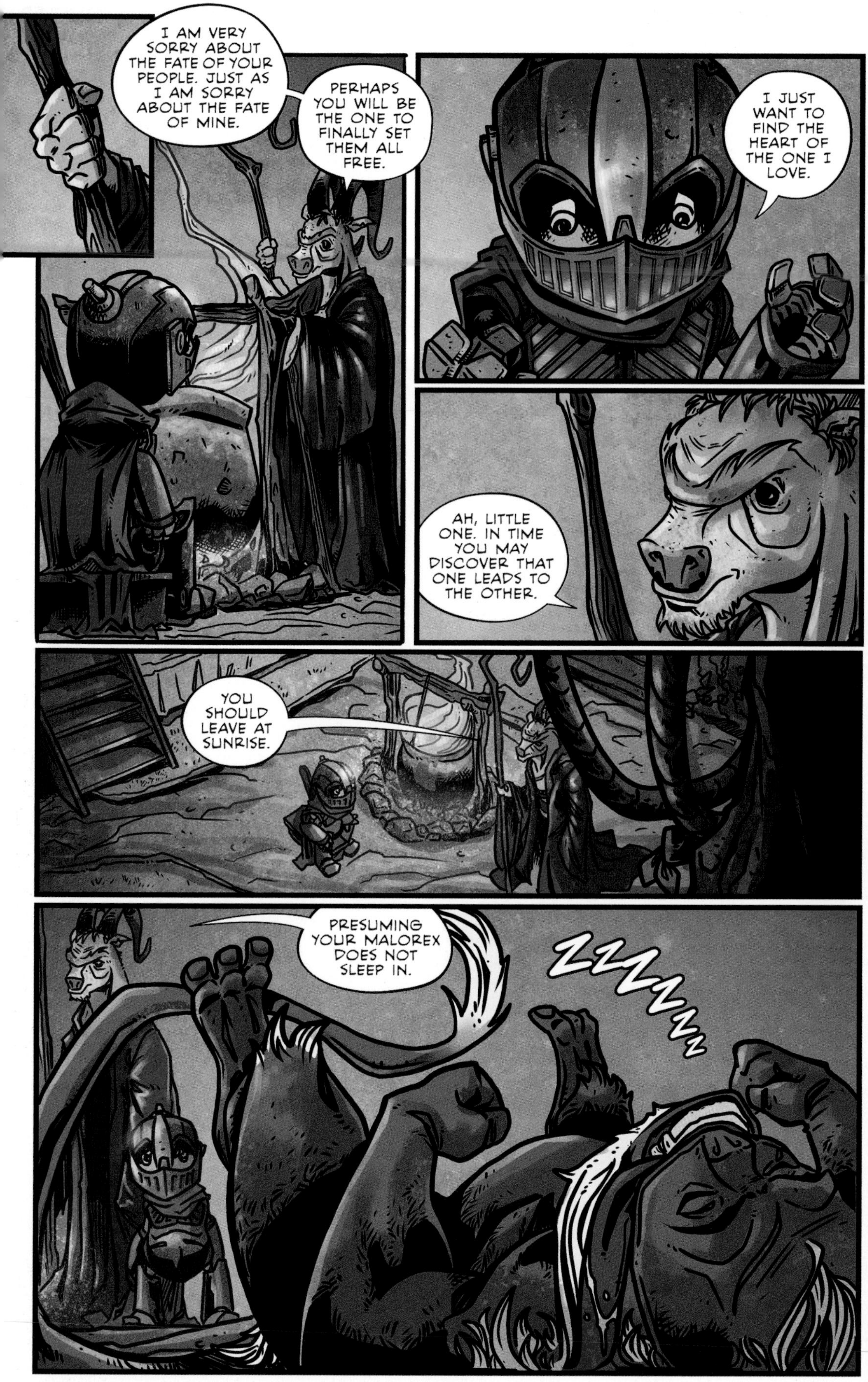
I AM VERY SORRY ABOUT THE FATE OF YOUR PEOPLE. JUST AS I AM SORRY ABOUT THE FATE OF MINE.
PERHAPS YOU WILL BE THE ONE TO FINALLY SET THEM ALL FREE.
I JUST WANT TO FIND THE HEART OF THE ONE I LOVE.
AH, LITTLE ONE. IN TIME YOU MAY DISCOVER THAT ONE LEADS TO THE OTHER.
YOU SHOULD LEAVE AT SUNRISE.
PRESUMING YOUR MALOREX DOES NOT SLEEP IN.
ZZZZZZZ

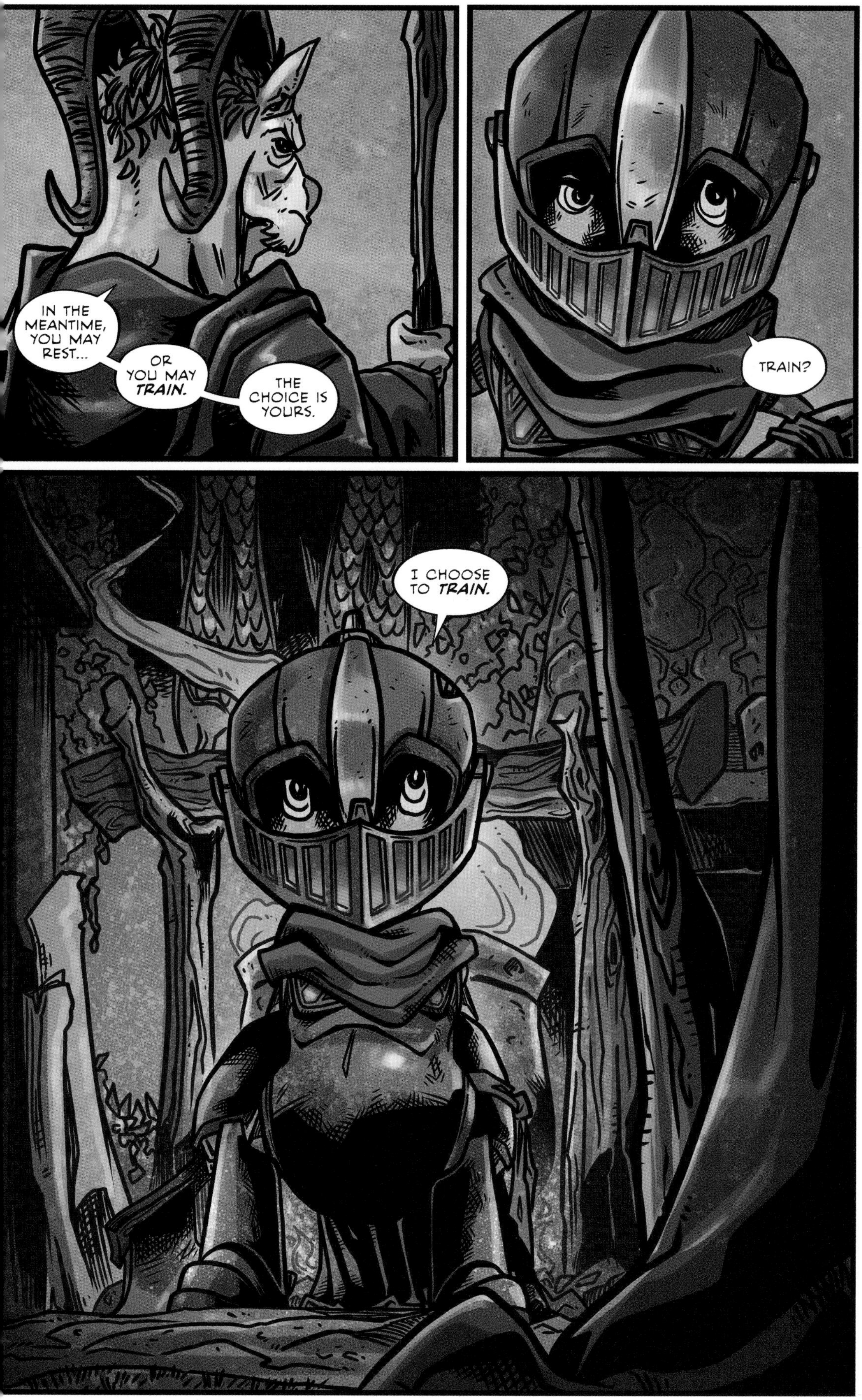
IN THE MEANTIME, YOU MAY REST...
OR YOU MAY *TRAIN.*
THE CHOICE IS YOURS.
TRAIN?
I CHOOSE TO *TRAIN.*

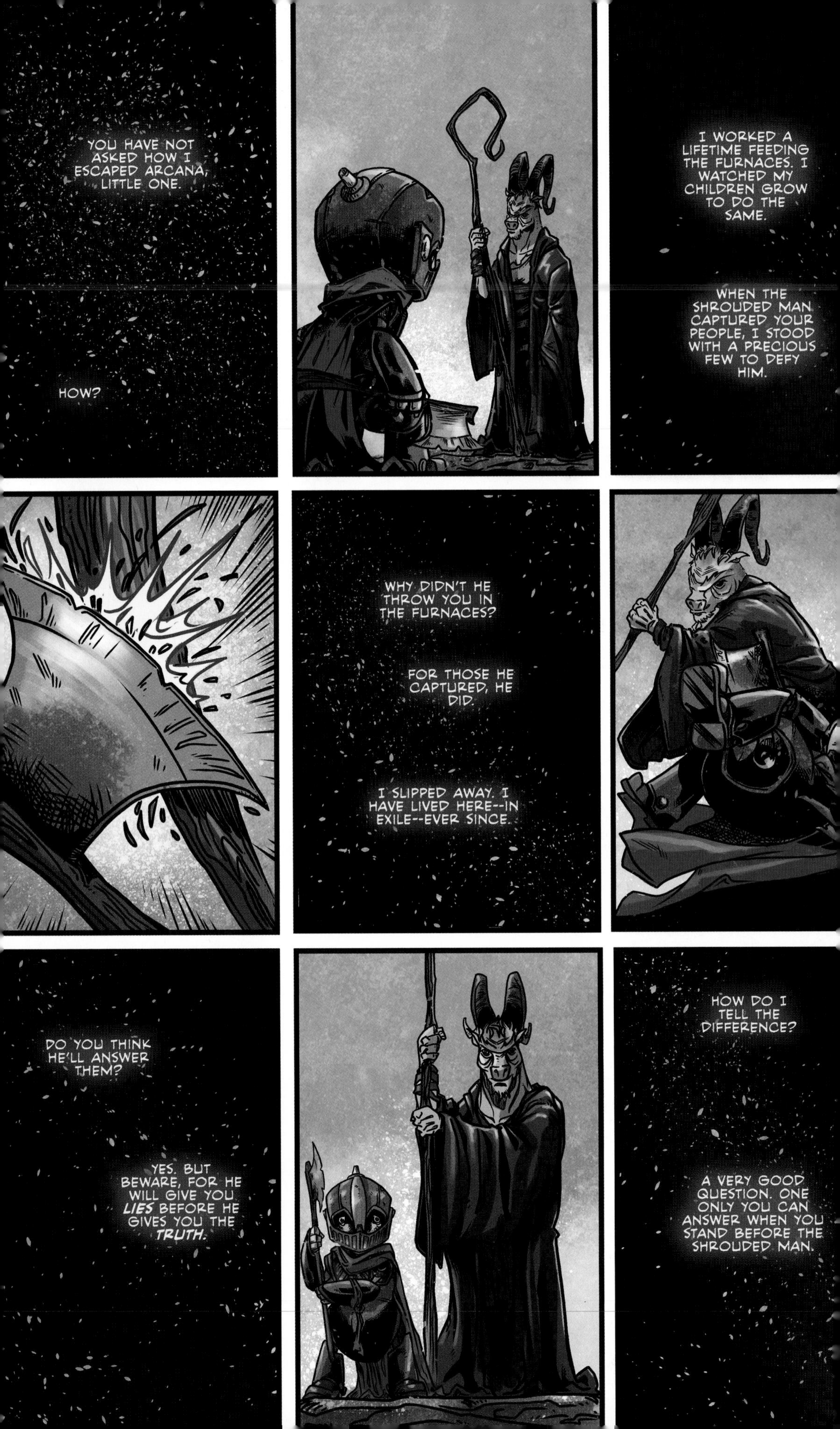

YOU HAVE NOT ASKED HOW I ESCAPED ARCANA, LITTLE ONE.
HOW?
I WORKED A LIFETIME FEEDING THE FURNACES. I WATCHED MY CHILDREN GROW TO DO THE SAME.
WHEN THE SHROUDED MAN CAPTURED YOUR PEOPLE, I STOOD WITH A PRECIOUS FEW TO DEFY HIM.
WHY DIDN'T HE THROW YOU IN THE FURNACES?
FOR THOSE HE CAPTURED, HE DID.
I SLIPPED AWAY. I HAVE LIVED HERE--IN EXILE--EVER SINCE.
DO YOU THINK HE'LL ANSWER THEM?
YES. BUT BEWARE, FOR HE WILL GIVE YOU *LIES* BEFORE HE GIVES YOU THE *TRUTH*.
HOW DO I TELL THE DIFFERENCE?
A VERY GOOD QUESTION. ONE ONLY YOU CAN ANSWER WHEN YOU STAND BEFORE THE SHROUDED MAN.

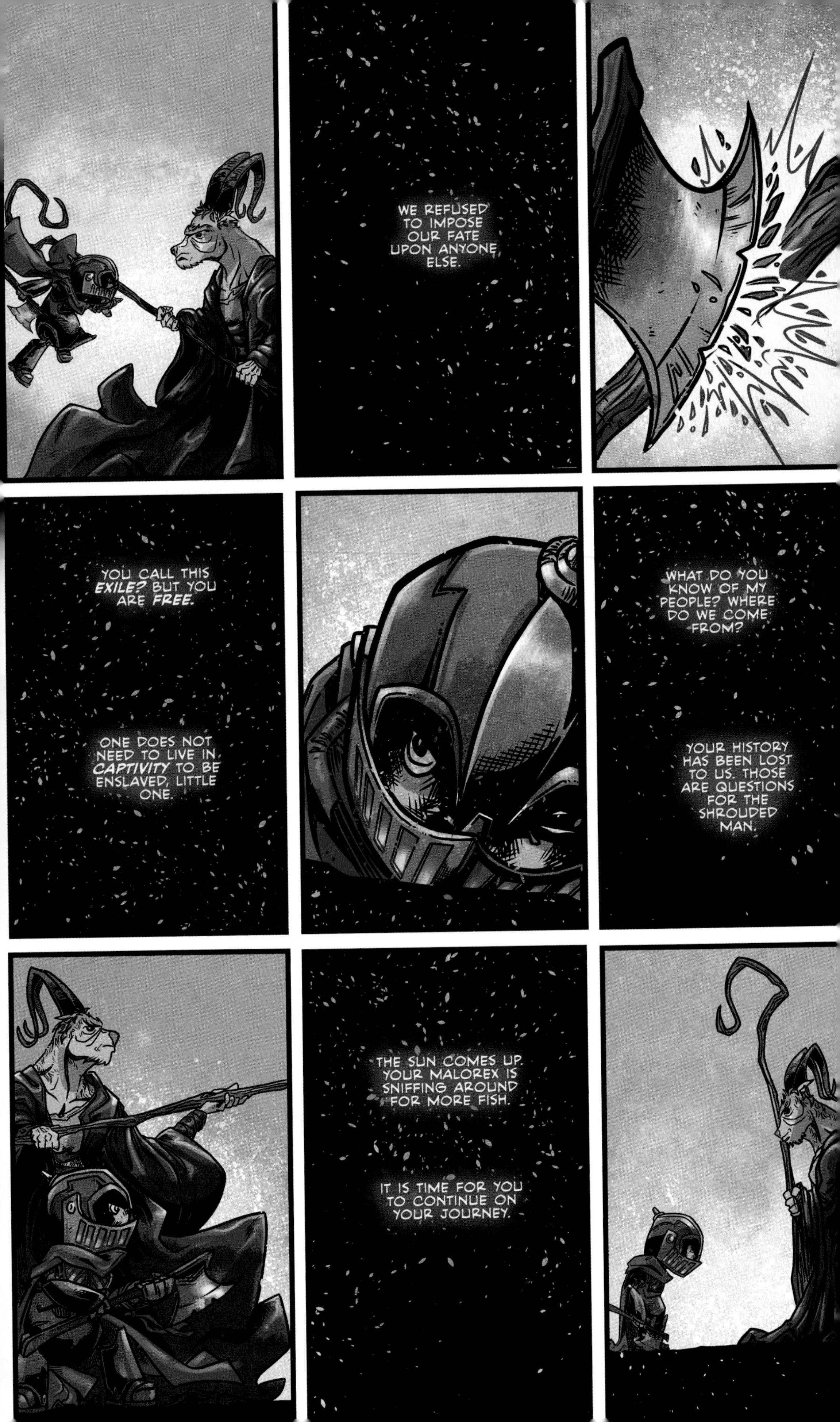
WE REFUSED TO IMPOSE OUR FATE UPON ANYONE ELSE.
YOU CALL THIS *EXILE?* BUT YOU ARE *FREE.*
ONE DOES NOT NEED TO LIVE IN *CAPTIVITY* TO BE ENSLAVED, LITTLE ONE.
WHAT DO YOU KNOW OF MY PEOPLE? WHERE DO WE COME FROM?
YOUR HISTORY HAS BEEN LOST TO US. THOSE ARE QUESTIONS FOR THE SHROUDED MAN.
THE SUN COMES UP. YOUR MALOREX IS SNIFFING AROUND FOR MORE FISH.
IT IS TIME FOR YOU TO CONTINUE ON YOUR JOURNEY.

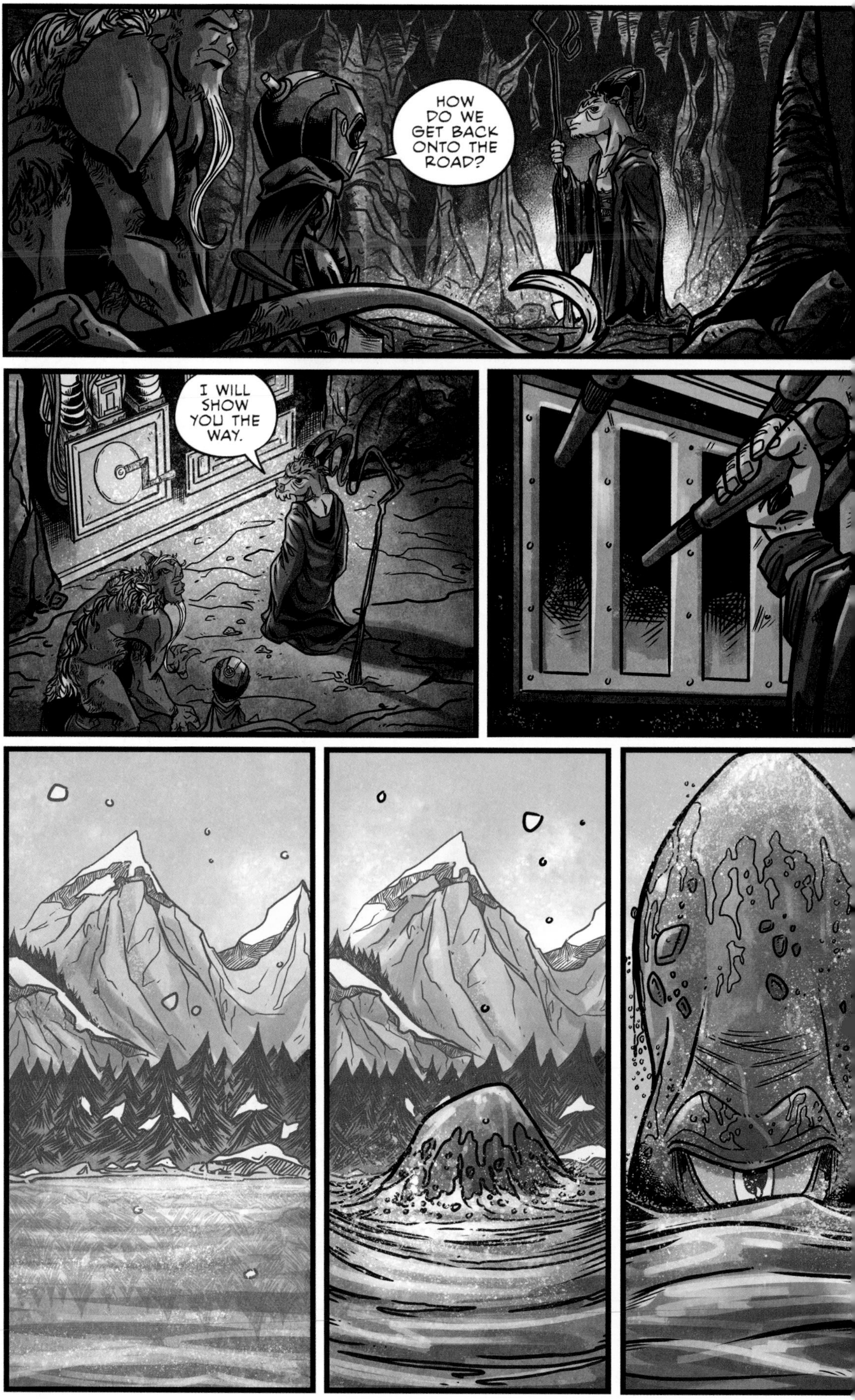
HOW DO WE GET BACK ONTO THE ROAD?
I WILL SHOW YOU THE WAY.

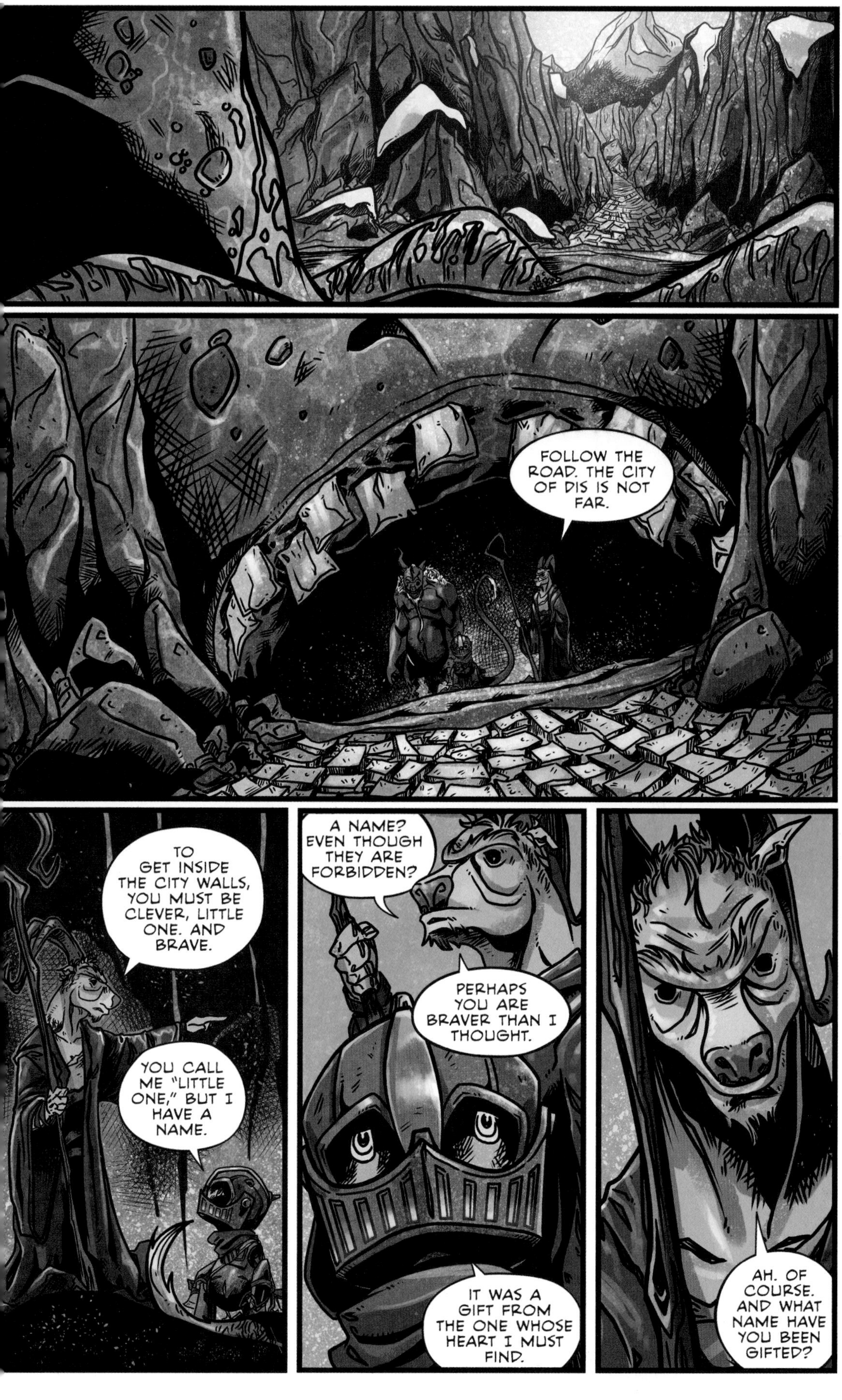
FOLLOW THE ROAD. THE CITY OF DIS IS NOT FAR.
TO GET INSIDE THE CITY WALLS, YOU MUST BE CLEVER, LITTLE ONE. AND BRAVE.
YOU CALL ME "LITTLE ONE," BUT I HAVE A NAME.
A NAME? EVEN THOUGH THEY ARE FORBIDDEN?
PERHAPS YOU ARE BRAVER THAN I THOUGHT.
IT WAS A GIFT FROM THE ONE WHOSE HEART I MUST FIND.
AH. OF COURSE. AND WHAT NAME HAVE YOU BEEN GIFTED?

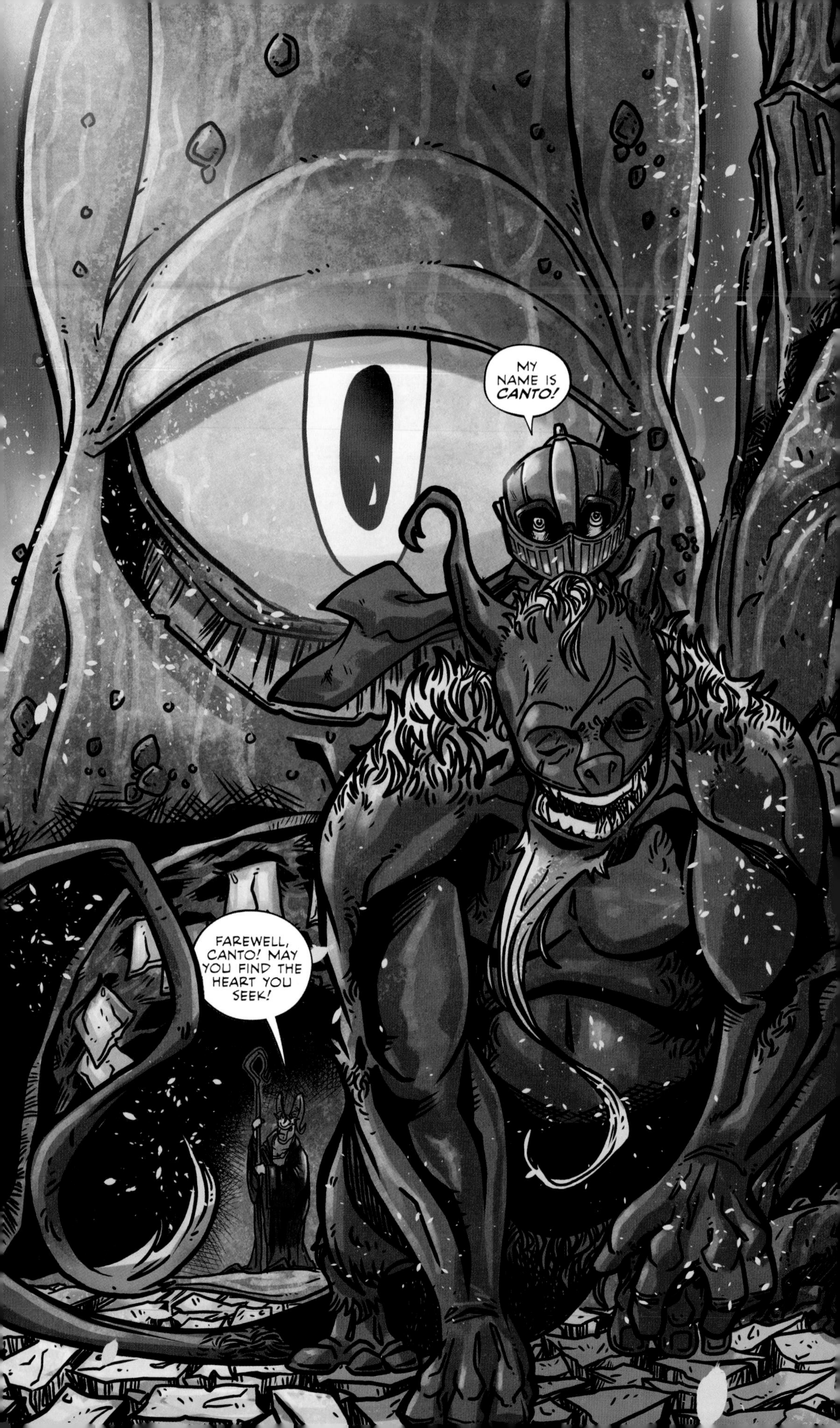
MY NAME IS *CANTO!*
FAREWELL, CANTO! MAY YOU FIND THE HEART YOU SEEK!

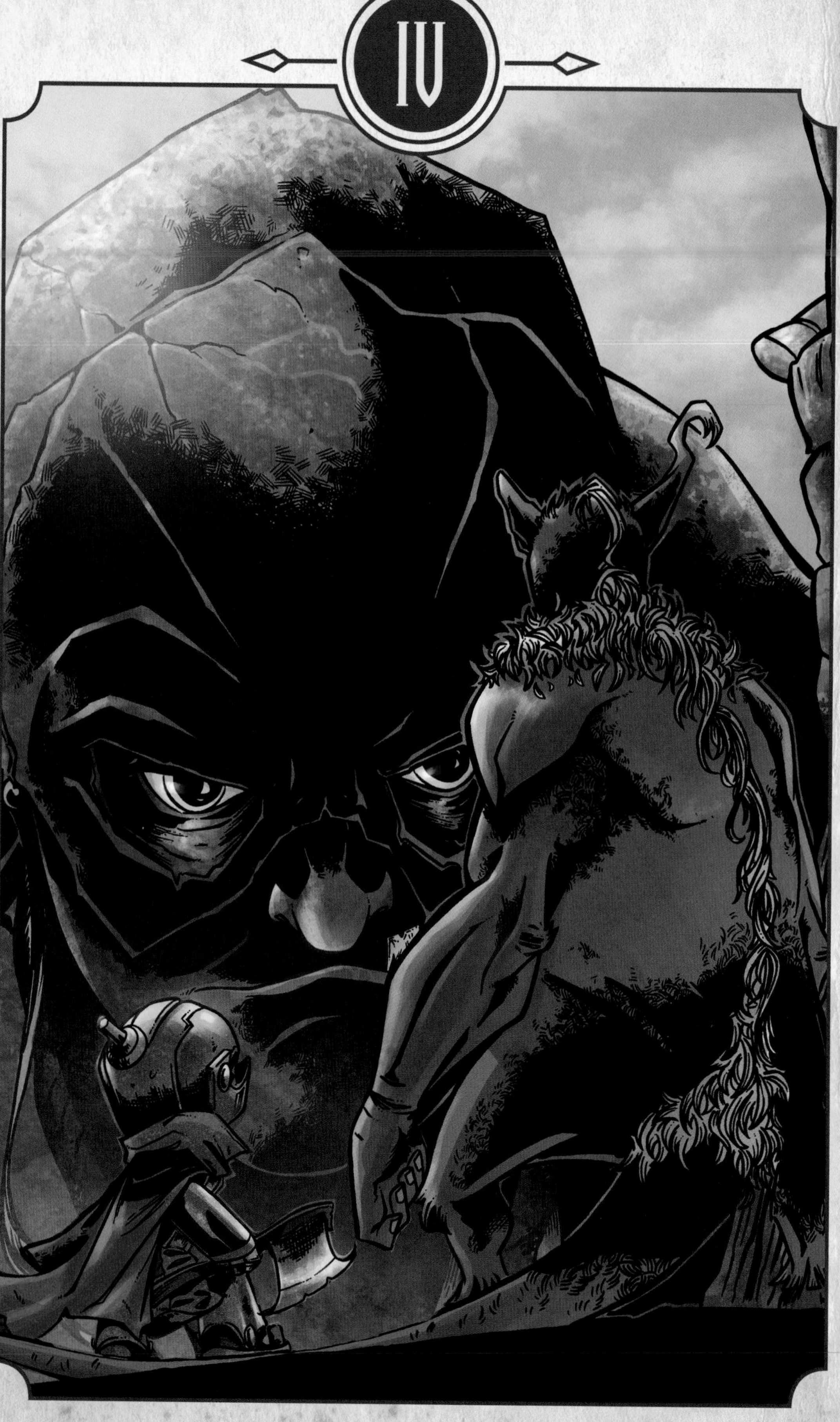

Art by **Drew Zucker**, *Colors by* **Vittorio Astone**

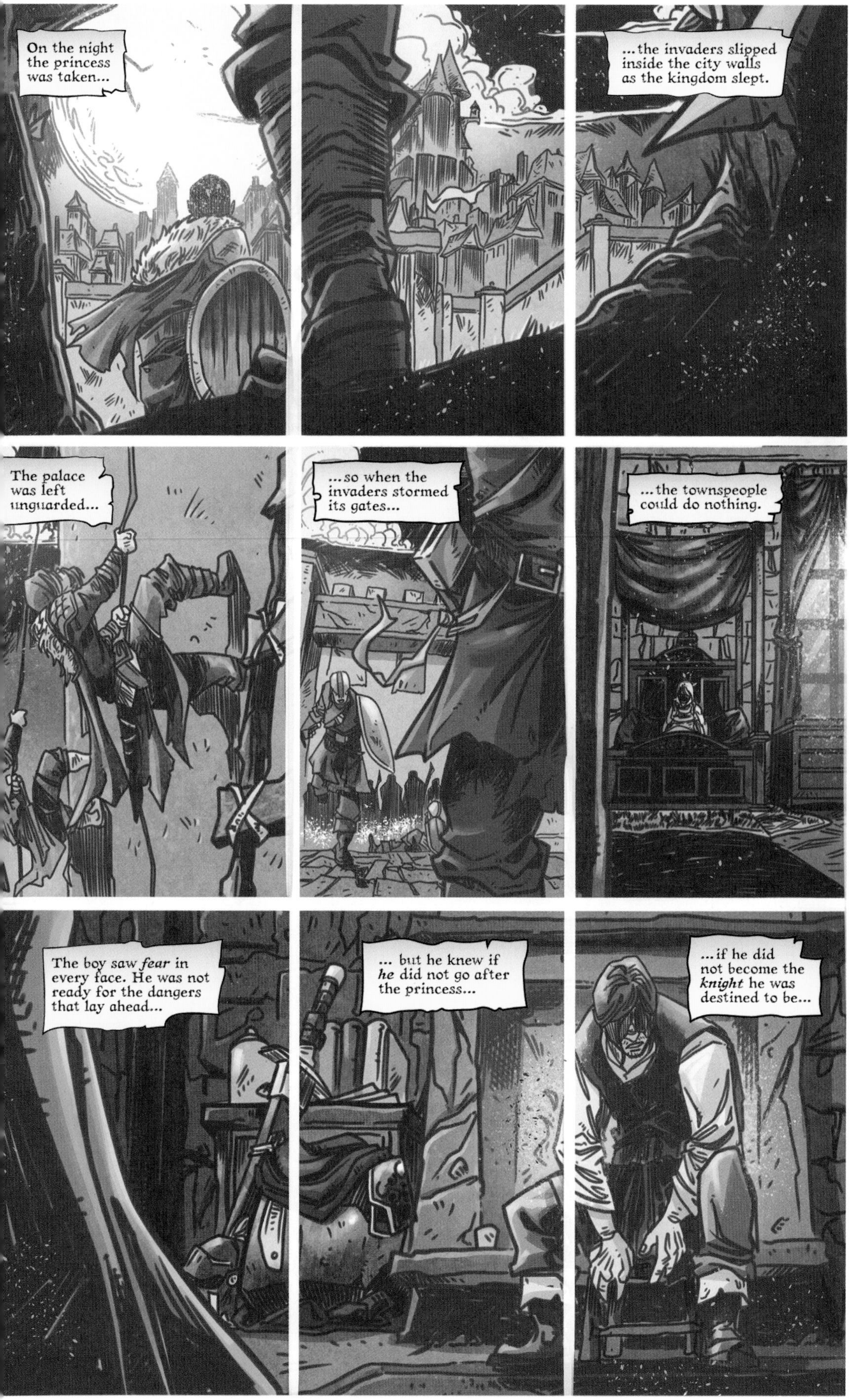
On the night the princess was taken...
...the invaders slipped inside the city walls as the kingdom slept.
The palace was left unguarded...
...so when the invaders stormed its gates...
...the townspeople could do nothing.
The boy saw *fear* in every face. He was not ready for the dangers that lay ahead...
... but he knew if *he* did not go after the princess...
...if he did not become the *knight* he was destined to be...

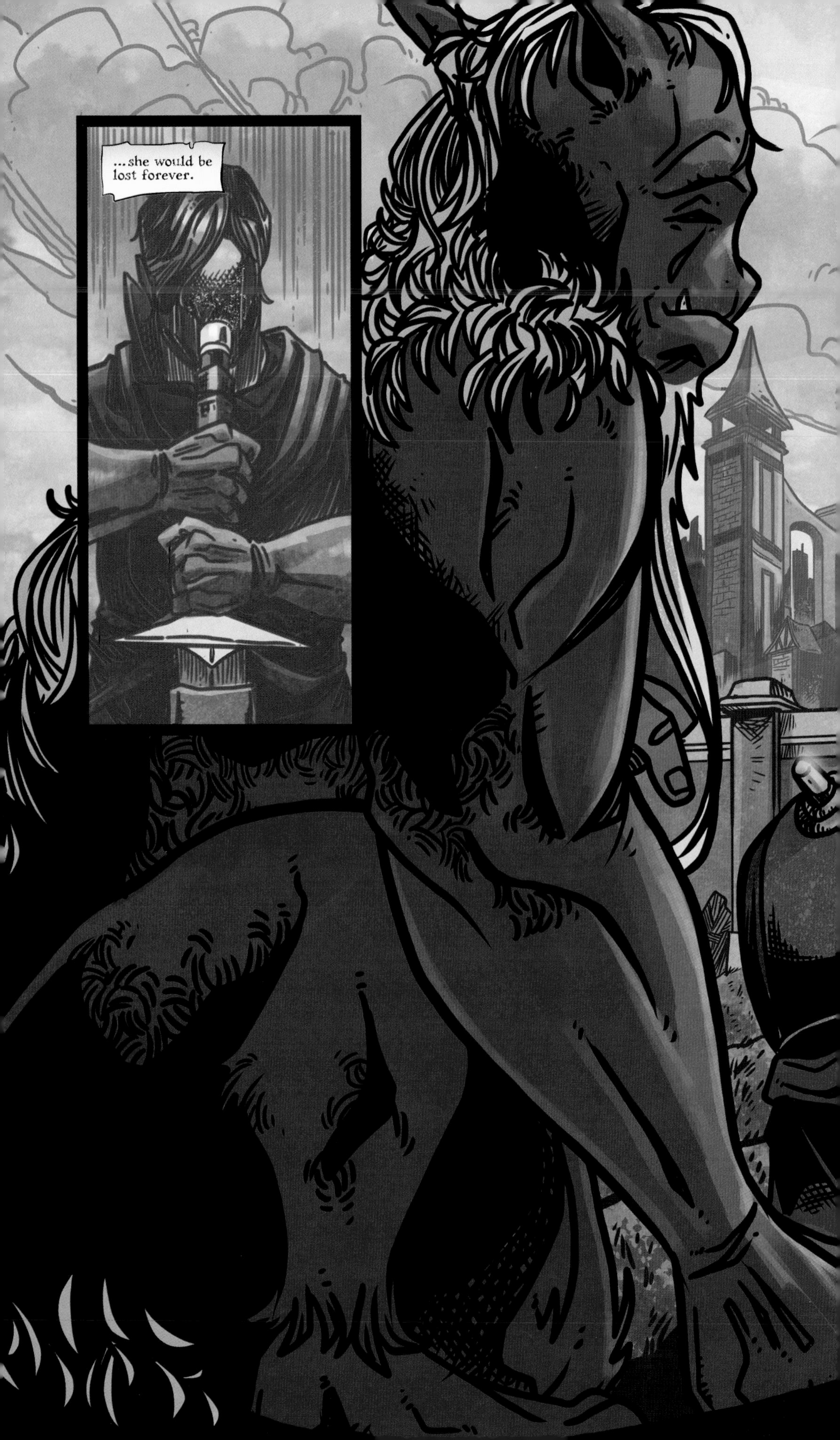
...she would be lost forever.

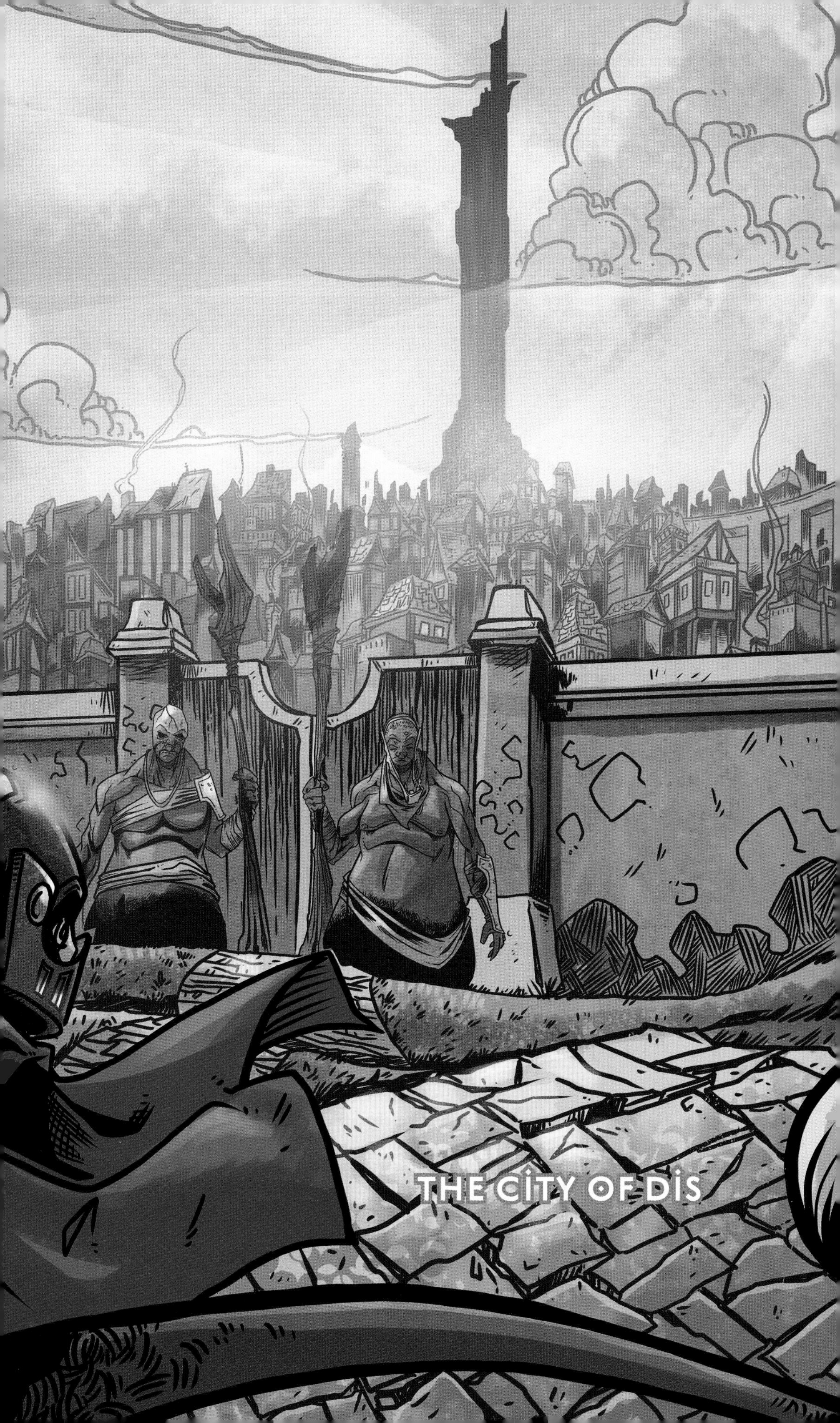
THE CITY OF DIS

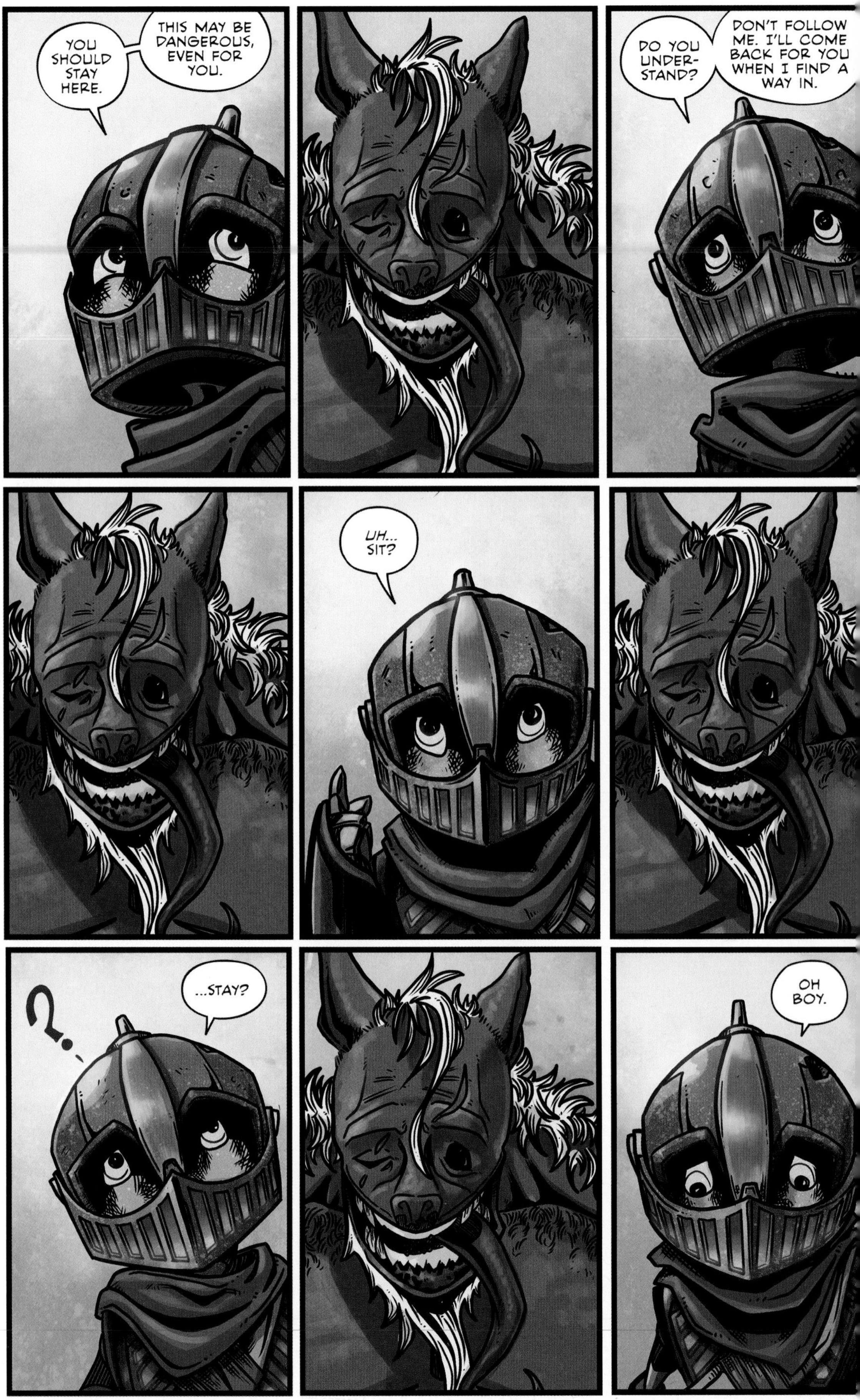
YOU SHOULD STAY HERE.
THIS MAY BE DANGEROUS, EVEN FOR YOU.
DO YOU UNDER-STAND?
DON'T FOLLOW ME. I'LL COME BACK FOR YOU WHEN I FIND A WAY IN.
UH... SIT?
...STAY?
?
OH BOY.

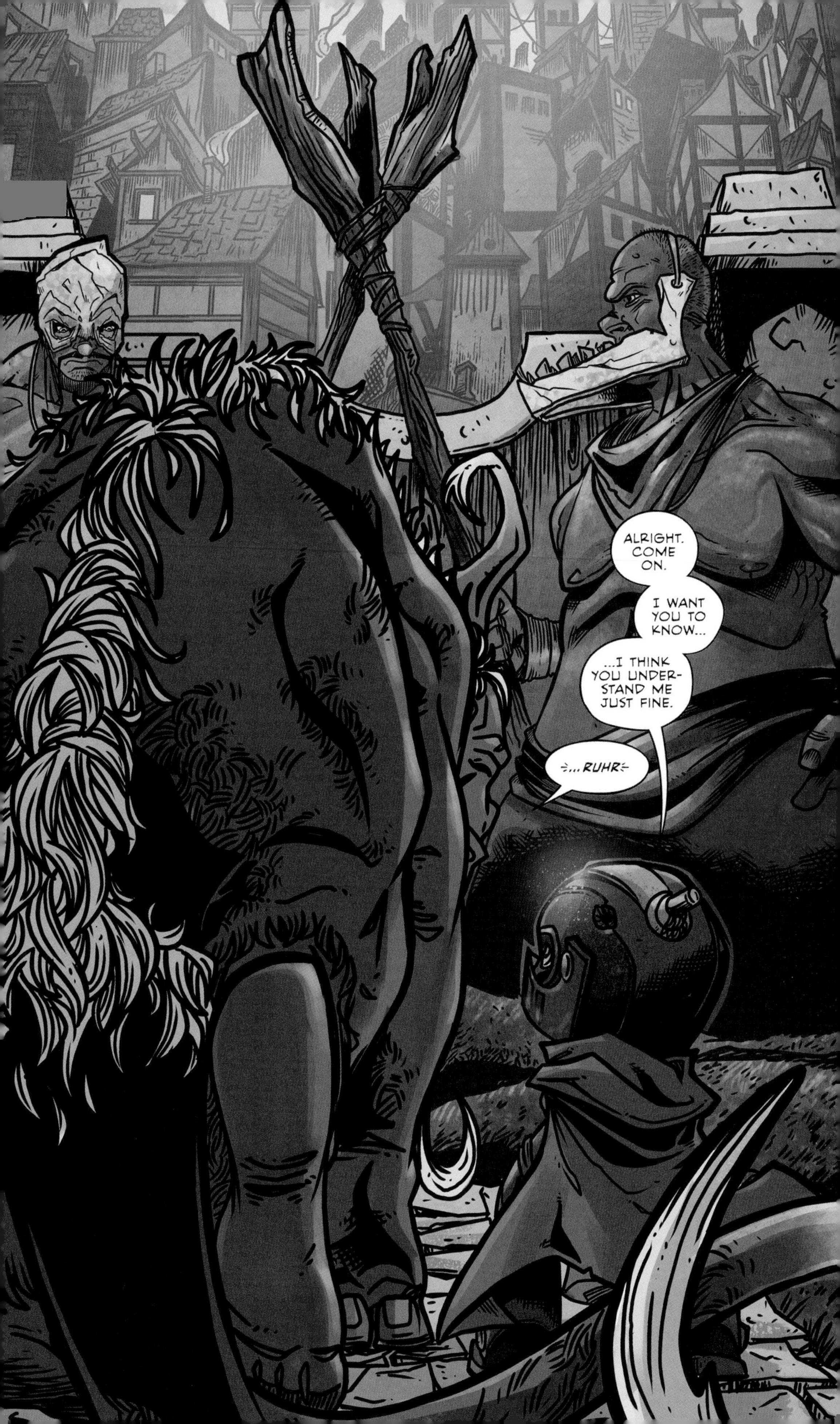
ALRIGHT. COME ON.
I WANT YOU TO KNOW...
...I THINK YOU UNDER-STAND ME JUST FINE.
...RUHR

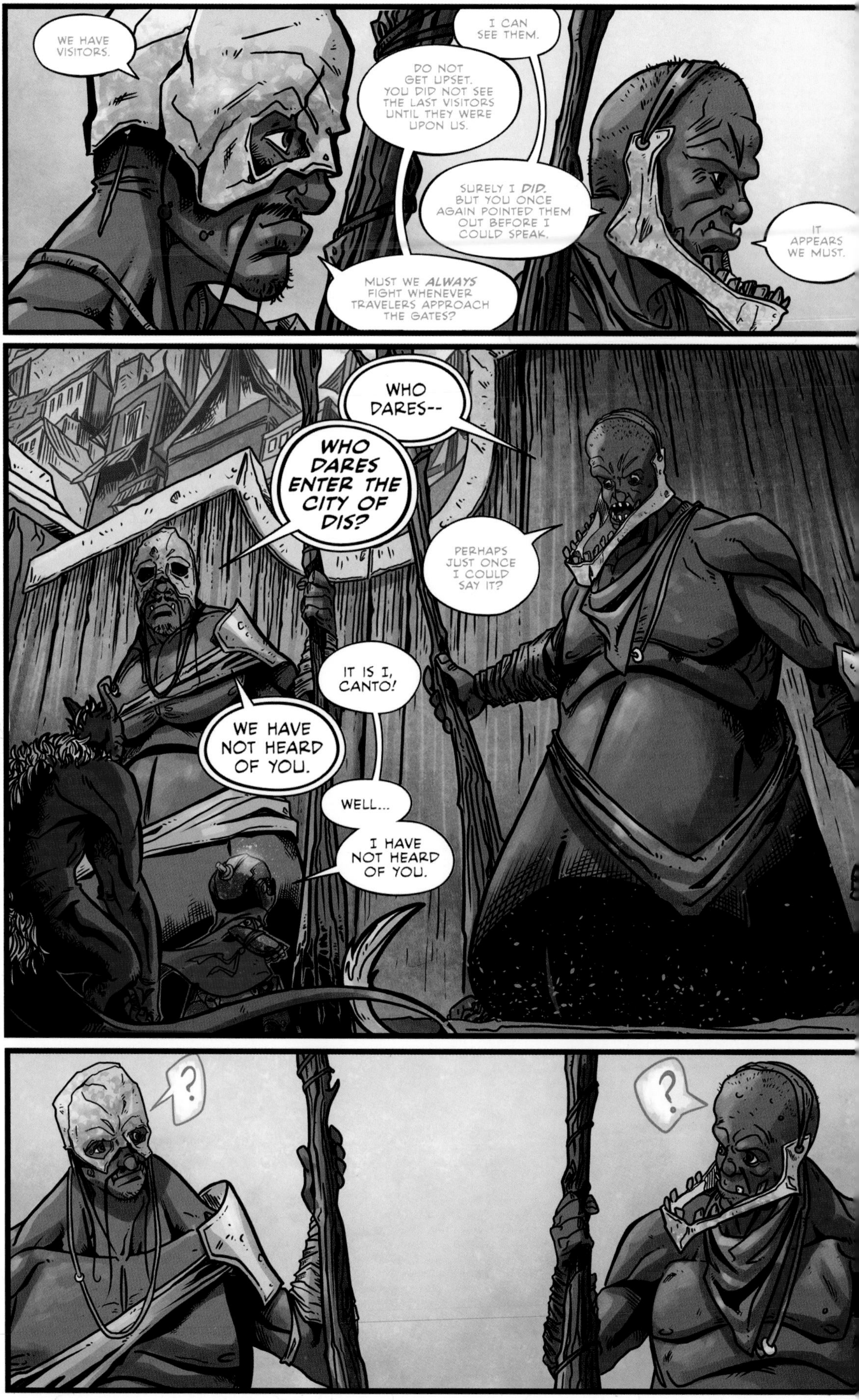
WE HAVE VISITORS.
I CAN SEE THEM.
DO NOT GET UPSET. YOU DID NOT SEE THE LAST VISITORS UNTIL THEY WERE UPON US.
SURELY I *DID*. BUT YOU ONCE AGAIN POINTED THEM OUT BEFORE I COULD SPEAK.
MUST WE *ALWAYS* FIGHT WHENEVER TRAVELERS APPROACH THE GATES?
IT APPEARS WE MUST.
WHO DARES--
WHO DARES ENTER THE CITY OF DIS?
PERHAPS JUST ONCE I COULD SAY IT?
IT IS I, CANTO!
WE HAVE NOT HEARD OF YOU.
WELL...
I HAVE NOT HEARD OF YOU.
?
?

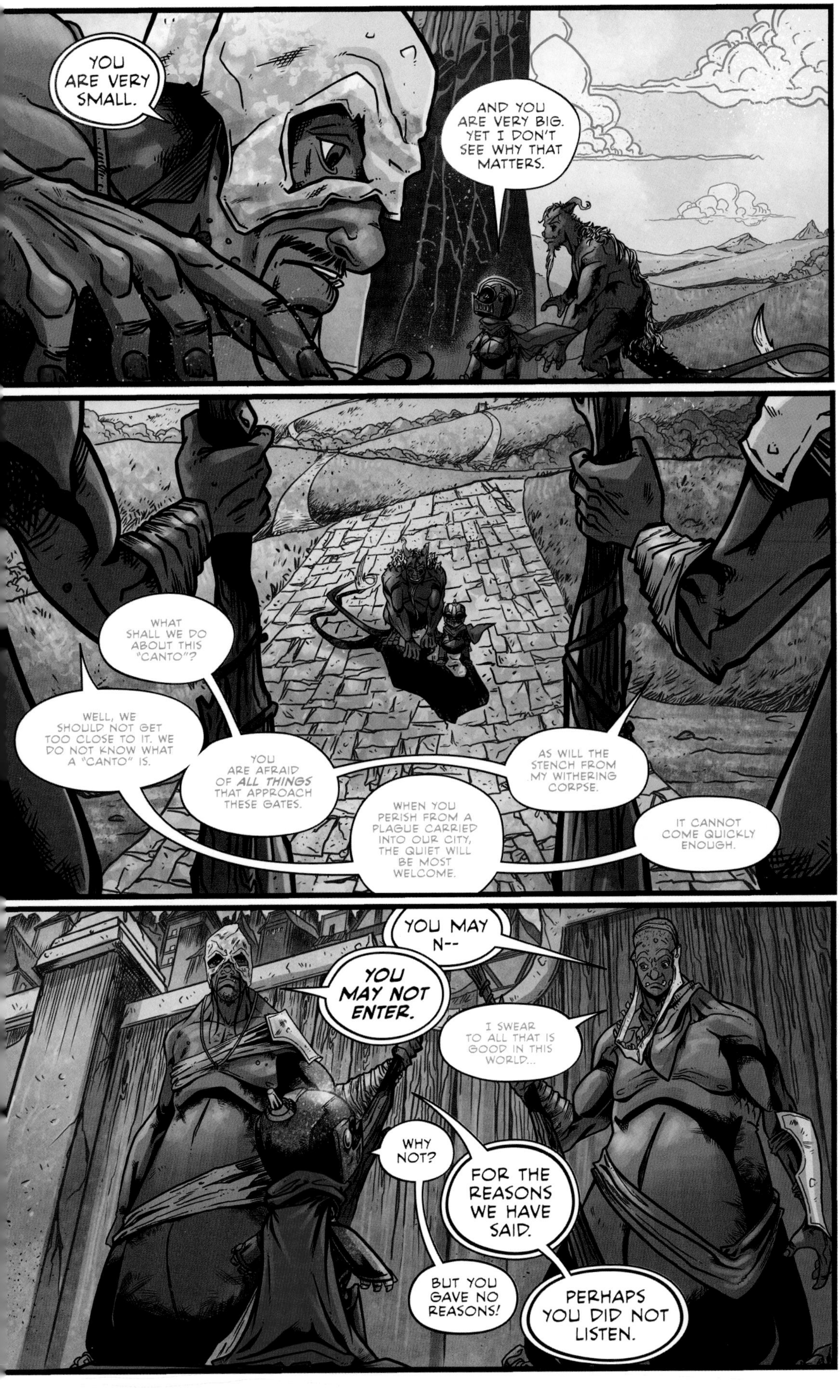
YOU ARE VERY SMALL.
AND YOU ARE VERY BIG. YET I DON'T SEE WHY THAT MATTERS.
WHAT SHALL WE DO ABOUT THIS "CANTO"?
WELL, WE SHOULD NOT GET TOO CLOSE TO IT. WE DO NOT KNOW WHAT A "CANTO" IS.
YOU ARE AFRAID OF *ALL THINGS* THAT APPROACH THESE GATES.
WHEN YOU PERISH FROM A PLAGUE CARRIED INTO OUR CITY, THE QUIET WILL BE MOST WELCOME.
AS WILL THE STENCH FROM MY WITHERING CORPSE.
IT CANNOT COME QUICKLY ENOUGH.
YOU MAY N--
YOU MAY NOT ENTER.
I SWEAR TO ALL THAT IS GOOD IN THIS WORLD...
WHY NOT?
FOR THE REASONS WE HAVE SAID.
BUT YOU GAVE NO REASONS!
PERHAPS YOU DID NOT LISTEN.

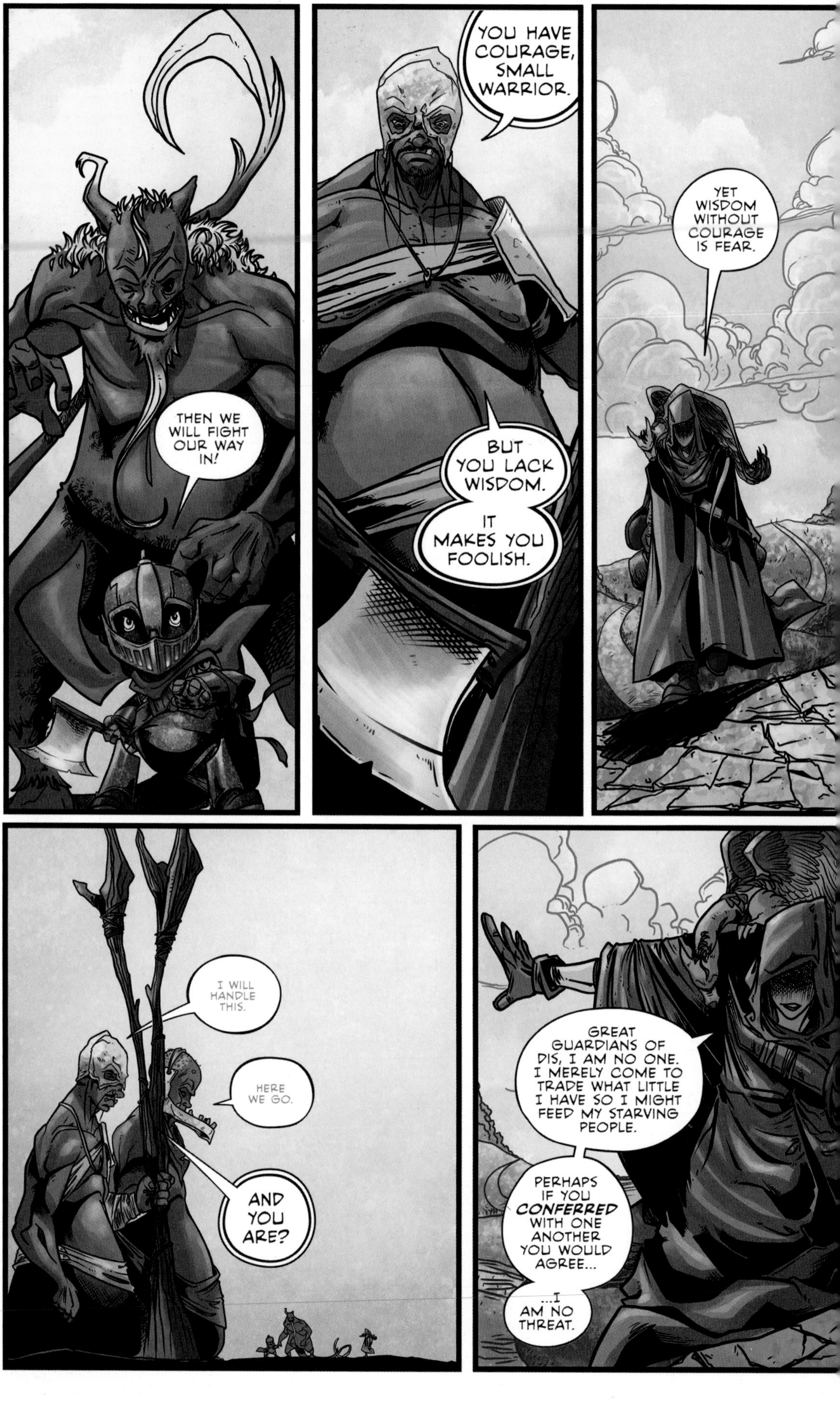
THEN WE WILL FIGHT OUR WAY IN!
YOU HAVE COURAGE, SMALL WARRIOR.
BUT YOU LACK WISDOM.
IT MAKES YOU FOOLISH.
YET WISDOM WITHOUT COURAGE IS FEAR.
I WILL HANDLE THIS.
HERE WE GO.
AND YOU ARE?
GREAT GUARDIANS OF DIS, I AM NO ONE. I MERELY COME TO TRADE WHAT LITTLE I HAVE SO I MIGHT FEED MY STARVING PEOPLE.
PERHAPS IF YOU CONFERRED WITH ONE ANOTHER YOU WOULD AGREE...
...I AM NO THREAT.

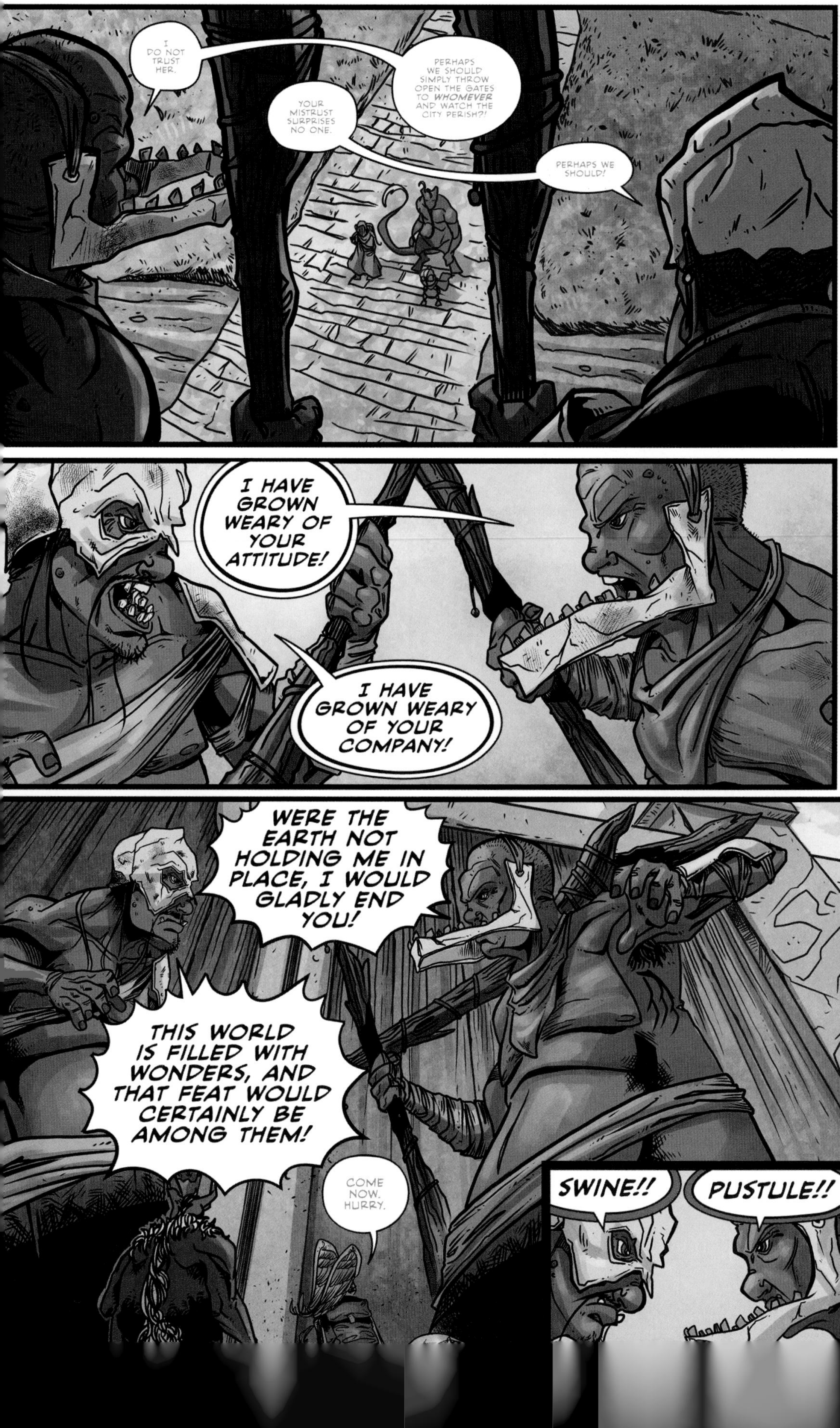
I DO NOT TRUST HER.
PERHAPS WE SHOULD SIMPLY THROW OPEN THE GATES TO WHOMEVER AND WATCH THE CITY PERISH?!
YOUR MISTRUST SURPRISES NO ONE.
PERHAPS WE SHOULD!
I HAVE GROWN WEARY OF YOUR ATTITUDE!
I HAVE GROWN WEARY OF YOUR COMPANY!
WERE THE EARTH NOT HOLDING ME IN PLACE, I WOULD GLADLY END YOU!
THIS WORLD IS FILLED WITH WONDERS, AND THAT FEAT WOULD CERTAINLY BE AMONG THEM!
COME NOW. HURRY.
SWINE!!
PUSTULE!!

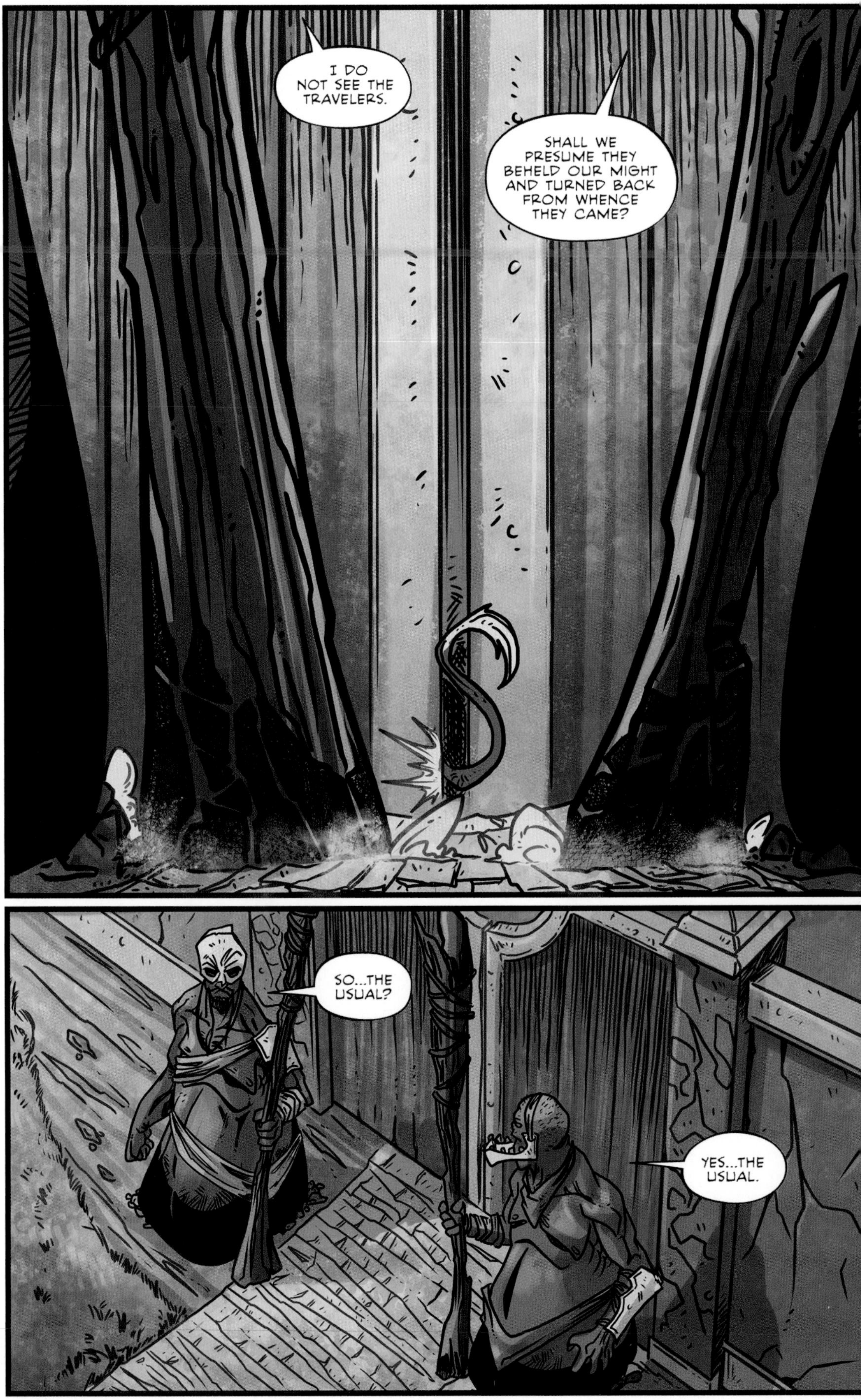
I DO NOT SEE THE TRAVELERS.
SHALL WE PRESUME THEY BEHELD OUR MIGHT AND TURNED BACK FROM WHENCE THEY CAME?
SO...THE USUAL?
YES...THE USUAL.

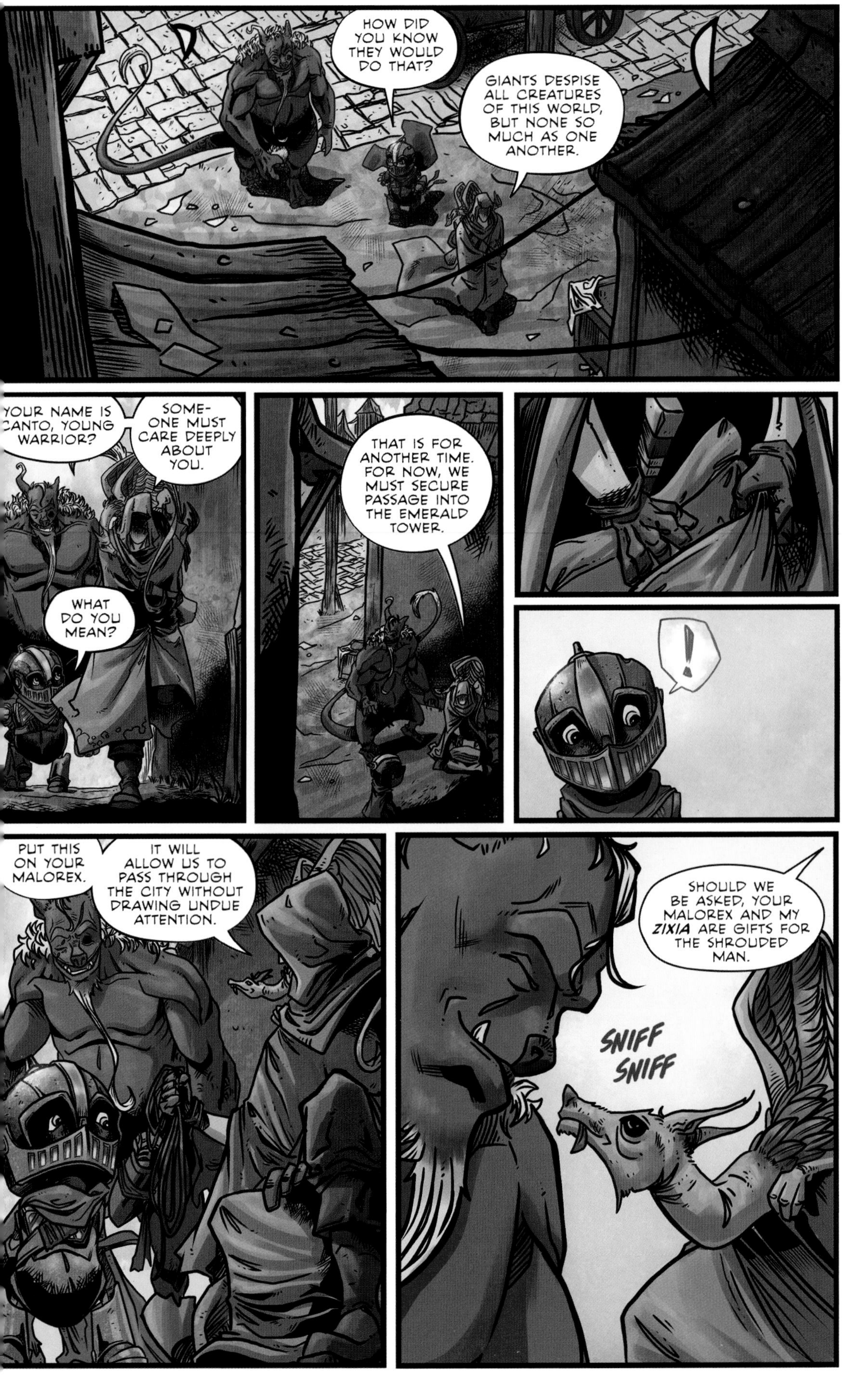
HOW DID YOU KNOW THEY WOULD DO THAT?
GIANTS DESPISE ALL CREATURES OF THIS WORLD, BUT NONE SO MUCH AS ONE ANOTHER.
YOUR NAME IS CANTO, YOUNG WARRIOR?
SOME-ONE MUST CARE DEEPLY ABOUT YOU.
WHAT DO YOU MEAN?
THAT IS FOR ANOTHER TIME. FOR NOW, WE MUST SECURE PASSAGE INTO THE EMERALD TOWER.
!
PUT THIS ON YOUR MALOREX.
IT WILL ALLOW US TO PASS THROUGH THE CITY WITHOUT DRAWING UNDUE ATTENTION.
SHOULD WE BE ASKED, YOUR MALOREX AND MY *ZIXIA* ARE GIFTS FOR THE SHROUDED MAN.
SNIFF SNIFF

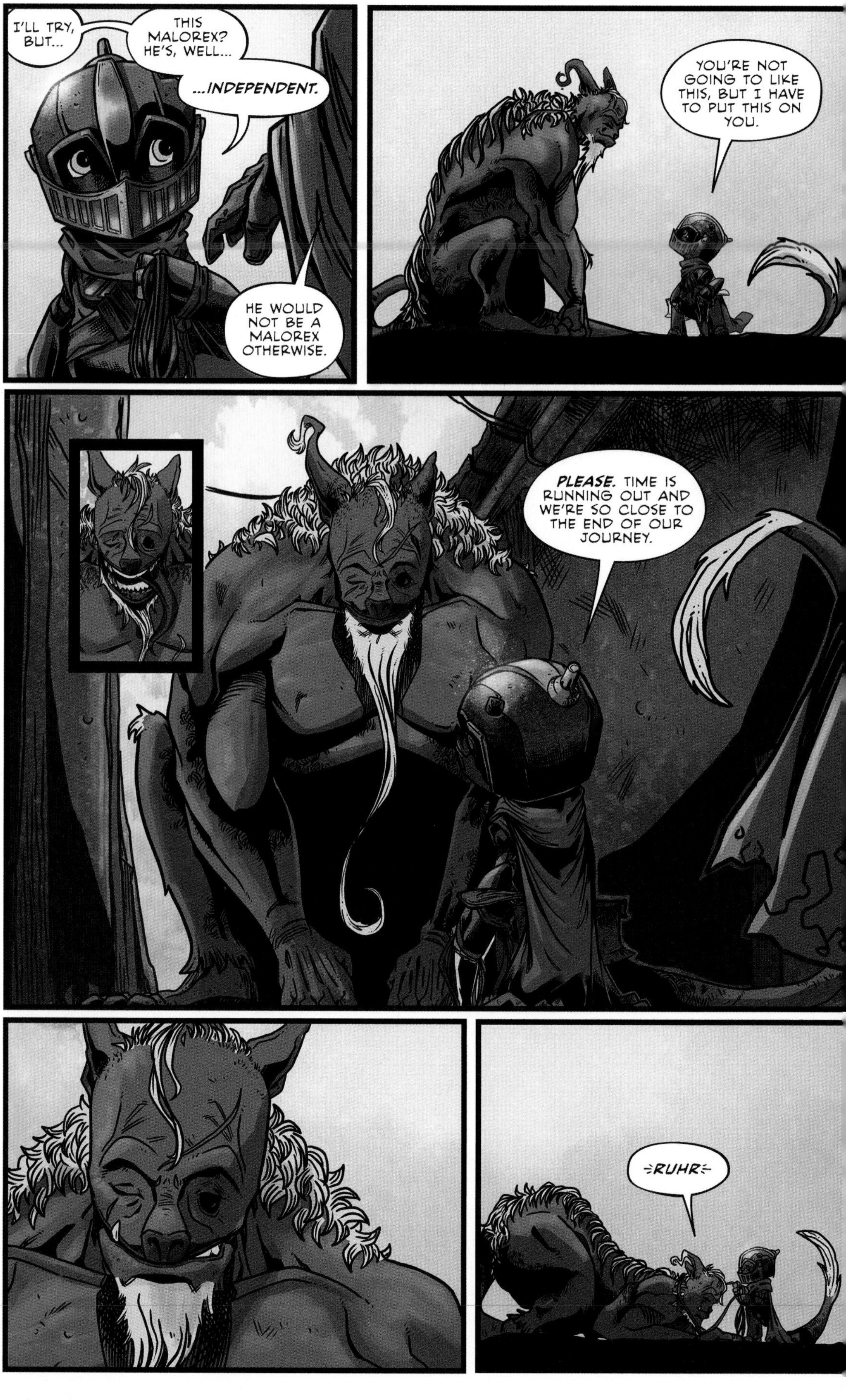

I'LL TRY, BUT...
THIS MALOREX? HE'S, WELL...
...INDEPENDENT.
HE WOULD NOT BE A MALOREX OTHERWISE.
YOU'RE NOT GOING TO LIKE THIS, BUT I HAVE TO PUT THIS ON YOU.
PLEASE. TIME IS RUNNING OUT AND WE'RE SO CLOSE TO THE END OF OUR JOURNEY.
RUHR

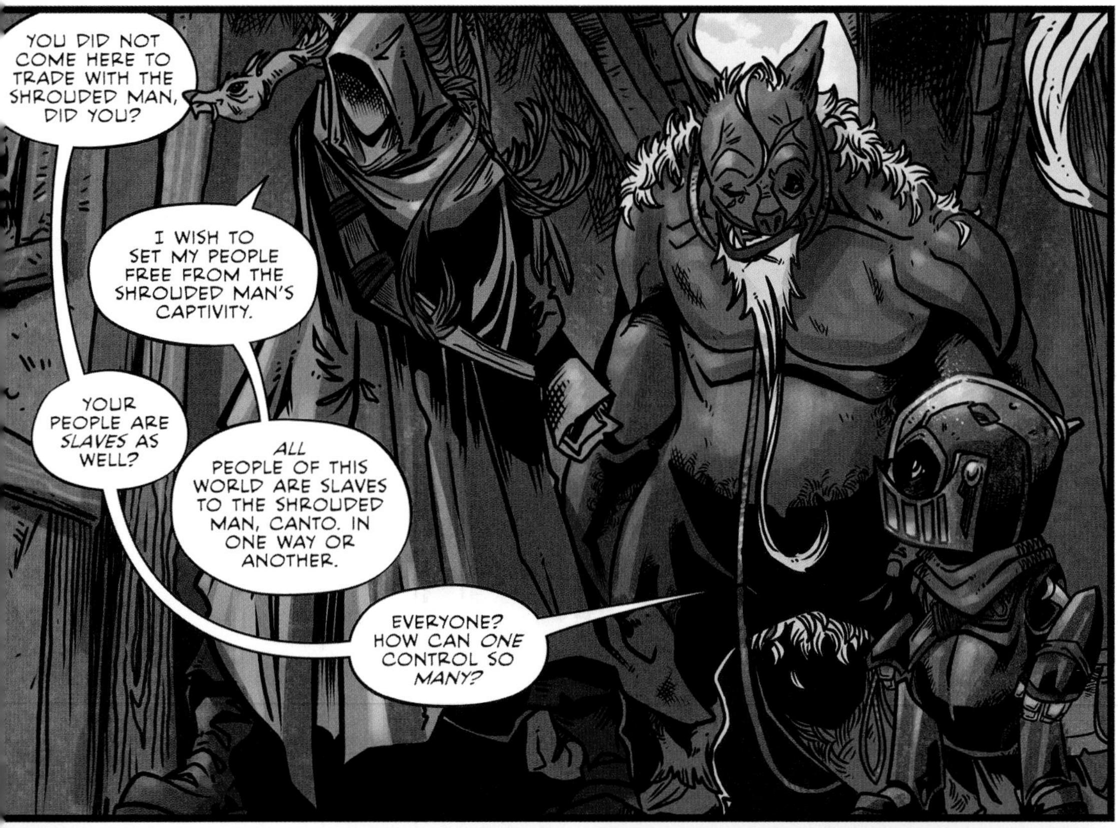
YOU DID NOT COME HERE TO TRADE WITH THE SHROUDED MAN, DID YOU?
I WISH TO SET MY PEOPLE FREE FROM THE SHROUDED MAN'S CAPTIVITY.
YOUR PEOPLE ARE *SLAVES* AS WELL?
ALL PEOPLE OF THIS WORLD ARE SLAVES TO THE SHROUDED MAN, CANTO. IN ONE WAY OR ANOTHER.
EVERYONE? HOW CAN *ONE* CONTROL SO *MANY?*

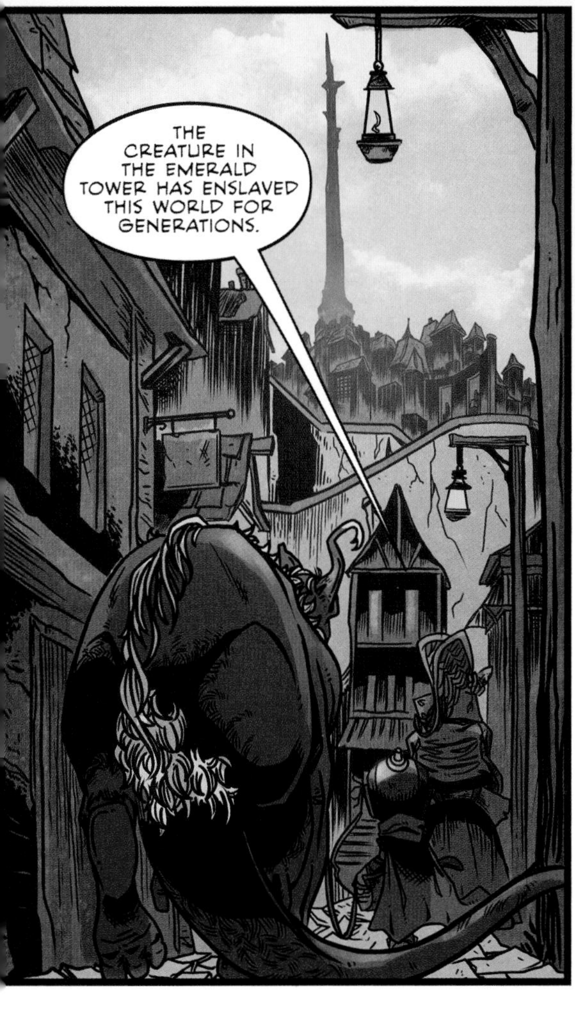
THE CREATURE IN THE EMERALD TOWER HAS ENSLAVED THIS WORLD FOR GENERATIONS.

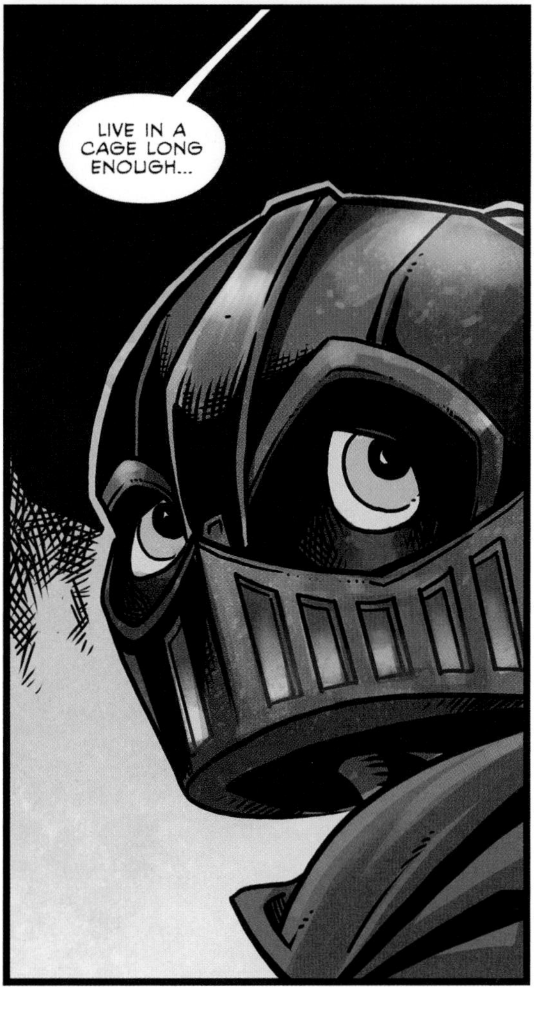
LIVE IN A CAGE LONG ENOUGH...

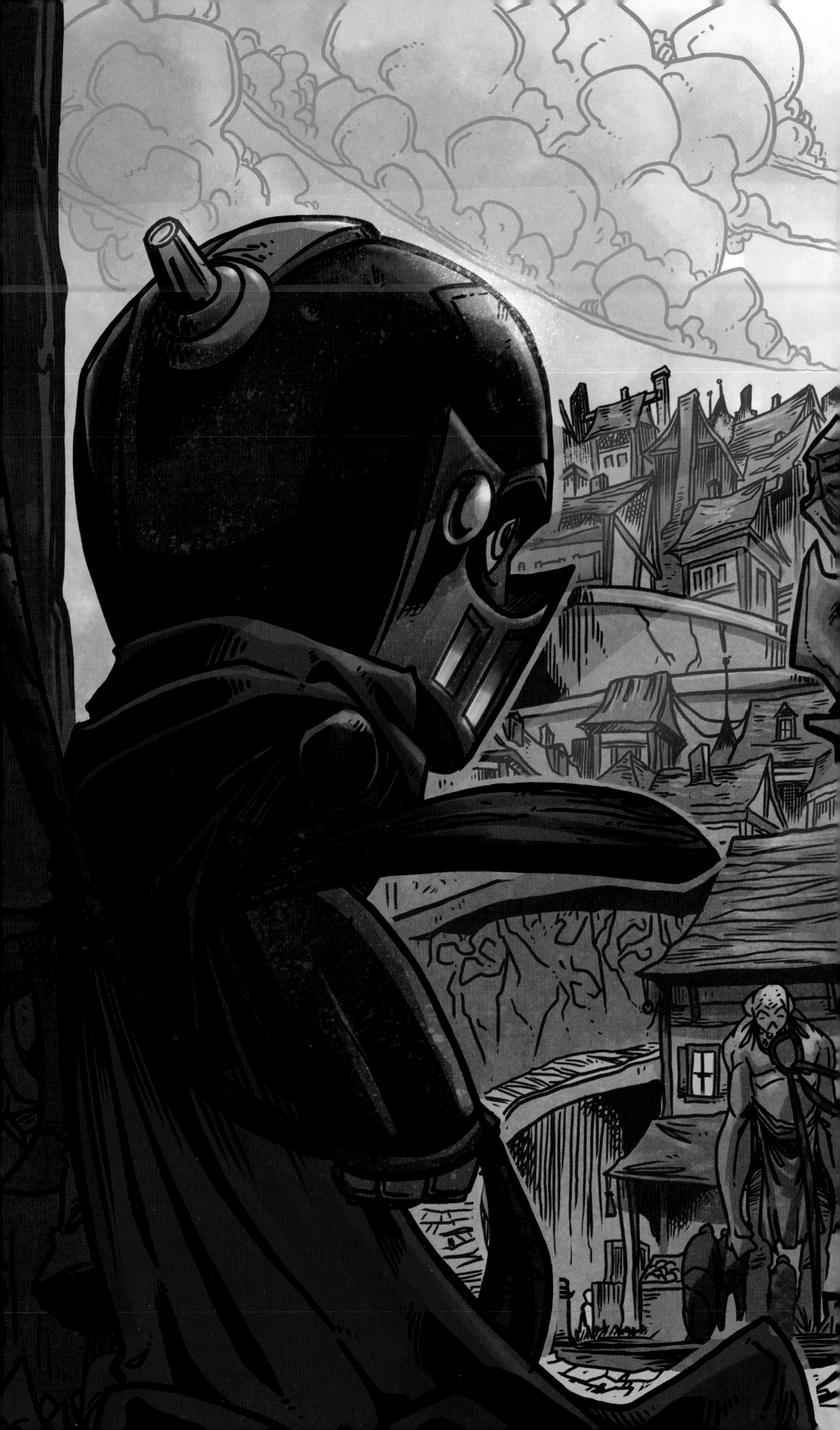

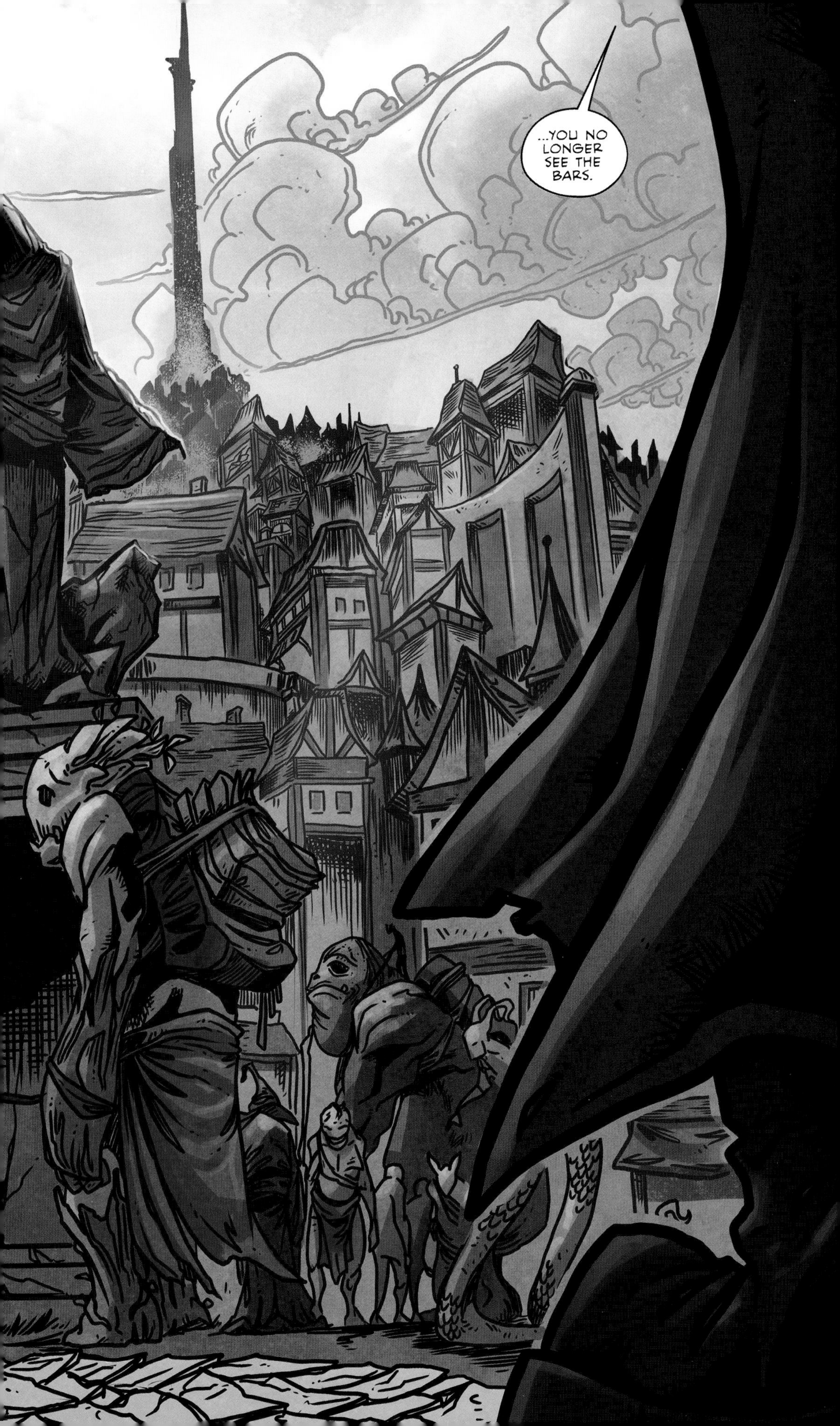
...YOU NO LONGER SEE THE BARS.

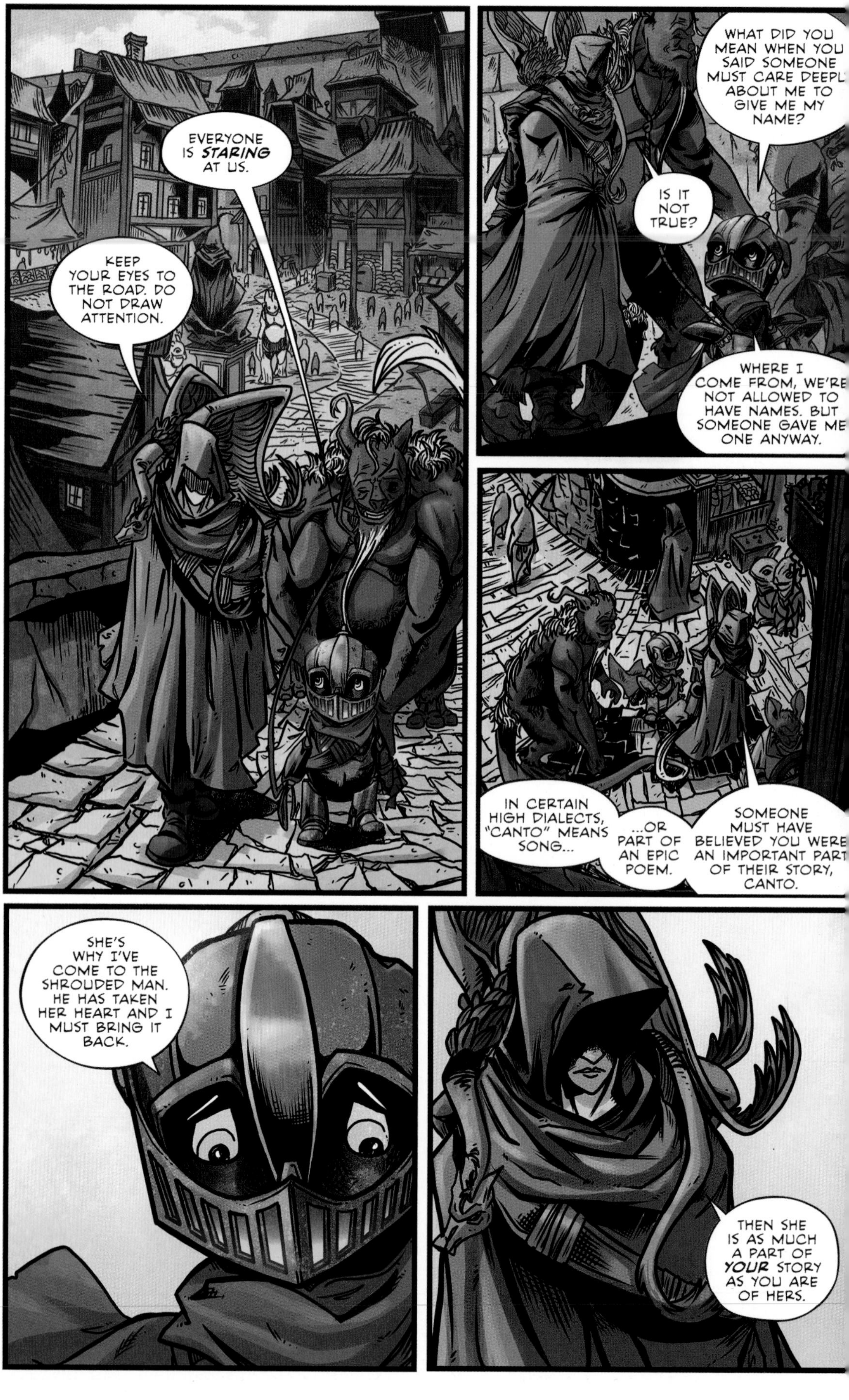
EVERYONE IS *STARING* AT US.
KEEP YOUR EYES TO THE ROAD. DO NOT DRAW ATTENTION.
WHAT DID YOU MEAN WHEN YOU SAID SOMEONE MUST CARE DEEPL ABOUT ME TO GIVE ME MY NAME?
IS IT NOT TRUE?
WHERE I COME FROM, WE'RE NOT ALLOWED TO HAVE NAMES. BUT SOMEONE GAVE ME ONE ANYWAY.
IN CERTAIN HIGH DIALECTS, "CANTO" MEANS SONG...
...OR PART OF AN EPIC POEM.
SOMEONE MUST HAVE BELIEVED YOU WERE AN IMPORTANT PART OF THEIR STORY, CANTO.
SHE'S WHY I'VE COME TO THE SHROUDED MAN. HE HAS TAKEN HER HEART AND I MUST BRING IT BACK.
THEN SHE IS AS MUCH A PART OF *YOUR* STORY AS YOU ARE OF HERS.

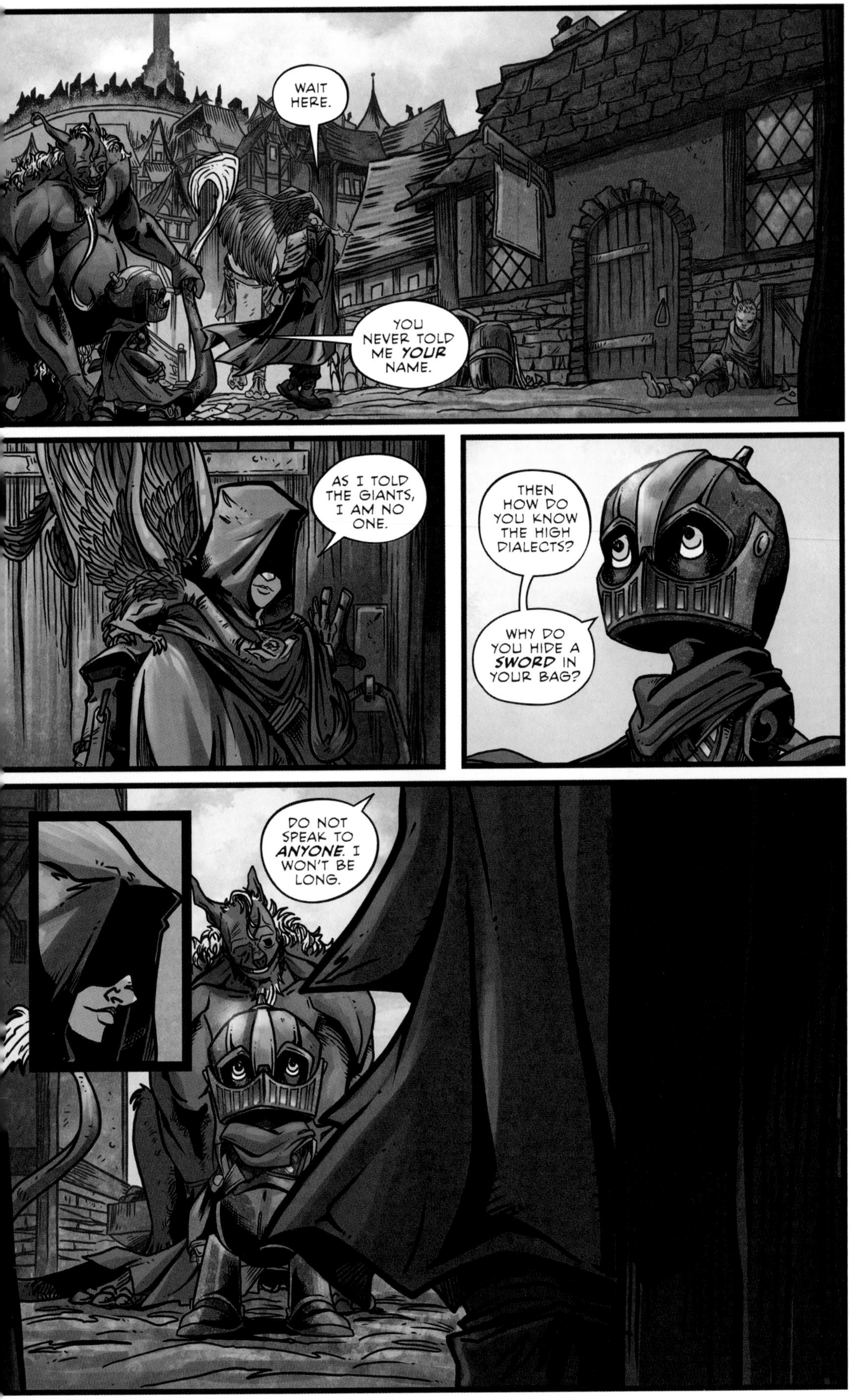
WAIT HERE.
YOU NEVER TOLD ME YOUR NAME.
AS I TOLD THE GIANTS, I AM NO ONE.
THEN HOW DO YOU KNOW THE HIGH DIALECTS?
WHY DO YOU HIDE A SWORD IN YOUR BAG?
DO NOT SPEAK TO ANYONE. I WON'T BE LONG.

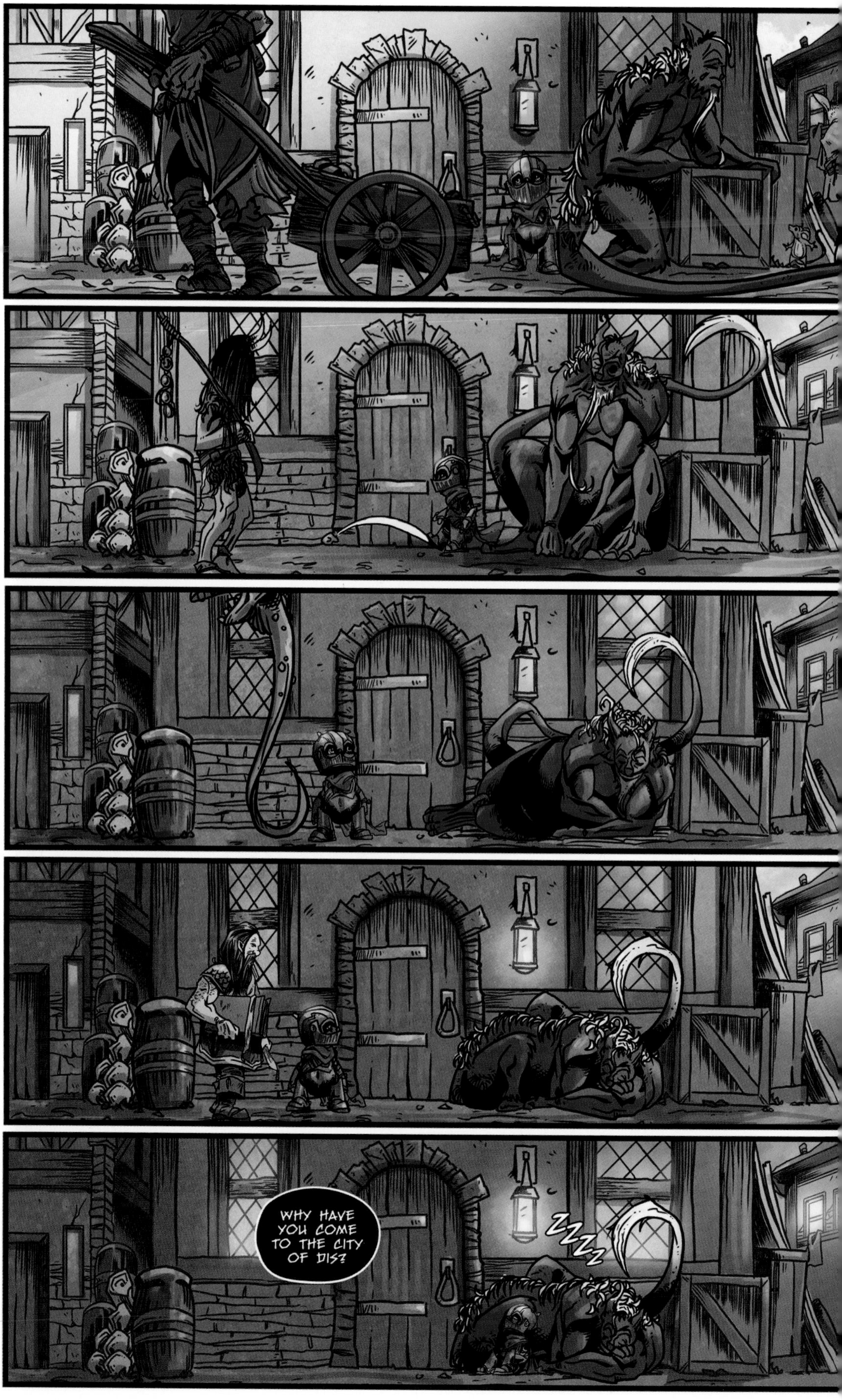
WHY HAVE YOU COME TO THE CITY OF DIS?
ZZZZ

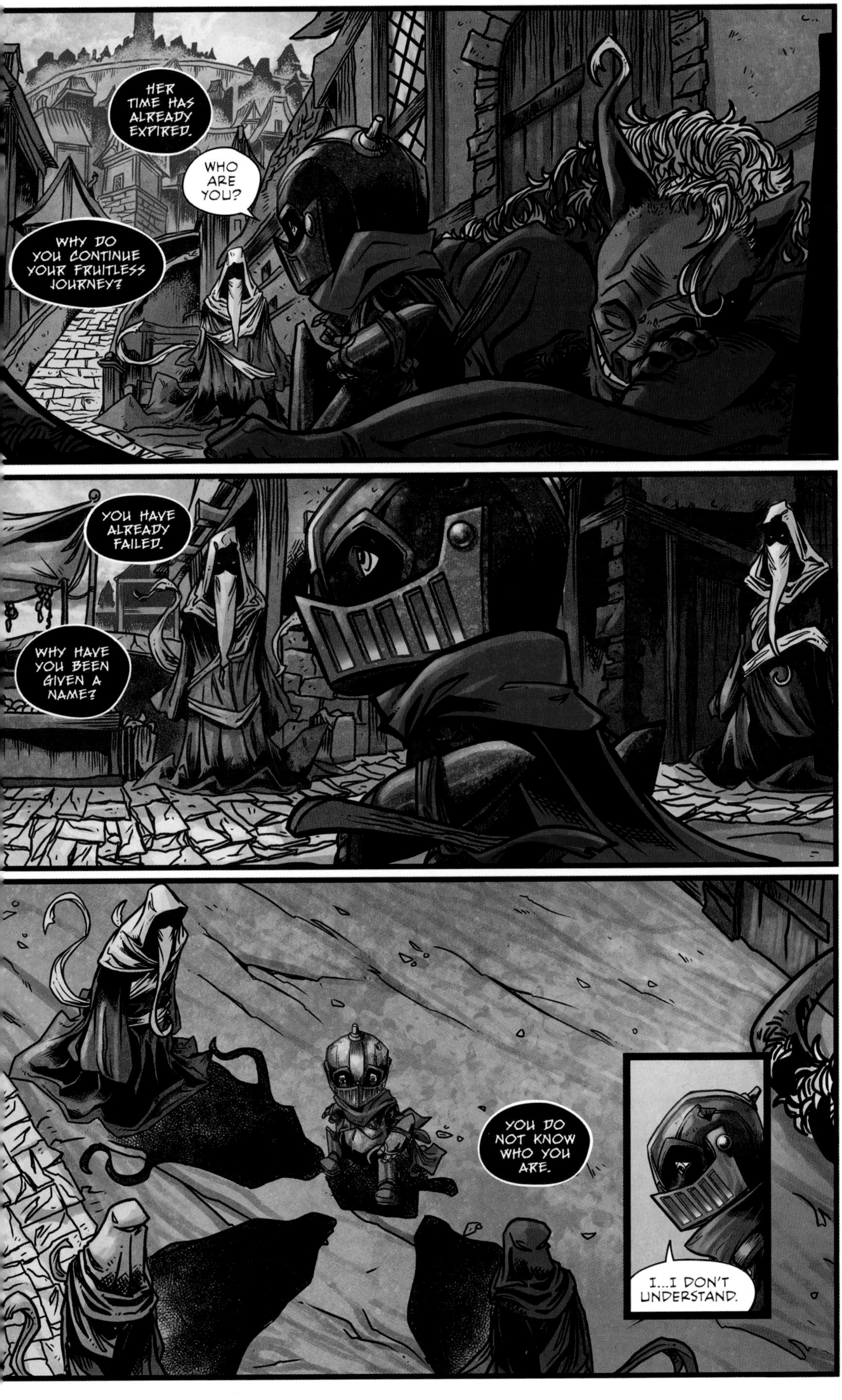
HER TIME HAS ALREADY EXPIRED.
WHO ARE YOU?
WHY DO YOU CONTINUE YOUR FRUITLESS JOURNEY?
YOU HAVE ALREADY FAILED.
WHY HAVE YOU BEEN GIVEN A NAME?
YOU DO NOT KNOW WHO YOU ARE.
I...I DON'T UNDERSTAND.

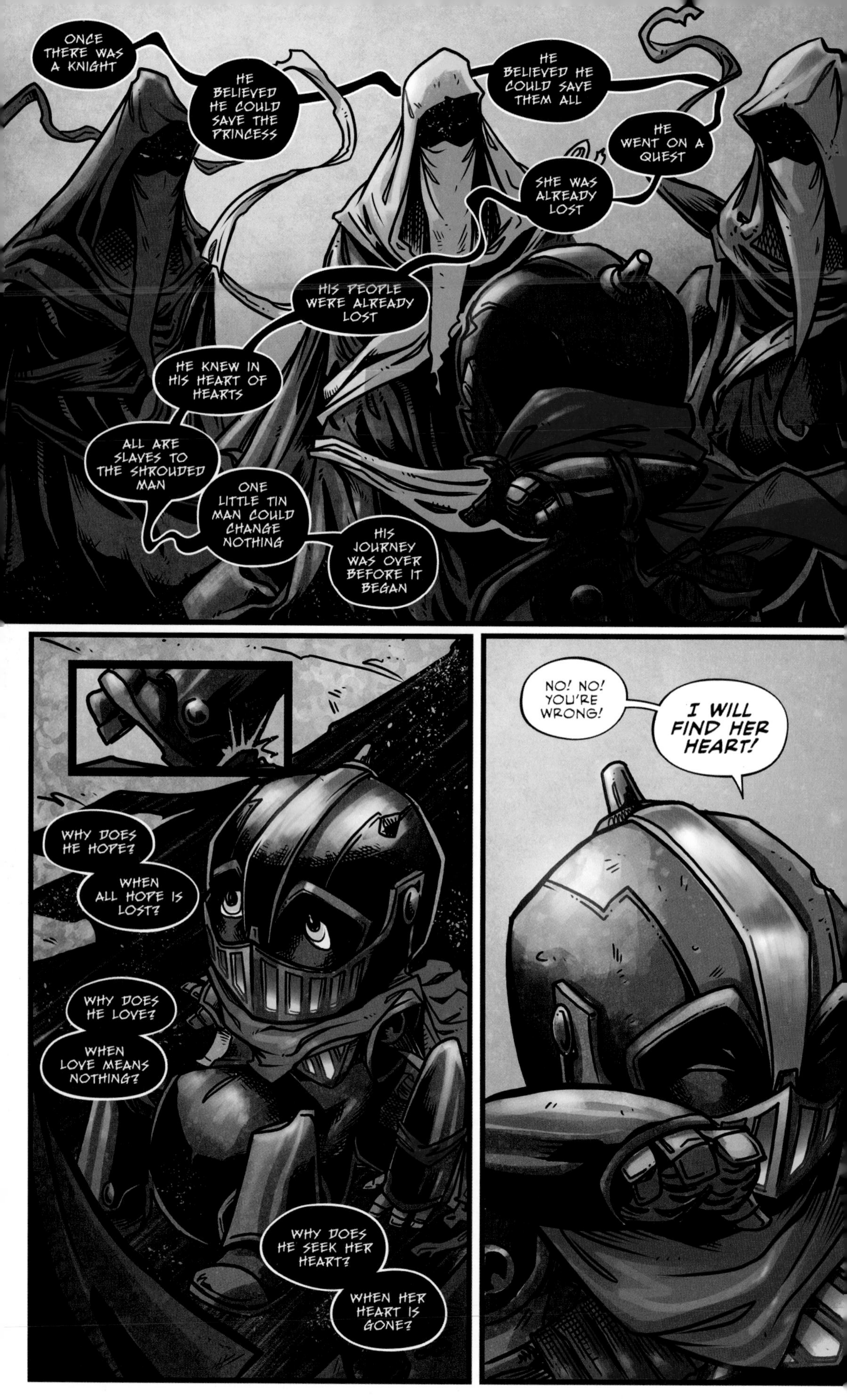
ONCE THERE WAS A KNIGHT
HE BELIEVED HE COULD SAVE THE PRINCESS
HE BELIEVED HE COULD SAVE THEM ALL
HE WENT ON A QUEST
SHE WAS ALREADY LOST
HIS PEOPLE WERE ALREADY LOST
HE KNEW IN HIS HEART OF HEARTS
ALL ARE SLAVES TO THE SHROUDED MAN
ONE LITTLE TIN MAN COULD CHANGE NOTHING
HIS JOURNEY WAS OVER BEFORE IT BEGAN
WHY DOES HE HOPE?
WHEN ALL HOPE IS LOST?
WHY DOES HE LOVE?
WHEN LOVE MEANS NOTHING?
WHY DOES HE SEEK HER HEART?
WHEN HER HEART IS GONE?
NO! NO! YOU'RE WRONG!
I WILL FIND HER HEART!

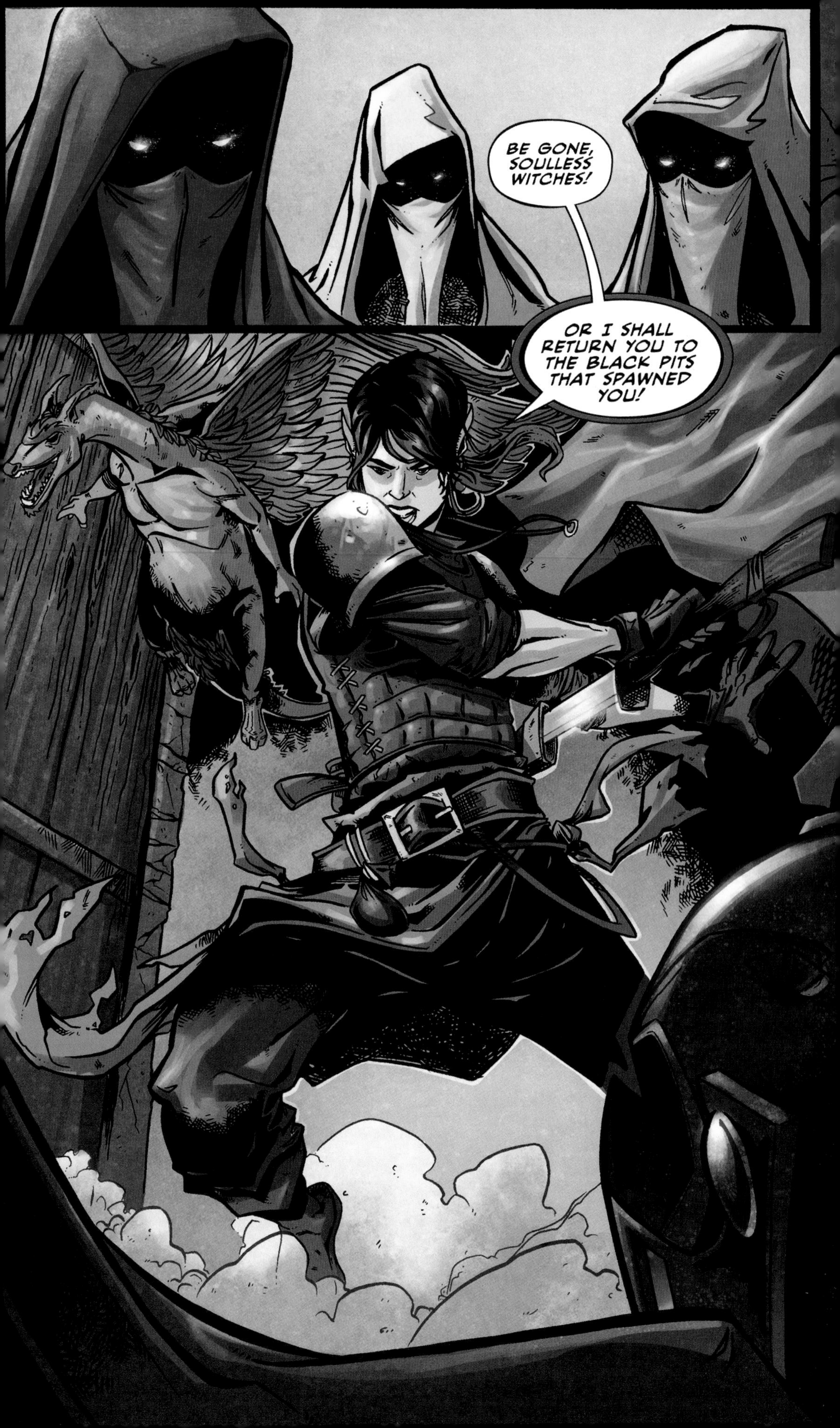
BE GONE, SOULLESS WITCHES!
OR I SHALL RETURN YOU TO THE BLACK PITS THAT SPAWNED YOU!

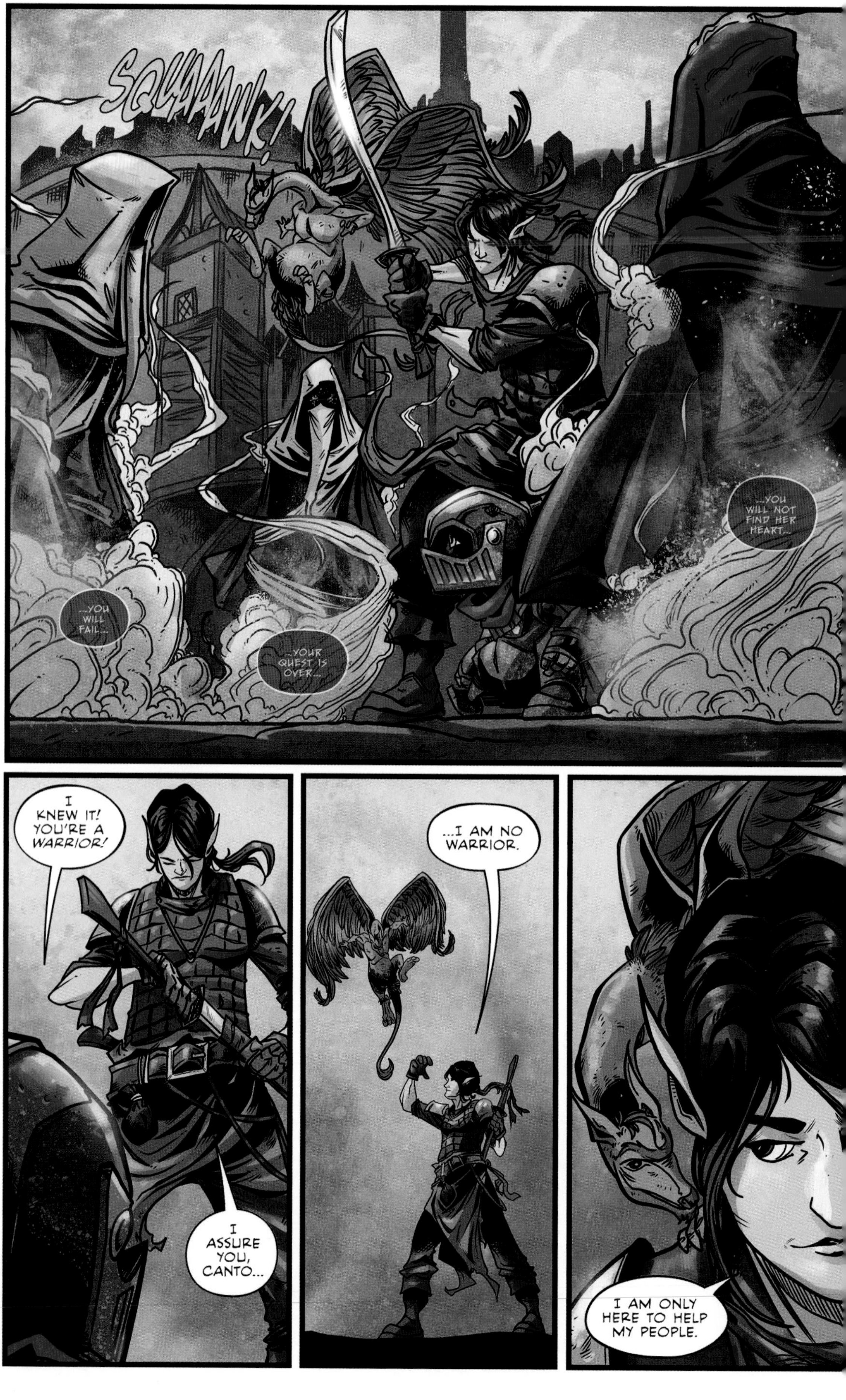
SQUAAAWK!
...YOU WILL FAIL...
...YOUR QUEST IS OVER...
...YOU WILL NOT FIND HER HEART...
I KNEW IT! YOU'RE A WARRIOR!
I ASSURE YOU, CANTO...
...I AM NO WARRIOR.
I AM ONLY HERE TO HELP MY PEOPLE.

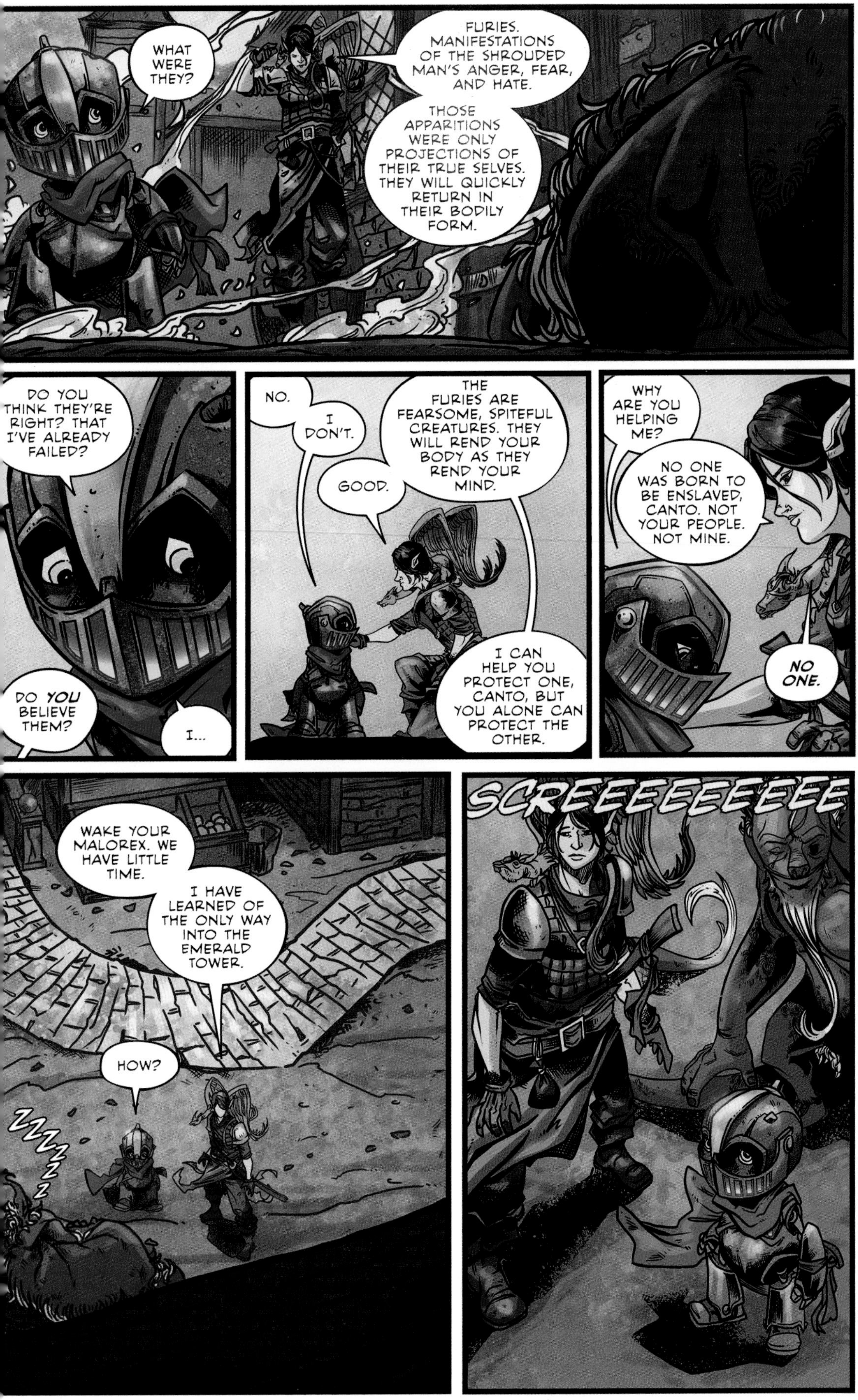
WHAT WERE THEY?
FURIES. MANIFESTATIONS OF THE SHROUDED MAN'S ANGER, FEAR, AND HATE.
THOSE APPARITIONS WERE ONLY PROJECTIONS OF THEIR TRUE SELVES. THEY WILL QUICKLY RETURN IN THEIR BODILY FORM.
DO YOU THINK THEY'RE RIGHT? THAT I'VE ALREADY FAILED?
DO YOU BELIEVE THEM?
I...
NO.
I DON'T.
GOOD.
THE FURIES ARE FEARSOME, SPITEFUL CREATURES. THEY WILL REND YOUR BODY AS THEY REND YOUR MIND.
I CAN HELP YOU PROTECT ONE, CANTO, BUT YOU ALONE CAN PROTECT THE OTHER.
WHY ARE YOU HELPING ME?
NO ONE WAS BORN TO BE ENSLAVED, CANTO. NOT YOUR PEOPLE. NOT MINE.
NO ONE.
WAKE YOUR MALOREX. WE HAVE LITTLE TIME.
I HAVE LEARNED OF THE ONLY WAY INTO THE EMERALD TOWER.
HOW?
ZZZZZZ
SCREEEEEEEEEEE

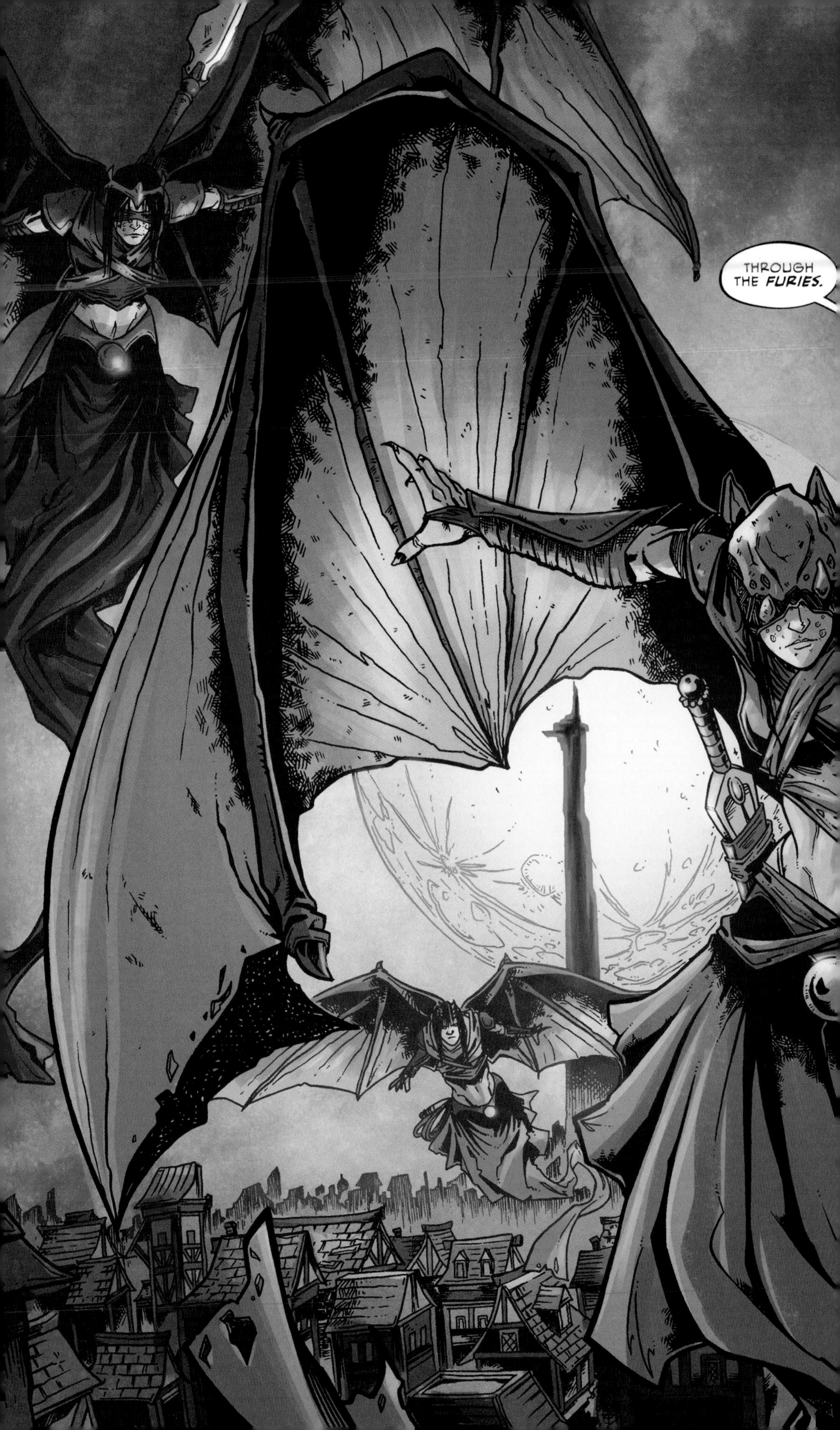
THROUGH THE *FURIES.*

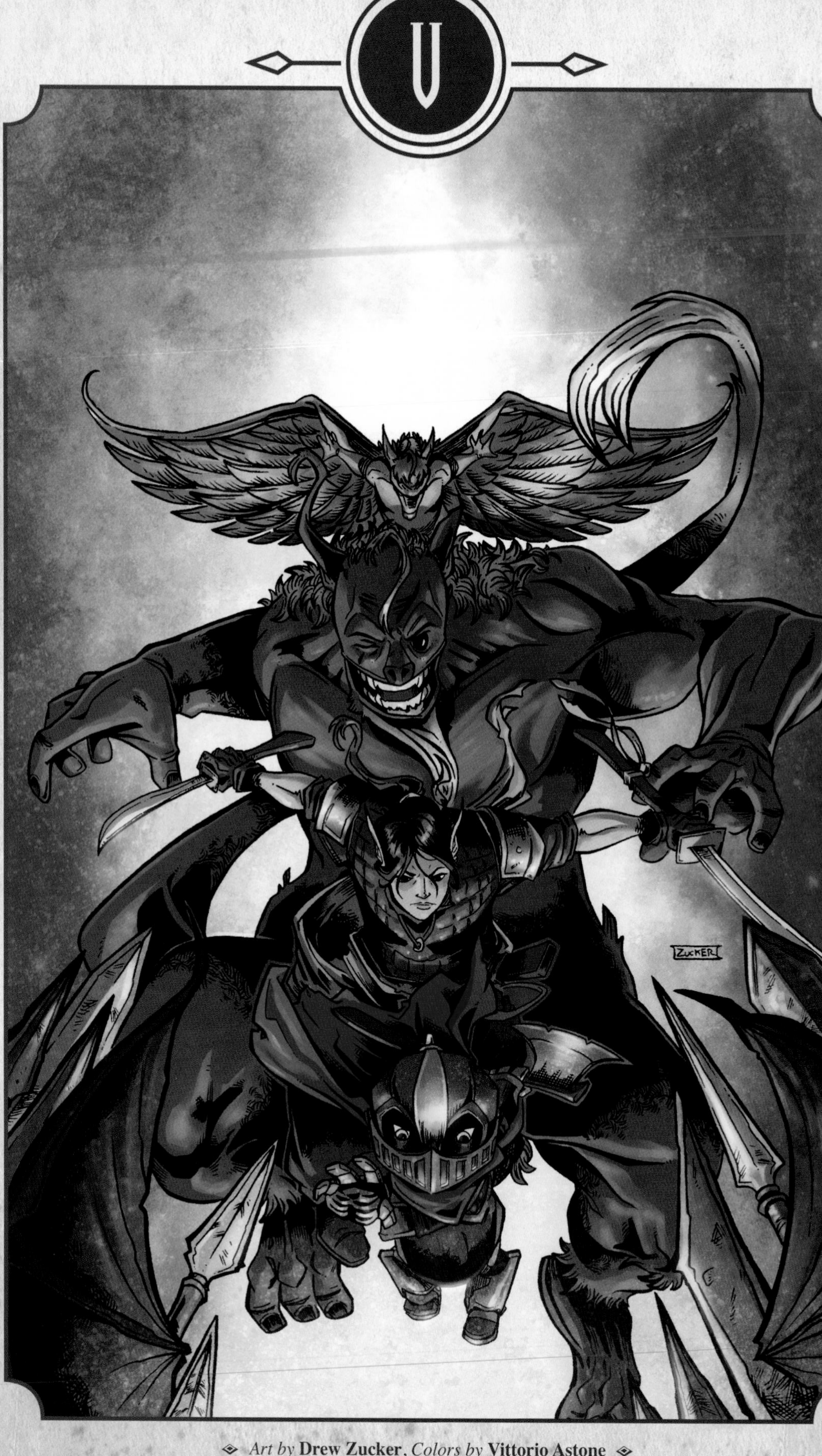
V
ZUCKER

Art by **Drew Zucker**, *Colors by* **Vittorio Astone**

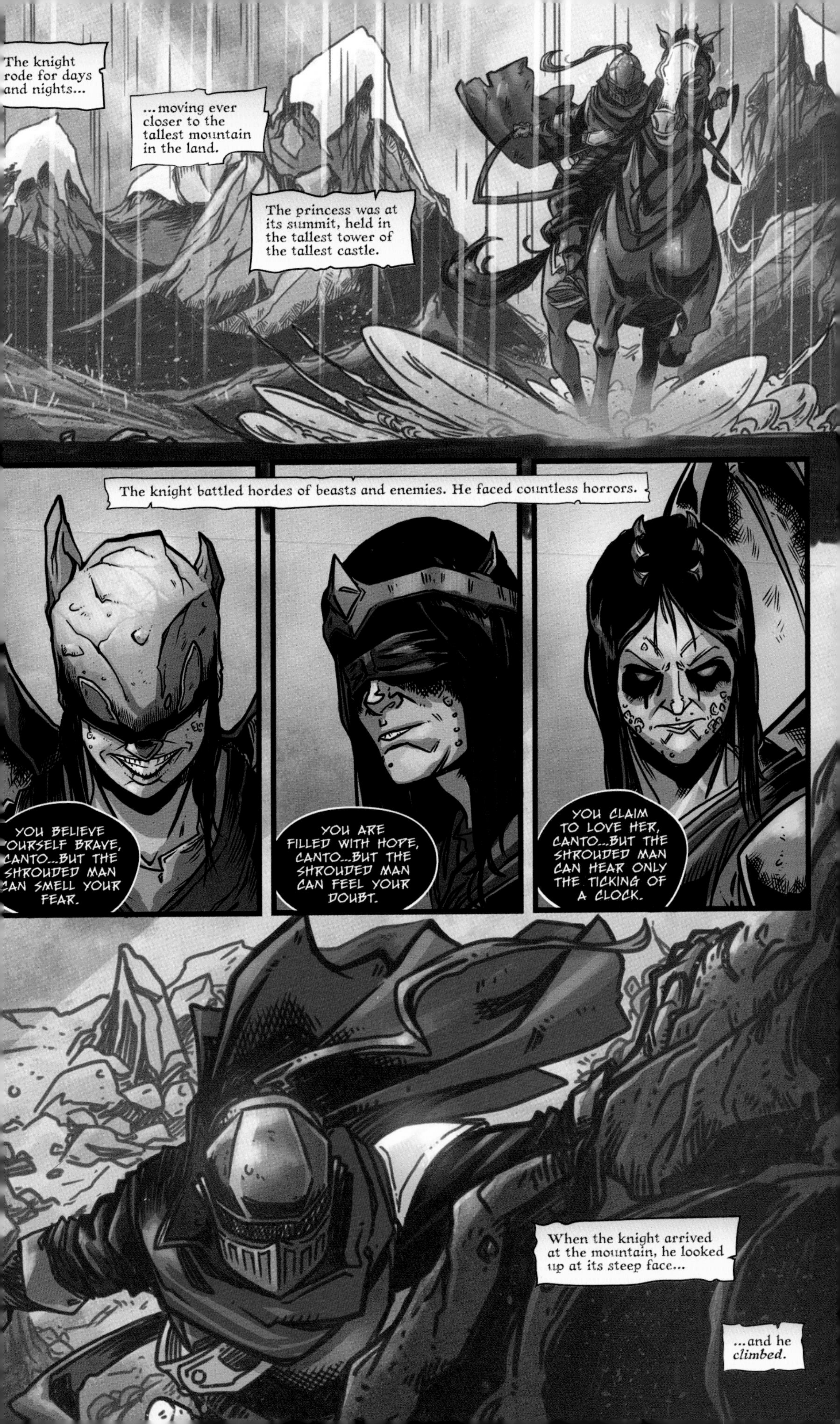

The knight rode for days and nights...
...moving ever closer to the tallest mountain in the land.
The princess was at its summit, held in the tallest tower of the tallest castle.
The knight battled hordes of beasts and enemies. He faced countless horrors.
YOU BELIEVE YOURSELF BRAVE, CANTO...BUT THE SHROUDED MAN CAN SMELL YOUR FEAR.
YOU ARE FILLED WITH HOPE, CANTO...BUT THE SHROUDED MAN CAN FEEL YOUR DOUBT.
YOU CLAIM TO LOVE HER, CANTO...BUT THE SHROUDED MAN CAN HEAR ONLY THE TICKING OF A CLOCK.
When the knight arrived at the mountain, he looked up at its steep face...
...and he *climbed*.

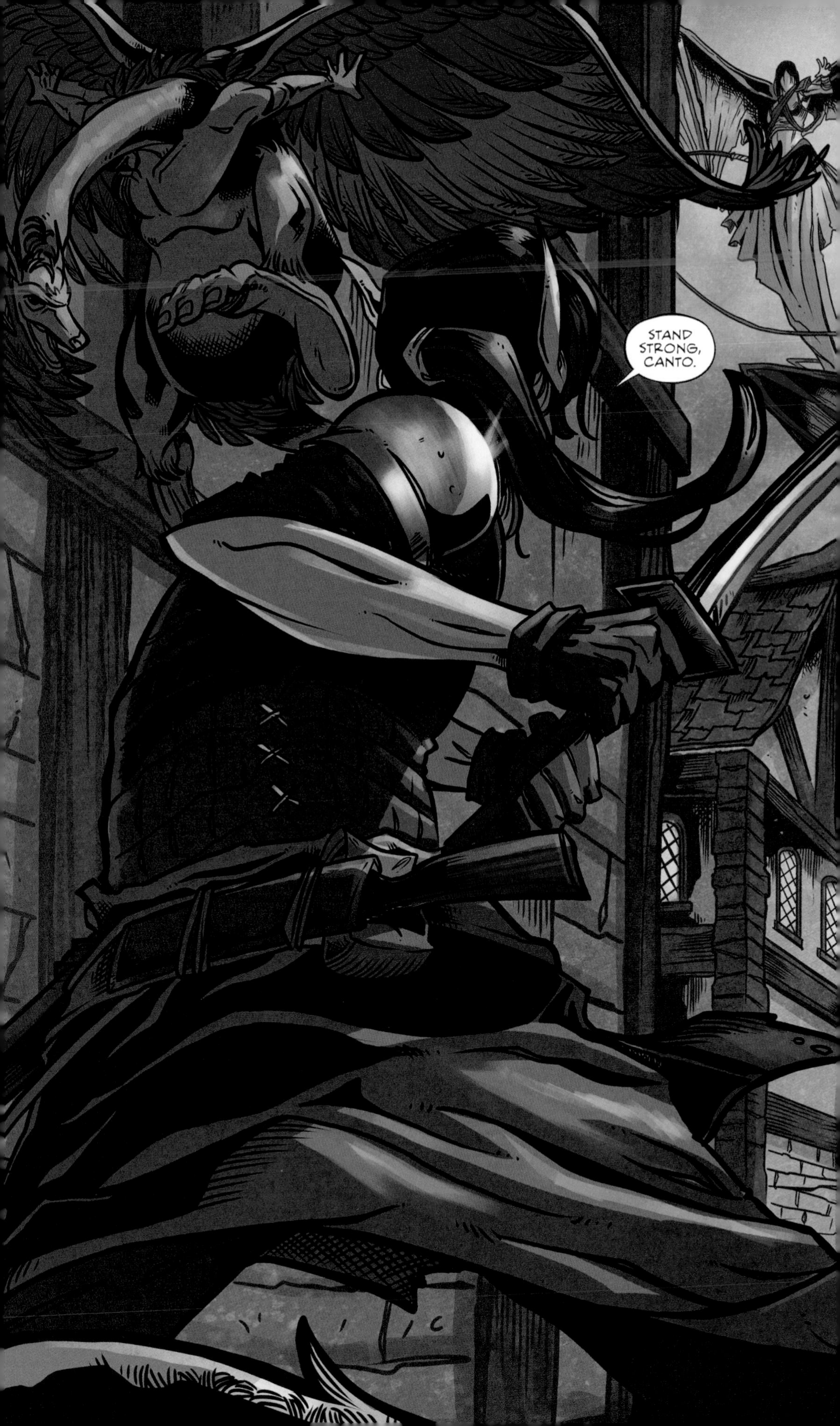
STAND STRONG, CANTO.

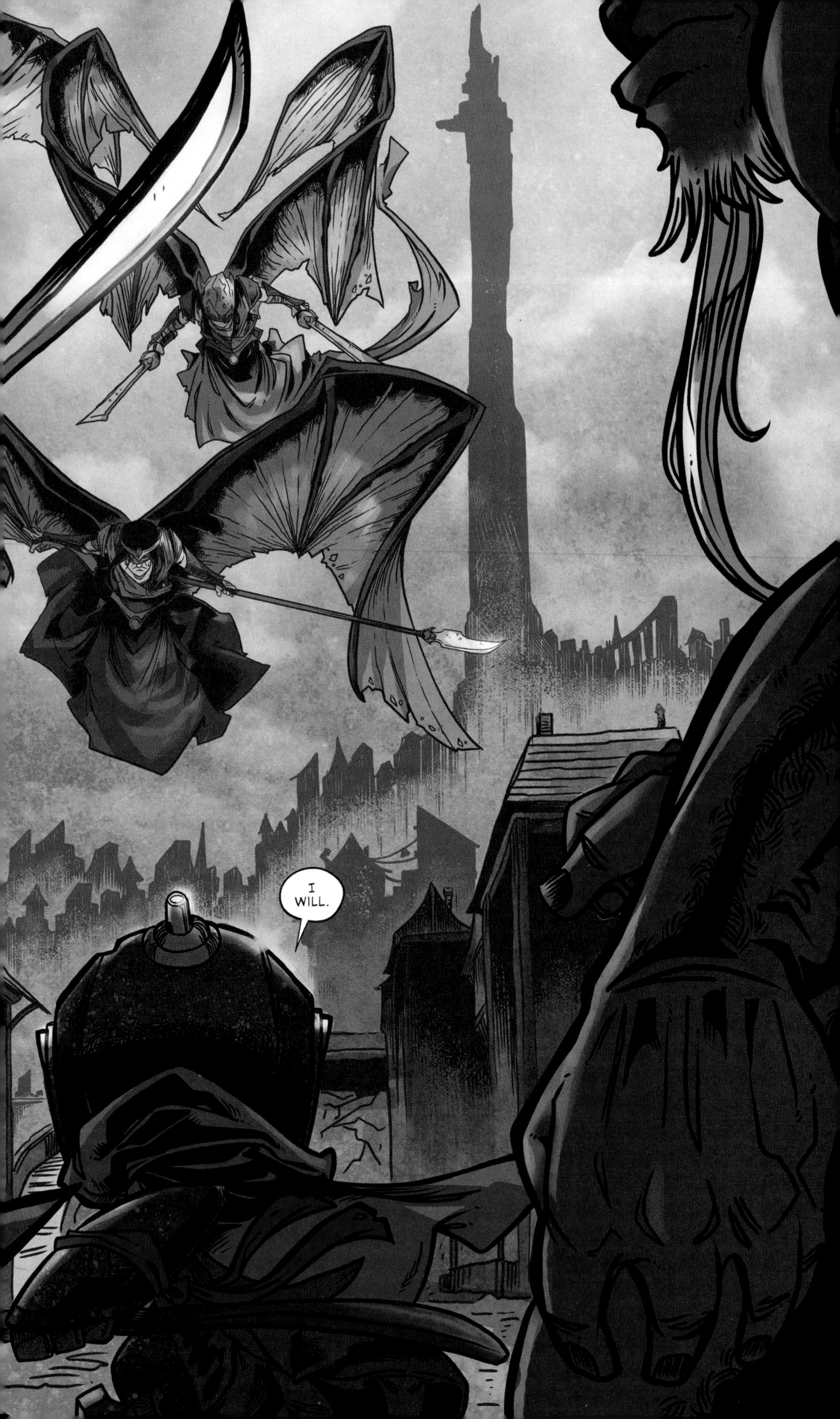
I WILL.

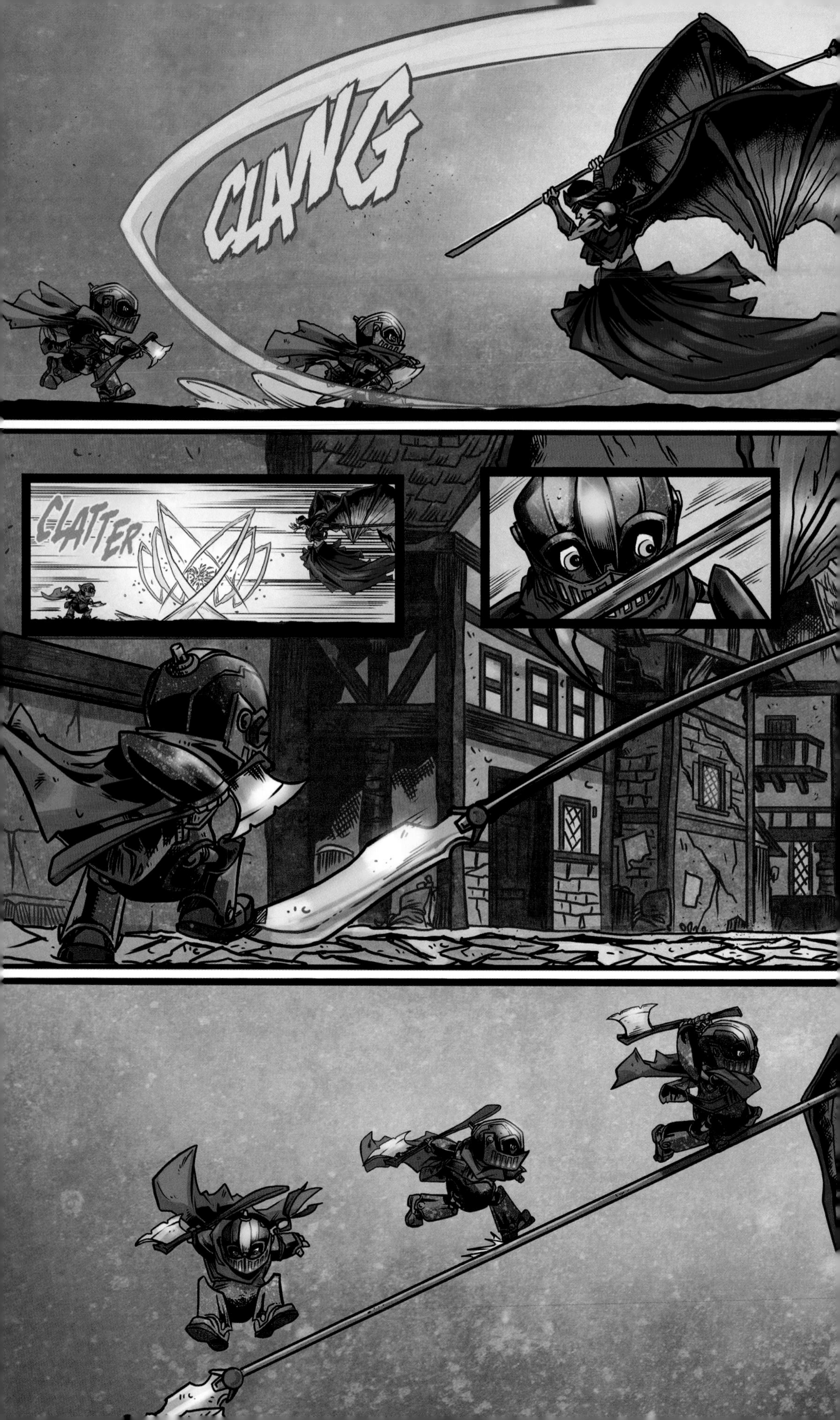
CLANG
CLATTER

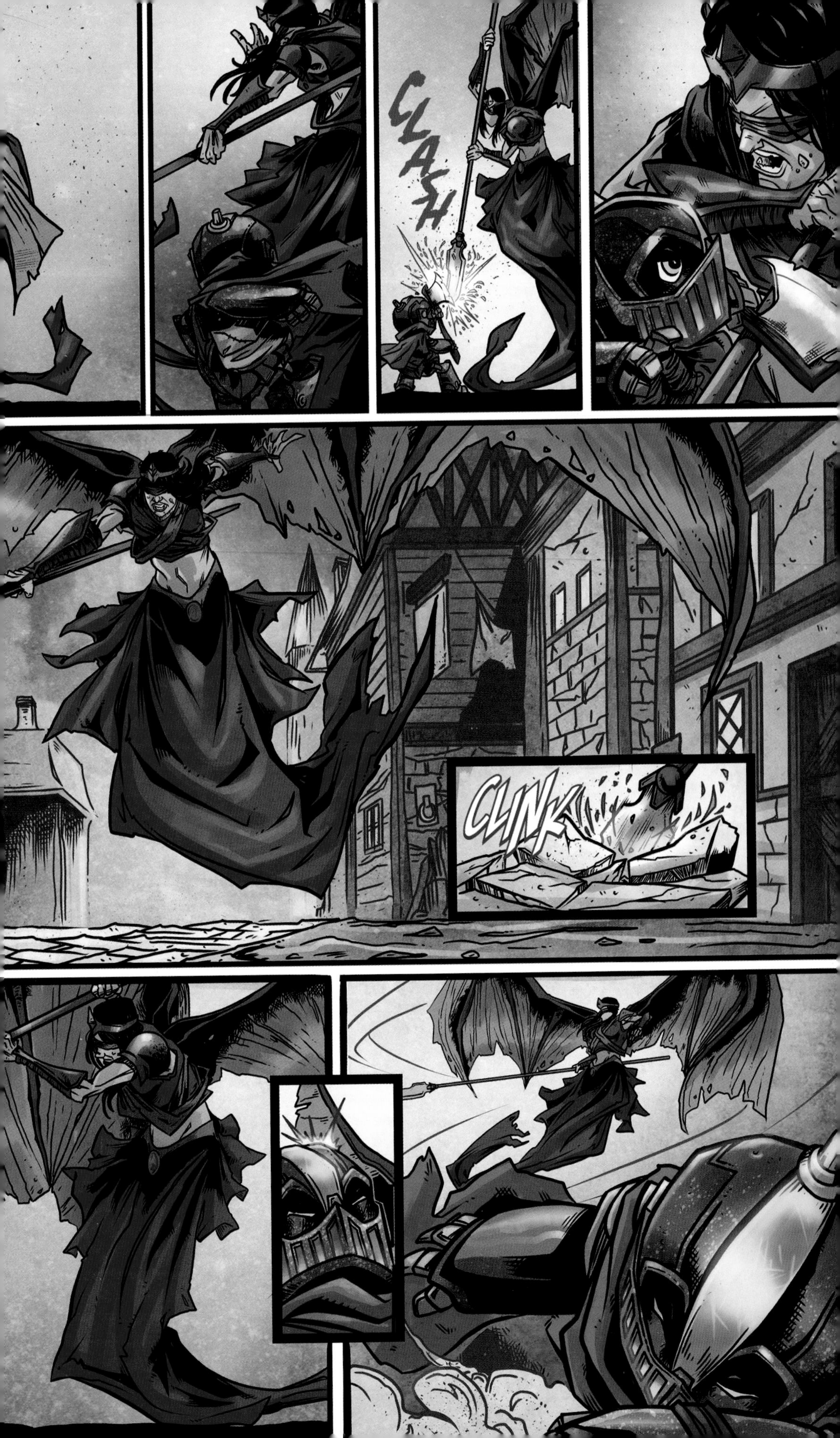
CLASH
CLINK

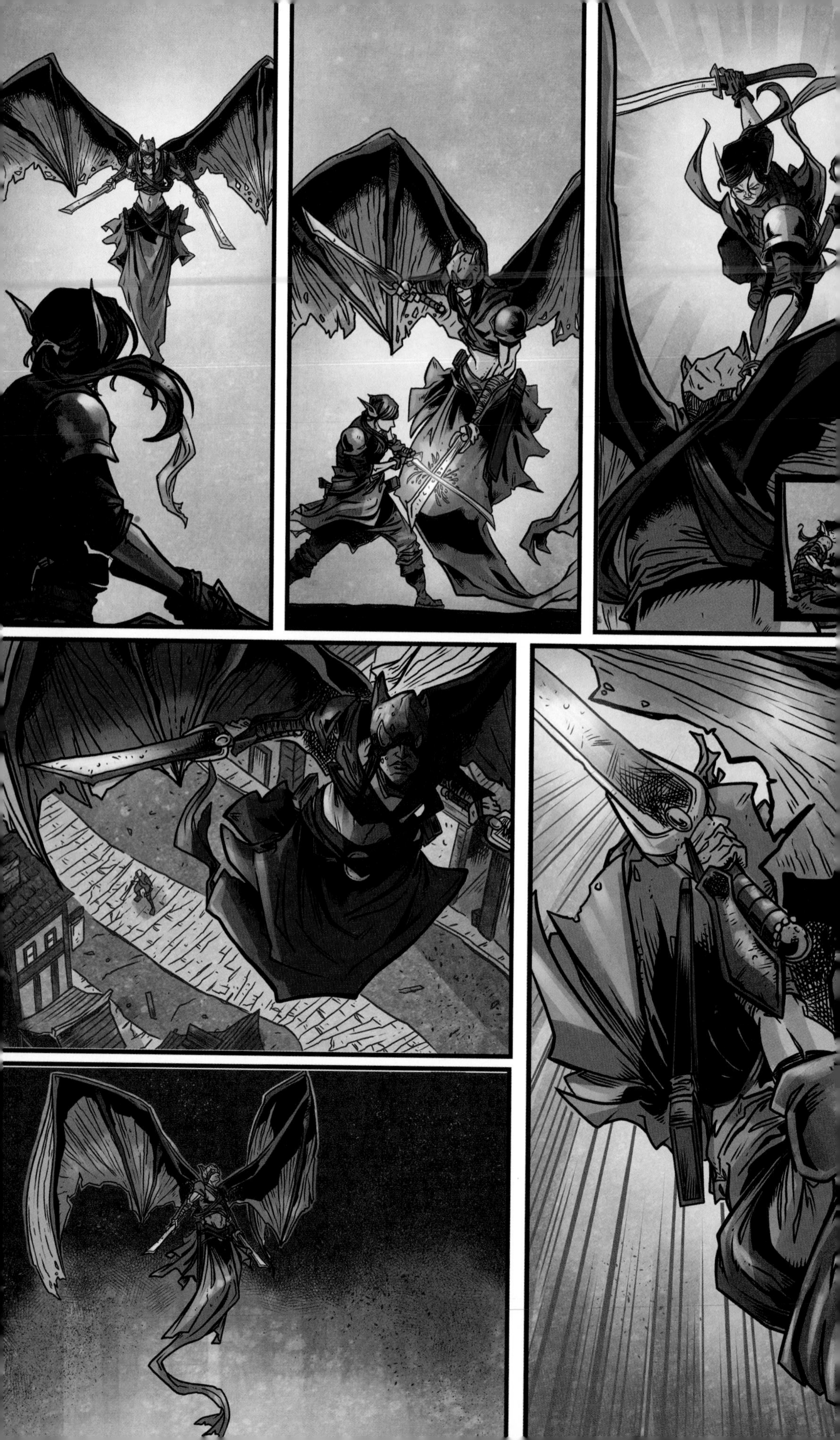

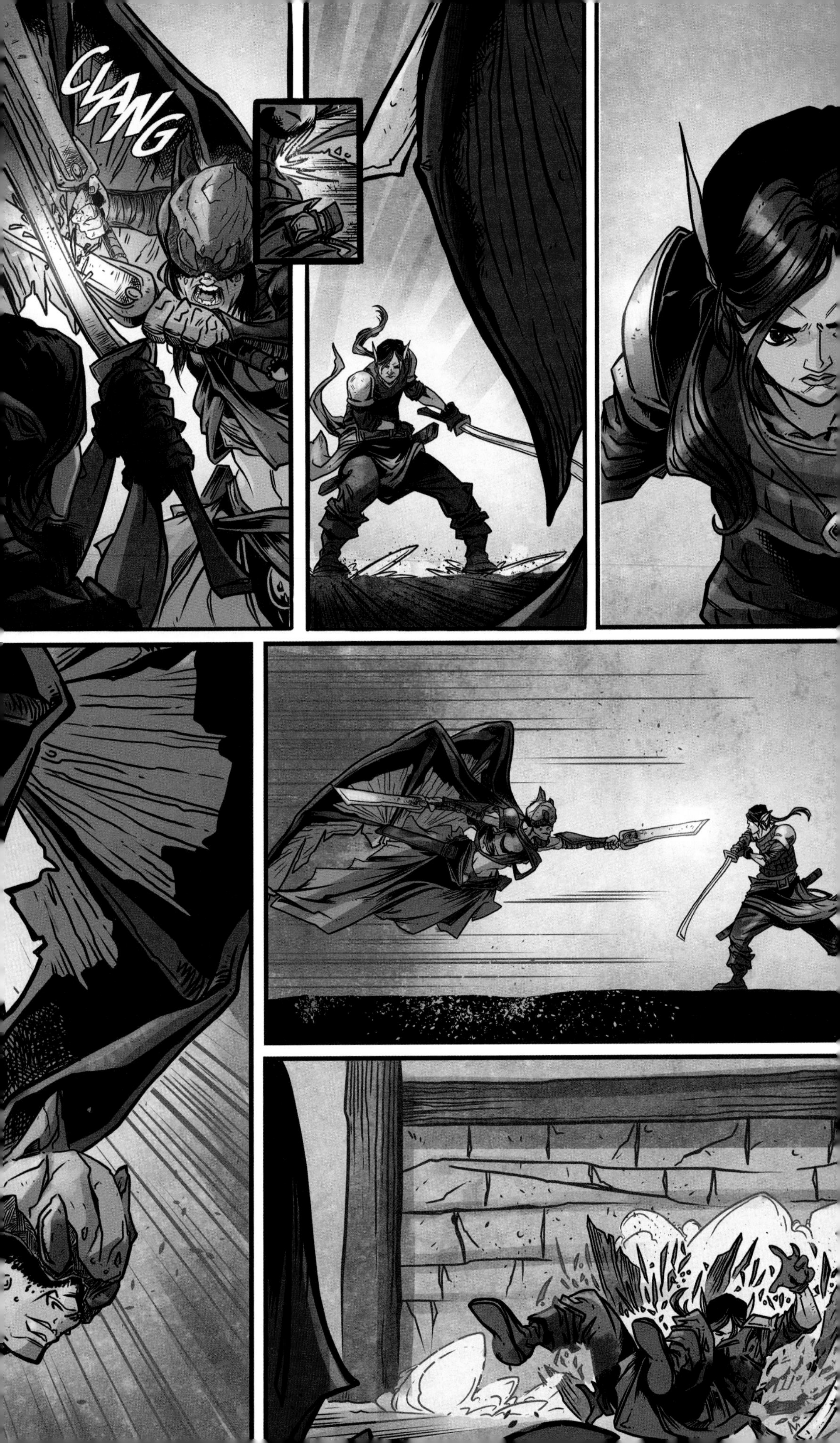
CLANG

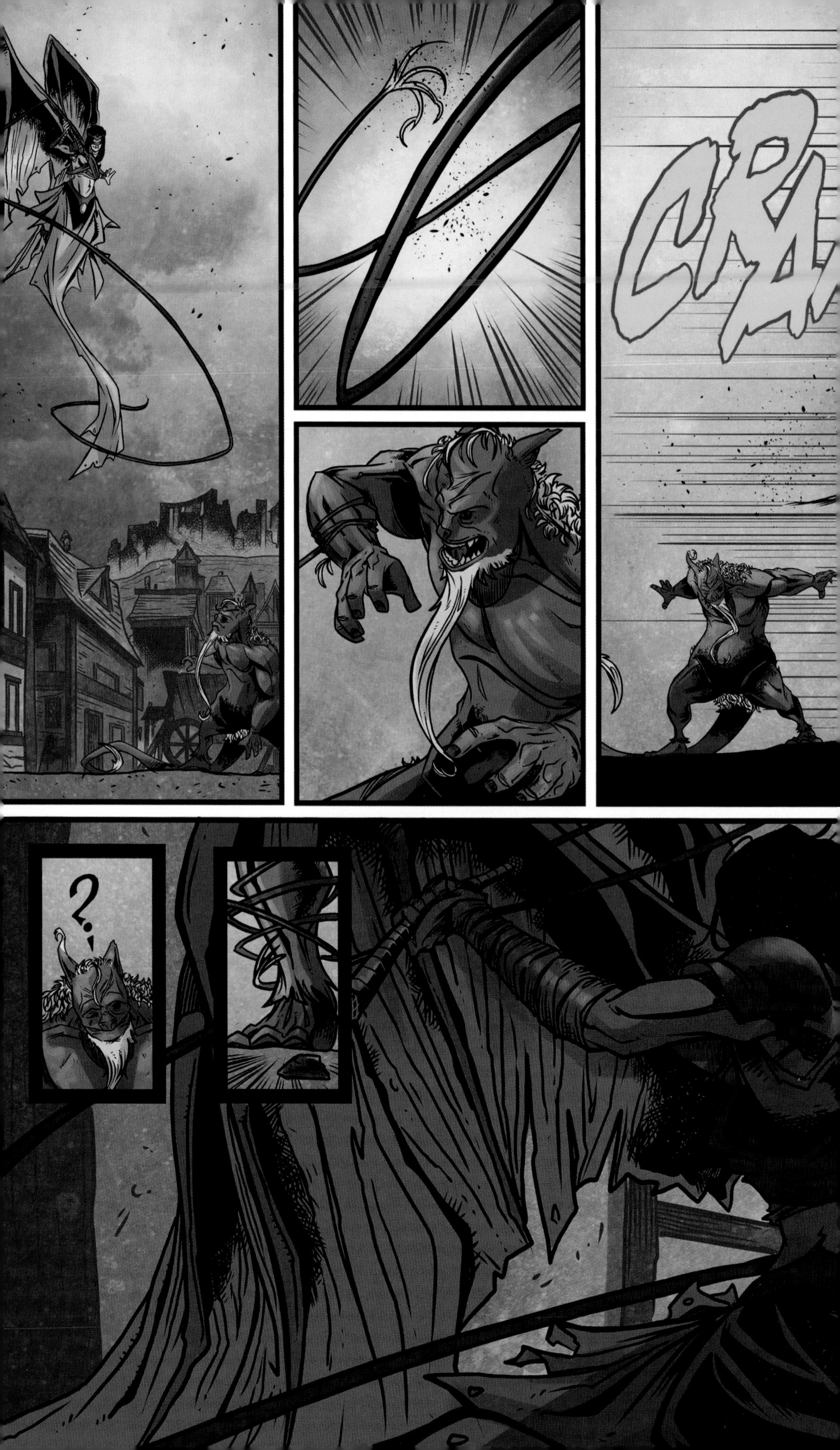
CRA
?

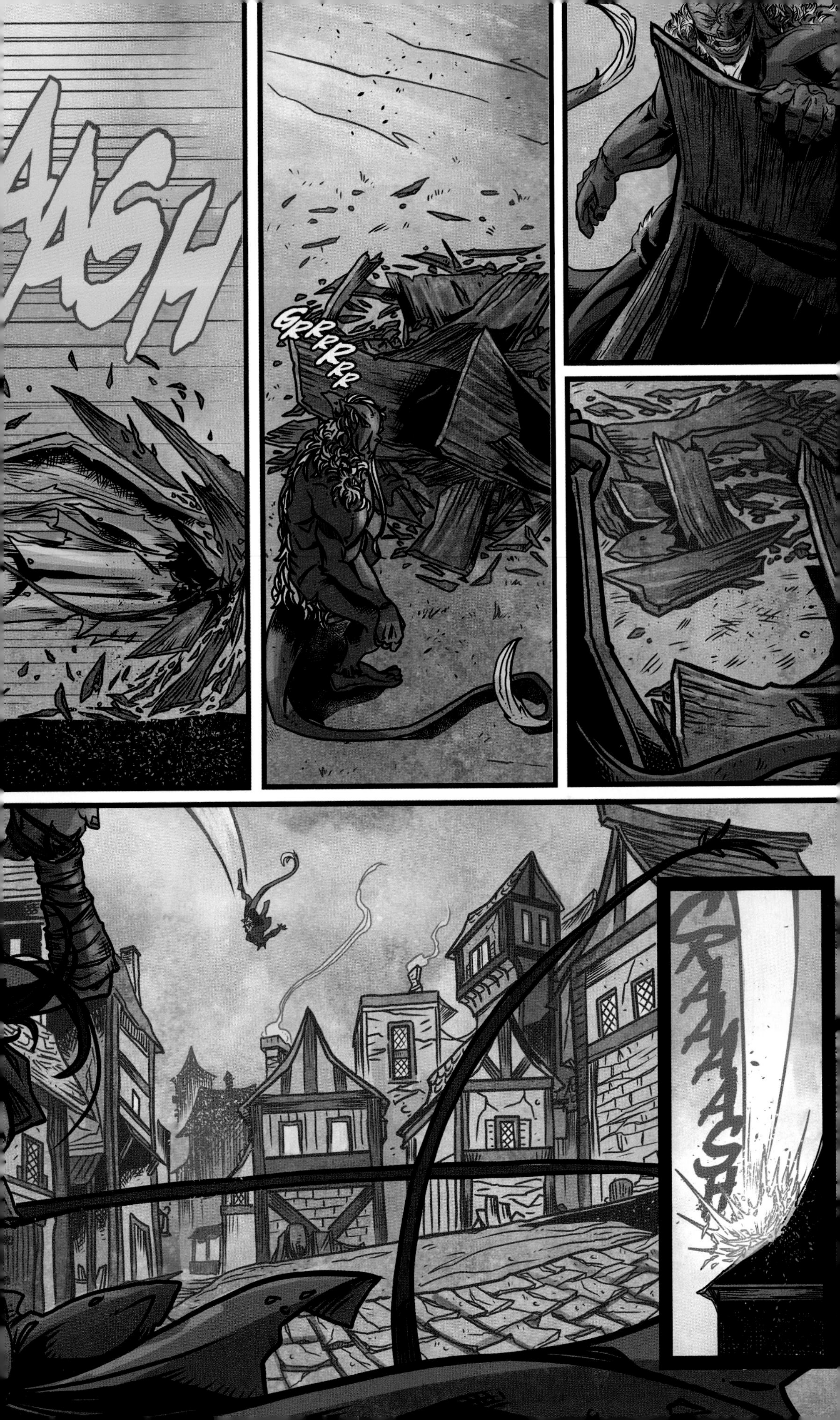
ASH
GRRRRR
CRAAASH

I HEAR THE CLOCK IN YOUR CHEST, LITTLE WARRIOR. IT HAS ALREADY BEGUN TO SLOW.

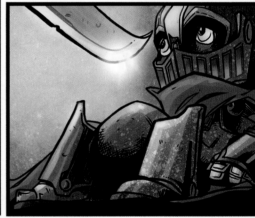

WHY DO YOU CONTINUE TO STRUGGLE?

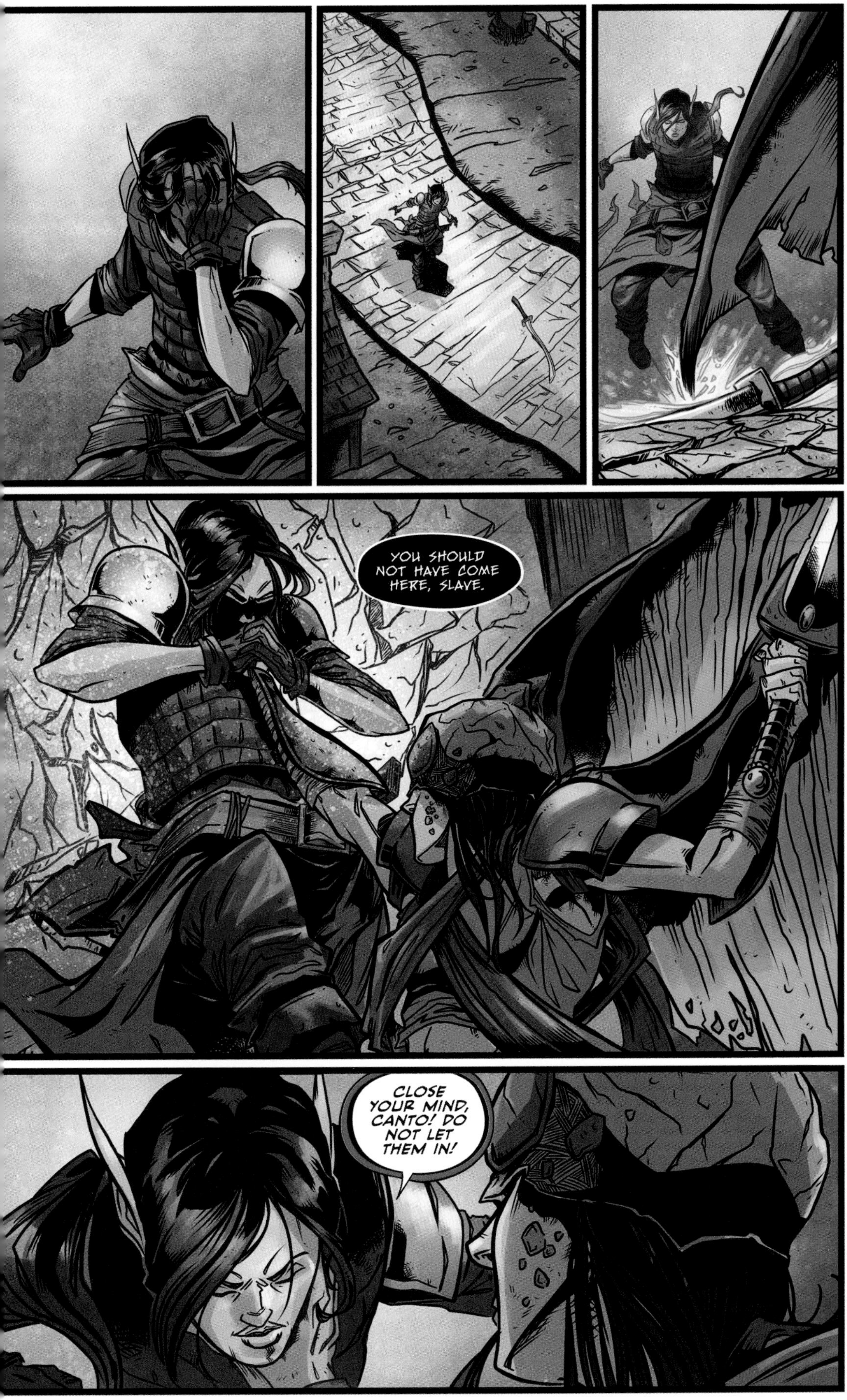
YOU SHOULD NOT HAVE COME HERE, SLAVE.
CLOSE YOUR MIND, CANTO! DO NOT LET THEM IN!

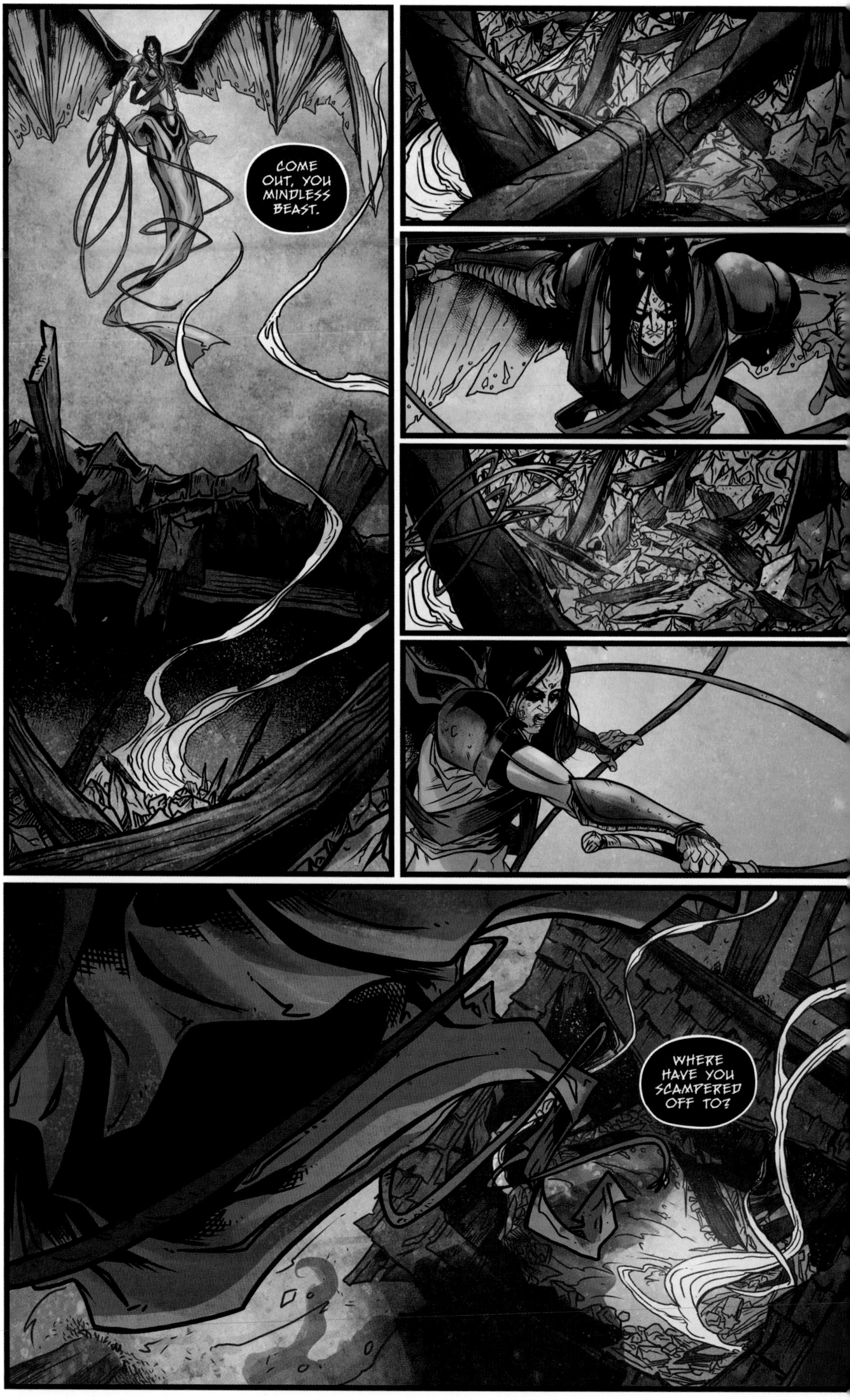
COME OUT, YOU MINDLESS BEAST.
WHERE HAVE YOU SCAMPERED OFF TO?

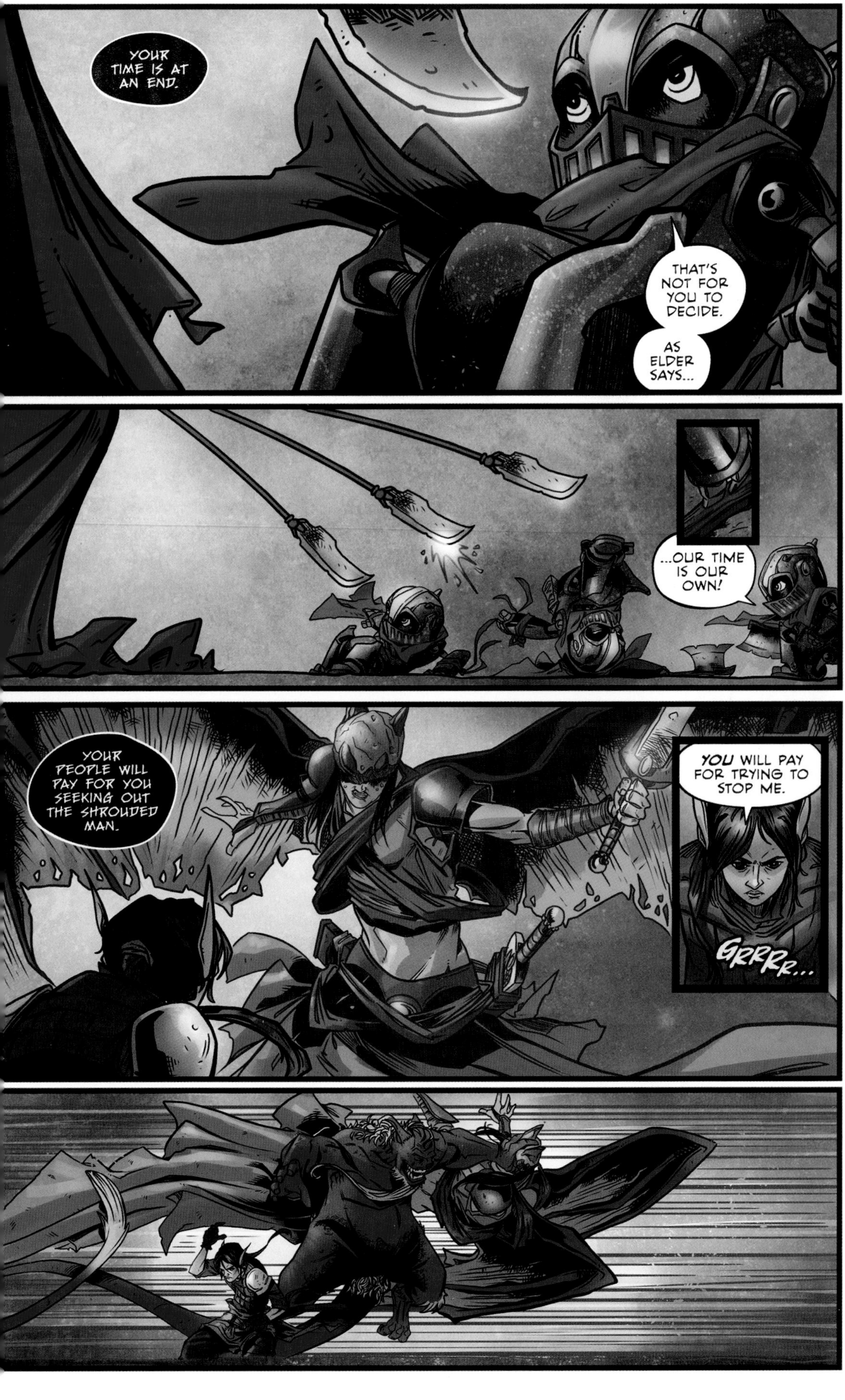
YOUR TIME IS AT AN END.
THAT'S NOT FOR YOU TO DECIDE.
AS ELDER SAYS...
...OUR TIME IS OUR OWN!
YOUR PEOPLE WILL PAY FOR YOU SEEKING OUT THE SHROUDED MAN.
YOU WILL PAY FOR TRYING TO STOP ME.
GRRRR...

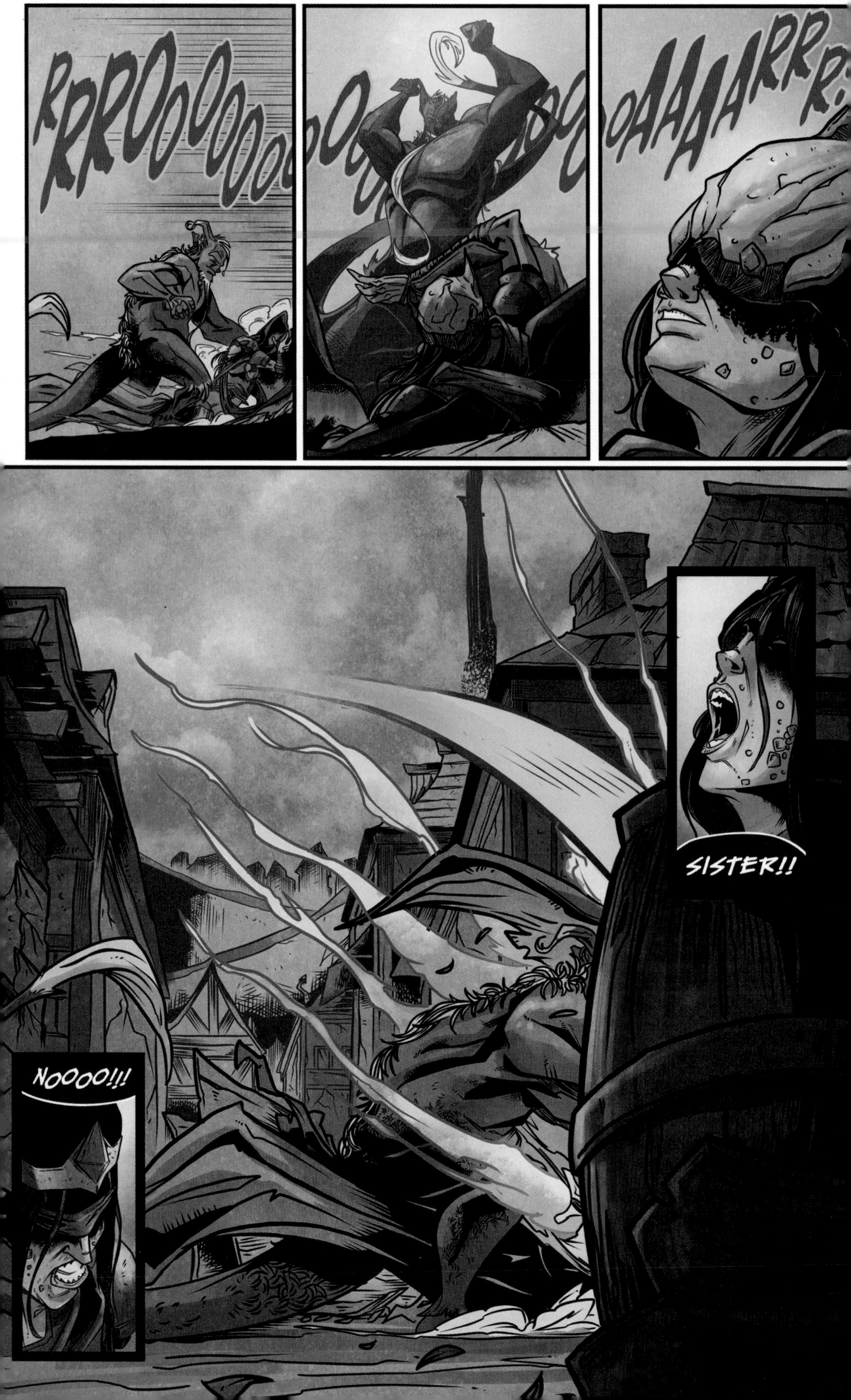
RRROOOOOOOOOOOOOOOOOOOOOOOOAAAAARRRR!
SISTER!!
NOOOO!!!

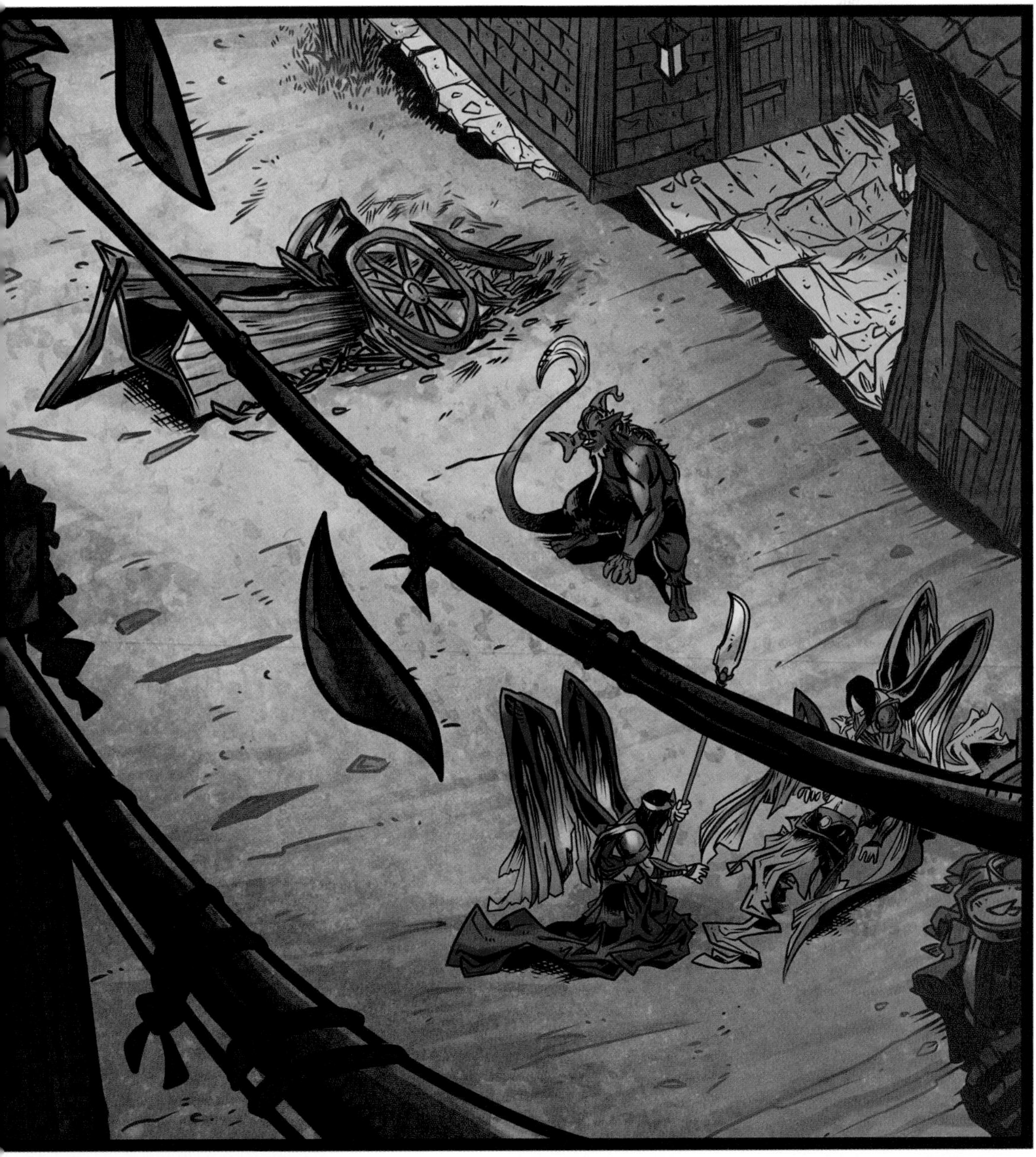

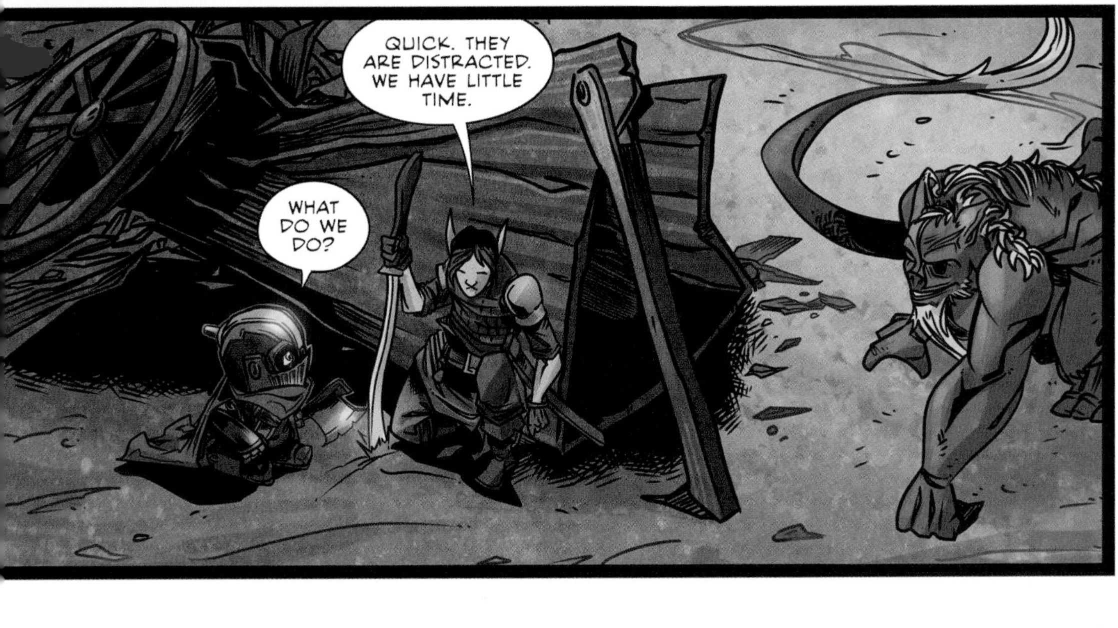
QUICK. THEY ARE DISTRACTED. WE HAVE LITTLE TIME.
WHAT DO WE DO?

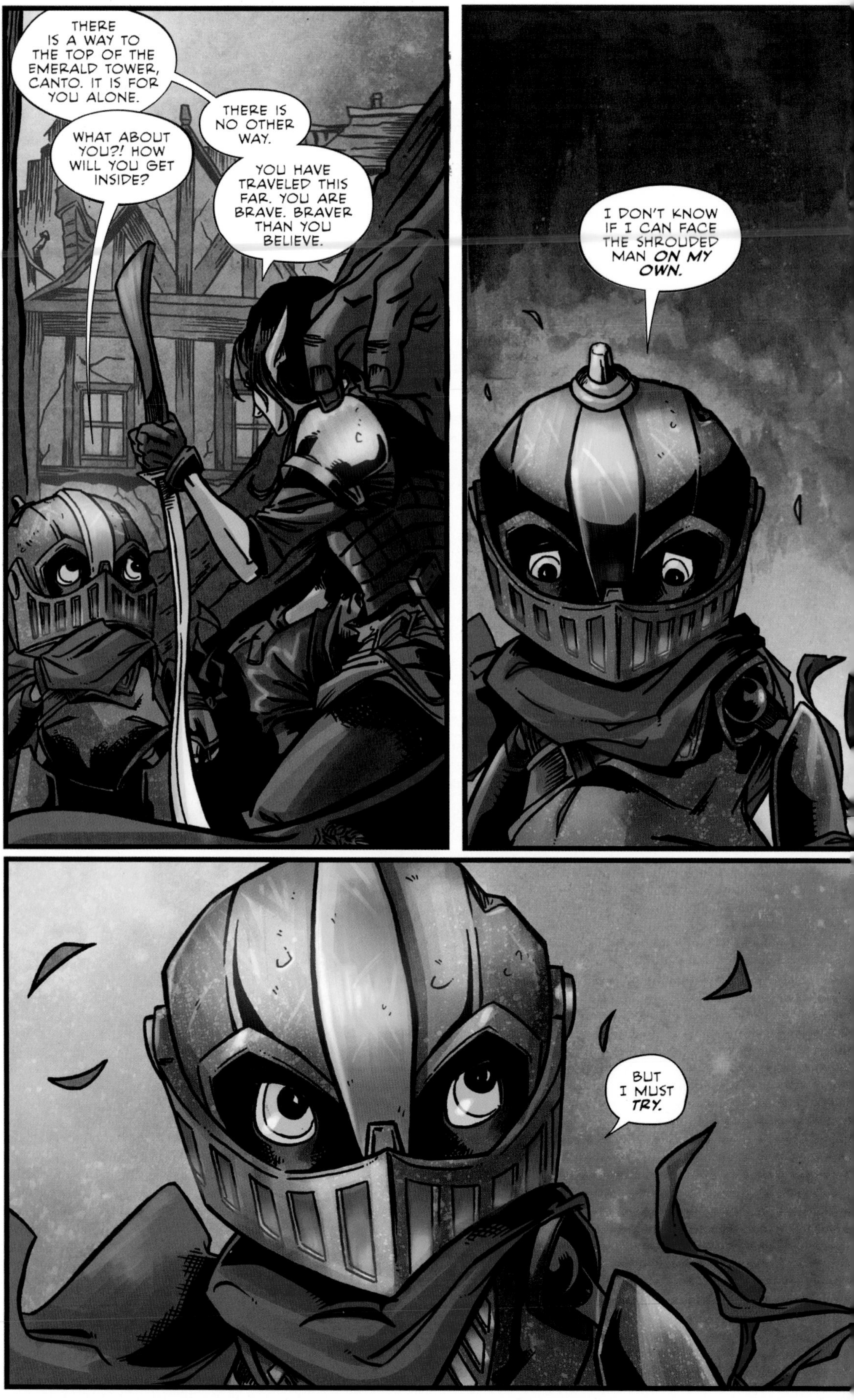
THERE IS A WAY TO THE TOP OF THE EMERALD TOWER, CANTO. IT IS FOR YOU ALONE.
WHAT ABOUT YOU?! HOW WILL YOU GET INSIDE?
THERE IS NO OTHER WAY.
YOU HAVE TRAVELED THIS FAR. YOU ARE BRAVE. BRAVER THAN YOU BELIEVE.
I DON'T KNOW IF I CAN FACE THE SHROUDED MAN *ON MY OWN.*
BUT I MUST *TRY.*

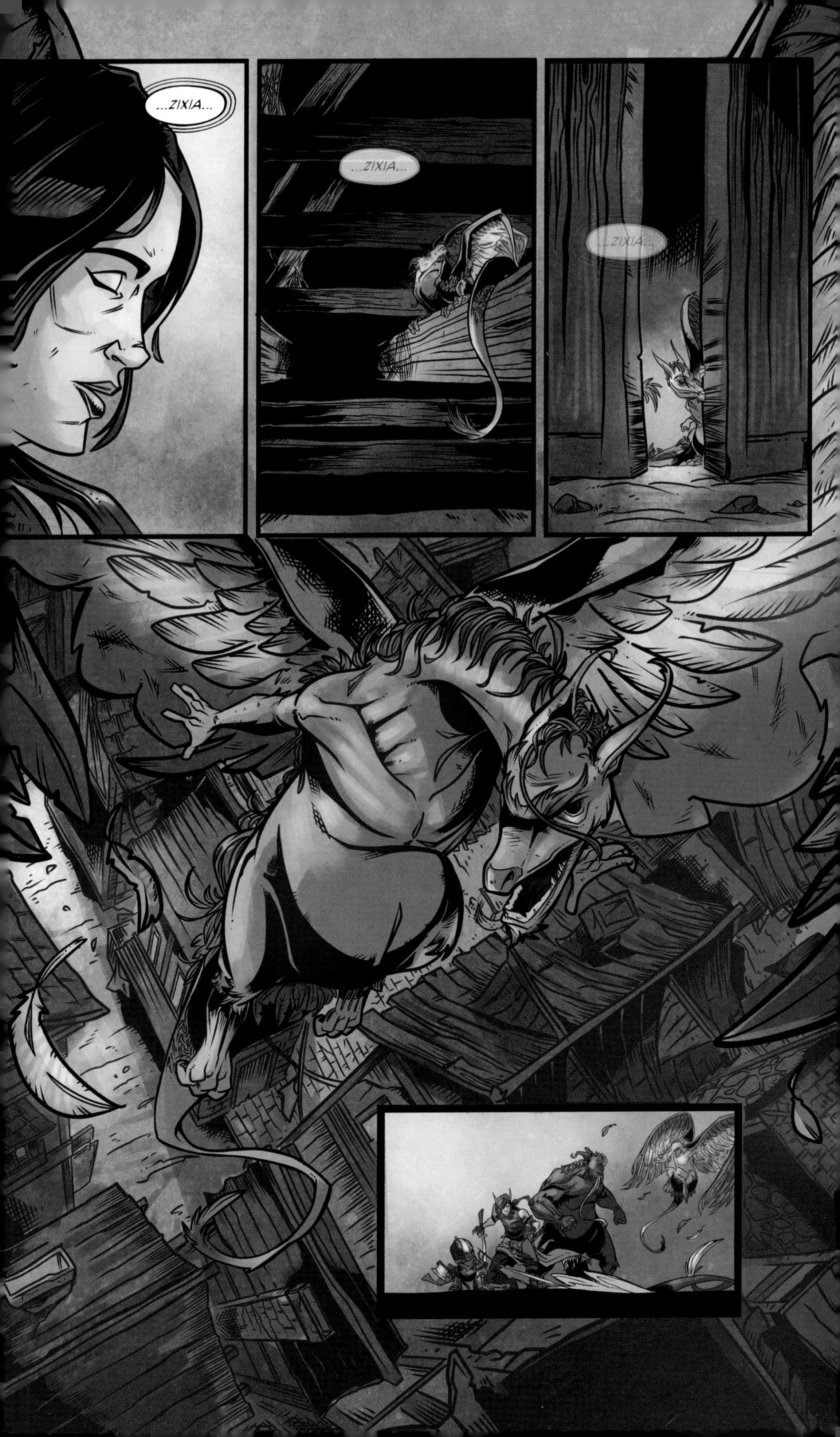
...ZIXIA...
...ZIXIA...
...ZIXIA...

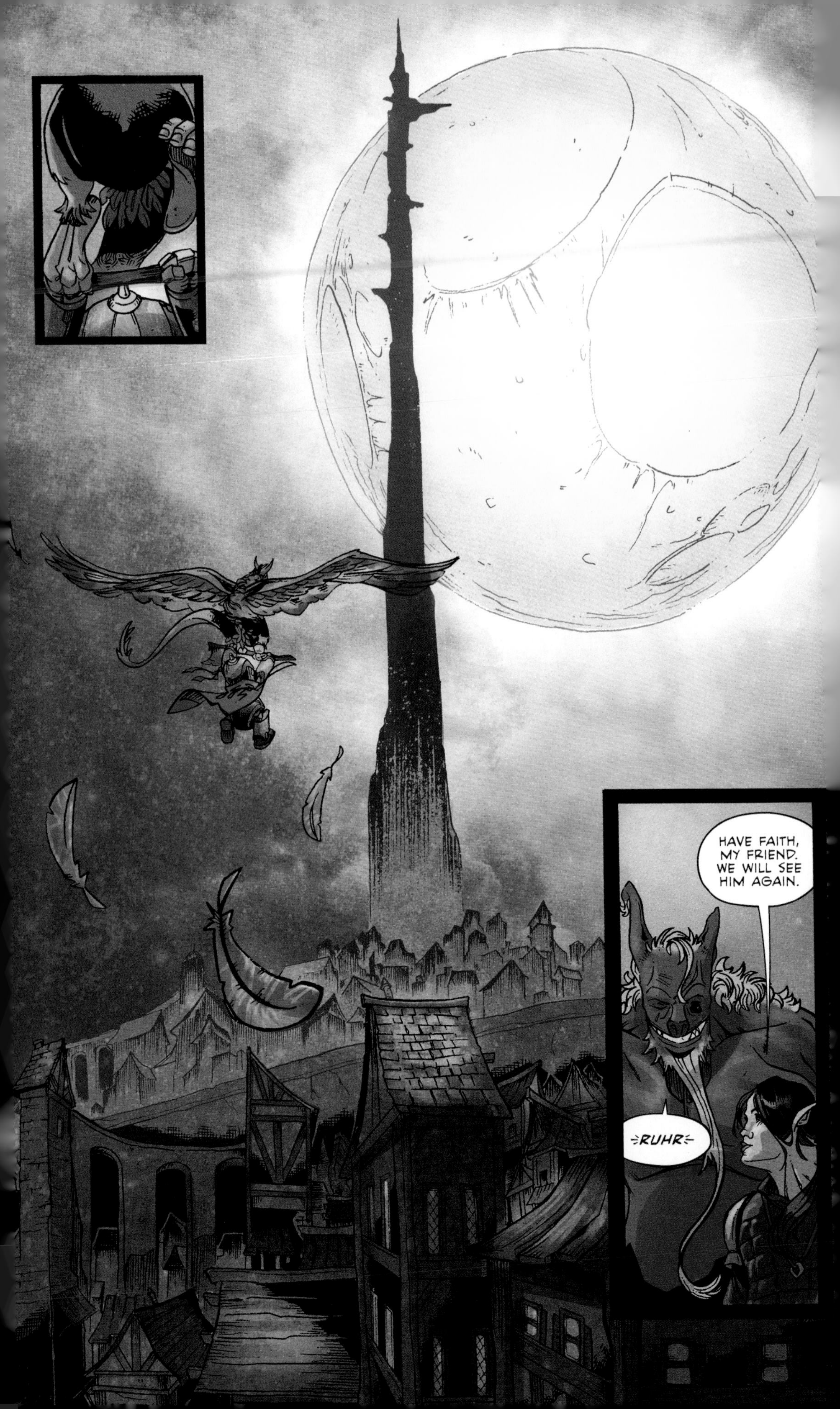
HAVE FAITH, MY FRIEND. WE WILL SEE HIM AGAIN.
RUHR

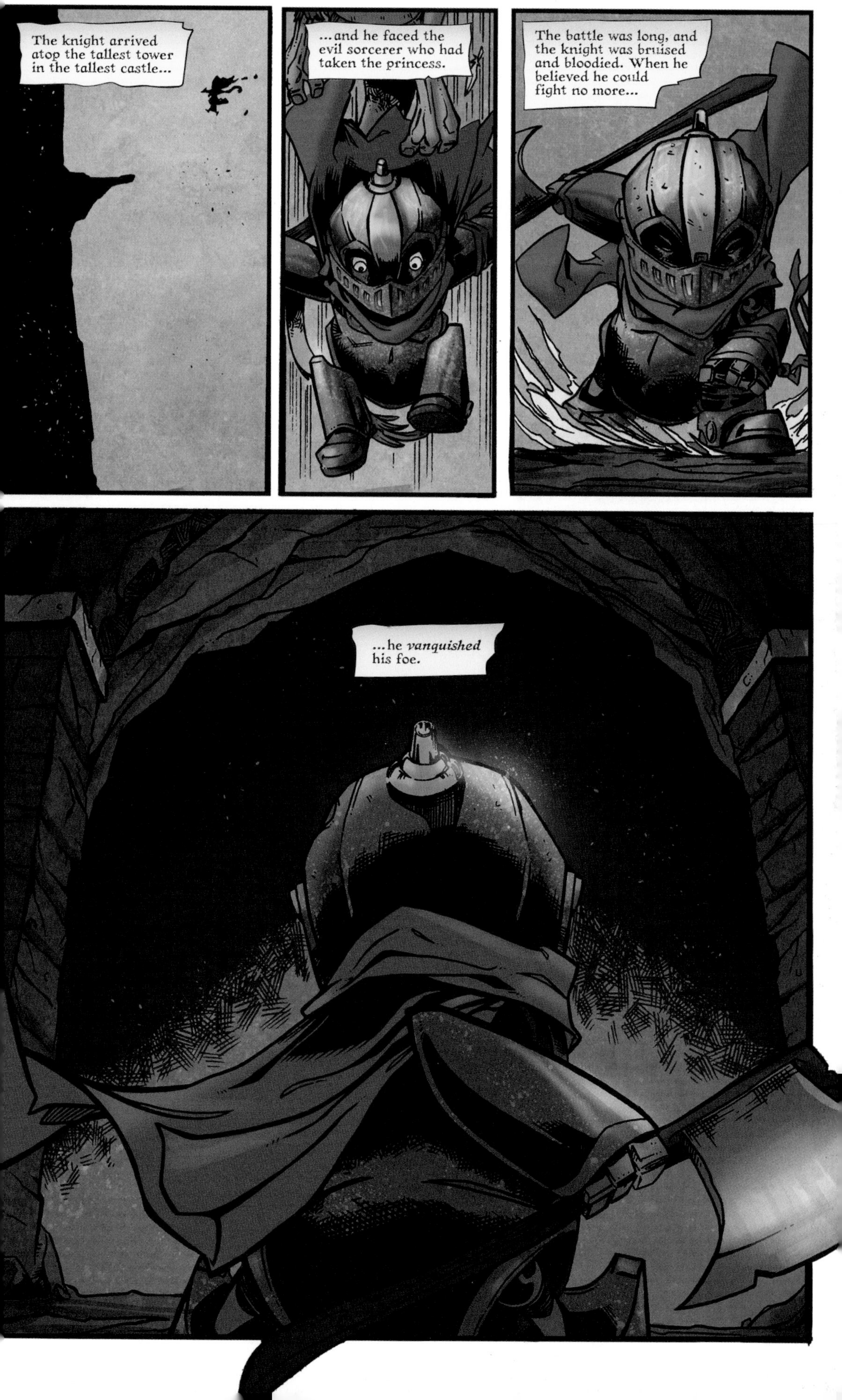
The knight arrived atop the tallest tower in the tallest castle...
...and he faced the evil sorcerer who had taken the princess.
The battle was long, and the knight was bruised and bloodied. When he believed he could fight no more...
...he *vanquished* his foe.

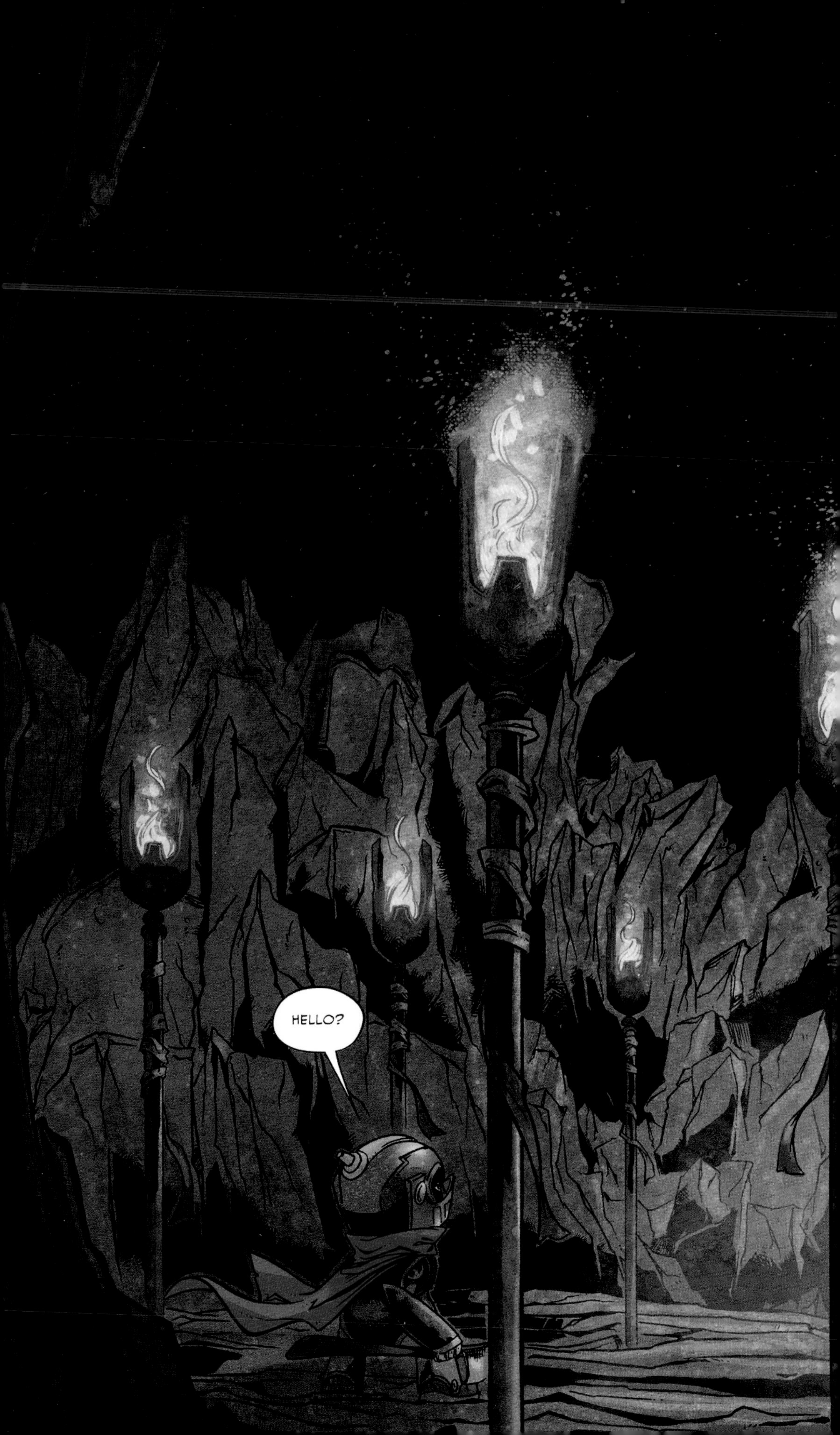
HELLO?

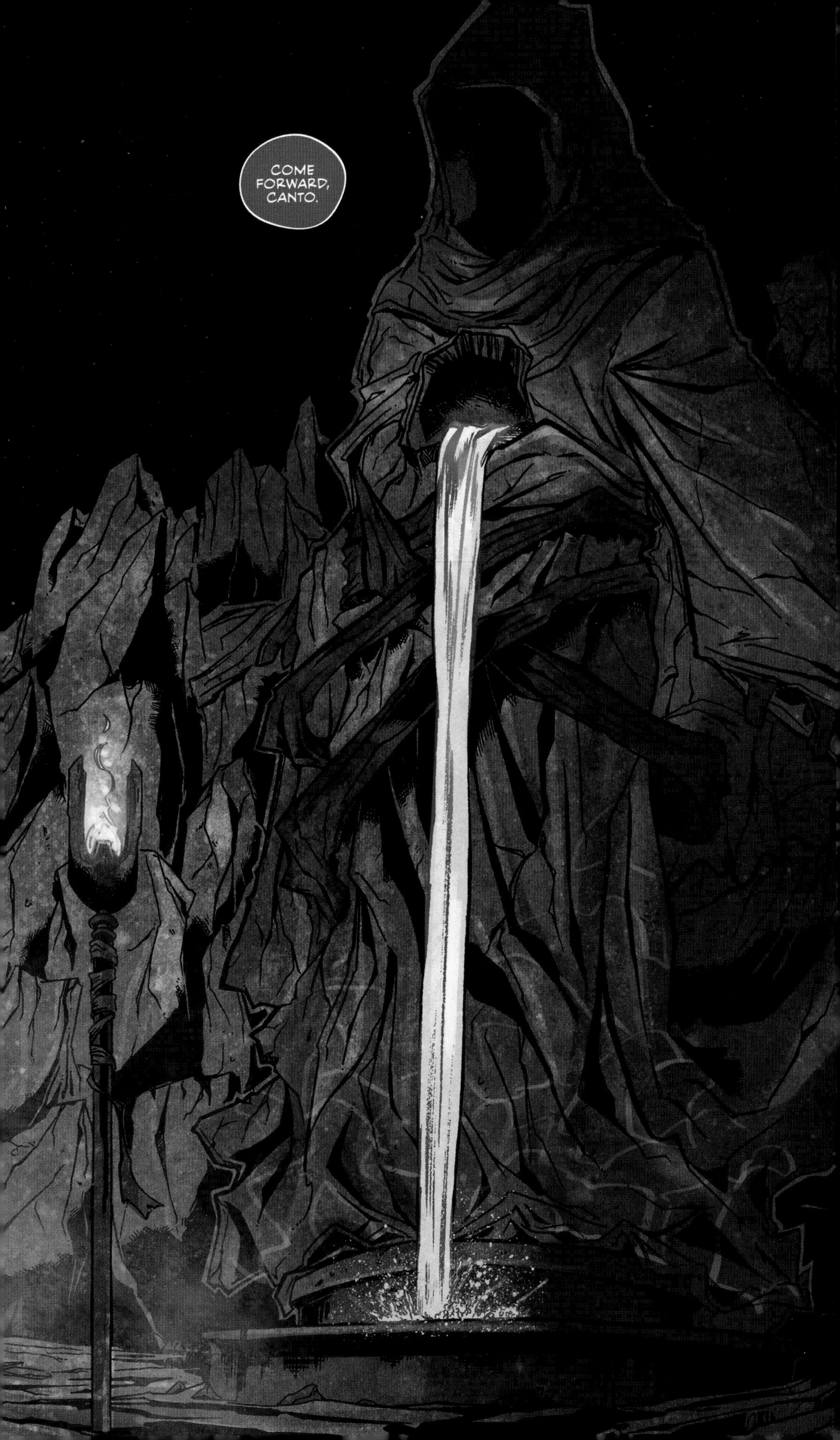
COME FORWARD, CANTO.

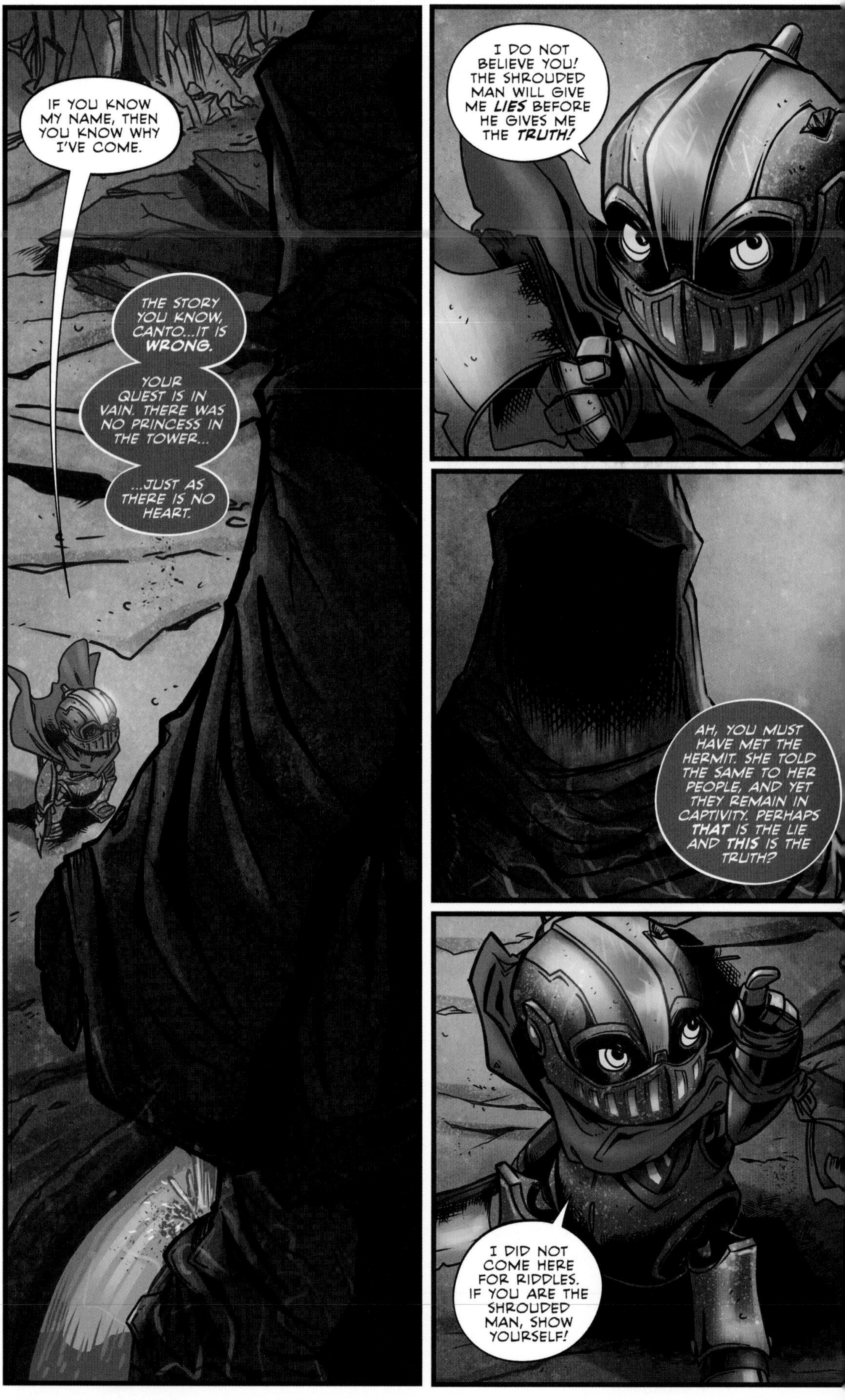
IF YOU KNOW MY NAME, THEN YOU KNOW WHY I'VE COME.
THE STORY YOU KNOW, CANTO...IT IS **WRONG.**
YOUR QUEST IS IN VAIN. THERE WAS NO PRINCESS IN THE TOWER...
...JUST AS THERE IS NO HEART.
I DO NOT BELIEVE YOU! THE SHROUDED MAN WILL GIVE ME ***LIES*** BEFORE HE GIVES ME THE ***TRUTH!***
AH, YOU MUST HAVE MET THE HERMIT. SHE TOLD THE SAME TO HER PEOPLE, AND YET THEY REMAIN IN CAPTIVITY. PERHAPS **THAT** IS THE LIE AND **THIS** IS THE TRUTH?
I DID NOT COME HERE FOR RIDDLES. IF YOU ARE THE SHROUDED MAN, SHOW YOURSELF!

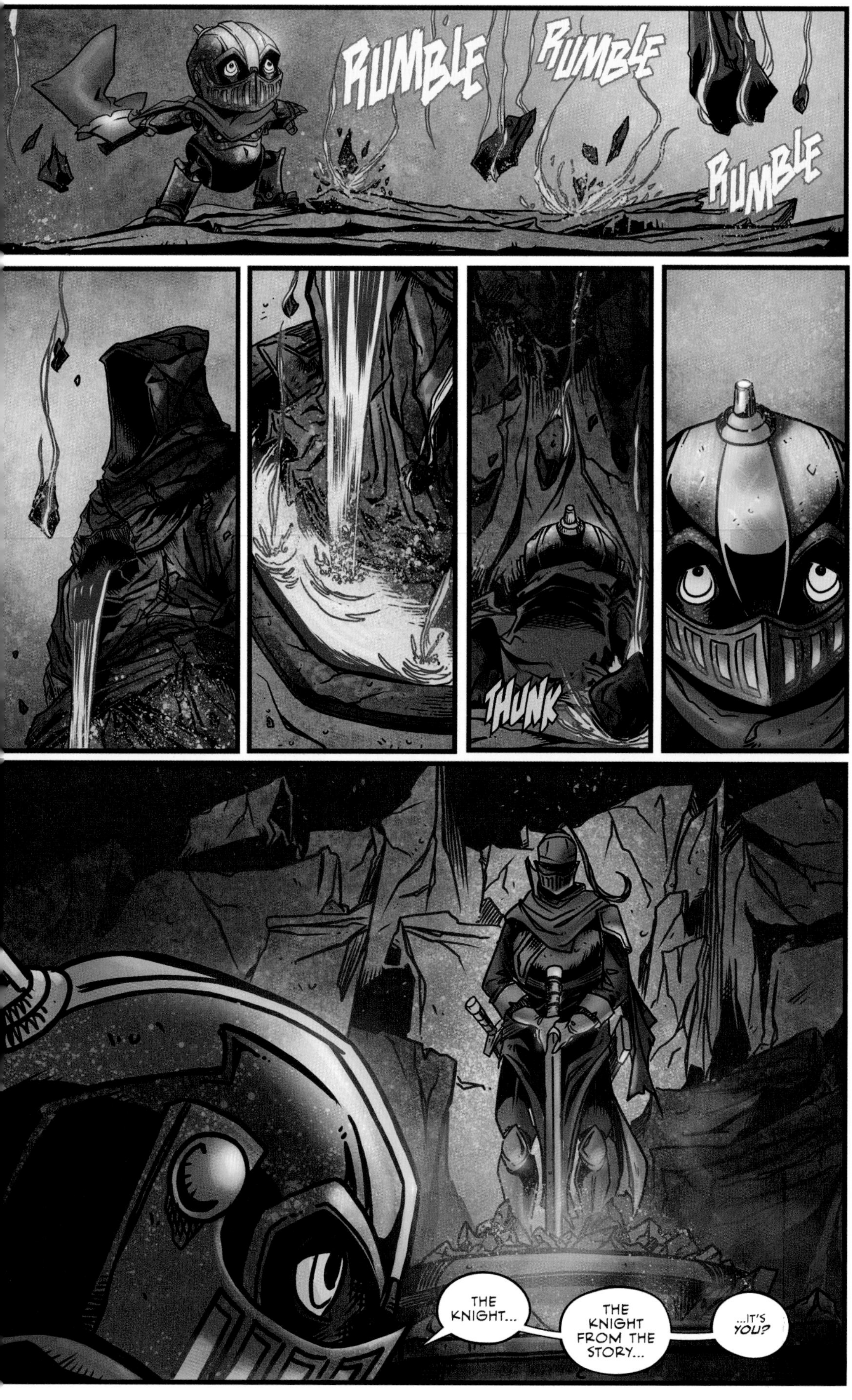
RUMBLE
RUMBLE
RUMBLE
THUNK
THE KNIGHT...
THE KNIGHT FROM THE STORY...
...IT'S YOU?

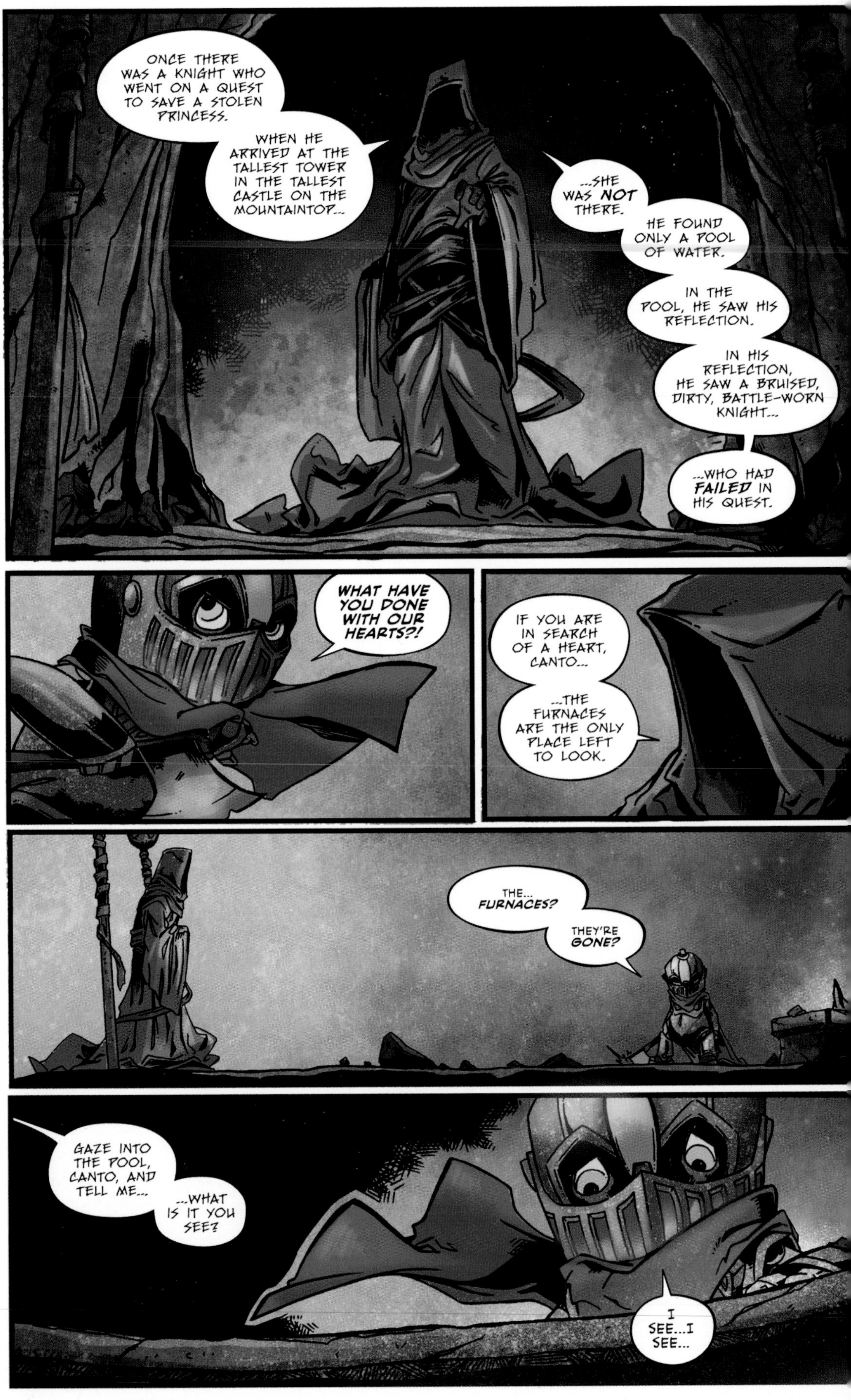
ONCE THERE WAS A KNIGHT WHO WENT ON A QUEST TO SAVE A STOLEN PRINCESS.
WHEN HE ARRIVED AT THE TALLEST TOWER IN THE TALLEST CASTLE ON THE MOUNTAINTOP...
...SHE WAS NOT THERE.
HE FOUND ONLY A POOL OF WATER.
IN THE POOL, HE SAW HIS REFLECTION.
IN HIS REFLECTION, HE SAW A BRUISED, DIRTY, BATTLE-WORN KNIGHT...
...WHO HAD FAILED IN HIS QUEST.
WHAT HAVE YOU DONE WITH OUR HEARTS?!
IF YOU ARE IN SEARCH OF A HEART, CANTO...
...THE FURNACES ARE THE ONLY PLACE LEFT TO LOOK.
THE... FURNACES?
THEY'RE GONE?
GAZE INTO THE POOL, CANTO, AND TELL ME...
...WHAT IS IT YOU SEE?
I SEE...I SEE...

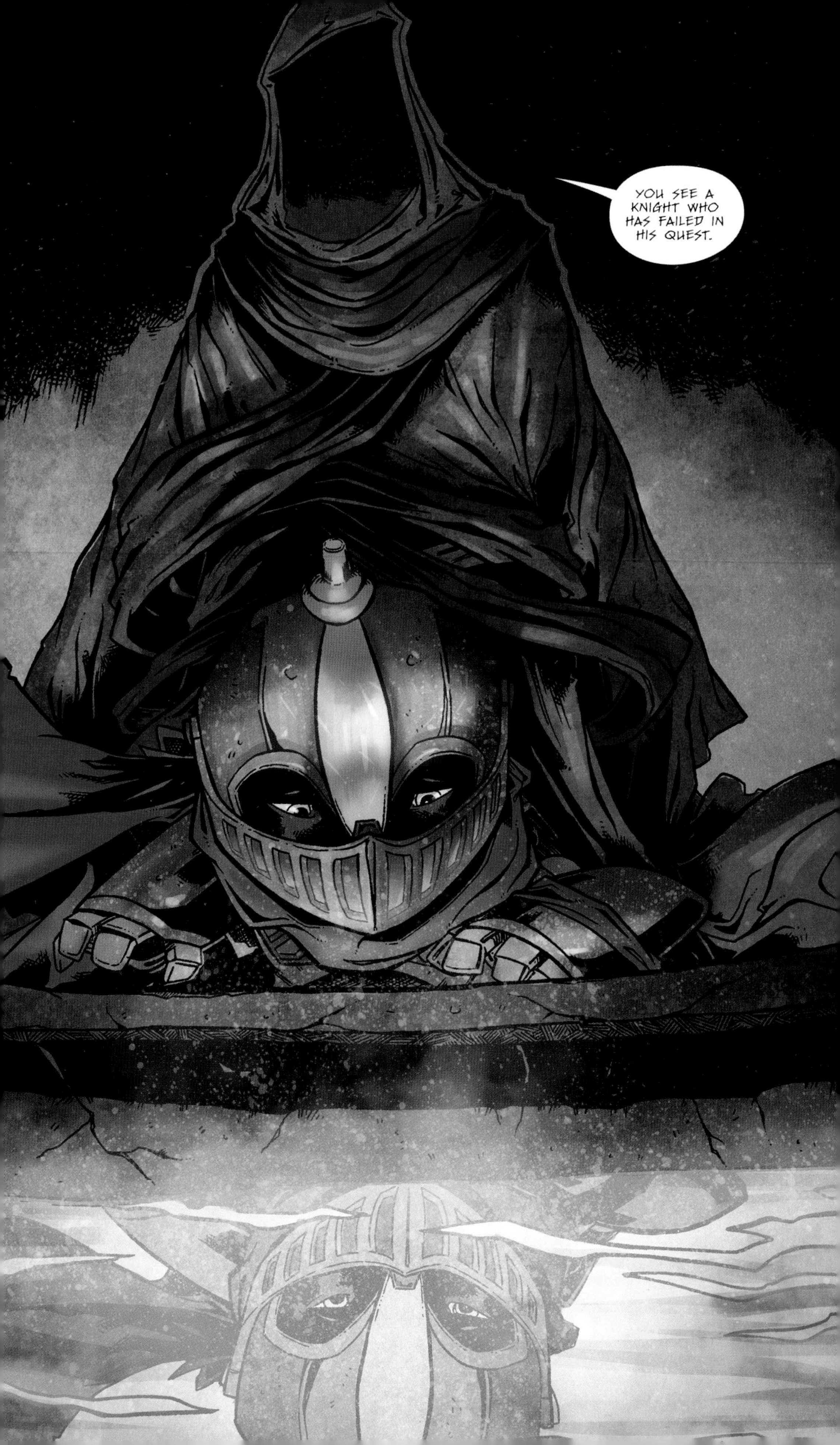
YOU SEE A KNIGHT WHO HAS FAILED IN HIS QUEST.

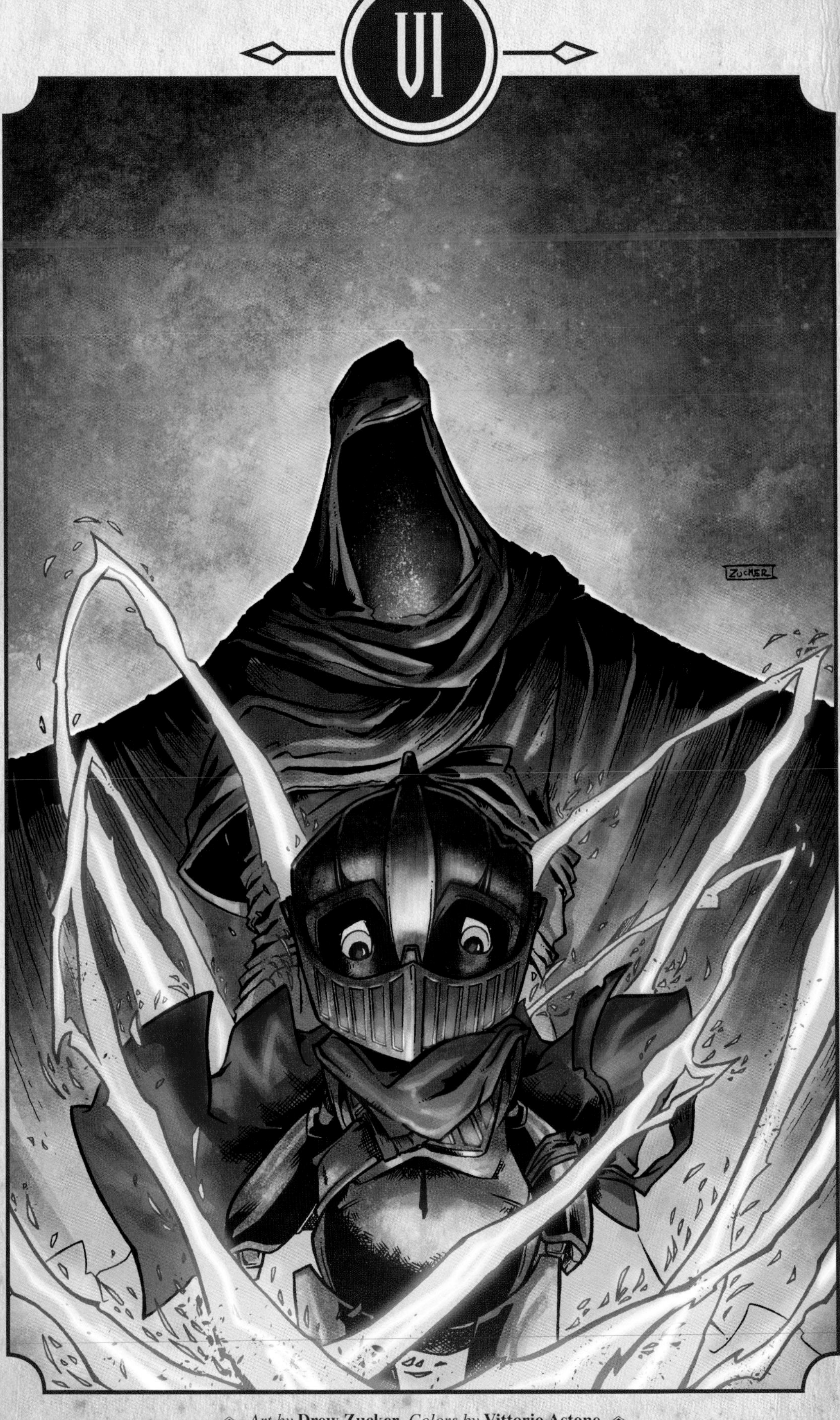
VI
ZUCKER

Art by **Drew Zucker**, *Colors by* **Vittorio Astone**

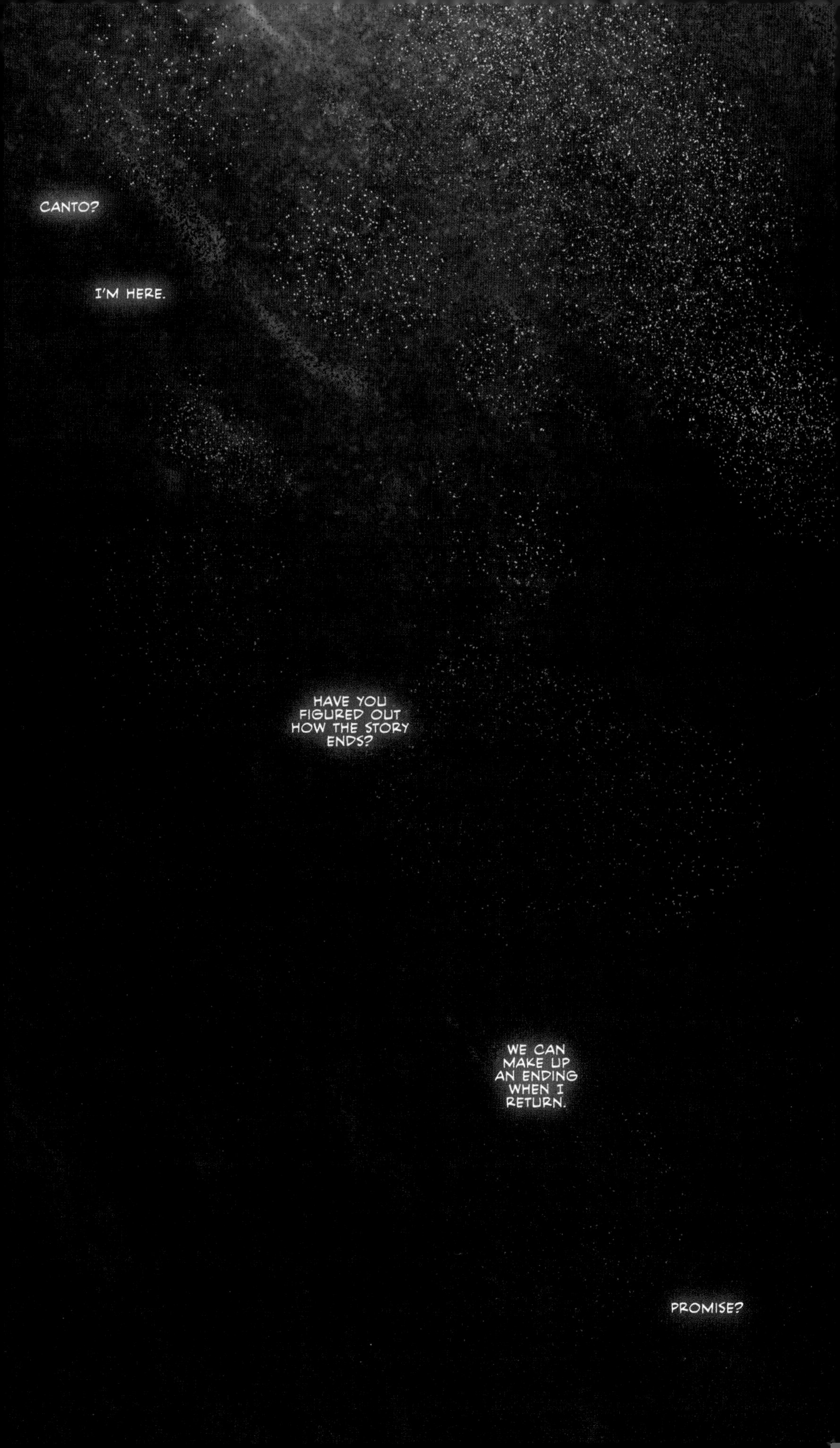
CANTO?
I'M HERE.
HAVE YOU FIGURED OUT HOW THE STORY ENDS?
WE CAN MAKE UP AN ENDING WHEN I RETURN.
PROMISE?

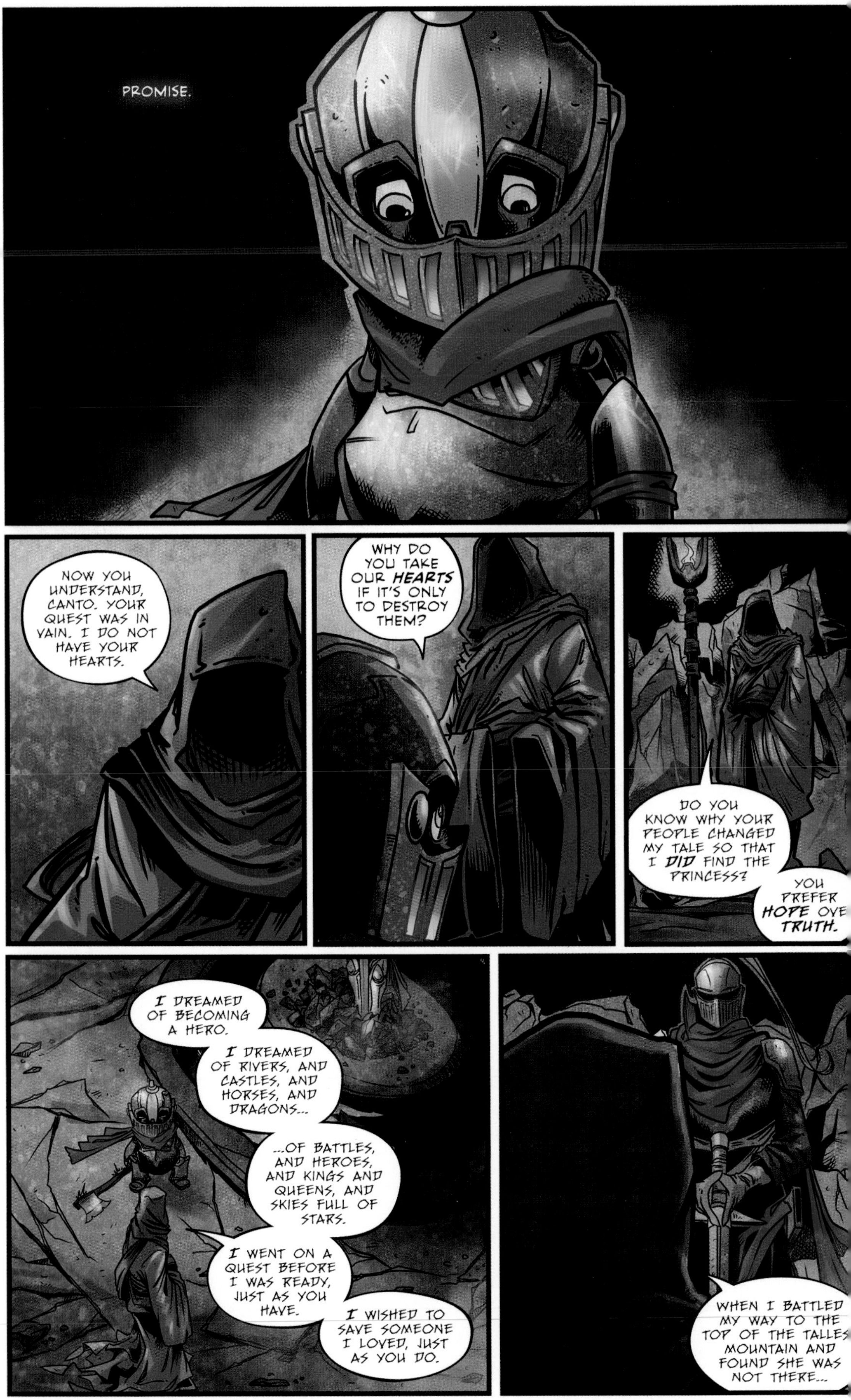
PROMISE.
NOW YOU UNDERSTAND, CANTO. YOUR QUEST WAS IN VAIN. I DO NOT HAVE YOUR HEARTS.
WHY DO YOU TAKE OUR HEARTS IF IT'S ONLY TO DESTROY THEM?
DO YOU KNOW WHY YOUR PEOPLE CHANGED MY TALE SO THAT I DID FIND THE PRINCESS?
YOU PREFER HOPE OVE TRUTH.
I DREAMED OF BECOMING A HERO.
I DREAMED OF RIVERS, AND CASTLES, AND HORSES, AND DRAGONS...
...OF BATTLES, AND HEROES, AND KINGS AND QUEENS, AND SKIES FULL OF STARS.
I WENT ON A QUEST BEFORE I WAS READY, JUST AS YOU HAVE.
I WISHED TO SAVE SOMEONE I LOVED, JUST AS YOU DO.
WHEN I BATTLED MY WAY TO THE TOP OF THE TALLES MOUNTAIN AND FOUND SHE WAS NOT THERE...

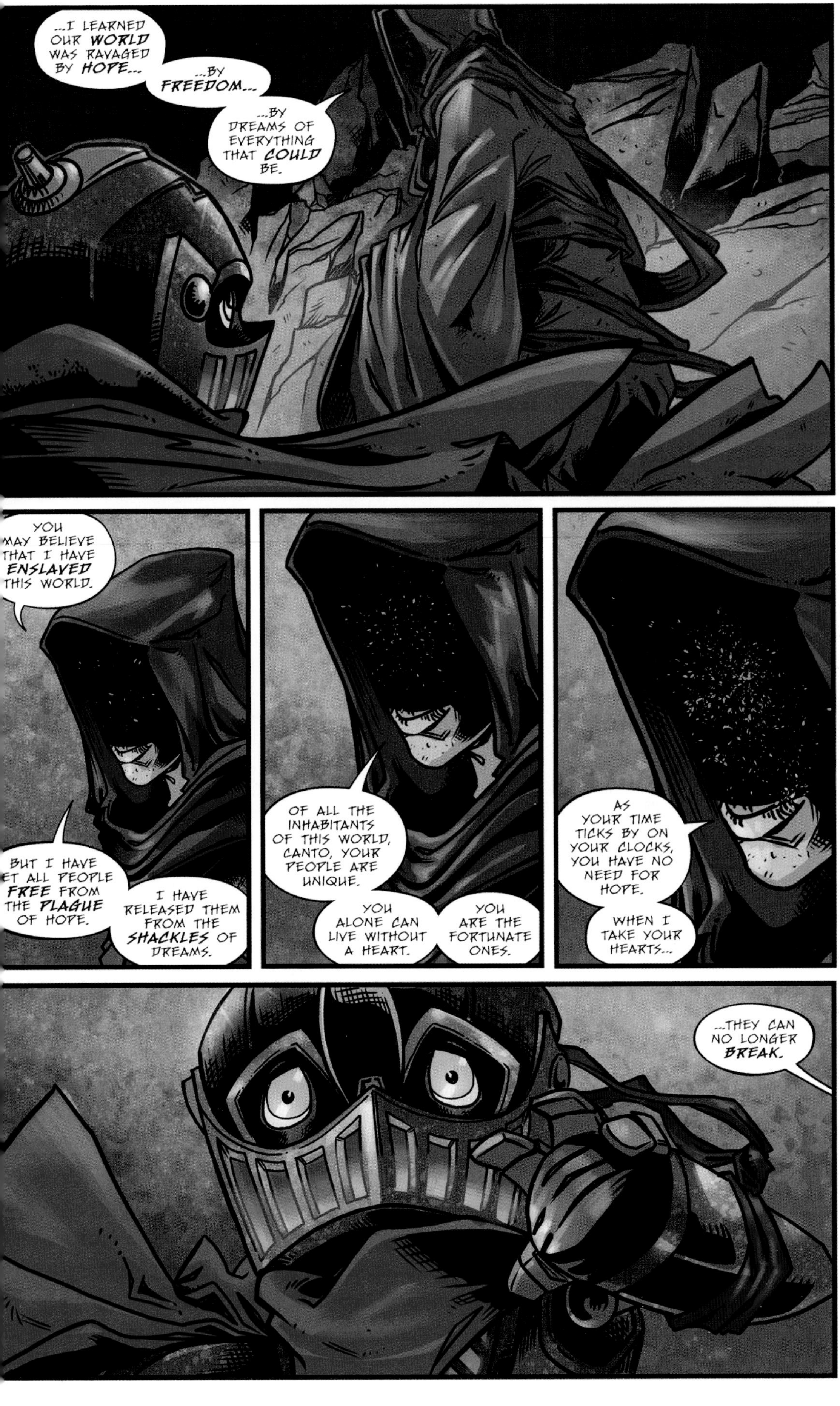
...I LEARNED OUR WORLD WAS RAVAGED BY HOPE...
...BY FREEDOM...
...BY DREAMS OF EVERYTHING THAT COULD BE.
YOU MAY BELIEVE THAT I HAVE ENSLAVED THIS WORLD.
BUT I HAVE ET ALL PEOPLE FREE FROM THE PLAGUE OF HOPE.
I HAVE RELEASED THEM FROM THE SHACKLES OF DREAMS.
OF ALL THE INHABITANTS OF THIS WORLD, CANTO, YOUR PEOPLE ARE UNIQUE.
YOU ALONE CAN LIVE WITHOUT A HEART.
YOU ARE THE FORTUNATE ONES.
AS YOUR TIME TICKS BY ON YOUR CLOCKS, YOU HAVE NO NEED FOR HOPE.
WHEN I TAKE YOUR HEARTS...
...THEY CAN NO LONGER BREAK.

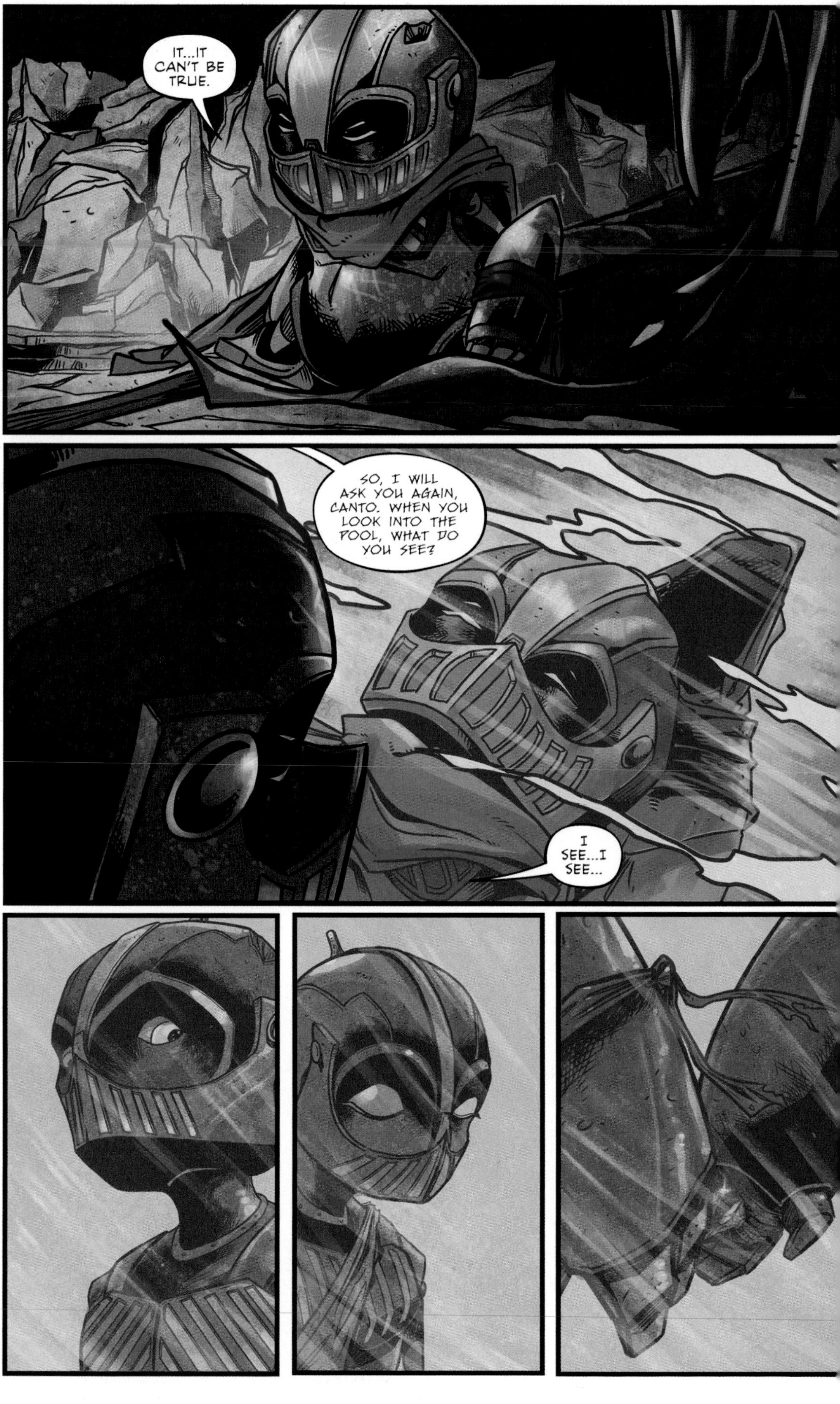
IT...IT CAN'T BE TRUE.
SO, I WILL ASK YOU AGAIN, CANTO. WHEN YOU LOOK INTO THE POOL, WHAT DO YOU SEE?
I SEE...I SEE...

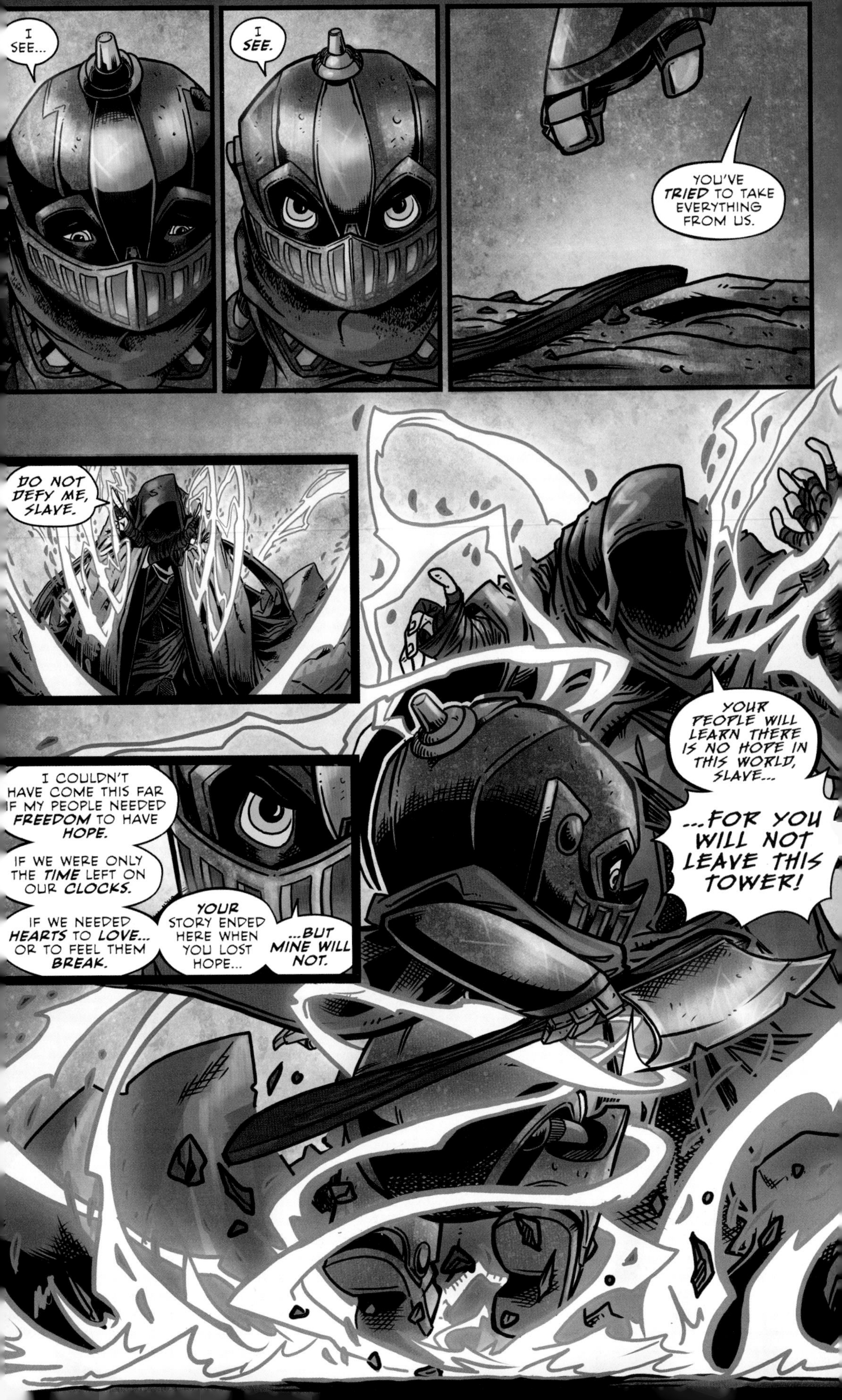

I SEE...
I SEE.
YOU'VE TRIED TO TAKE EVERYTHING FROM US.
DO NOT DEFY ME, SLAVE.
I COULDN'T HAVE COME THIS FAR IF MY PEOPLE NEEDED FREEDOM TO HAVE HOPE.
IF WE WERE ONLY THE TIME LEFT ON OUR CLOCKS.
IF WE NEEDED HEARTS TO LOVE... OR TO FEEL THEM BREAK.
YOUR STORY ENDED HERE WHEN YOU LOST HOPE...
...BUT MINE WILL NOT.
YOUR PEOPLE WILL LEARN THERE IS NO HOPE IN THIS WORLD, SLAVE...
...FOR YOU WILL NOT LEAVE THIS TOWER!

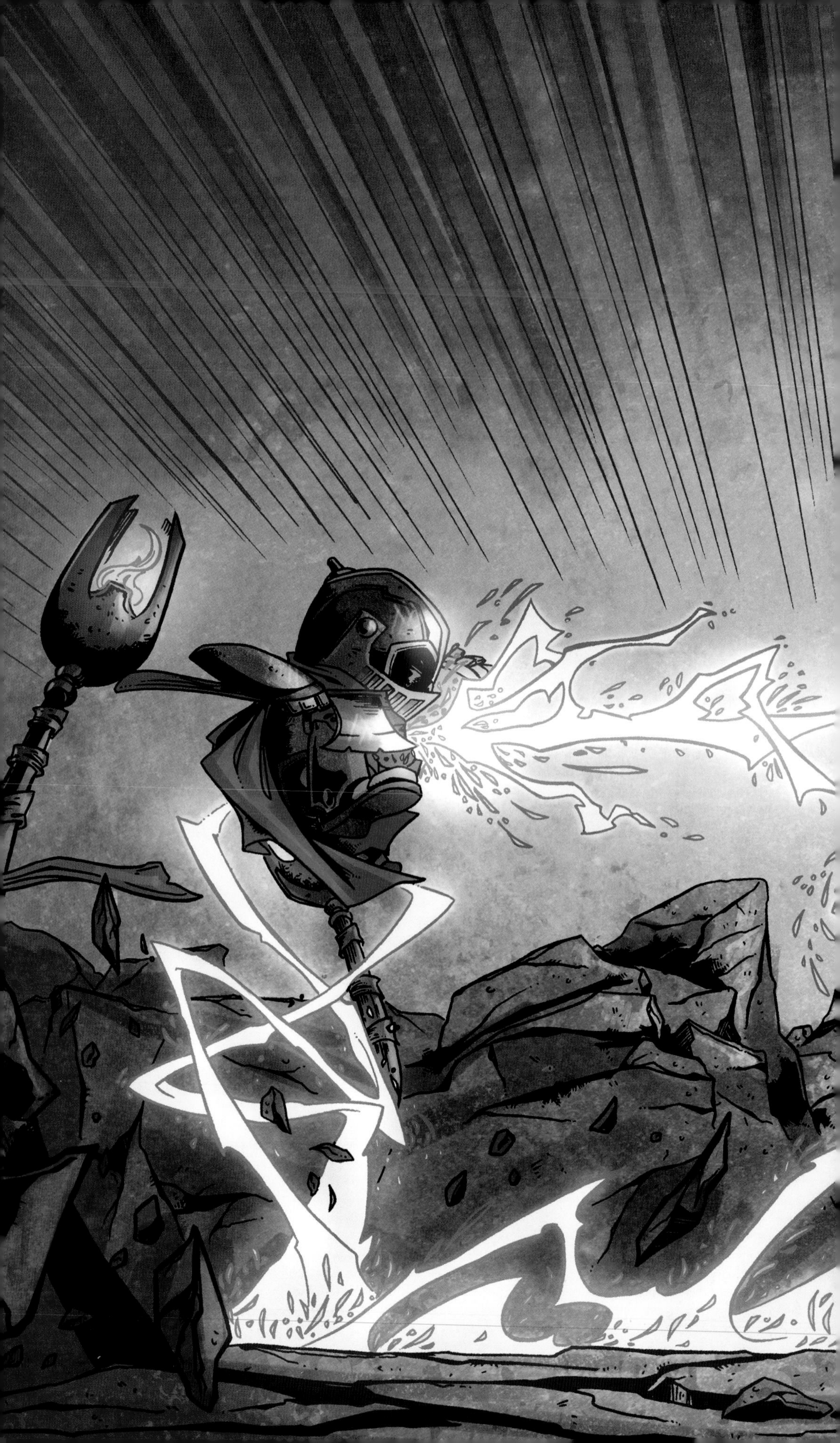

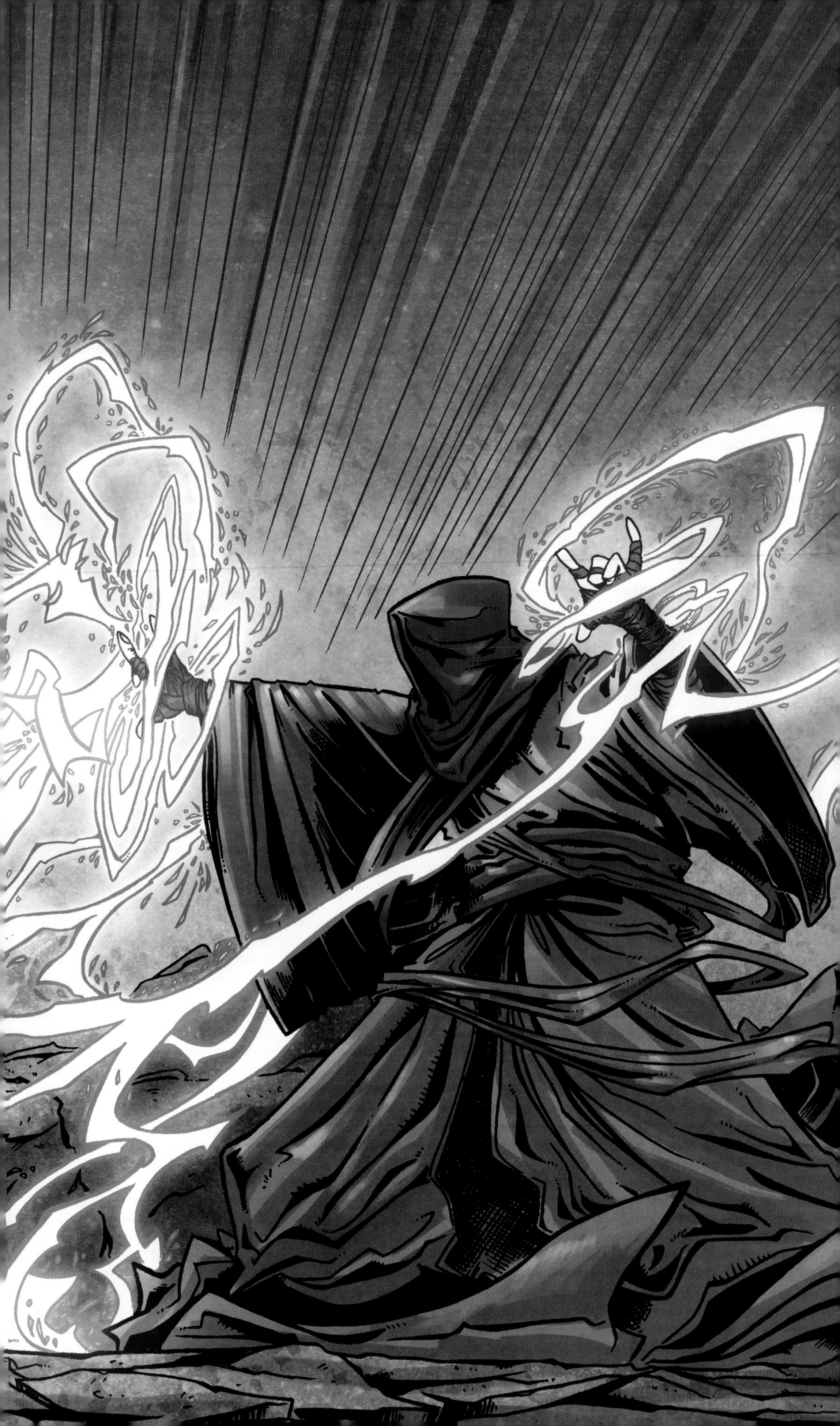

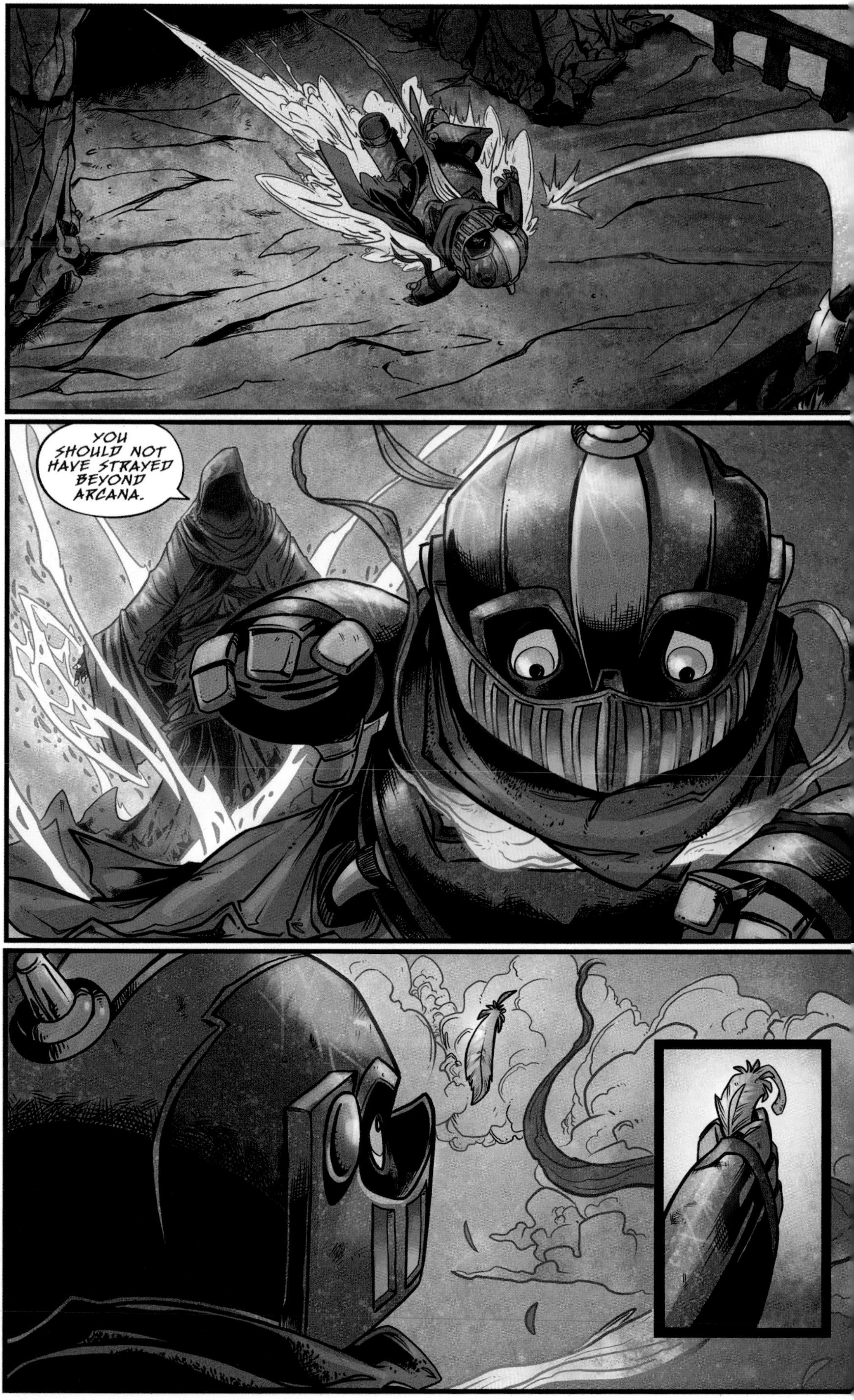
YOU SHOULD NOT HAVE STRAYED BEYOND ARCANA.

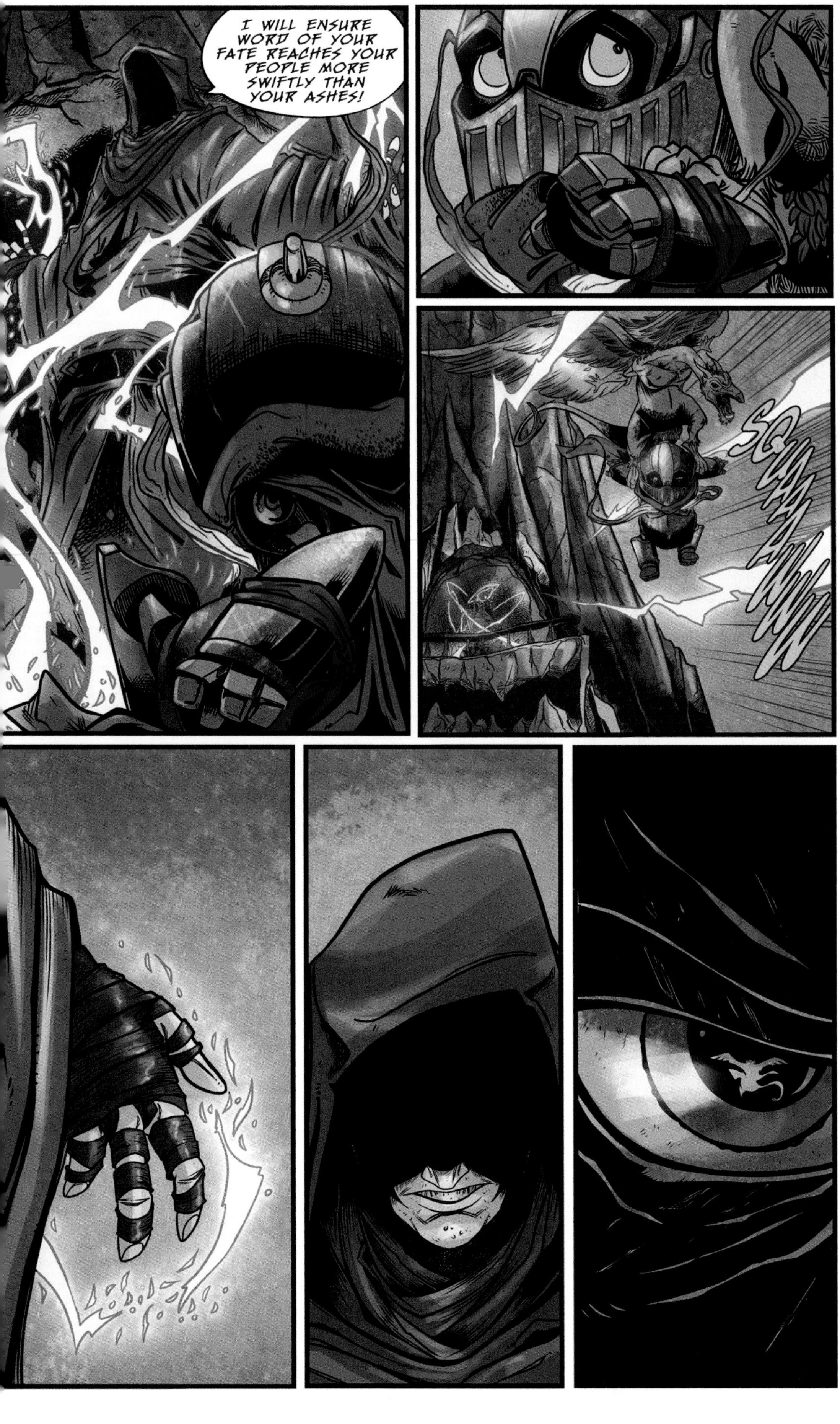
I WILL ENSURE WORD OF YOUR FATE REACHES YOUR PEOPLE MORE SWIFTLY THAN YOUR ASHES!

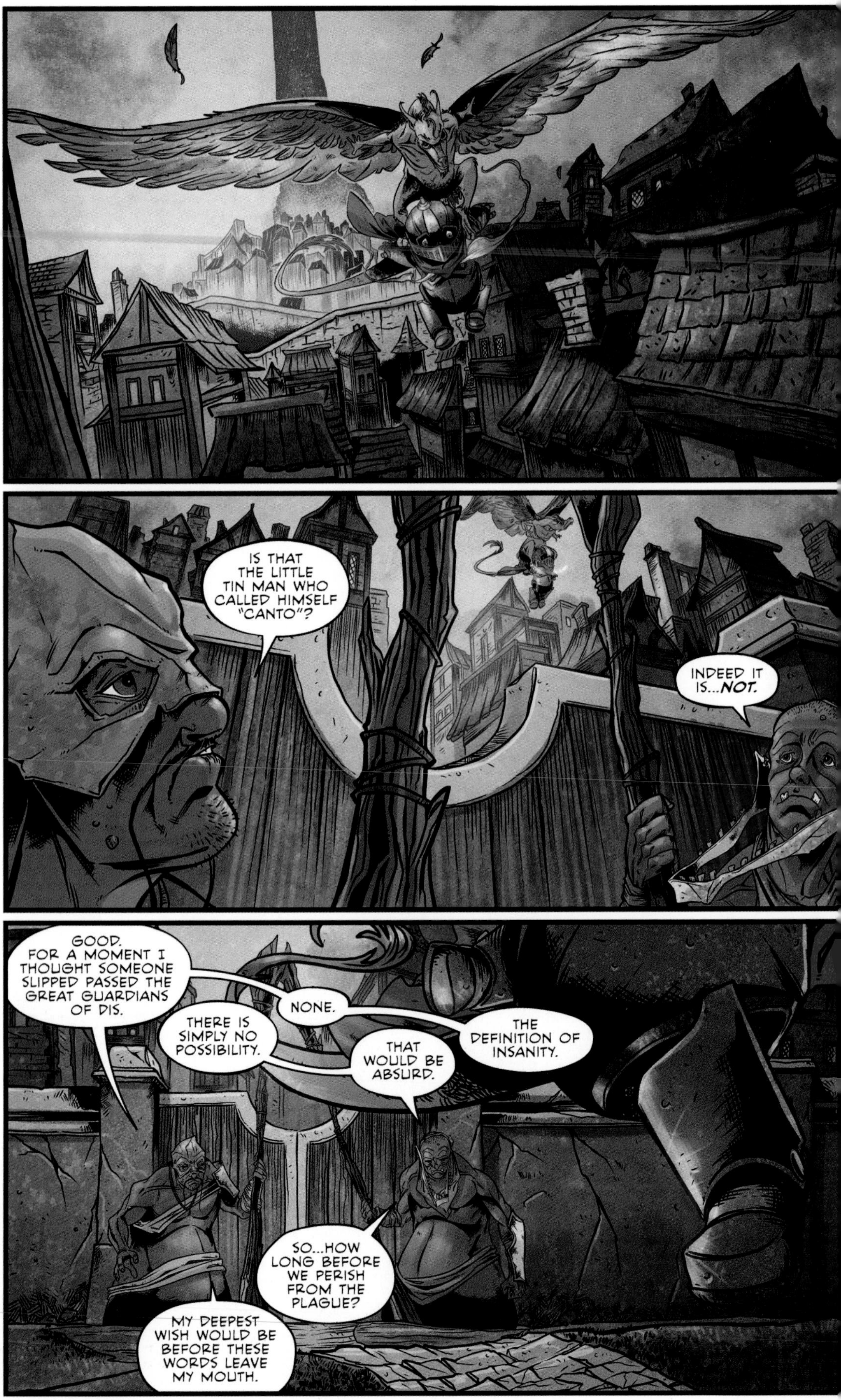
IS THAT THE LITTLE TIN MAN WHO CALLED HIMSELF "CANTO"?
INDEED IT IS...***NOT.***
GOOD. FOR A MOMENT I THOUGHT SOMEONE SLIPPED PASSED THE GREAT GUARDIANS OF DIS.
NONE.
THE DEFINITION OF INSANITY.
THERE IS SIMPLY NO POSSIBILITY.
THAT WOULD BE ABSURD.
SO...HOW LONG BEFORE WE PERISH FROM THE PLAGUE?
MY DEEPEST WISH WOULD BE BEFORE THESE WORDS LEAVE MY MOUTH.

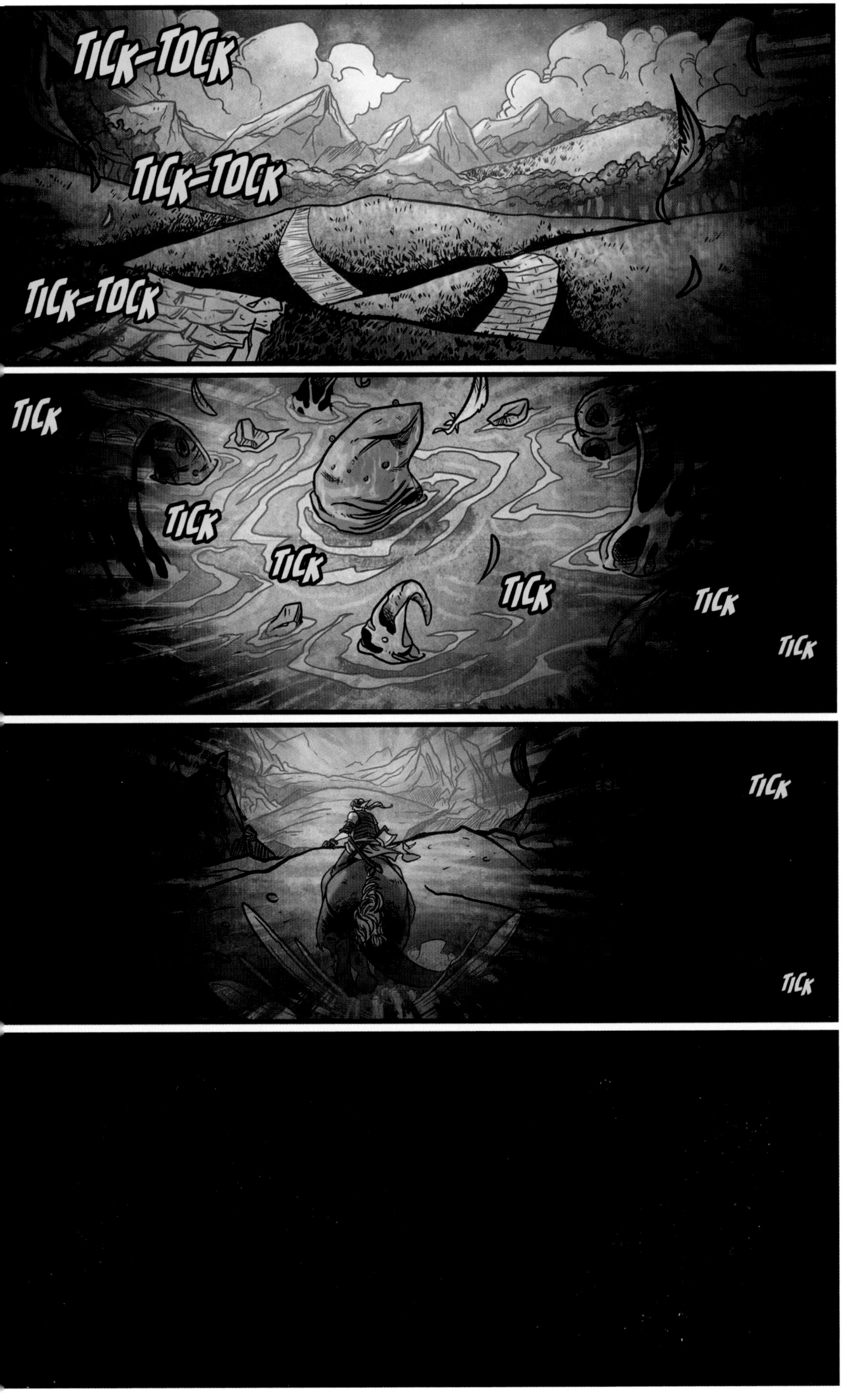
TICK-TOCK
TICK-TOCK
TICK-TOCK
TICK
TICK
TICK
TICK
TICK
TICK
TICK
TICK

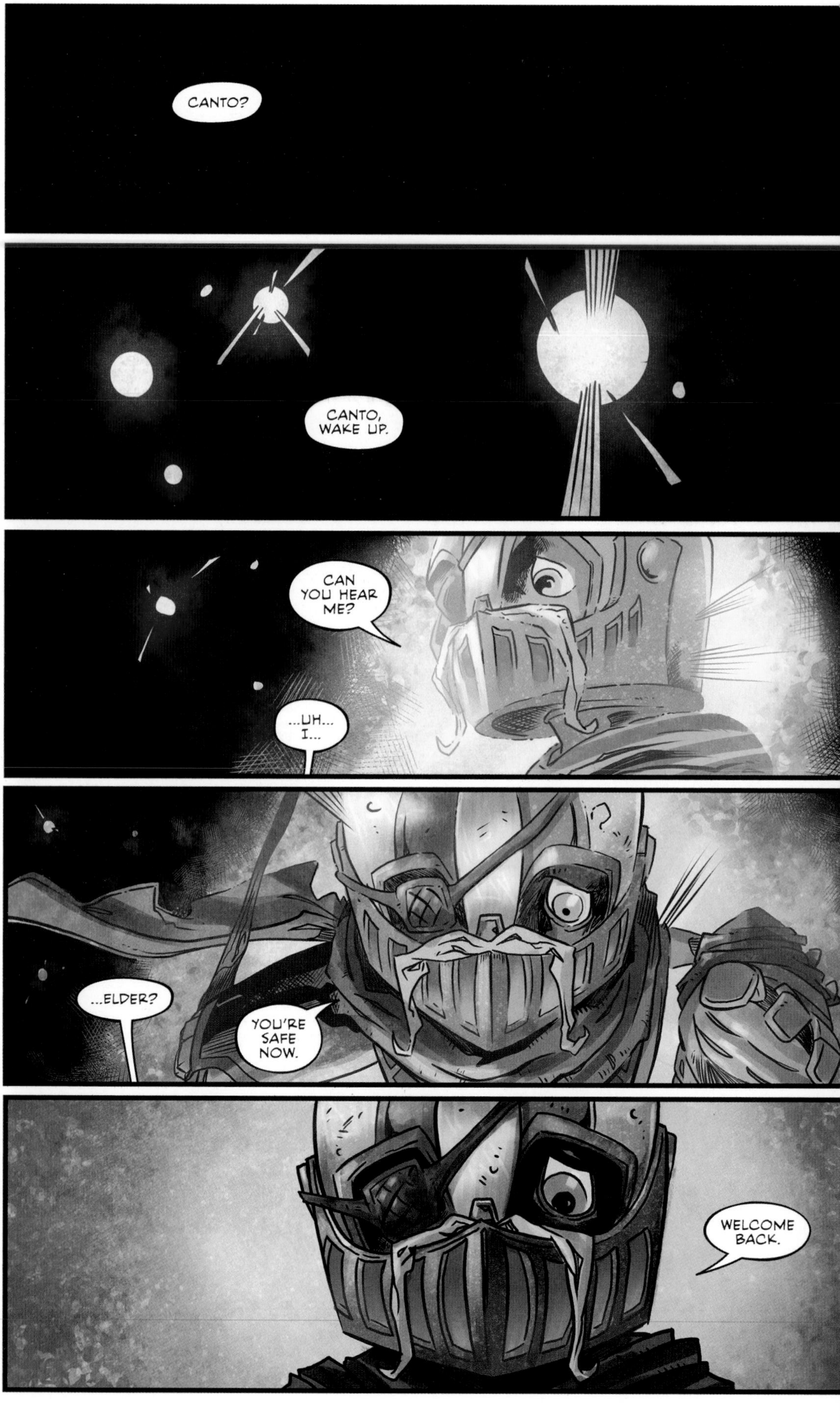
CANTO?
CANTO, WAKE UP.
CAN YOU HEAR ME?
...UH... I...
...ELDER?
YOU'RE SAFE NOW.
WELCOME BACK.

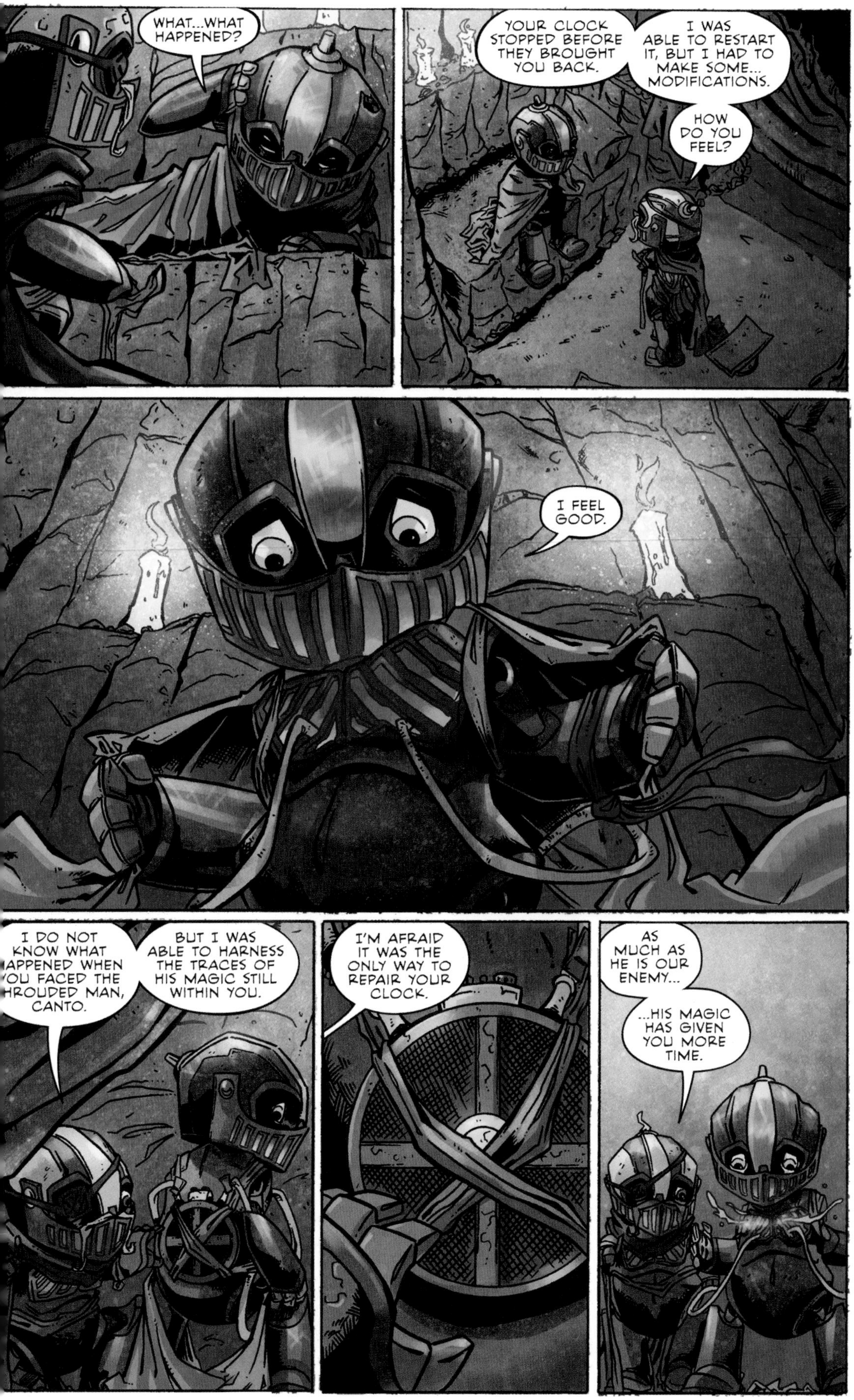
WHAT...WHAT HAPPENED?
YOUR CLOCK STOPPED BEFORE THEY BROUGHT YOU BACK.
I WAS ABLE TO RESTART IT, BUT I HAD TO MAKE SOME... MODIFICATIONS.
HOW DO YOU FEEL?
I FEEL GOOD.
I DO NOT KNOW WHAT APPENDED WHEN OU FACED THE HROUDED MAN, CANTO.
BUT I WAS ABLE TO HARNESS THE TRACES OF HIS MAGIC STILL WITHIN YOU.
I'M AFRAID IT WAS THE ONLY WAY TO REPAIR YOUR CLOCK.
AS MUCH AS HE IS OUR ENEMY...
...HIS MAGIC HAS GIVEN YOU MORE TIME.

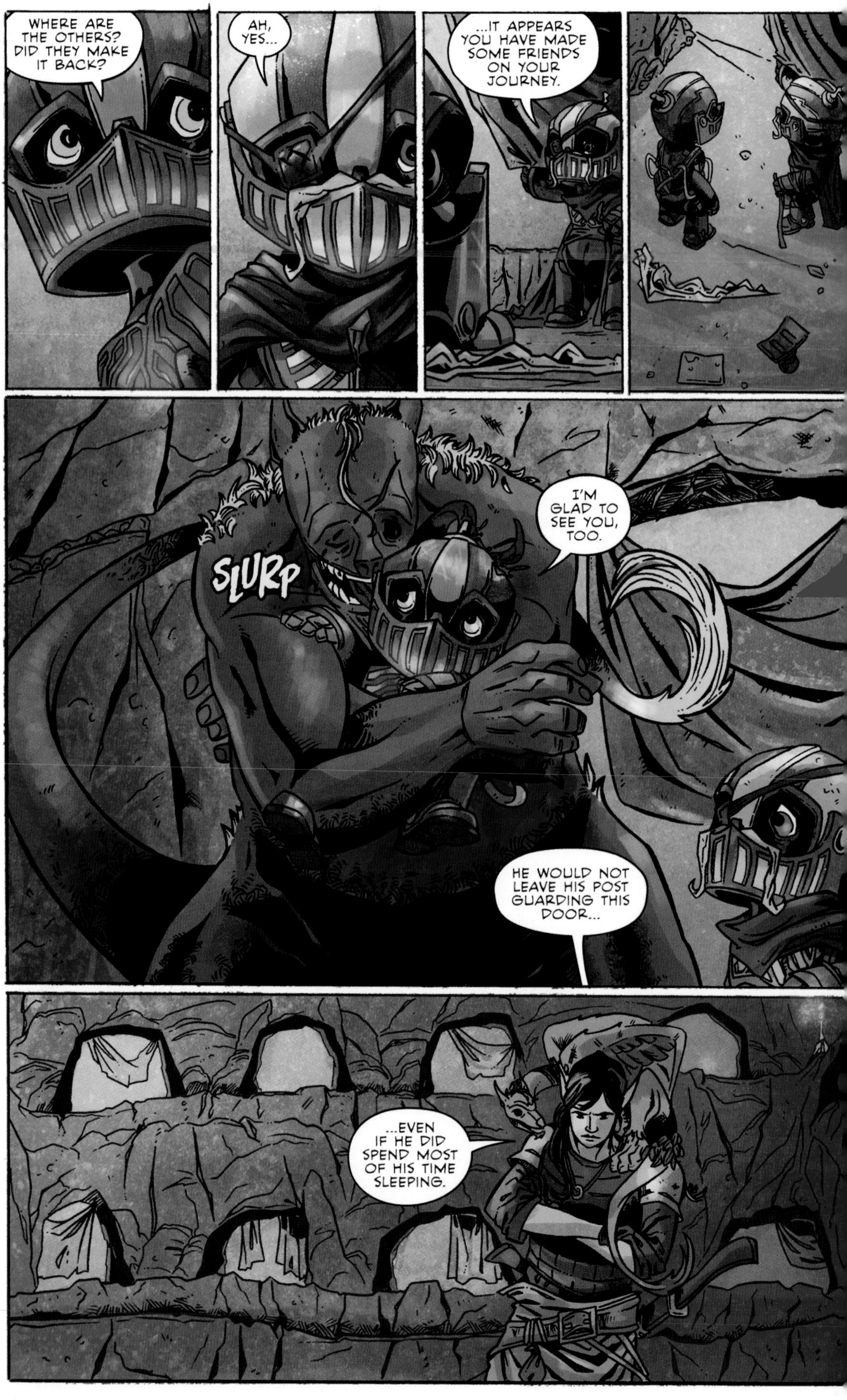
WHERE ARE THE OTHERS? DID THEY MAKE IT BACK?
AH, YES...
...IT APPEARS YOU HAVE MADE SOME FRIENDS ON YOUR JOURNEY.
SLURP
I'M GLAD TO SEE YOU, TOO.
HE WOULD NOT LEAVE HIS POST GUARDING THIS DOOR...
...EVEN IF HE DID SPEND MOST OF HIS TIME SLEEPING.

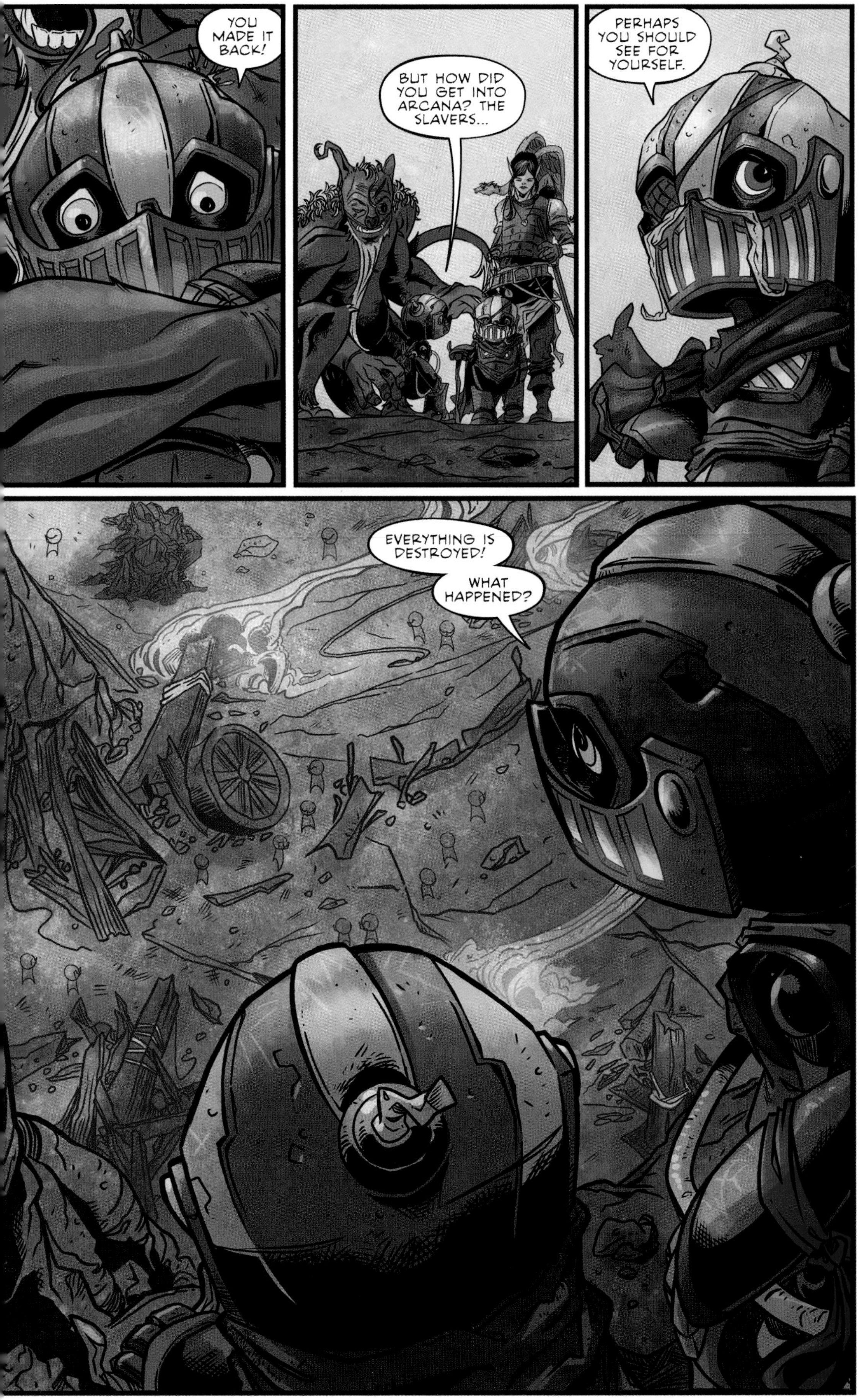
YOU MADE IT BACK!
BUT HOW DID YOU GET INTO ARCANA? THE SLAVERS...
PERHAPS YOU SHOULD SEE FOR YOURSELF.
EVERYTHING IS DESTROYED!
WHAT HAPPENED?

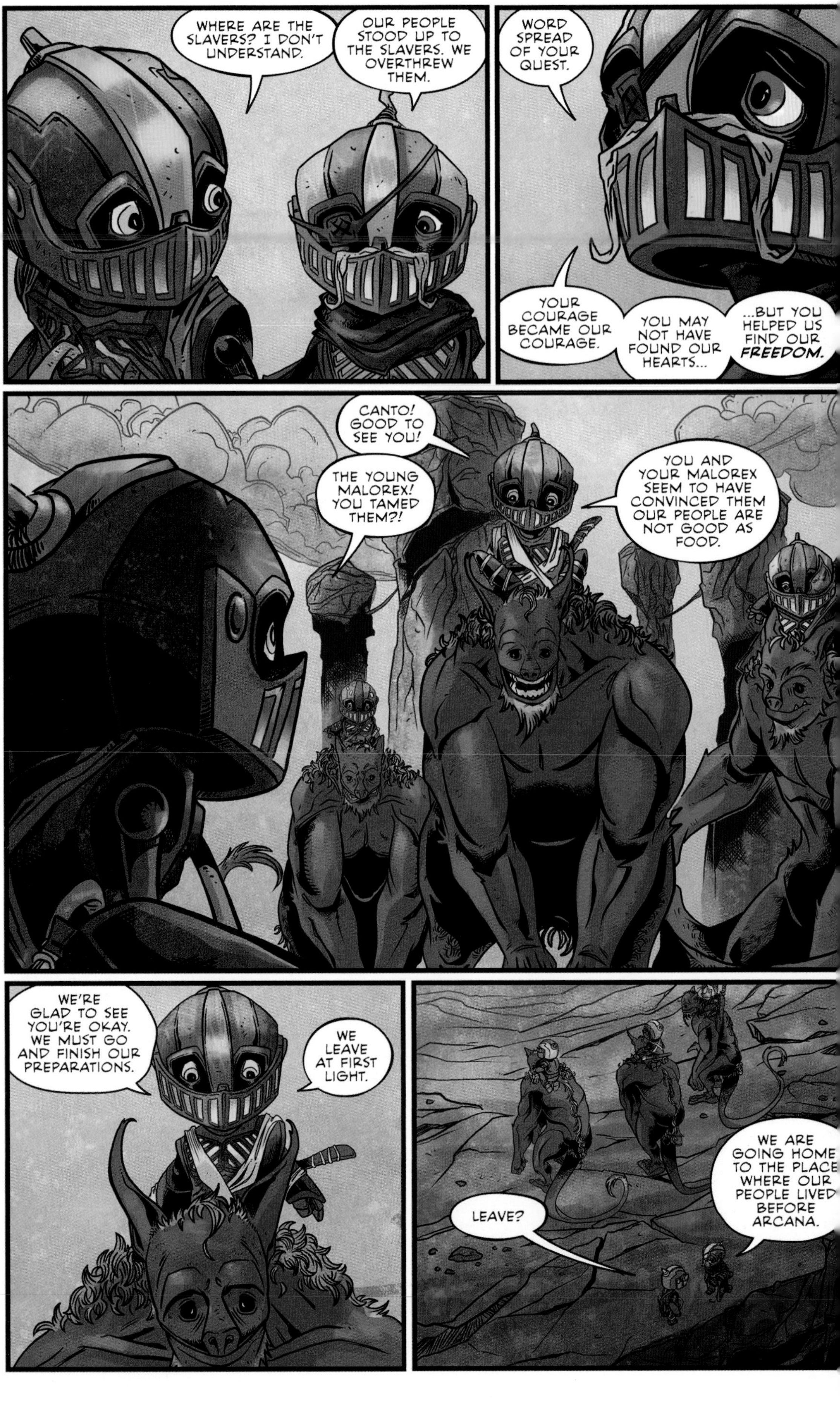
WHERE ARE THE SLAVERS? I DON'T UNDERSTAND.
OUR PEOPLE STOOD UP TO THE SLAVERS. WE OVERTHREW THEM.
WORD SPREAD OF YOUR QUEST.
YOUR COURAGE BECAME OUR COURAGE.
YOU MAY NOT HAVE FOUND OUR HEARTS...
...BUT YOU HELPED US FIND OUR *FREEDOM.*
CANTO! GOOD TO SEE YOU!
THE YOUNG MALOREX! YOU TAMED THEM?!
YOU AND YOUR MALOREX SEEM TO HAVE CONVINCED THEM OUR PEOPLE ARE NOT GOOD AS FOOD.
WE'RE GLAD TO SEE YOU'RE OKAY. WE MUST GO AND FINISH OUR PREPARATIONS.
WE LEAVE AT FIRST LIGHT.
LEAVE?
WE ARE GOING HOME TO THE PLACE WHERE OUR PEOPLE LIVED BEFORE ARCANA.

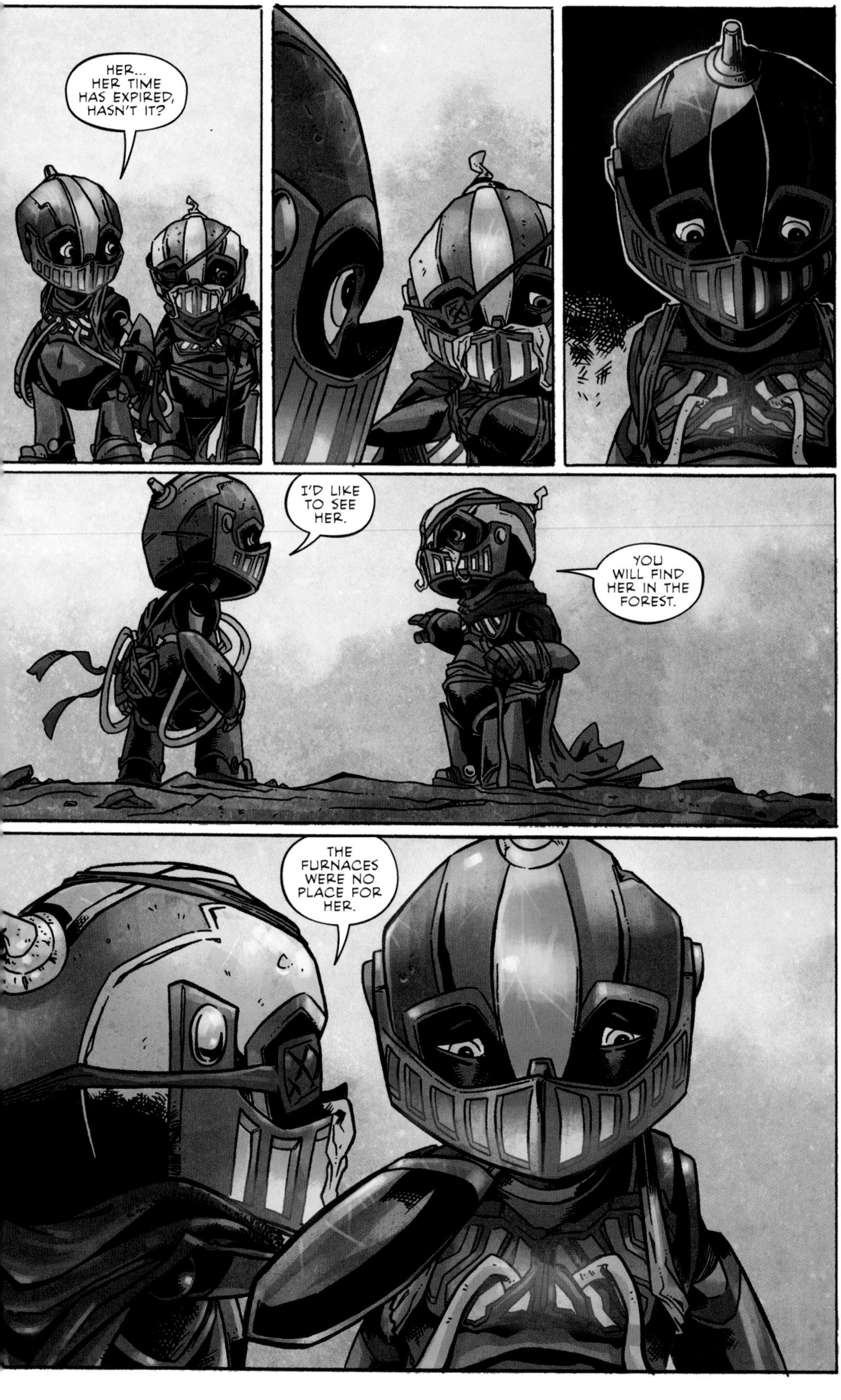

HER... HER TIME HAS EXPIRED, HASN'T IT?
I'D LIKE TO SEE HER.
YOU WILL FIND HER IN THE FOREST.
THE FURNACES WERE NO PLACE FOR HER.

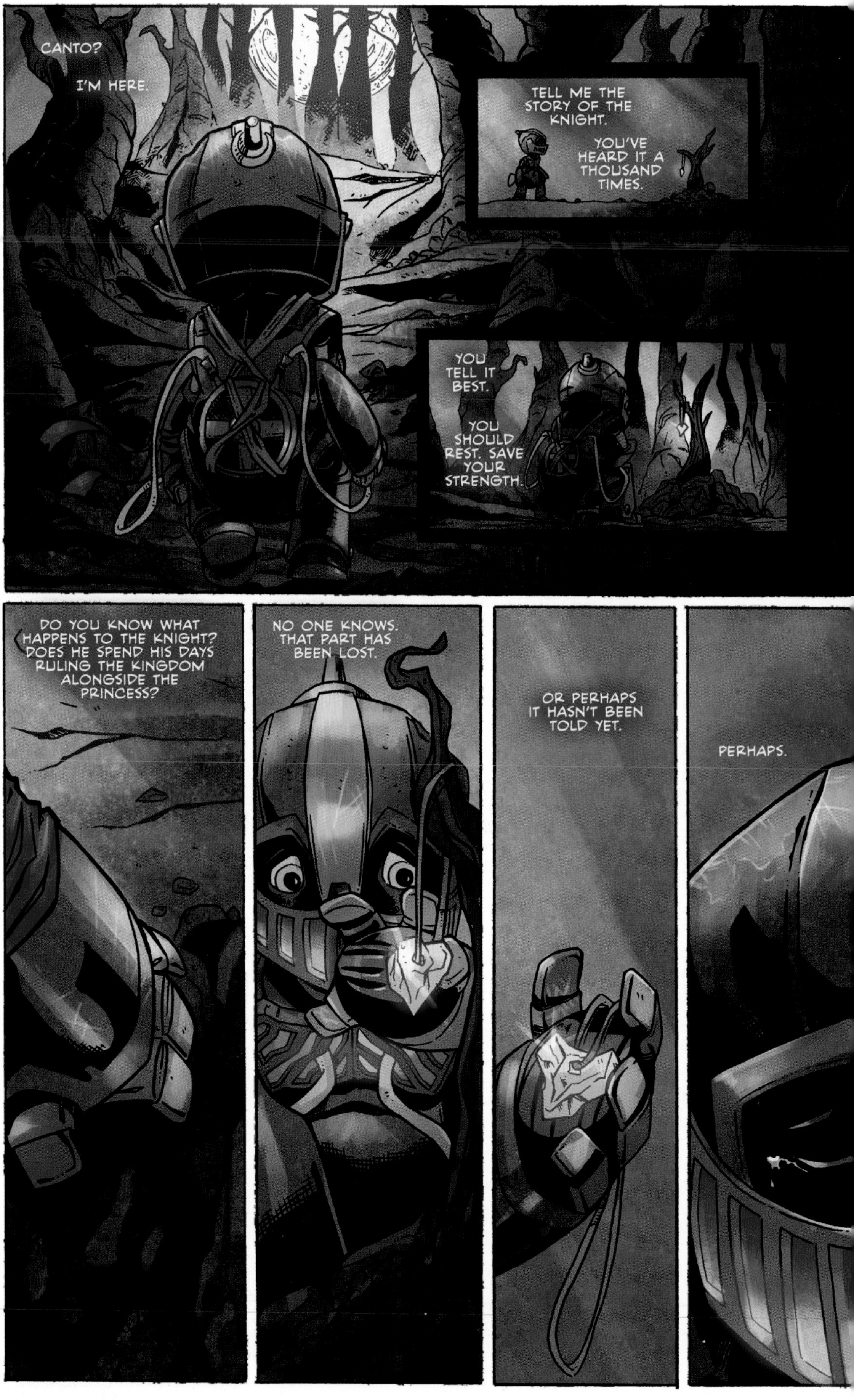
CANTO?
I'M HERE.
TELL ME THE STORY OF THE KNIGHT.
YOU'VE HEARD IT A THOUSAND TIMES.
YOU TELL IT BEST.
YOU SHOULD REST. SAVE YOUR STRENGTH.
DO YOU KNOW WHAT HAPPENS TO THE KNIGHT? DOES HE SPEND HIS DAYS RULING THE KINGDOM ALONGSIDE THE PRINCESS?
NO ONE KNOWS. THAT PART HAS BEEN LOST.
OR PERHAPS IT HASN'T BEEN TOLD YET.
PERHAPS.

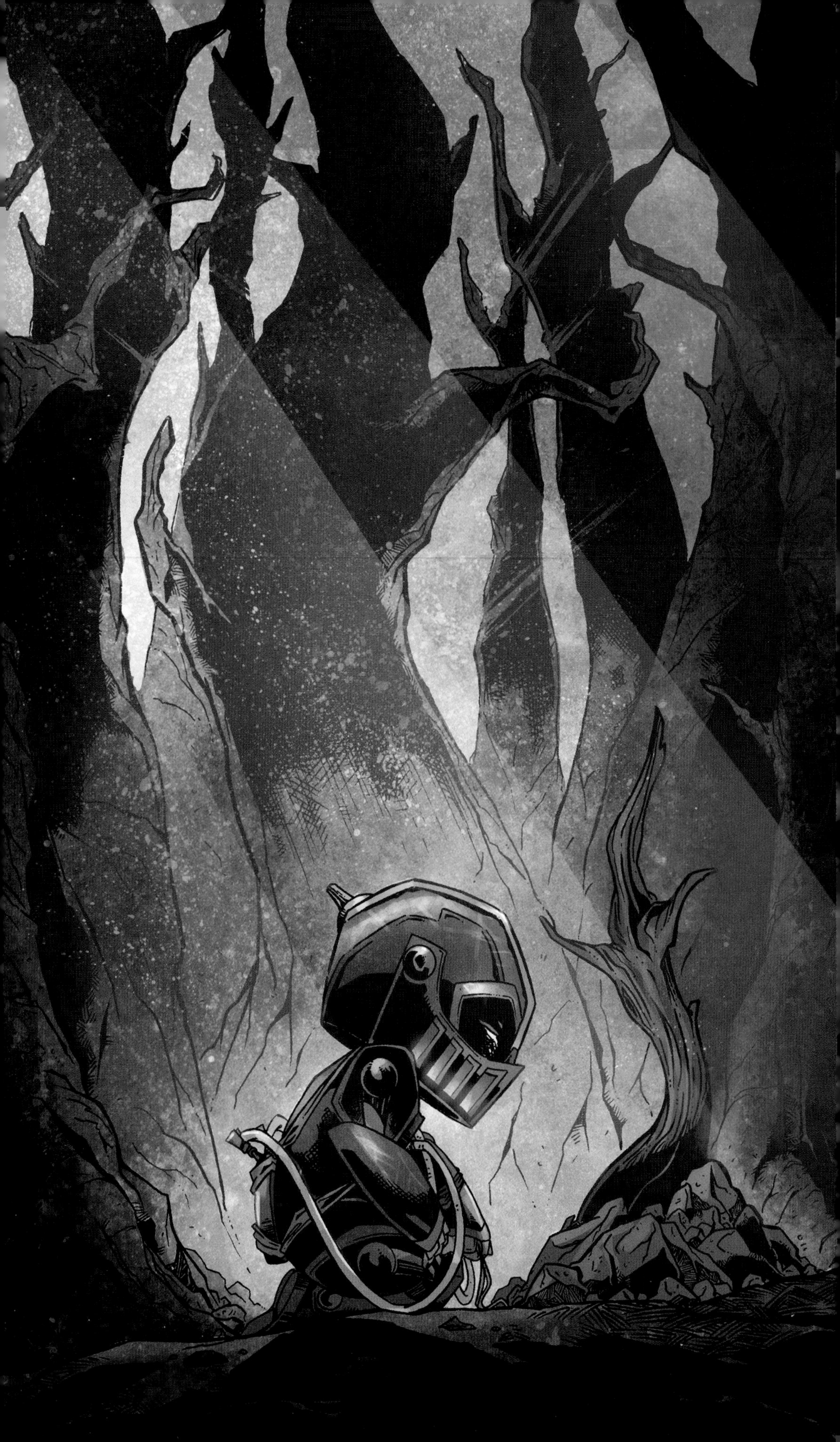

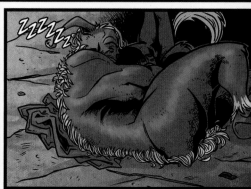

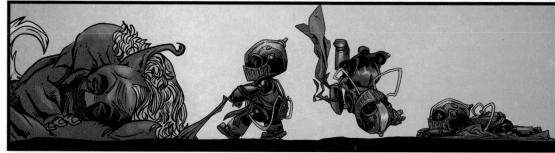

HOW A CREATURE CAN SLEEP SO MUCH, I'LL NEVER KNOW.

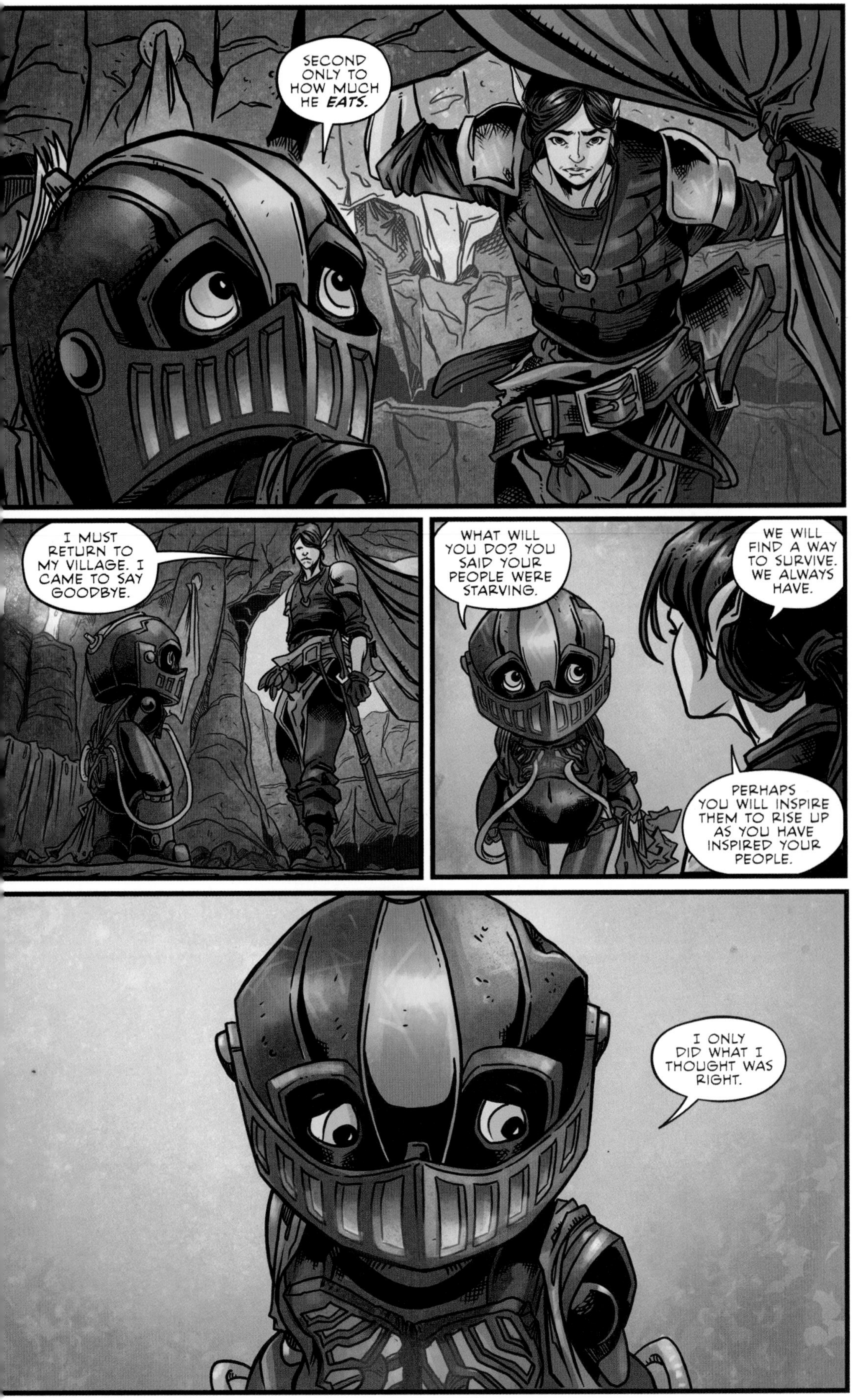
SECOND ONLY TO HOW MUCH HE *EATS.*
I MUST RETURN TO MY VILLAGE. I CAME TO SAY GOODBYE.
WHAT WILL YOU DO? YOU SAID YOUR PEOPLE WERE STARVING.
WE WILL FIND A WAY TO SURVIVE. WE ALWAYS HAVE.
PERHAPS YOU WILL INSPIRE THEM TO RISE UP AS YOU HAVE INSPIRED YOUR PEOPLE.
I ONLY DID WHAT I THOUGHT WAS RIGHT.

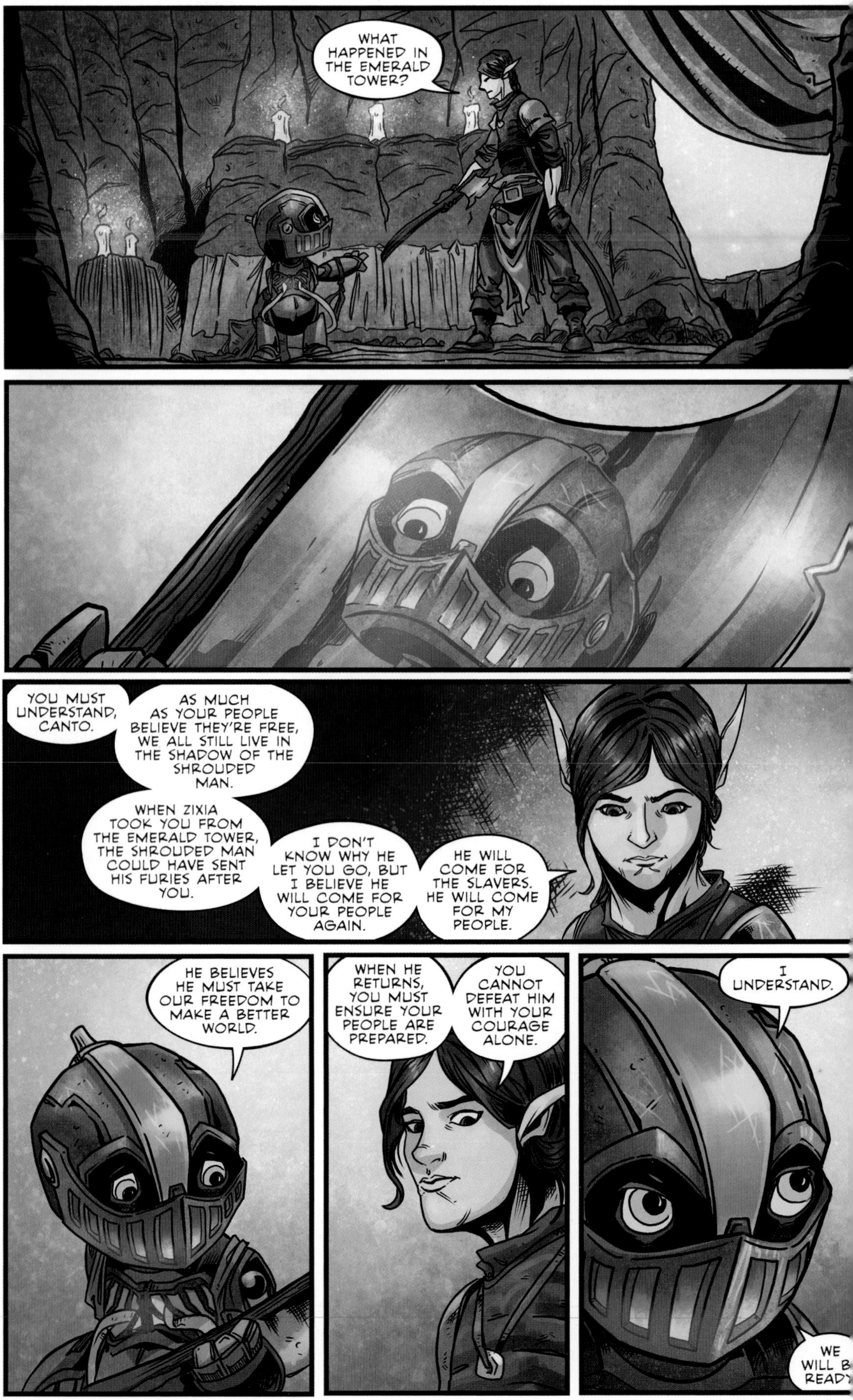

WHAT HAPPENED IN THE EMERALD TOWER?
YOU MUST UNDERSTAND, CANTO.
AS MUCH AS YOUR PEOPLE BELIEVE THEY'RE FREE, WE ALL STILL LIVE IN THE SHADOW OF THE SHROUDED MAN.
WHEN ZIXIA TOOK YOU FROM THE EMERALD TOWER, THE SHROUDED MAN COULD HAVE SENT HIS FURIES AFTER YOU.
I DON'T KNOW WHY HE LET YOU GO, BUT I BELIEVE HE WILL COME FOR YOUR PEOPLE AGAIN.
HE WILL COME FOR THE SLAVERS. HE WILL COME FOR MY PEOPLE.
HE BELIEVES HE MUST TAKE OUR FREEDOM TO MAKE A BETTER WORLD.
WHEN HE RETURNS, YOU MUST ENSURE YOUR PEOPLE ARE PREPARED.
YOU CANNOT DEFEAT HIM WITH YOUR COURAGE ALONE.
I UNDERSTAND.

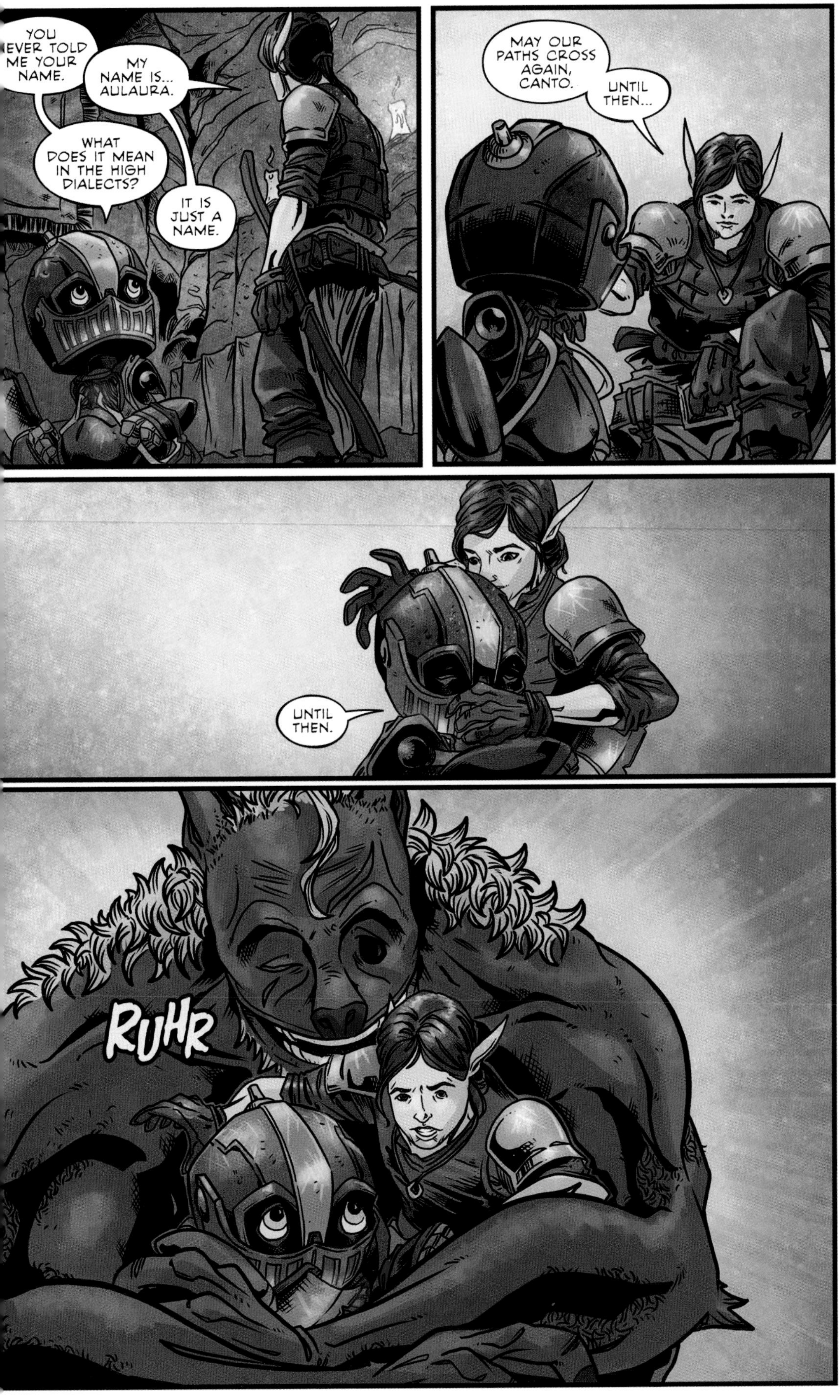
YOU EVER TOLD ME YOUR NAME.
MY NAME IS... AULAURA.
WHAT DOES IT MEAN IN THE HIGH DIALECTS?
IT IS JUST A NAME.
MAY OUR PATHS CROSS AGAIN, CANTO.
UNTIL THEN...
UNTIL THEN.
RUHR

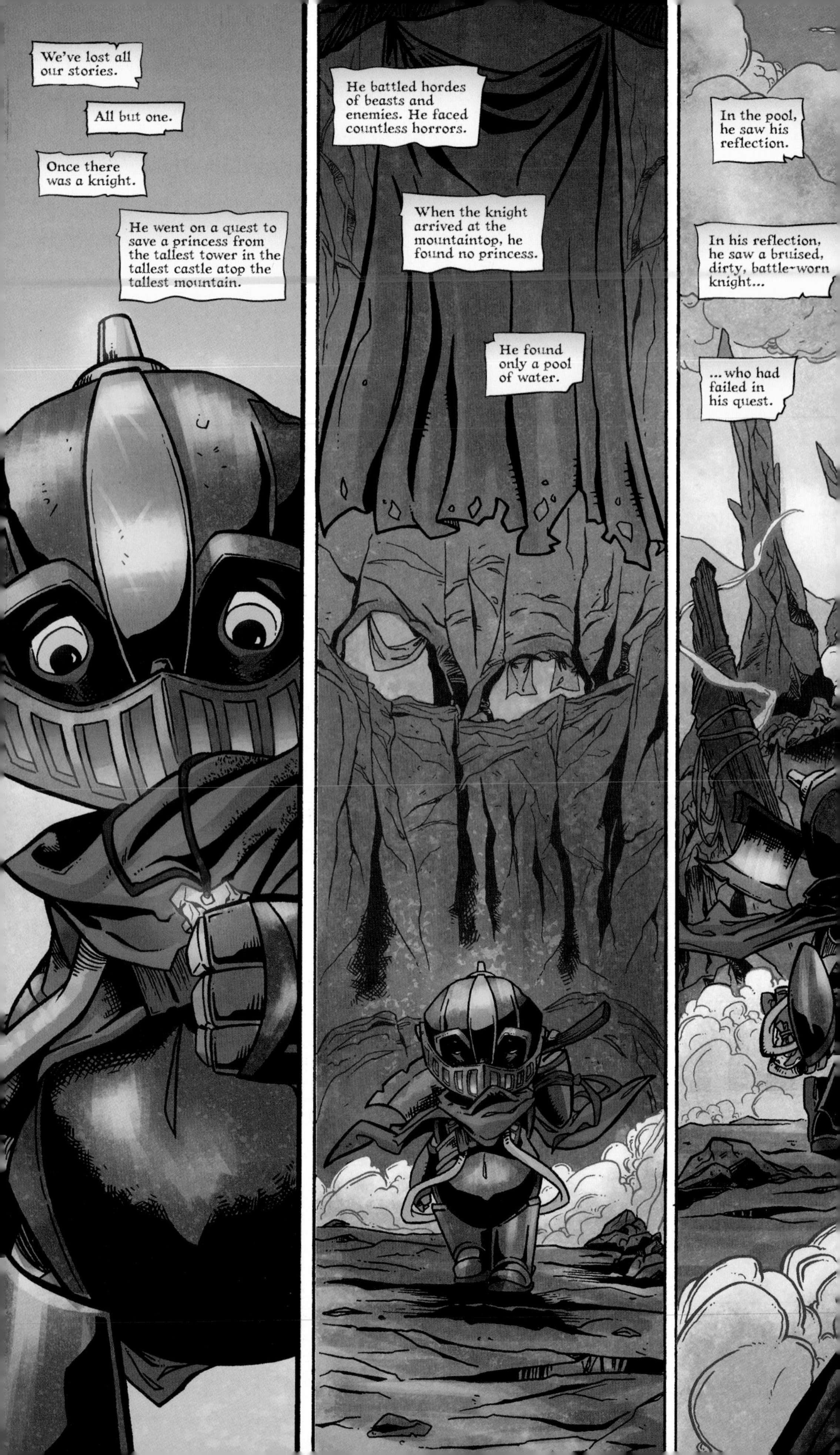
We've lost all our stories.
All but one.
Once there was a knight.
He went on a quest to save a princess from the tallest tower in the tallest castle atop the tallest mountain.
He battled hordes of beasts and enemies. He faced countless horrors.
When the knight arrived at the mountaintop, he found no princess.
He found only a pool of water.
In the pool, he saw his reflection.
In his reflection, he saw a bruised, dirty, battle-worn knight...
...who had failed in his quest.

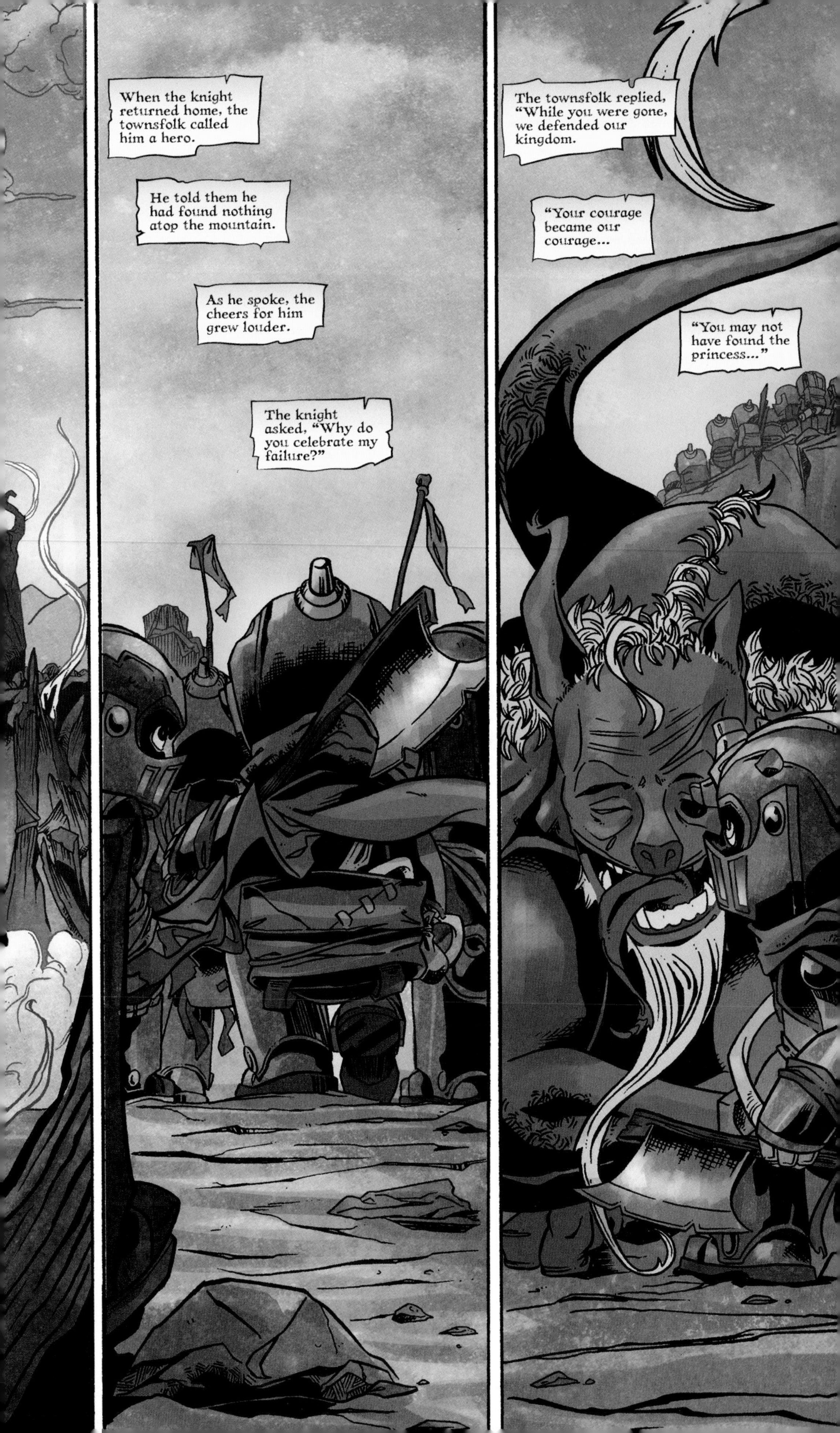
When the knight returned home, the townsfolk called him a hero.
He told them he had found nothing atop the mountain.
As he spoke, the cheers for him grew louder.
The knight asked, "Why do you celebrate my failure?"
The townsfolk replied, "While you were gone, we defended our kingdom.
"Your courage became our courage...
"You may not have found the princess..."

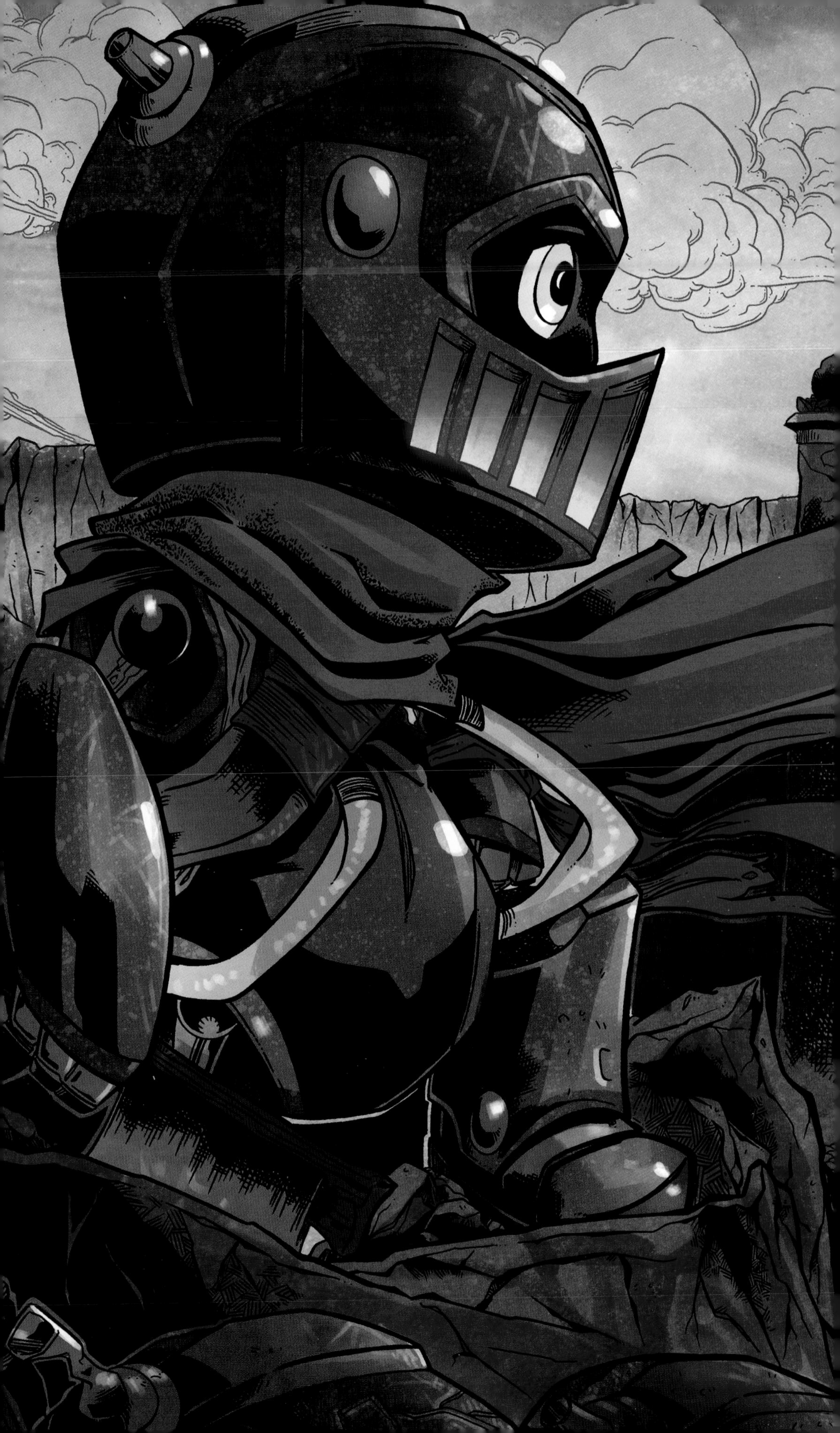

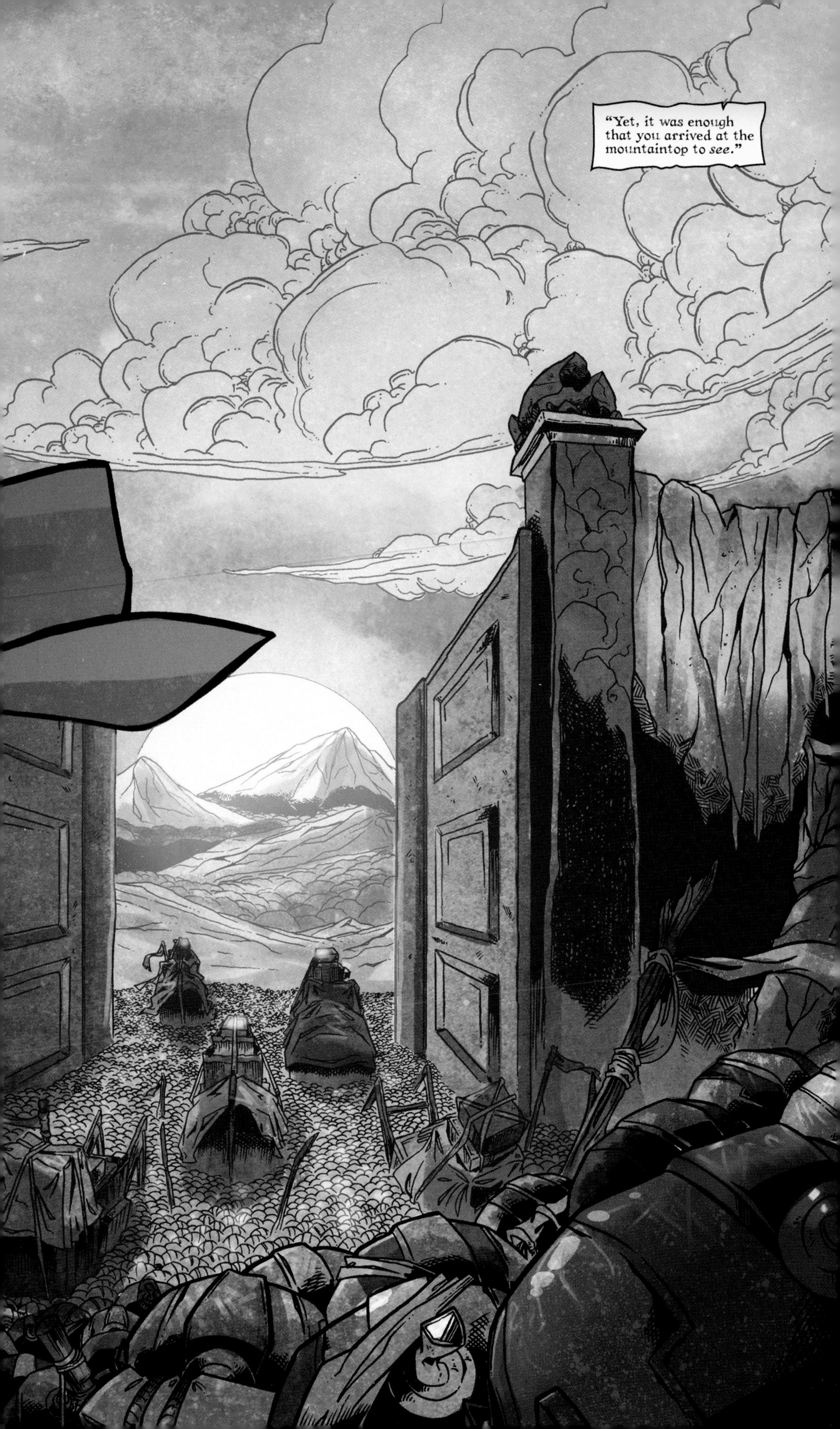
"Yet, it was enough that you arrived at the mountaintop to *see*."

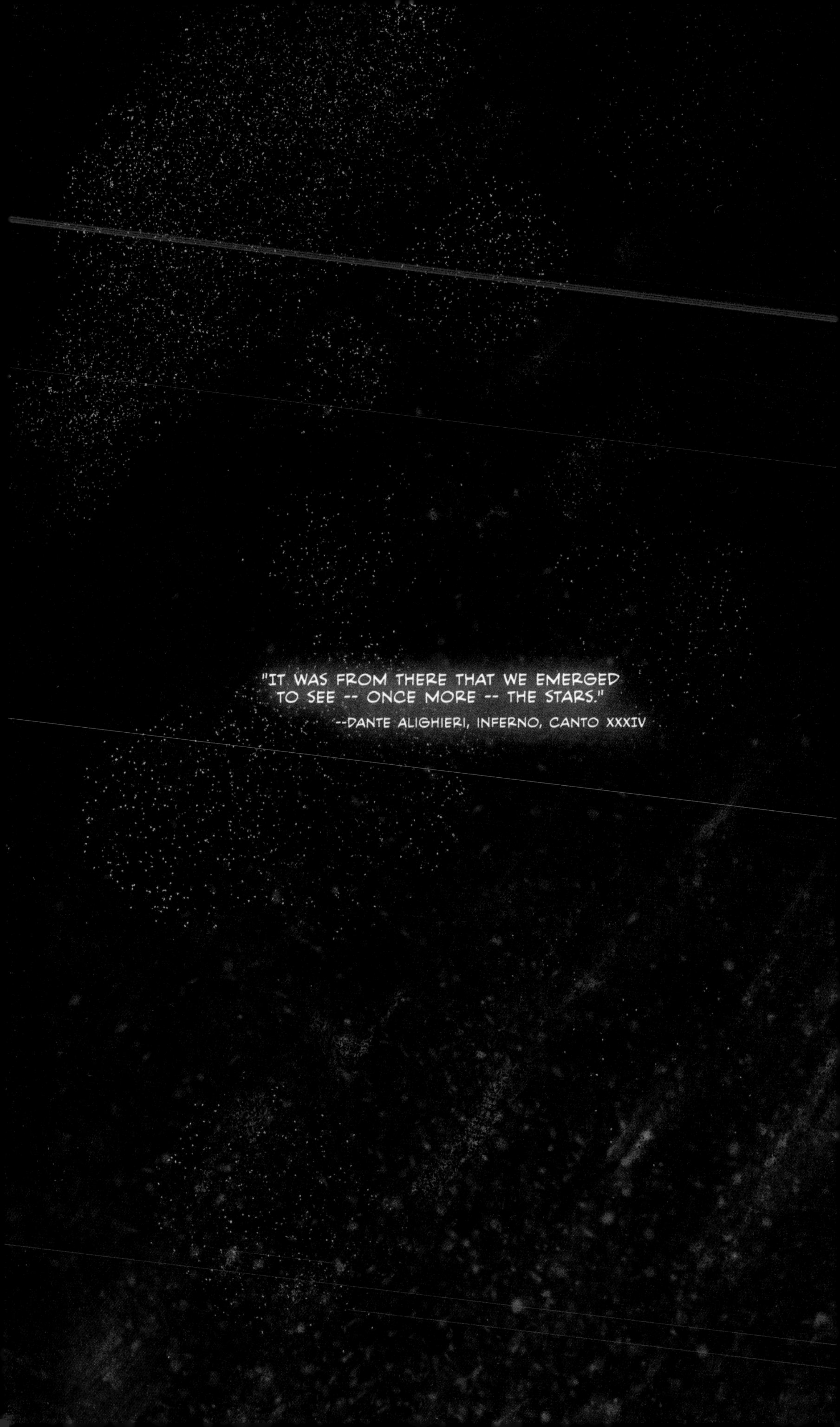
"IT WAS FROM THERE THAT WE EMERGED TO SEE -- ONCE MORE -- THE STARS."
--DANTE ALIGHIERI, INFERNO, CANTO XXXIV

WONDER TALES

The Skeksis from *The Dark Crystal*. Gmork the wolf from *The Neverending Story*. The junk lady from *Labyrinth*. The Wheelers from *Return to Oz*.

Like so many of us, these modern fairy tales filled my childhood. They were my childhood. Dark. Unsettling. And to a 12-year-old kid... glorious.

I don't have many things left from my childhood, but when I was 12, I found this vintage copy of *The Wonderful Wizard of Oz* at my local library's book sale. Dated 1901. I've collected more books in the series over the years, but that first one means the world to me.

In that original volume, L. Frank Baum's introduction rejected the dark morality of Grimm's and Anderson's fables. He believed "the time has come for a series of newer 'wonder tales' in which the stereotyped genie, dwarf and fairy are eliminated, together with all the horrible and bloodcurdling incident devised by their authors to point a fearsome moral to each tale." Dorothy's journey through Oz "was written solely to pleasure children of today. It aspires to being a modernized fairy tale, in which the wonderment and joy are retained and the heart-aches and nightmares are left out."

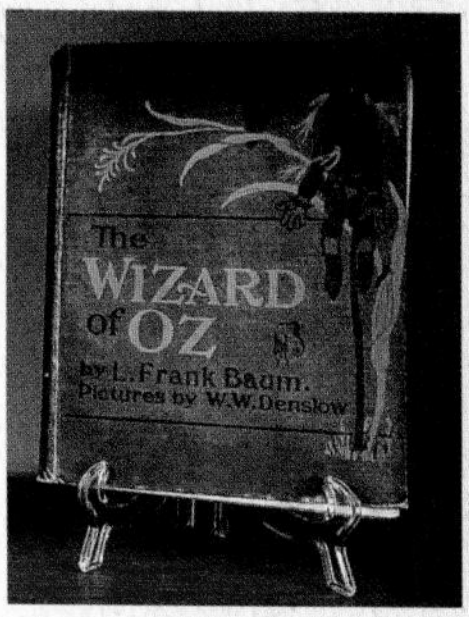
The
WIZARD
of OZ
by L. Frank Baum.
Pictures by W.W. Denslow

Despite his intent, the darkness remained in his story of a lost young girl wandering in a strange land, stalked by a fearsome witch, deceived by a huckster wizard, and befriended by a tin man without a heart, a talking lion, and a sentient scarecrow. But that's the nature of the best stories, and maybe that's what Baum was getting at—when there's darkness, there should also be light.

Canto's mix of darkness and hope was born out of this fertile soil. A newer wonder tale for the 21st century. My deepest hope is that you, dear reader, will find Canto's dangerous journey stays with you long past the final page. There will be more adventures for Canto. With more darkness, no doubt. But also with more light.

I believe Baum, the father of the "modernized fairy tale," would be pleased.

David M. Booher
Los Angeles, March, 2020

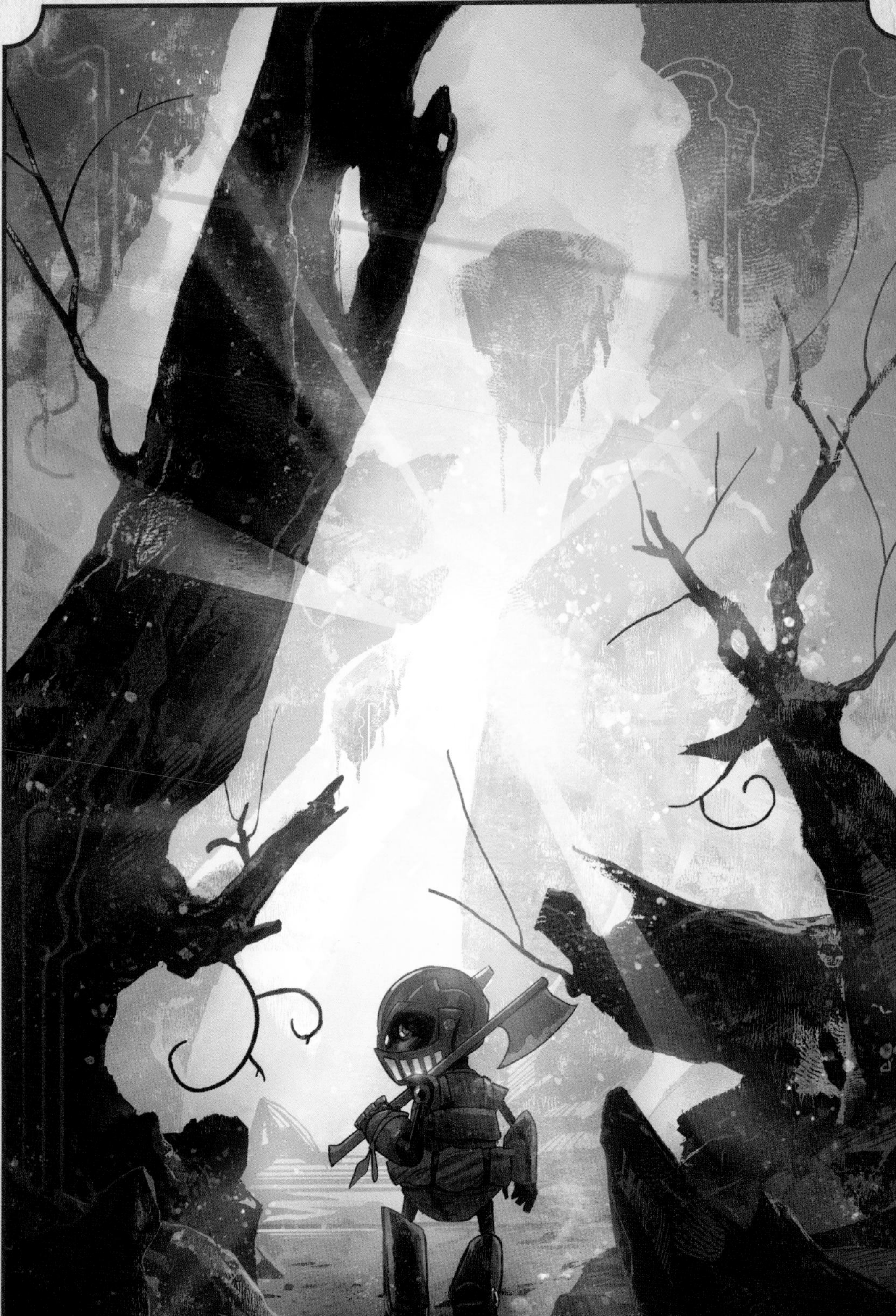

Art by **Nick Robles**

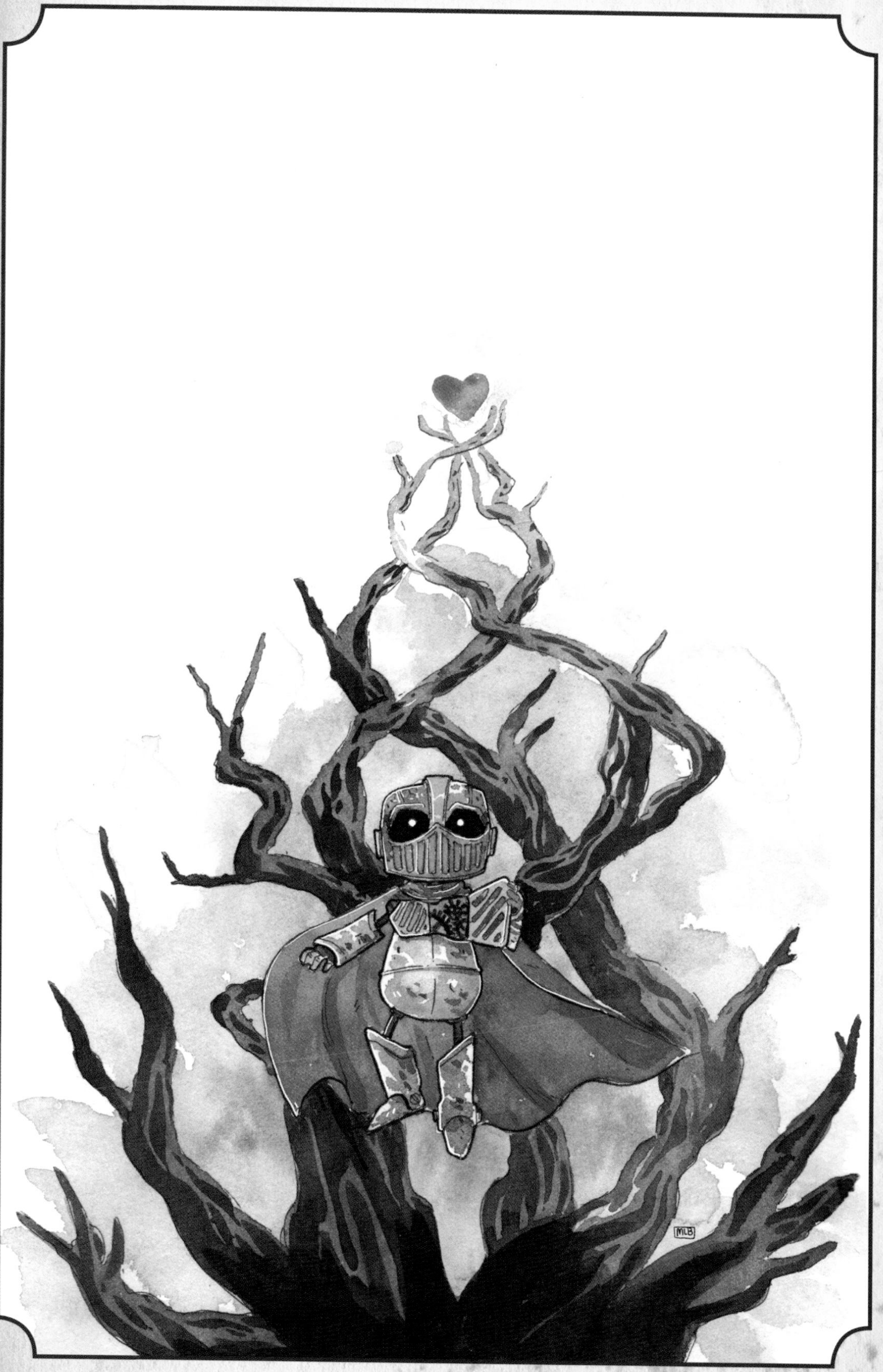

Art by **Morgan Beem**

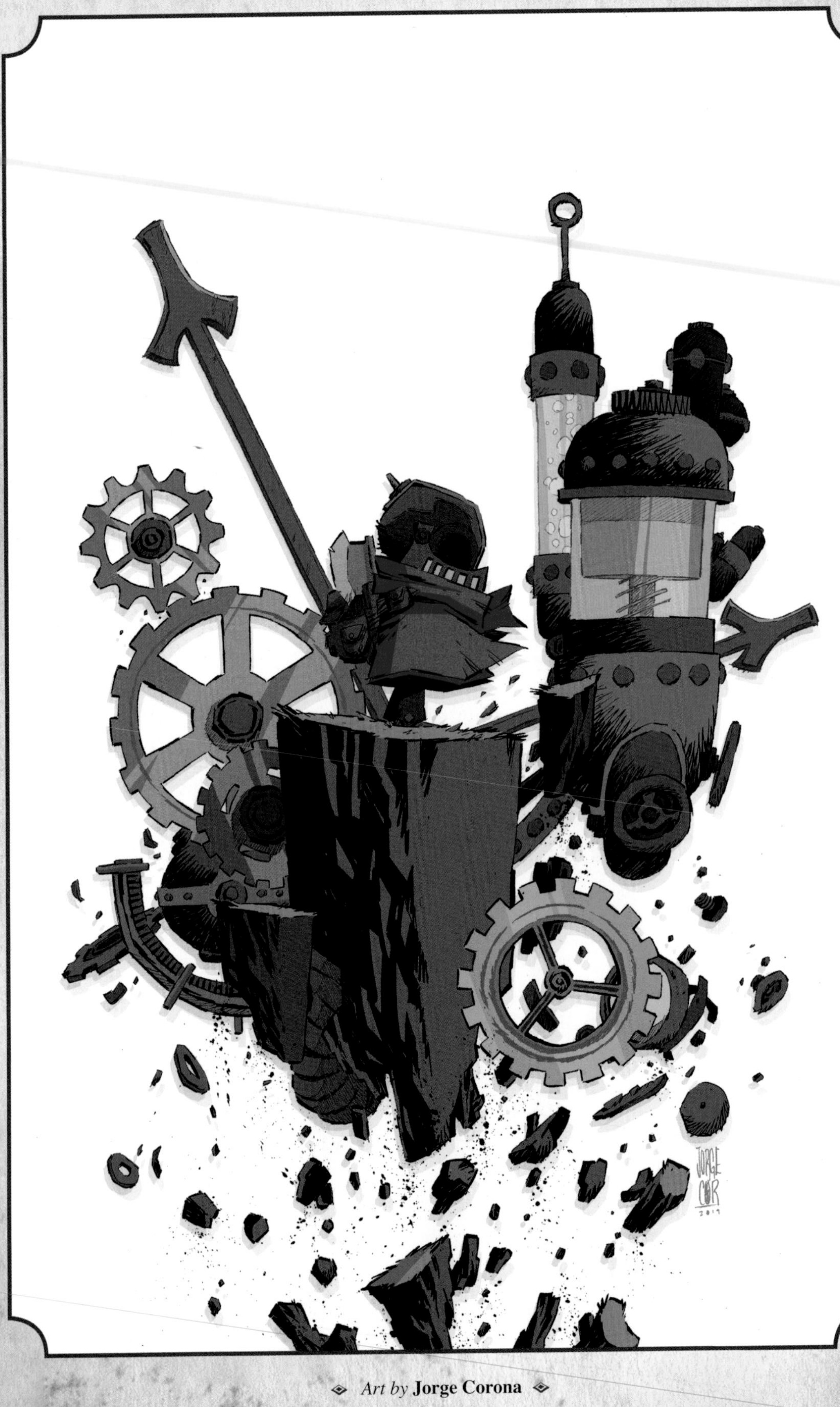

Art by **Jorge Corona**

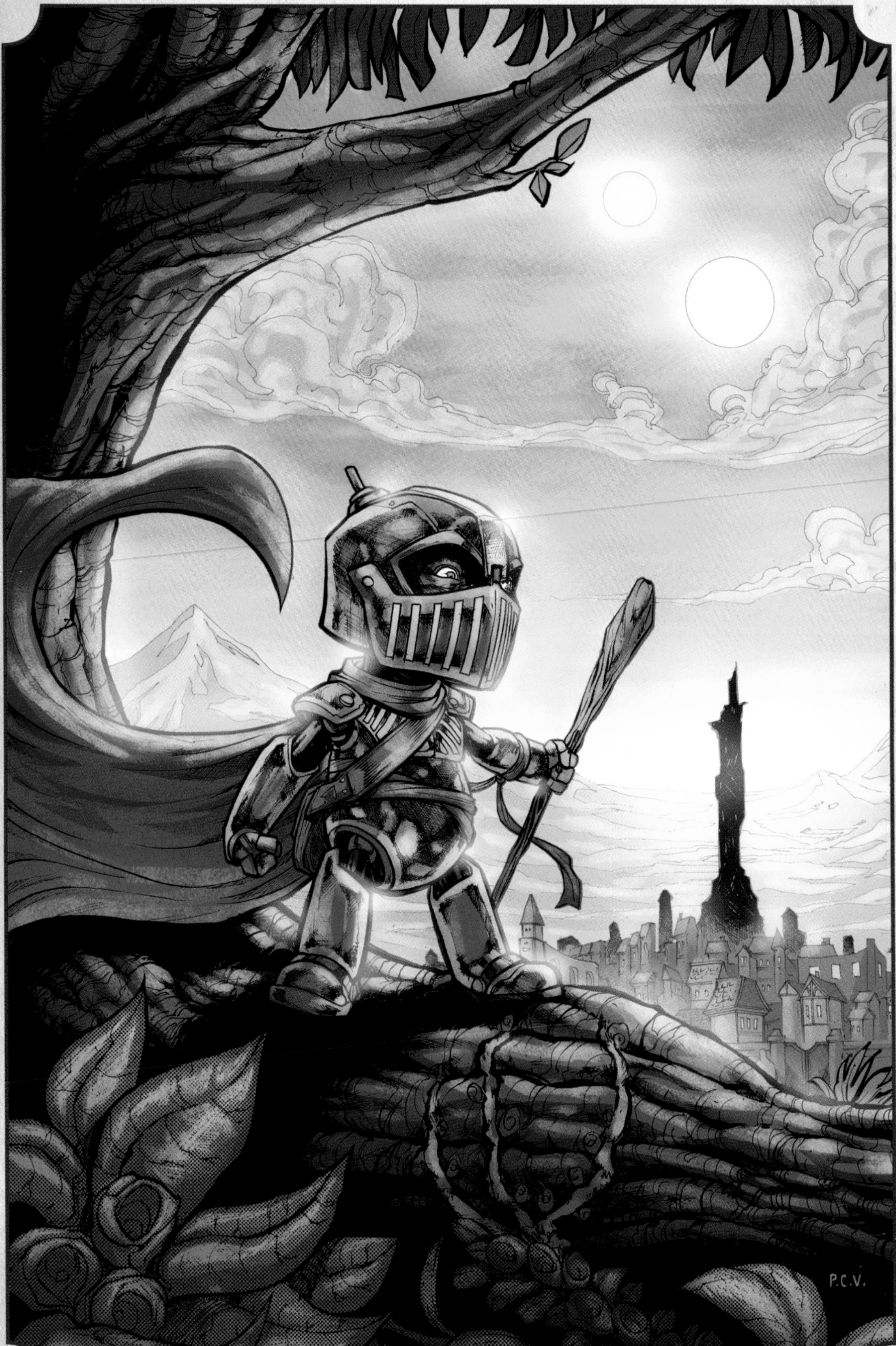
P.C.V.

Art by **Phillip Sevy**

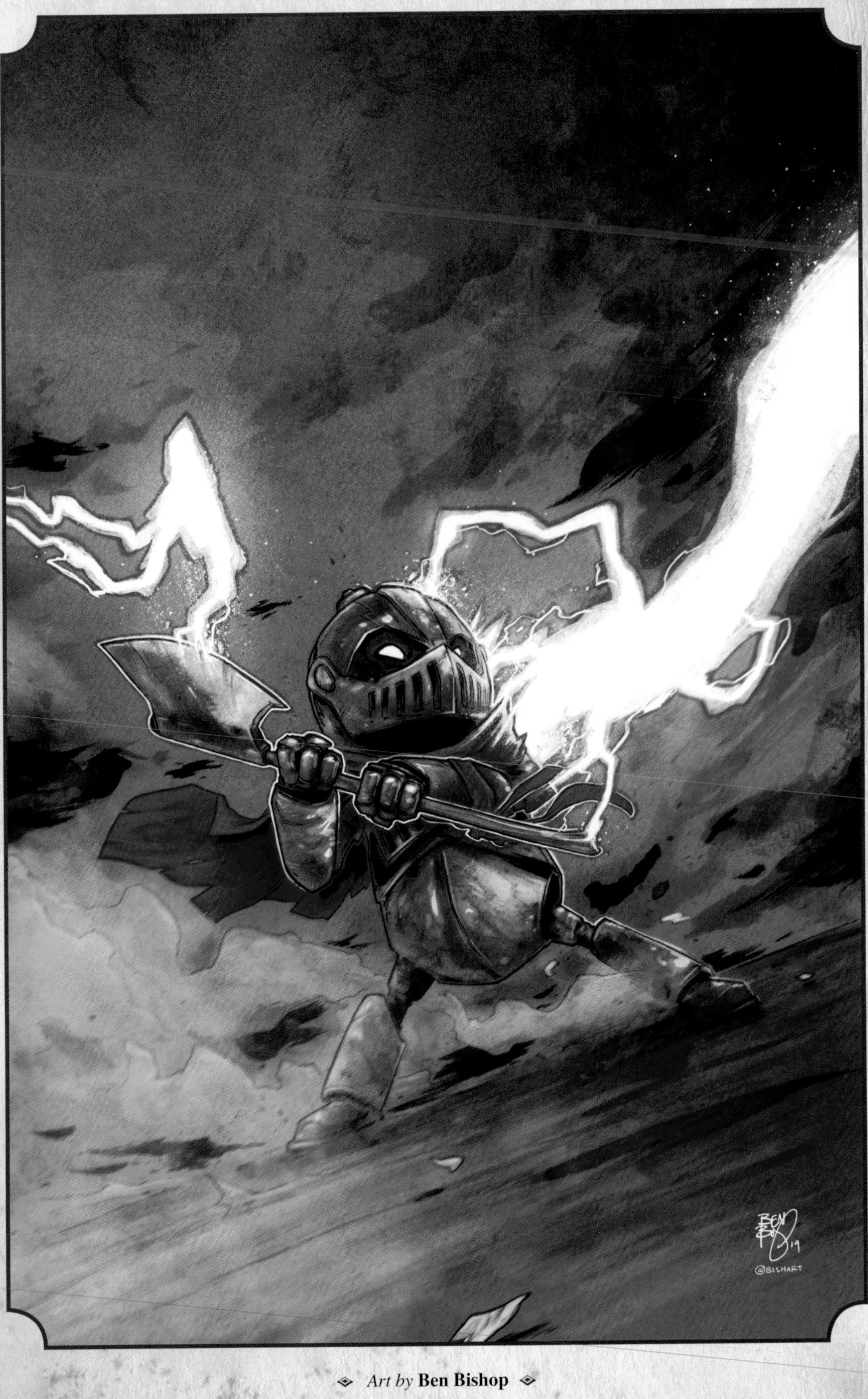
@BISHART

Art by **Ben Bishop**

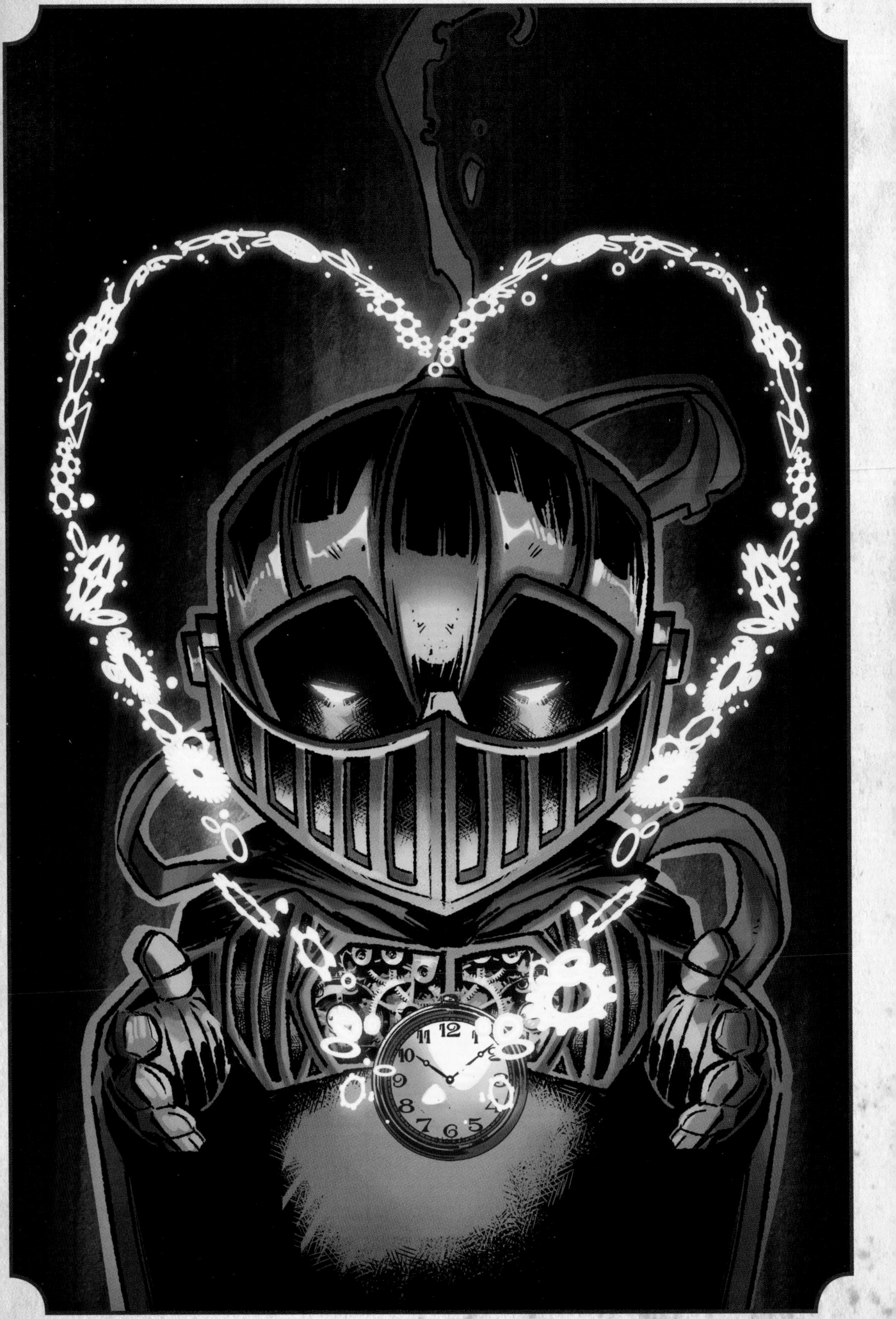

◈ *Art by* **Roberta Ingranata**, *Colors by* **Warnia Sahadewa** ◈

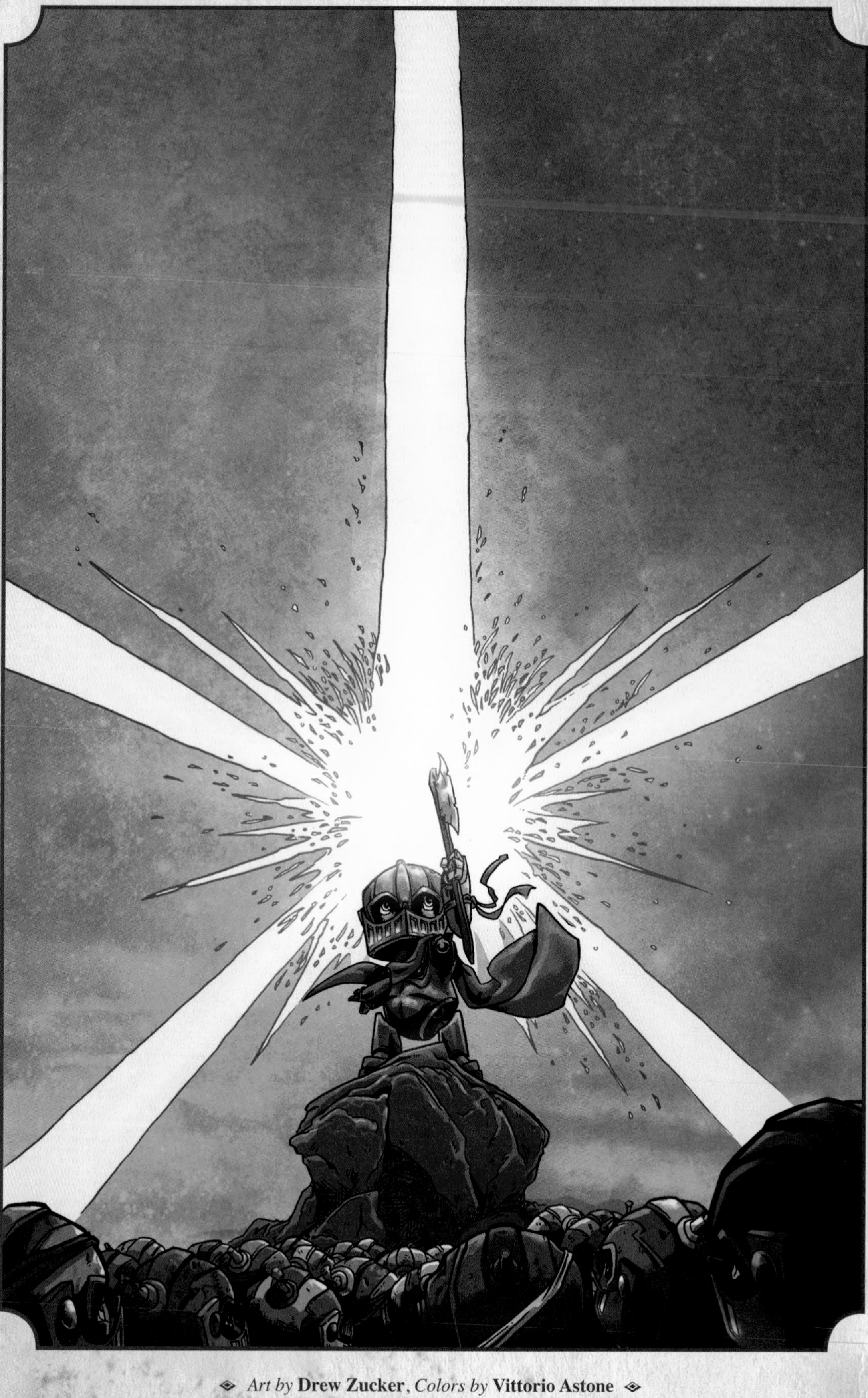

Art by **Drew Zucker**, *Colors by* **Vittorio Astone**

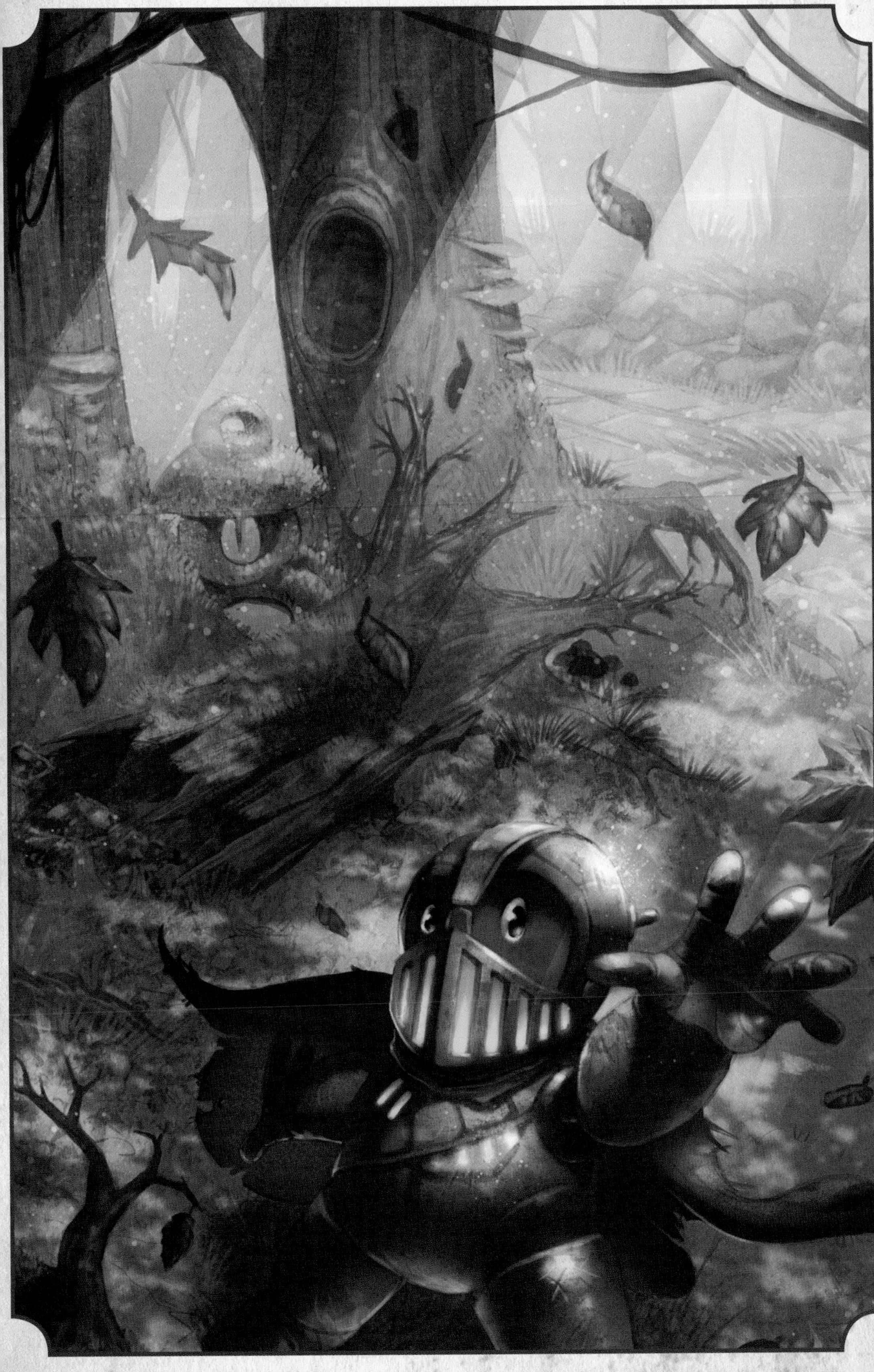

Art by **Vittorio Astone**

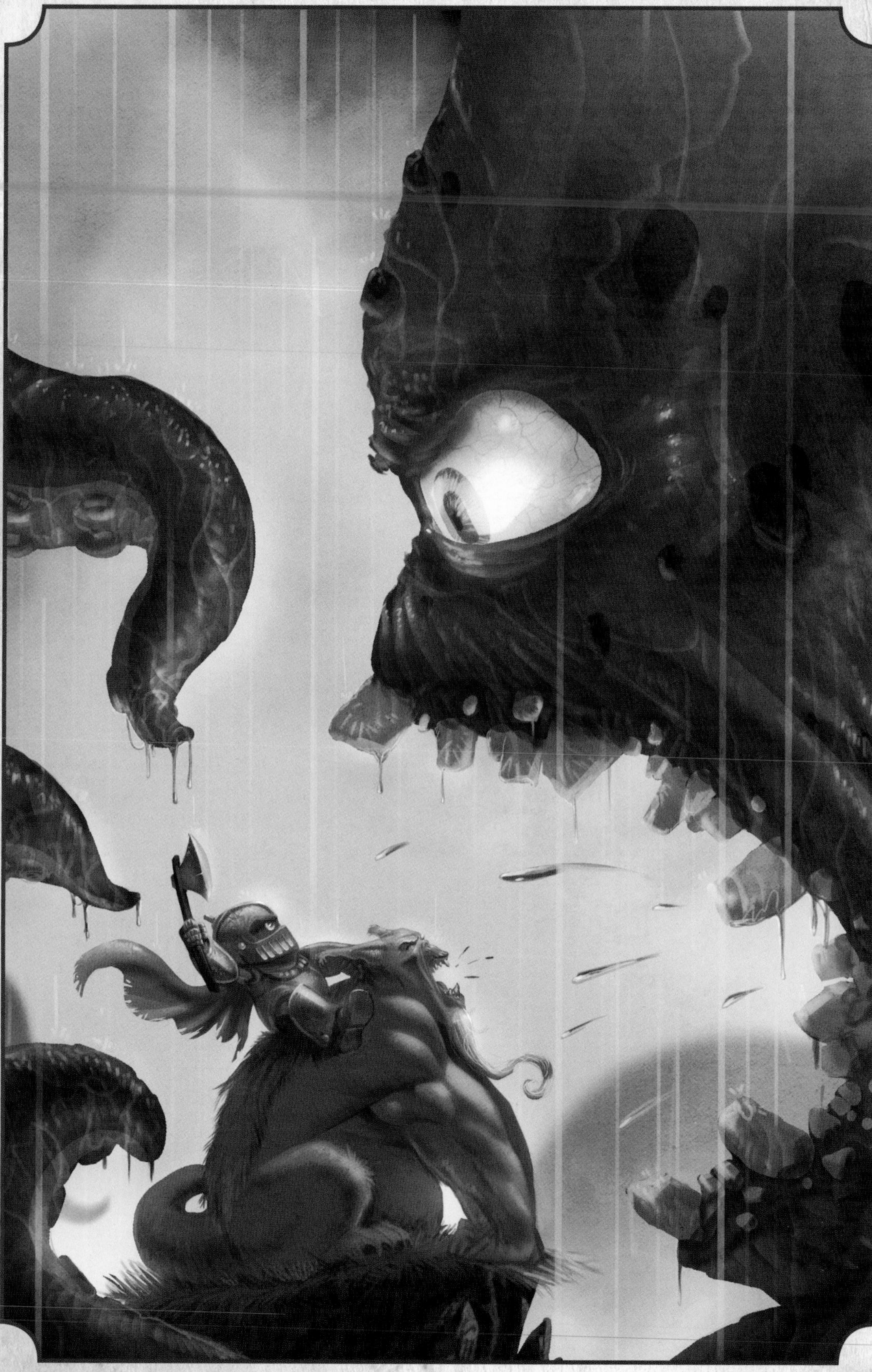

Art by Vittorio Astone

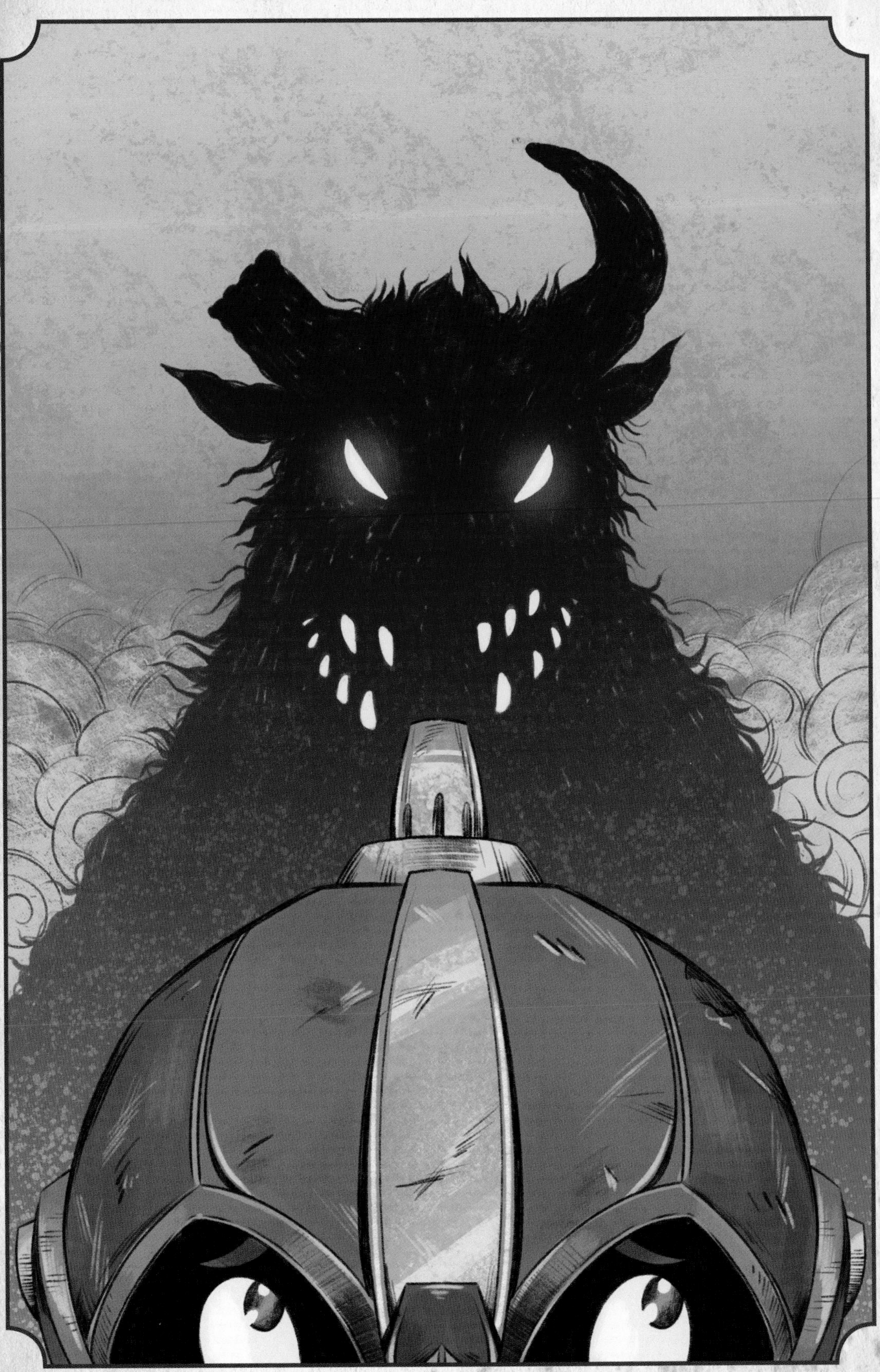

Art by **Nicole Goux**

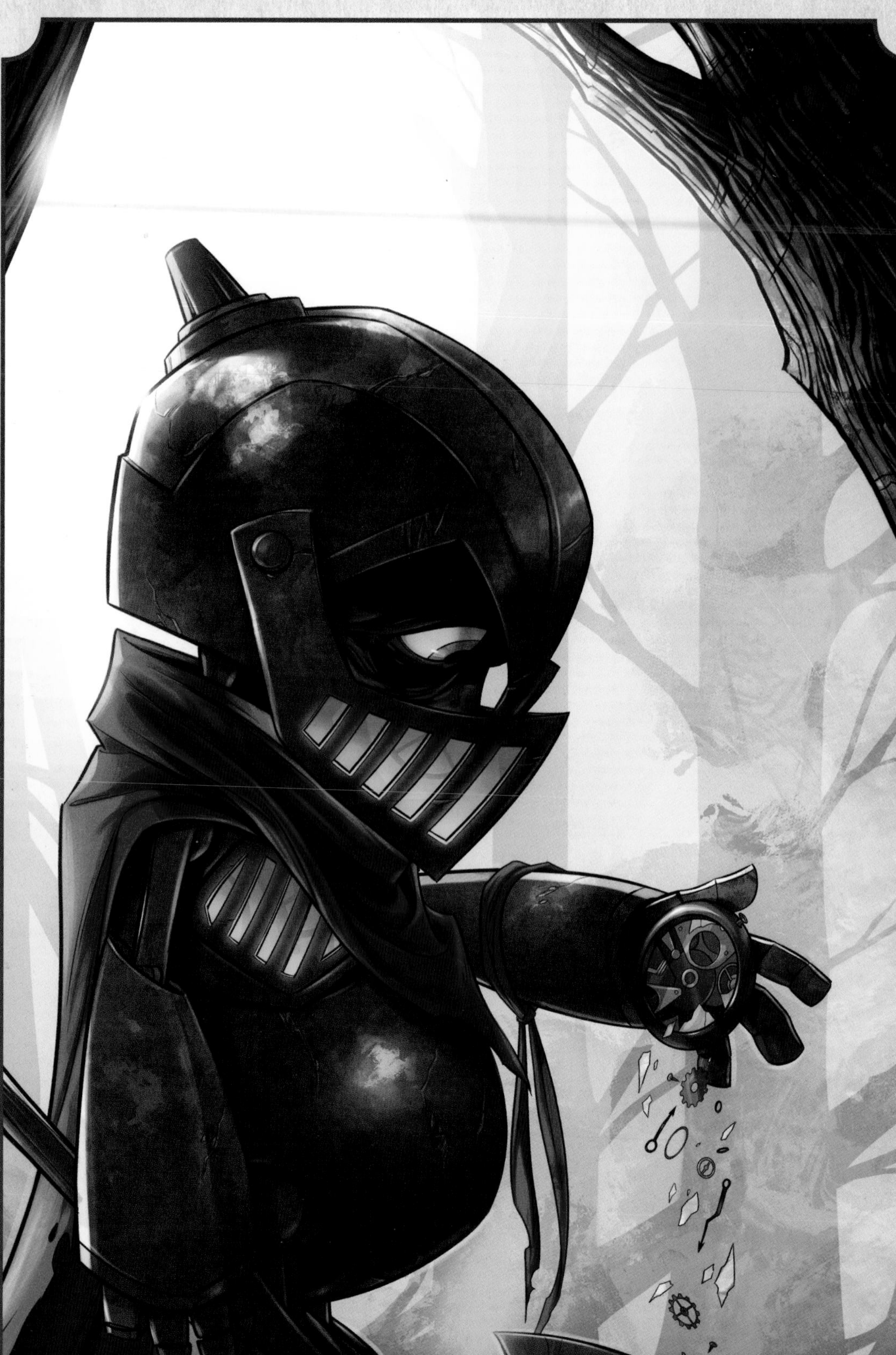

Art by **Chris Ables**

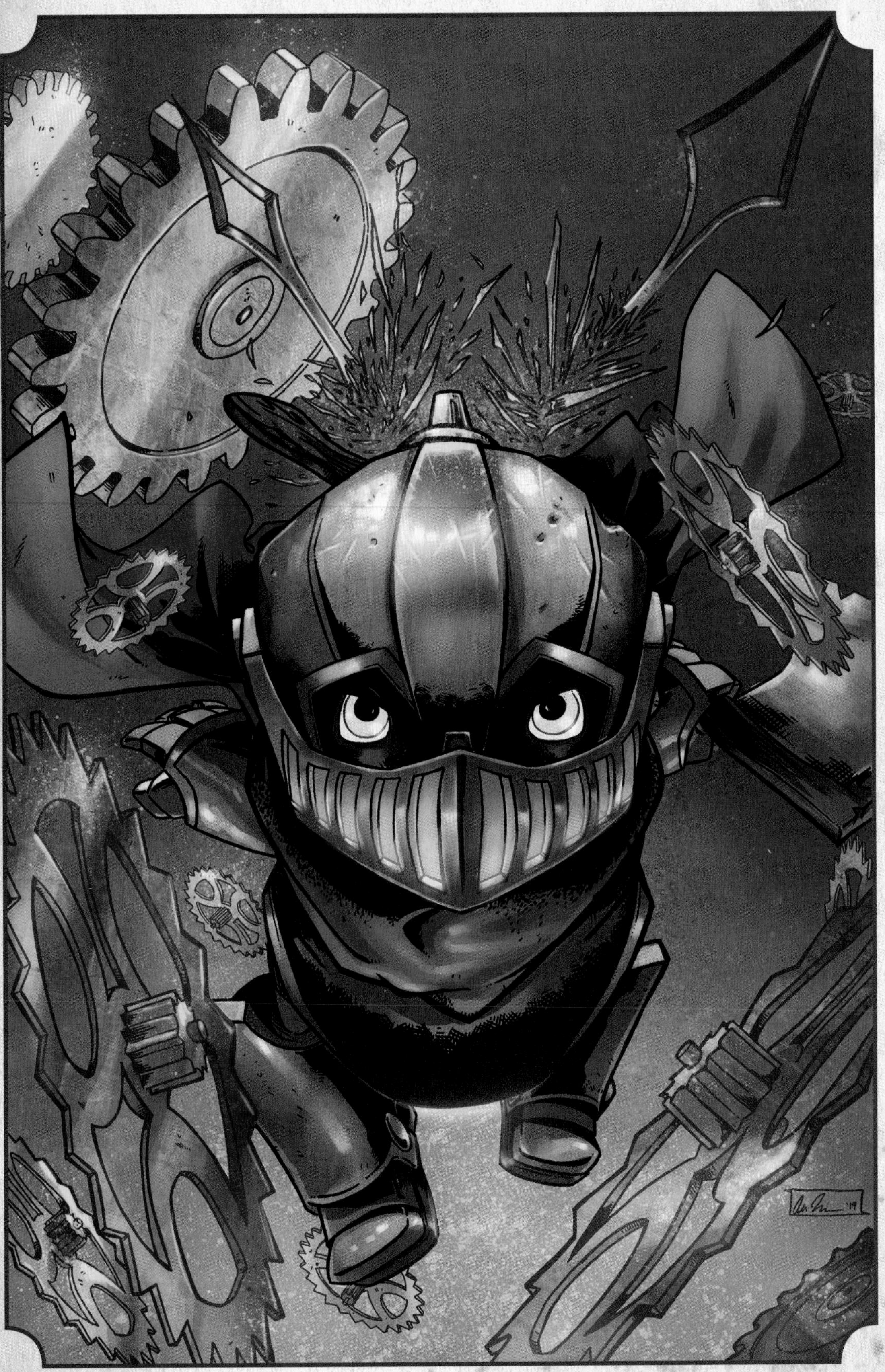

◈ *Art by* **Drew Zucker**, *Colors by* **Vittorio Astone** ◈

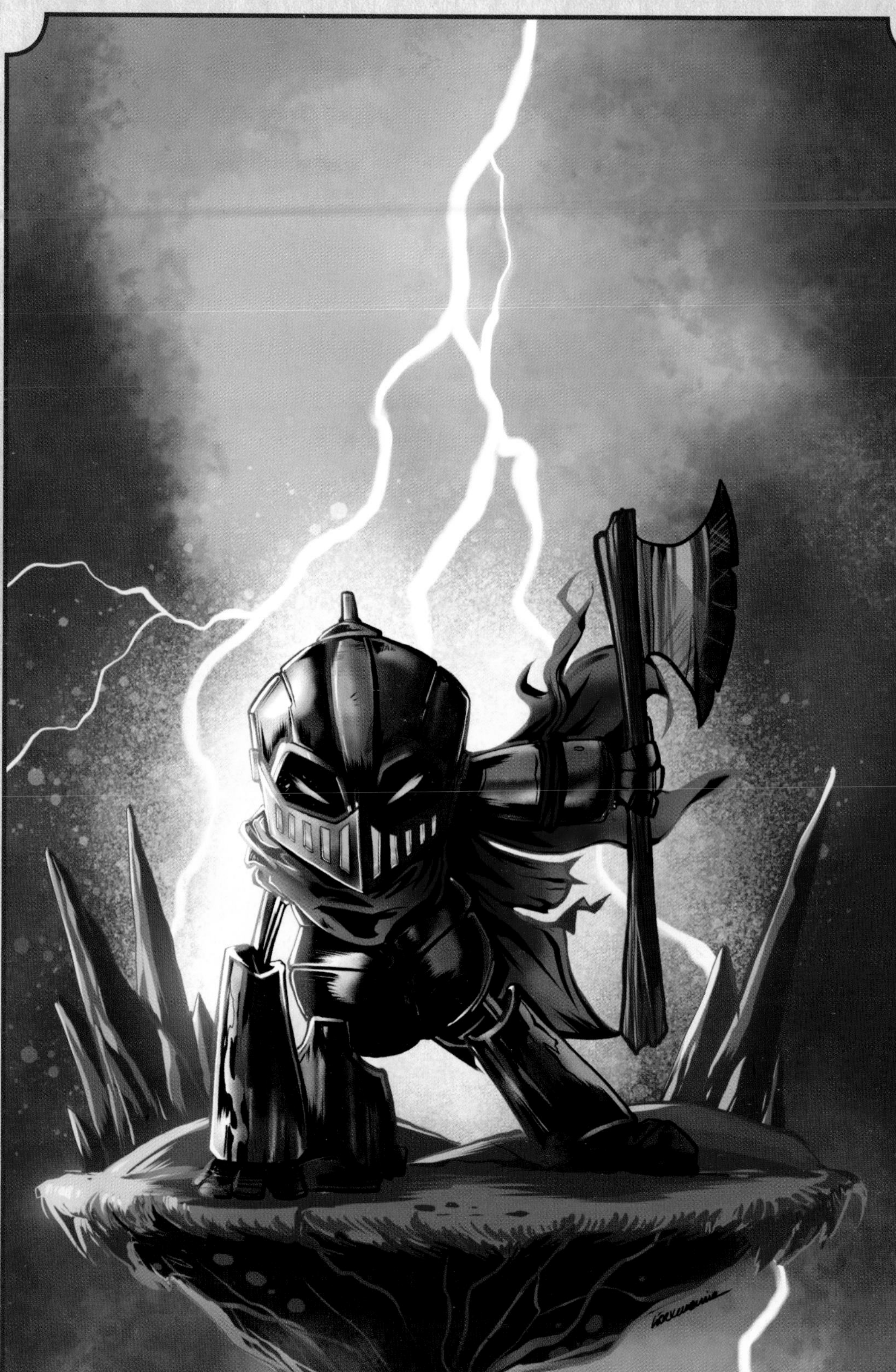

Art by **Görkem Demir**